WHISPERS OF PASSION

"India." She loved the way he said her name.

"He is still there, in the shadows, watching us," Theuderic said, so softly she could just hear the words. "If I kiss you now, he will believe that what he suggested about us is the truth."

"Isn't it?" Her voice was as soft as his had been, but he heard it, and he dropped his hand.

"Go inside," he said. "I'll follow in a little while. If anyone asks for me, say our paths crossed coming and going from the latrine."

"Don't send me away."

"Go now. Leave me or I'll take you here in the snow and not care if the groom watches us. Sleep next to Eudon tonight."

"Theu—"

"Go!" There was such passion, and so much pain in that one word, that she fled from him into the hall, to smoky warmth and masculine laughter and at least the semblance of safety.

Other books by Flora Speer:

VIKING PASSION
DESTINY'S LOVERS
MUCH ADO ABOUT LOVE
VENUS RISING
BY HONOR BOUND

A TIME TO LOVE AGAIN

FLORA SPEER

LOVE SPELL ◆ **NEW YORK CITY**

LOVE SPELL®

August 1993

Published by

Dorchester Publishing Co., Inc.
276 Fifth Avenue
New York, NY 10001

The name ''Love Spell'' and its logo are trademarks of Dorchester Publishing Co., Inc.

Printed in the United States of America.

My thanks to my daughter Beth and my son-in-law Kevin, who were my advisers on the subject of computers—a subject upon which, like my heroine India, I do not know enough to keep myself out of serious trouble.

To everything there is a season, and a time to every purpose…A time to be born, and a time to die…A time to love….

Ecclesiastes 3:1-2,8

Chapter One

Connecticut, December, 1991.

"India, you really ought to rejoin the twentieth century." Willi put down her hamburger, wiped a spot of catsup off her chin with a paper napkin, and reached for her soda. "When Professor Moore retires at the end of the year and the new department head arrives, you will be expected to know how to use a computer. Professor Moore may tolerate you using that old typewriter, but I don't think the new man will. He's younger, he'll be more up-to-date, so you'll have to be up-to-date, too, kid."

Willi always called India *kid*, even though she was three months younger than India. And the question of who would replace India's elderly, revered boss as chairman of the Department of

History and Political Science had for months been the subject of speculation and rumor for every faculty member or employee at Cheswick University.

"I know perfectly well how to use a computer. I did all that work for Robert using one." India fell silent, wishing she had gone directly home after work instead of letting Willi talk her into this Christmas shopping expedition. She had bought Willi's present weeks before, and there was no one else to buy a gift for this year except Robert's cat, Charlemagne. Considering Charlemagne's uncanny ability to locate his favorite mood-altering substance within seconds, purchase of his catnip mouse was best left until Christmas Eve.

"That's just what I mean," Willi said. "Robert has been dead for over a year, but you are still living like a recluse in that big old house with only a cat for company and your job as your only social activity."

"We've had this discussion before." India sighed. Her appetite gone, she pushed aside her salad and the crackers that went with it. She and Willi had brought their trays from the fast-food take-out counter to the quietest corner of the food court and sat down at a table near the oversized fountain that was the centerpiece of the Greater Cheswick Mall. The sound of falling water muffled at least some of the noise made by the crowd of Christmas shoppers, but India could still hear the music being played on the public address system. She reflected with gloomy cynicism that the song she most hated at that particular moment was *The Little Drummer Boy*. She sighed again, acknowledging that she was totally lacking in holiday spirit.

"Hank says he's willing to help you refresh your computer skills," Willi announced.

"Hank who?" India was baffled at first, until she remembered the man. "You mean the resident computer genius of Cheswick U? I've barely met him. Why would he do a favor like that for me?"

"Well," Willi looked a bit like Charlemagne after he had destroyed his catnip mouse, "I kind of like him, and he says he likes me."

"Somehow I don't see you and Mr. Marsh as close friends," India said. "I don't think you are at all alike."

"Maybe that's the attraction."

Willi looked so happy that India decided to keep to herself her reservations about Hank Marsh. She could see nothing at all romantic about him, or about his work, but then, Willi's taste in men had always been different from hers. Not to mention her taste in clothing.

Willi wore a silver-studded black leather jacket over a dark blue turtleneck sweater and a black leather miniskirt. Black opaque tights and high-heeled black leather boots encased her plump legs. Willi's dark hair was styled in a spiky cut, her eyelashes were heavy with mascara, and her lips and fingertips were bright red. Next to her dearest friend, India felt like a dowdy old lady in her practical grey wool suit and bowed white blouse.

The piped-in music shifted to a string rendition of *Greensleeves*. At the first strains of the ancient melody, India's mood lifted as if by magic. She had a sudden urge to pull her hair out of its carefully arranged French twist and let it hang down below her shoulders in the style she had favored as a young girl.

"It's time for you to start living again," Willi said, her words echoing India's thoughts. "You have refused to touch a computer since Robert got too sick to work anymore, and heaven knows, his research was weird—all that seventh and eighth century stuff—and you were as immersed in it as he was. You need an update, professionally and personally."

"You're right," India said, sipping her tea.

"I am? Without any more argument than that?" Willi stared for a minute, then grinned, her old, irrepressible smile that India remembered so well from their childhood. "Well, it's about time you came to your senses again."

"What I want," India said, knowing her next words would be the best Christmas gift she could possibly give her friend, "is some of your good advice. I *am* dreadfully out of touch. When do you think Hank could make time for my first lesson?"

"Nine o'clock Saturday morning, his office," Willi replied without missing a beat. "Now, about your clothes. Grey is not your color, kid. I see you in a nice, deep red. . . ."

"Wow." Hank Marsh stared at India, who was clothed in a cranberry wool jersey skirt, matching sweater, and stylish shoes. "When Willi talked about a transformation, she wasn't joking. You look great, Mrs. Baldwin."

The after-work shopping session had resulted in the purchase of two new outfits, a pair of elegant suede pumps, a pair of fashionable boots, and a complete makeover at a cosmetics counter. The following day, Willi had escorted India to a lunch-hour appointment with her hairdresser. India's forehead was now covered by side-swept bangs and her hair hung in a straight fall of glossy golden brown that stopped just short of her shoulders, with the ends turned under in a casual pageboy style.

"The change is mostly Willi's doing. And call me India, please." Aware of Willi's interest in this man, India looked at him more carefully than she had on the few previous occasions when they had met. Hank was shorter than she was, and skinny in a loose-limbed, adolescent way. His youthful looks were deceiving. India had heard enough about him to know that behind the tousled blond hair and light blue eyes, behind the boyish face with its perennially suspicious expression, a brilliant mind never stopped working.

"I can't understand how you and Willi became friends." Hank flushed a bit, as if he thought he might have accidentally said something insulting, but India understood what he meant.

"We met in the fourth grade," she said. "Our class was seated alphabetically, so Wilhemina Jones was placed just behind India Johnson. We have been friends since that first day, and it has always seemed to me that the ways in which we are different only bind us closer together."

"Complementary opposites." Hank nodded. "It makes sense to me. She told me how great you were after her father ran off with that waitress and left Mrs. Jones with four children younger than Willi to raise."

"Did she also mention the way she stood by me when my parents were killed in an automobile accident? Or all the helpful things she did while my husband was sick? Willi was wonderful to both of us for those two dreadful years, even though she thought my marriage to Robert was a big mistake, because he was so much older than I. Willi is the best friend I have ever had," India told him.

"I know about your husband's work," Hank said. "The early Middle Ages aren't everyone's meat, but he was famous here at the university for his interesting lectures. Willi tells me you were his research assistant, and that it was you who convinced him to use a computer, so you can't be completely ignorant about my baby, even if you are a couple of years out of practice."

Hank caressed the keyboard of his own computer with a loving gesture.

Only now did India look around his office. It was a monument to neatness, with books and papers precisely arranged and not a speck of dust to be seen. Willi had warned her about Hank's insistence that no food or drink be brought into the room, lest spills disrupt the working of his beloved computer. This electronic wonder, which Hank had personally modified to suit his needs, dominated the room. India recognized the display terminal, keyboard, and printer, but most of the other components looked like nothing she had ever seen attached to a computer before.

"Willi mentioned that you are working on a special project," she remarked, taking in the curious additions to what appeared to be an ordinary office instrument. Thinking of the way in which her work with Robert had drawn them closer together, she added, "Does Willi help you?"

"She's far happier in Art History," Hank replied. Willi was secretary to the chairman of that department, her office just down the hall from India's. "Willi is not interested in exploring the many mysteries of the space-time continuum."

"Space-time continuum?" India repeated, not sure what he meant. Then, because Hank looked as if he expected some further comment from her, she added, "I remember something about that from my one and only college physics course. Wasn't it Albert Einstein's idea?"

"I guess you could say so, but I've taken a different direction," Hank said, blithely dismissing the great scientist. "I'm working on the direct manipulation of time. Have you ever wanted to change something in the past?"

"That sounds dangerous." A chill shivered up India's spine. "If you could change the past, wouldn't you change the present and the future, too? Hank, you can't be serious about this."

"Don't look so scared," he said, laughing at her objections. "So far, it's all just speculation, the sort of thing people like me sit around and talk about late at night. It stimulates the imagination, but unfortunately I haven't been able to prove my theory yet. Incidentally, there is another theory that the further back in time those changes are made, the less likely you would be to alter the present. Does that calm your ethical fears?"

"It might if I could understand what you have been talking about," she replied, strangely disturbed by what Hank had just said.

"It's too complicated for me to try to explain any more than I have," he told her with a touch of arrogance in his manner. "Willi can't understand what I am trying to do, and neither could you."

She had the oddest feeling that Hank thought he had revealed too much about his work. But if that work really was purely speculative, then it could be of no concern to her. What mattered to her at the moment was learning to use the computer again.

"O.K.," Hank said, gesturing to her to sit in the chair placed in front of the keyboard, "let's see what we can do about making you better at your job before the new boss gets here."

"Theodore Brant, Ph.D," India murmured, relieved to find the conversation veering away from Hank's incomprehensible work and back to solid ground again.

"Brant—Brand? As in firebrand?" said Hank. "That sounds interesting. I wonder if his personality matches his name."

Hank proved to be a surprisingly good teacher. After a long Saturday morning with him India felt she had come a long way toward updating her computer skills, but still she wanted to practice on her own for a while, with no one looking over her shoulder to correct any mistakes she might make.

"If you don't mind, I would like to come back tomorrow," she told Hank when they stopped shortly after one o'clock. "Actually, I'd like to bring in some of Robert's material to work on. I ought to do something with all that data he collected. I'm sure the janitor will let me in, so you won't have to be here."

"You can use my computer," Hank said, "just as long as you don't disturb these two piles of paper or turn on the switch on this component."

"I won't touch it," India promised, "but will I be in your way at all?"

"I'll probably be in late tomorrow," he replied. "I have a date with Willi tonight."

"In that case, I'll get here early in the morning, and work until you come."

"Fair enough. But be careful of my baby." Hank sat down in the chair India had vacated. "I don't·let just anyone use her. This is a special favor, because of Willi."

"I understand, and I appreciate your generosity. I promise I'll be careful." She wasn't sure he heard her, or even that he was aware of her when she said good-bye and left. All of his concentration was on the screen where, as she glanced back before closing the office door, India could see the strange swirls of three-dimensional color graphics and a series of numbers that looked like some kind of complicated mathematical equation.

Chapter Two

India was up early on Sunday morning. After feeding Charlemagne his favorite tuna breakfast and making a cup of black coffee for herself, she dressed with care. Willi's lectures during the past week, coupled with the process of trying on and deciding about new clothing, had reawakened the vanity she had so sternly put aside three years previously, when she had decided that nothing mattered except her terminally ill husband. She had always liked nice clothes and had relished the sensation of rich fabrics against her skin. This morning she put on a lacy bra and a silk teddy trimmed in matching lace. The salesclerk had called the pale color *antique gold*. It suited India's golden brown hair and light brown eyes. She applied brown and green eyeshadow, added black mascara to her naturally thick lashes, and finished her makeup with a warm peach lipstick. Then she pulled on one of her new outfits, a tunic and narrow trousers of dark green. The wristwatch Robert had given her was at the jeweler's for cleaning, and none of her earrings suited her costume. At a loss for accessories, she rummaged through her small collection of jewelry until she found the necklace that had been Robert's first gift.

"I wish I could give you the real thing instead of just a museum reproduction," he had said when she opened the box. "It's from the eighth century."

The round pendant was about two inches across, its gold surface decorated with bright red, green, blue, and yellow enamels. The center design was a four-petaled flower, like a cross. This was surrounded by bands of color, each band divided into triangles and squares, and the piece was finished with a gold border. The chain was of heavy gold-plated links.

"Perfect." India slipped the chain over her head and adjusted the pendant, noticing that the green enamel exactly matched the color of her tunic. Then she stood still, looking at her left hand in the mirror. "Robert, you told me not to mourn you forever, and Willi has recently told me the same thing. It's time I took the advice of the two people I love most. I'll never forget you and the wonderful life we had, but it's time for me to start living again." With a feeling of complete serenity, knowing somewhere deep in her heart that what she was doing was right and Robert would approve, she removed her engagement ring and wedding band and laid them in the jewelry box, closing the lid firmly on them.

Picking up her purse, she walked downstairs to the back parlor of the old house to the room they had converted into an office for Robert's historical research. The shelves were still crowded with his books and papers, the only empty spot being the place where the computer had once sat. India had sold it shortly after Robert's death. After a quick search she found what she wanted—a notebook and two floppy disks. Stuffing them into her purse, she returned to the living room, frowning at what she beheld.

The house needed some Christmas brightness. It was only three days until the holiday, and she hadn't even hung a wreath on the door. Picking her keys off the hall table and heading toward the garage, India decided she would visit the mall again that afternoon. She wanted some new decorations, and she also wanted to buy a gift for Hank, who had been so patient with her the day before. She still did not think he was the right man for Willi because he was too involved with his work—work that India simply could not understand. She doubted if many people could understand what Hank was trying to do, which must have been frustrating for him. Feeling a bit sorry for him, she resolved to invite him and Willi to dinner one night during the coming week.

She was in an upbeat mood as she backed

her car out of the driveway. She had the feeling that something wonderful was going to happen. Her life had begun to change, and unlike her recent holidays, this was going to be a happy season.

The university was not as deserted as she had expected. Most of the students had gone home for the holiday break, but as she followed the janitor toward Hank's office, India met several professors she knew, all of them carrying armloads of the blue books that contained the students' answers to the just-completed final exams. Grades had to be posted by Monday evening, so everyone she met passed her with only a hurried greeting. Remembering how distracted Robert could become at the end of a semester, India thought with some amusement, as the janitor opened Hank's office door and let her in, that everyone except the janitor would very likely forget having seen her.

Sitting down at the computer, she got right to work, checking the material on the first floppy disk against Robert's handwritten notes. Soon she was immersed in the old familiar world of eighth century Francia, the land that would by modern times become partly France and partly Germany. She could speak the language of that world, after a fashion, for Robert had tried his best to teach it to her.

A few hours later, she stopped to stretch her muscles. While walking around the office wriggling her shoulders and flexing her fingers and wrists, her eyes fell upon a pile of printout material Hank had left. On the top sheet was the word *Time*, followed by a mathematical equation that looked vaguely familiar. She picked up the paper, sinking back into the chair as she read it over, trying to make some sense of it. In spite of its apparent familiarity, the meaning of the formula was beyond her.

"Space and time," she muttered, frowning at the numbers.

Recalling with a guilty pang that Hank wanted his papers left untouched, she reached across one of the new pieces of equipment to lay the sheet back on the pile. As she did so, her left hand accidentally brushed against the switch Hank had warned her not to touch. The mysterious piece of equipment hummed into life.

"Oh, dear." At first, India snatched her hand away from the switch, then, almost immediately, she leaned forward again to turn it off. But she froze before she made contact with it, mesmerized by the bright peach-colored glow now emanating from the screen in front of her. As she watched, the green letters of the data she had been working on disappeared into the growing brilliance of that light. Within another second, the light had eclipsed the components of Hank's entire system.

India knew she ought to turn the computer off, but she could no longer see the switch, and she was afraid of an electrical shock if she put her hand into the light and started fumbling around. Still seated, she scooted the chair backward, wondering how best to deal with this unexpected problem. She thought about diving beneath the work station to find the plug and pull it out, but she wasn't sure where the plug was—possibly behind a heavy section she wouldn't be able to move—and she wasn't absolutely certain there was only one plug. Hank might have arranged more than one electrical connection when he modified the computer.

All of this she thought about within a moment or two, before she remembered the janitor. He would know where the fuse box was, or the circuit breaker, or whatever gadget kept electricity streaming into the infernal machine now filling the office with an eerie shade of golden peach. The janitor might be able to cut off the electricity before whatever was happening could wipe out Hank's program and destroy all his work. She jumped out of the chair and headed for the hall, the peach light growing ever brighter behind her. Just as she stepped through the door, Hank appeared around a corner at the end of the hall.

"What have you done to my computer?" he shouted, racing to the doorway to stare wild-eyed at the now-pulsating light.

"It was an accident. I bumped the switch. I never meant to touch it. Oh, Hank, I'm sorry."

"Sorry? Oh, my God!" he swore, his eyes still fixed on the light.

"Can you turn it off?" India asked. "If I've ruined your program, I'll never forgive myself."

"Which switch did you turn on?" Hank demanded, throwing his parka on the floor and moving toward the computer.

"The one on this component." Seeing that he was not afraid to get closer to the peach-colored light, India reached through it, eager to undo the damage she had already done.

"Don't touch it!" Hank yelled.

But her groping fingertips had found the rounded top of the switch. She pushed at it. Nothing happened. She tried again, though she could see neither the switch nor her own hand, and she felt the strangest sensation, as if her arm were being pulled into the humming machinery.

"What's happening?" she cried. "Hank, you're fading out. Where are you?"

"India, get away from there!"

Hank's voice was fading, too, as though he spoke from an increasing distance, and she could just barely see him through the brilliant glow coming from the computer. Suddenly the air was sharp with the smell of ozone. She heard the crackle of electricity, and it seemed to her that numbers whirled about her head, forming and reforming into complicated equations.

"Innndiaaa—" Hank's frantic shout drew out into a long, sad whisper of sound. From somewhere beneath her, blackness grew and developed, an aching, empty void through which she was falling . . . falling . . . .

* * *

"What's going on here?" Willi stood in the open doorway, watching a singed and dirty Hank crawl out from between two sections of furniture. "I could hear you shouting from all the way down the hall. Did India blow a fuse? Where is she?"

"Gone." Pale and shaking, Hank pulled himself to his feet.

"She hasn't gone far," Willi said. "Her purse and coat are still here."

"She went"—Hank took a deep gulp of air—"she went into the computer."

"What are you saying?" Willi's puzzled expression showed just the beginning of fear.

"She's lost. Somehow she got mixed up in the program. She was working on her own data, and she turned this on." He gave the offending component a hard smack with one hand. "I never thought it would actually work. It was just one of my far-out ideas. I left my new computations in here last night. I warned her not to touch the switch, but she did, and when she tried to turn it off, she vanished."

"Are you crazy?" Willi's eyes were huge with dawning horror. "Or have you been reading too many of those weird scientific journals of yours? People don't vanish into computers!"

"India did. I saw it happen." Hank passed one hand across his face as if he would wipe out that awful sight. "She said it was an accident. I'm not sure what she did in here before I arrived."

Willi opened her mouth, then shut it, breathing deeply through her nose several times to steady herself before she could trust herself to speak.

"I am not going to waste precious time screaming or crying or having hysterics," she said in a tight little voice. "You are going to bring India back. If I can do anything to help, I will."

"That's just it," Hank cried. "I don't *know* what to do."

"Then you shouldn't be fooling around with this machine." Willi shook her head in disgust at his carelessness, then went to the table next to the keyboard, searching for anything that might offer a clue to India's exact whereabouts. "Look here. I know this, it's Robert's notebook. And here's one of his floppy disks."

"Yesterday she was talking about working on some of his notes," Hank offered, moving to stand next to her. "There's a date on it."

"Robert was such an old fuddy-duddy that he dated and cross-referenced everything," Willi told him. "See? This floppy disk is labeled *AD 777*."

"And this empty sleeve is dated *AD 778*," Hank added. "This must be the one she was using."

"Which means?" Willi asked, a hard edge to her voice.

"If what I think happened actually did happen, India may well have been sent to the year 778," Hank said, still looking down at the disk sleeve in his hand.

"Henry Adelbert Marsh." Willi's voice was slow and deadly now, and no one hearing her could possibly doubt that she meant every word she said. "I don't know what you have done with this stupid machine of yours to change it from an ordinary computer into this monster, or how you have done it, or what mad experiments you have been trying, but this I do know—you will bring India back from wherever you have sent her, and you will bring her back alive and healthy, or by heaven, you won't live to see Christmas Day."

Hank looked at the short, plump young woman in her black leather outfit. Mythology wasn't his field of expertise, but he knew an avenging fury when he saw one, and he believed Willi would do what she had threatened. Under her implacable stare he felt himself inundated by a wave of guilt. At the same time, he experienced a burst of excitement. Was it possible that his far-out theory was correct? Could he make India reappear and then duplicate what she had done? If so, he would be the author of one of the great discoveries of all time.

"I will do my best," he promised.

Chapter Three

India fell out of blackness to land right in the middle of a puddle of mud and ice. When she tried to stand up, someone bumped against her so hard that she was thrown to her knees again, down into trampled wet snow and dirty water. A dark fog enveloped her, making sight difficult. Her head ached and she felt sickeningly dizzy. Around her sounded loud cries and the clash of metal on metal. Wondering where on earth she was and what had happened, she blinked a few times, shook her head to clear her blurred vision, and then looked up into cold grey skies and drizzling rain.

A rough hand grabbed her arm, jerking her to her feet. An unshaven face was thrust into hers. She glimpsed a rounded metal helmet before she closed her eyes against the glare of a strange man's angry gaze.

"Idiot! Where is your sword?" The man spoke in a language she had heard only one other person use. But she recognized it, and she understood a good part of it.

"Sword? I don't—*sword*?" Her eyes flew open again. This time the black mist that had kept her from seeing clearly was gone. The dizziness was receding, too. The man who had hauled her upright was just a little taller than she, with dark brown hair showing beneath the gold-decorated rim of his helmet. His face was square-jawed and hard, his wide mouth firm. His upper body was covered with chain-mail armor and on his left arm he bore a large round shield. The man's eyes fell upon the necklace hanging around India's neck.

"What message from Charles?" he demanded, the language he was using making the name sound like a peculiar combination of the French pronunciation *Sharl* and the German *Karol*. "Speak quickly, boy, there isn't much time."

"What message? I don't understand."

"You wear the medallion of a royal messenger." He seemed to think that explained something. He peered more closely at her. "Answer me. Are you mad, or just ill? How did you appear here so suddenly? Never mind that now. Stay next to me. I'm bound to offer you what protection I can."

"I don't want or need your—oh!" India broke off, gaping in astonishment as a warrior clad in a fur cape over leather armor bore down on them, raising his battle-axe with deadly intent.

"Hugo! Marcion!" The man beside her shouted, and two more men sprang to his aid, swords bared and ready for action. "Here's a king's messenger alone and unarmed. Keep him safe."

"What happened to your companion?" one of the newcomers asked India. As he spoke, he slashed with his sword at the man in the fur cape. The man jumped backward, then raised his axe again, circling their little group of four, looking for an opening through which he could attack.

"I think I came here alone," India quavered, speaking in the language the men were using, not taking her eyes off the man with the axe.

Everything was happening so fast, and she was utterly confused by the strange sights and sounds. She saw that they were standing in a clearing in the midst of a forest. Nearby, a squalid-looking hut was burning, and she could distinguish men struggling with sword and axe. She watched a long, sharp-pointed spear fly through the air. Then she covered her eyes with her hands because she had just realized that she was in the middle of a battlefield.

For a minute or two, she entertained the hope that she had somehow wandered into a meeting of one of those societies that gathered periodically to recreate the Middle Ages for a weekend. The idea was driven out of her mind by a scream. When she lowered her hands from her face to see what had happened, the fur-caped man was on the ground. This time she clamped her hands over her mouth to keep herself from being sick, and she kept her eyes tightly shut from then on, until the noise of battle had ceased. Mercifully, it was soon over. India stood ankle-deep in mud, in a state of terrified shock.

"You're a weak-spirited lad," said a low voice.

She forced herself to open her eyes once more, but she refused to look at what she knew must surround her. She kept her attention on the grey-eyed man who stood before her, the same man who had called her a king's messenger.

"Cowardly," the man said, frowning at her. He looked her over from head to toe, his expression beneath the iron helmet conveying a deep aversion toward one so squeamish. "A puking child."

"I'm sorry. I've never seen bloodshed before," she responded, grateful for once in her life that her breasts were small, and doubly glad for the concealing fabric of her loose tunic, which made her look as slender as the boy this man imagined she was. Thinking she would be well advised to show some respect to one so heavily armed, she added, "Please, sir, can you tell me where I am and what has happened?"

"First tell me who you are and how you came here," the man replied. "What were you doing alone in this place where no unblooded lad should be?"

"My name is India Baldwin," she began.

"Baudoin?" The man stepped closer to her. "If this is some trick, I'll have you flayed alive."

She thought he probably would. He was frowning at her again, and she felt a thrill of fear. His arms beneath the chain mail *brunia* were heavily muscled, and the broad, double-edged sword he balanced lightly in his huge right hand was plainly no toy.

"I don't know how I got here," she informed him. That was true enough, for she did not understand the theory or the mechanism of what had happened to her in Hank's office. She could only hope that Hank would be able to reverse his computer's effect on her and quickly remove her from whatever this place was.

"I saw a man in this condition once," said the warrior Marcion, a handsome fellow whose curling dark hair was revealed when he pulled off his helmet. "That man was struck on the head in a fight. When he woke up, he could recall nothing about his own life, not even his name, until the swelling went away. Have you been hit on the head, boy?" His voice was not unkind, but when he reached out one hand to feel her scalp, India shrank away from him. Catching the hard look of the grey-eyed man who seemed to be the leader, she thought better of her reluctance and let Marcion search her head for bumps. He gave her a friendly smile before he ran his hand through her hair.

"Well?" the grey-eyed man asked when his friend had finished.

"No swellings." Marcion grunted, mystified

by his findings. "But have you noticed his face is painted?"

"A Greek, then," said the large-boned man called Hugo. "Byzantine men paint their faces and go clean-shaven like this stripling."

"He's a noble," said Marcion. "Look at his hands. No ordinary person would have such clean nails. Nor has he a scribe's inkstains on his fingers, though there's the bump on his right middle finger that all scribes have."

"A painted boy who claims the name of Baudoin and who can write," mused the leader. "Which Baudoin, boy? Of Noyon, or of Bordeaux?"

"Neither. I spoke of Robert Baldwin," India told him. "He was my—my master." Something in the expression of those unnerving grey eyes told her she ought to continue the deception and let these men believe she was a boy. The thought of what a heavily armed band of warriors, fresh from battle, might do to a defenseless woman was too horrible to consider. India saw a vast abyss of time and terror opening before her. Where was Hank? When would he retrieve her? *Could* he retrieve her, or would she be stuck here—wherever *here* was—forever?

"And where does this *Robair Baudoin* live?" asked the leader, his voice oddly soft.

"He does not live." India decided her safety lay in staying as close to the truth as she could. That way, she might not be tripped up in too many lies. "My master is dead. It was he who gave me this pendant."

"Ah, of course." Marcion smiled at her, nodding his curly head. "A loyal retainer, carrying out the final command of his dying lord. Now, that makes sense. And you got lost, didn't you, lad? Who wouldn't in this forsaken land? You've strayed into Saxony, boy, and just now you stumbled into one of those skirmishes the Saxons love to begin whenever they see a few Franks approaching. They will accept the True Faith in time, but until they do, we occasionally have to teach them a lesson in Christian forbearance." He looked out over the body-strewn field, nodding his acceptance of the story he had just woven around India's presence there.

"Who was this *Robair Baudoin*?" asked Hugo. "And why would a Greek be serving him?"

"I took a sacred vow," India responded, telling herself this was the truth, too. "I swore to remain with him until one of us died."

"And on his deathbed, he gave you a final mission?" asked the leader. "Or did he die in battle?"

"It was a long and painful illness," India said, adding the rest of the truth without further prompting. "He bore it bravely and died at peace with God and man." Unexpected tears threatened to overcome her, but she set her teeth and swallowed hard against the lump in her throat.

Hank, where are you? Get me out of here before

37

I say or do something that makes them kill me. Or before they realize I'm no boy, but a woman. Please, Hank. Please!

"To whom did this master of yours, this *Robair Baudoin*, send you?" asked the leader.

"What?" India stared at him, completely at a loss. She had no idea what to say next.

"It doesn't matter where he was supposed to go," Marcion countered his leader's probing question. "He's lost, and he's wearing the royal medallion. We are obligated to protect him and see that he's sheltered and fed. You can tell he's not himself yet after wandering into battle by accident. I can't blame the lad for that. I remember how I felt after my first experience in war. We'll take him along with us, and when he's fully recovered, we can set him on his way again."

"What if we are going in the wrong direction for him?" asked Hugo, who seemed to be having great difficulty in sorting out all that had been said. Raising both hands, Hugo removed his helmet to scratch his head in puzzlement.

"That's ridiculous," Marcion retorted, laughing. "No one would go deeper into Saxony without an army. You weren't going to Saxony, were you, boy?"

"I had no intention of being in Saxony at all," India responded with fervor.

"Nor should we be here, now that we've put down this minor revolt," remarked the leader. "Hugo, bring the horses. Marcion, find the others, report to me on who's wounded, and discover if we've lost anyone. And you, boy, come with me."

"Come where?" India stayed where she was, afraid to move, fearing that if she left the spot where she had first landed, Hank might never find her again.

"Were you so disrespectful to your late master?" snapped the leader. "Do as I say and don't question me."

"Obey him," Marcion advised, giving her a friendly push on one shoulder. "The Firebrand has a hot temper. Don't rouse it."

"Firebrand?" India repeated.

"We call him that for the ferocious way he fights, too. In the heat of battle, there is no one like him." Marcion spoke with deep and open respect.

"Does this paragon have a name?" asked India, eyeing the man who stood waiting impatiently for her to jump to his command.

"Don't you know him? He's Theuderic of Metz, fiercest warrior in all the Frankish armies, more than equal in valor to Count Hrulund himself. All right, don't flare up at me for praising your prowess, Theu. I'm going now. I will obey." With a wave of one hand and a laugh, Marcion suited action to his words, heading toward the field where a group of men was working. "I'll collect everyone. It looks to me as if we haven't many wounded to worry about," he called back.

Theu? *Firebrand*? *Count Hrulund*? India knew this could not be happening. It could not! But it was happening, and Theuderic of Metz had plans for her.

"Since you have no horse and since I do not trust you in spite of the royal sign you wear," Theuderic told her, "you will ride with me, on my horse."

"I am not accustomed to being called a liar." India faced him with her eyes blazing, determined not to move. "Furthermore, I do not wish to ride."

"I could tie you to my horse and let you walk behind us," Theuderic offered politely, a faint smile lurking at the corner of his mouth, "but just on the chance that a word or two of what you have said here is the truth, I am prepared to be generous and let you ride. I must admit, you sounded as if you did care about this Baudoin whom you claim was once your master. And I feel certain the story of how you got that medallion will prove to be an interesting one. You can tell it to me later. We are best gone from here quickly."

"What, are you afraid of a few Saxon savages?" She did not know why those insulting words passed her lips. She had never spoken so to any man before, but something about this bold warrior with his cold and arrogant stare infuriated her. He had called her a coward and a puking child. Considering what she had been through in the last couple of hours, she thought she deserved better treatment than that. She had not been sick at the sight of blood, she had not fainted or screamed while the battle raged around her. And she had managed not to lie. Twisting the facts a little to save her own skin was not a lie, it was a necessity. This crude man could never understand what had happened to her. In fact, if she tried to explain the truth, he would probably think she was mad or bewitched. Either way, she could be locked up— and possibly be put to death.

"*Boy.*" Theuderic's voice was soft again, and something in it made her shiver. "Here is Hugo with the horses. Will you ride with me for the next four days, or will you walk? The choice is yours."

"Four days?" She dared not go so far away from the spot where she had landed. How would Hank ever locate her? "I ought to stay here."

"I cannot allow that. Because of the medallion you wear, I am obligated to see you to safety. By what form of motion you get there is of small concern to me. I have never seen boots like yours before, but I do not think they will last for days of walking through forests and across rivers and streams, until I can provide a horse for you. I advise you to ride. Decide now, *boy*. This moment."

"I—I'll ride." Her decision was as much the result of the men now arriving as it was the effect of those cold and strangely knowing eyes that would not allow her to drop her own until he had broken the contact.

Theuderic's band of about a dozen warriors was dirty and bloodstained, but apparently only

41

a few minor injuries had been sustained in the brief battle they had fought, a remarkable feat considering their gear. Theuderic was the only man with chain mail. Marcion wore boiled-leather armor with metal scales sewn across chest and back. Hugo had plain boiled leather with no metal reinforcement, and the others made do with padded wool or plain woolen tunics. About half of them had rounded metal helmets. But every man was armed with sword, shield, knife, and battle-axe, and a few carried spears in addition to their other weapons.

At first, India was frightened by their appearance, but it was not long before she became fascinated by the warm way they greeted Theuderic, and then by the manner in which he spoke to each man, thanking them individually for their efforts, making certain that all were able to travel. Nor were the men particularly interested in India. After a comment or two on the mysterious appearance of a slender and attractive boy in their midst, they quickly went about the business of fastening onto the backs of their horses their weapons and what little plunder they had gathered from the dead. Before long most of them were mounted and ready to ride, and at that point the animals drew India's attention.

These were not the kind of horses she was used to seeing. With their thick coats and heavy legs, they looked more like sturdy farm horses than elegant riding steeds. She had ridden only twice in her life, and she did not look forward to this enforced journey. As she regarded Theuderic's grey and white mount with trepidation, the man himself stepped toward her, and without a word placed his hands on her waist. An instant later she was astride the horse's back, a moment more and Theuderic sat behind her. His brawny left arm came around her body to pull her back against him. The man was pure muscle, from his deep chest to unbelievably strong arms to thighs that were like tree trunks. She could feel those thighs move against her buttocks when he guided his horse forward. Disturbed by the motion, India sat rigid, her shoulders squared.

"There is nothing to fear." His warm breath stirred the lock of hair that fell against her cheek. "Not from my men, nor from me. I will keep you safe, and when we have reached Aachen, and you have had time to rest, you will tell me your story again. And this time, you will tell me the entire truth, *boy*." She turned her head sharply at that last, almost purred, syllable. The glint she saw in his eye generated a new concern in her heart. Either this man had penetrated her disguise or he had a yearning for young boys. She very much doubted it was the latter.

As for Hank, could he find her if she moved elsewhere? Would his peculiar theory about manipulating time allow for a change in position on her part? Would she ever see him, or Willi, again? For that matter, could she manage to stay alive until Hank might be able to arrange

43

something, compute a new formula, or get advice from one of his friends who also experimented with computers? And—what at that moment seemed to her to be the most urgent question of all—could she protect herself against the warrior who held her in such a firm grasp, who would surely soon understand that she was no boy, if he had not already discovered it?

Chapter Four

As Theuderic had warned, their way wound through forests and across rivers and streams. Winter had barely begun to loosen its grip on that thickly wooded, sparsely settled northern land. There was a thin layer of snow on the ground, and in the few bare spots mud oozed, while from frozen puddles shards of ice reared upward under the horses' hooves. The trees were bare, with spring's blossoming still several months away. The chill day was dampened by an occasional cold drizzle.

India's hands and feet grew numb and her nose began to run. Soon she was shivering in earnest. Then Theuderic took his blue wool cloak and wrapped it around them both, pulling her still closer to him in the process. She was too grateful for the warmth of his tough body to make any protest.

They rode until it began to grow dark, when they stopped at a spot where the stream they had been following widened into a little pool. There a pile of charred wood showed that men had camped in that place not long before, and by the comments of Marcion and Hugo, India learned it had been this very band, on its way into Saxony. She marveled how they could find their path through what looked to her like a trackless wilderness and then return to the same place.

Nor did the men seem over-tired after fighting and riding all day, though she nearly fell from weariness when Theuderic lifted her down from his horse. He stood for a moment with his hands resting lightly on her hips as if to steady her until she found her feet again. So it must have appeared to any who looked in their direction, but India was intensely aware of the forward pressure of those hands. Her own hands were still on his shoulders. She caught her breath, knowing without looking that his eyes were on her face, searching, searching. . . .

Unable to lift her own gaze from his mouth, she watched his firm lips tighten into a hard line. He had a nice mouth, and when he wasn't acting like the hardened leader of a warband, it often quirked into a half smile at one corner. It would be so easy to slide her arms around his neck, to pull his face down to hers. . . .

Appalled at her reaction to this rude, unlettered warrior, so different from any other man she had known, she jerked away from him. At once he removed his hands from her hips, releasing her.

"A pretty painted boy," he muttered under his breath.

"I wish you would call me by my name," she said.

"*Boy.*"

She did look upward then. What she saw unnerved her. In his grey glance, unanswered questions smoldered, along with a light that told her that he, too, had been affected by their momentary half-embrace. He turned from her with an oath, leading his horse aside without a backward look. She imagined with grim humor that he was disgusted with himself for feeling a stirring of interest toward what he thought was another male.

She moved around the clearing, trying to work out the stiffness in her legs. After a while she knelt by the pool to drink, wondering wryly if she would contract from the water some awful disease that could have been easily cured, or even prevented, in her own century. Which thought brought her to the vital question of exactly where she was—and *when*.

"If you want to relieve yourself," said Theuderic, kneeling beside her to scoop up a handful of the cold water, "as you must, after so long a ride, go behind those bushes. You will have privacy there. I'll see to it."

"Thank you." It was a need that she suddenly

realized was imperative. She rose and started toward the bushes he had indicated. Halfway across the clearing she understood what his offer must mean. *He knew! Theuderic was fully aware that she was no boy.* She could think of no other explanation for what he had said. She spun around, wanting to catch his eye when he did not expect it, but he was not looking at her. He was helping Marcion to stack branches and twigs into a mound for their campfire, while Hugo used flint and a few dry leaves to start a flame.

The spot behind the bushes was damp, with a moldy smell from last autumn's rotted leaves. It was cold, it was uncomfortable, and it was decidedly unsanitary, but she had no choice. When she had finished, she went to the stream to wash her hands.

"A very particular boy," said Theuderic behind her.

"What do you want of me?" She spoke sharply, hoping to elicit from him some admission of his knowledge about her, but his expression revealed nothing.

"The truth would be helpful," he said.

"I have told you no lies."

"If not, then you have surely left out a goodly portion of your story. I suspect that what you have not said is more important than what you have admitted."

"What does that mean?"

"I have met a Byzantine Greek or two, and

none of them spoke our tongue with your accent. In fact, the Greeks I have known have considered themselves so superior to Franks that they disliked having to learn our language."

"Then you may assume that I am not a Byzantine Greek."

"I have already done so," he told her. "The question remains—who and what are you? I will know the answers, *boy*. It would be better for you if you tell me now."

"Are you threatening one who wears the royal medallion?" She was surprised at her own nerve, but the man terrified her. The feeling had nothing to do with fear of physical violence from him, for she did not believe he would harm her—at least not until he had the answers he wanted. It was rather the sheer physicality of his hard body and the straightforward, practical thinking he had shown in the way he led his men that awed her. Having spent most of her life among scholars, she did not know how to deal with this kind of man, or how to stop her unwanted response to everything he did or said. At least she would not be in the same close proximity to him during the night as she had been forced to endure all day.

Unfortunately for her self-possession, she was soon disabused of this belief. The evening meal of dried meat and somewhat stale bread was scarcely washed down with bad ale before the men began to roll themselves into their cloaks for the night. Hugo added more logs to the fire, then went to stand guard with Marcion. It was then that Theuderic approached India with a length of hide rope in one hand.

"You will stay beside me tonight," he said, catching her right hand. "This will make certain you follow my orders."

"What are you doing?" she cried, trying to pull her hand out of his grasp. He was too strong for her to offer more than a puny resistance. Her wrist was ensnared by the rope and securely tied in a way that left two long ends of rope dangling. These Theuderic wrapped around his waist, pulling his armor and his shirt up high to fasten the knot next to his skin on his right side.

"Now," he said, "you cannot free yourself without waking me. Stop struggling unless you want the others to laugh at you and make unseemly remarks about your hairless cheeks. There are one or two in this band who would not hesitate to make nasty sport of a pretty boy. I doubt if you would welcome their embraces or the uses they would invent for your soft and delicate flesh."

She stood perfectly still, too shocked to speak or move. Theuderic nodded, apparently satisfied that she was properly cowed.

"Lie down here, where I have spread my cloak," he ordered, "and I will lie next to you. We'll keep each other warm, lad, and if you have any idea of trying to escape in spite of the precautions I've taken, I tell you now that my men have been ordered to kill you if you leave this spot without my express permission."

"Why would any guest ever want to leave your gracious hospitality?" she retorted, furious at the way she was being treated.

"Lie down." He did not shout. He did not have to.

The rope he had left between them was long enough for her to kneel on the cloak without forcing him to join her. She did as he had commanded, sitting on the blue wool. He stood over her, his muscular legs spread wide, fists planted on his hips, watching her. He was only an inch or so taller than India, but from her present subservient position he looked huge. He had removed his helmet, revealing straight dark brown hair cut just below his ears. It was matted and sweaty from the helmet, and there was a faint red line across his forehead where the metal edge had rested. He looked as though he had not shaved for four or five days. Beneath the square neck and elbow-length sleeves of his chain mail *brunia*, she saw his heavy linen shirt, its sleeves extending to his wrists. His grey trousers were strapped with leather thongs to hold them close to his legs, and his leather shoes were laced to the ankle. He took off his wide belt and sword, laying the weapon to one side of the cloak. She looked at the sword, then back at him. The spark in his eyes dared her to snatch up the blade and try to use it on him.

"Why do you distrust me so?" she asked.

"Because you appeared suddenly in a place where you ought not to be, and because I have not survived for twenty-seven years without knowing when a person speaks the truth and when that person is evading or lying," he said.

She flushed at that, then stiffened under a look that examined her from the crown of her head to her folded knees to her mudstained boots, a look that seemed to remove every garment she wore and search out each curve of her body. Looking back at him, she felt heat flowing through all her veins and arteries, weakening her muscles, turning her bones to molten jelly. So burning was his glance that when he dropped to one knee beside her, she half expected him to throw her to the ground and fling himself on top of her. And she, who had once responded with tender warmth to her husband's gentle caresses, was deeply shaken to find herself longing now for the fever of this barbarian's embrace.

"I said lie down, lad." Commanded by that hoarse whisper, she stretched out her legs and sank back, never taking her eyes from his. He bent over her, pulling one edge of the cloak across her body.

"Do you sleep in your chain mail?" she murmured.

"It is safer thus."

She knew he meant not only safer from possible attack by Saxons lurking in the woods around them, but safer from her as well. A tiny glimmer of triumph pierced the gloom of her growing concern over her situation. This tough, totally masculine creature was afraid of her effect on him.

He lay beside her, pulling part of his cloak up and over them both. Suddenly, before she could protest or fend him off, he rose on his left elbow, his right arm still holding the hem of his cloak. His face was so close. . . . He tucked the cloak around her shoulder, then touched her hair. His callused, blunt fingers moved slowly across her cheek, one fingertip tracing the lower margin of her mouth, and then the bow of her upper lip. She caught her breath and held it, unable to move, unable to do anything but stare back into his fathomless eyes. He spoke her name, translating it into his own accent.

"Een-dee-ahh." The sound was a whisper, a promise, and an acknowledgment of the tension rising between them. His eyes were on her mouth now, where his fingertip still lingered, caressing the sensitive flesh there. She moaned, the faintest of notes, while she ached for the kiss he had not offered.

Then his hand fell to her upper arm, encircling it, fettering her to his side with flesh that was like a manacle of strongest steel. He lowered his head, pillowing it on his arm, and in the firelight she saw his eyes close.

"Good night, boy," he said, and was silent.

India lay stiffly, willing herself not to tremble because she did not want him to know how strongly he had affected her. She had never wanted any man but Robert, and their lovemaking had ended more than a year before his death, because his energy had been sapped by surgery and chemotherapy. She had put aside desire as she had put aside so much else at that time, refusing even to think about her sexual needs. And now, projected out of her own century into a time and place she could not yet locate exactly, she was panting with longing for a man she did not know, just because he had a magnificently muscled body, a commanding manner, and magical eyes that held her entranced every time he looked directly at her.

Theuderic probably could not read or write; he certainly knew nothing of the art, literature, music, or history that had been so important in her own life; he was a bloodthirsty warrior without gentleness or good manners, and—heaven help her!—she wanted him. Having admitted it, she suffered through a dreadful few minutes, fearing for her sanity, until she decided that her inability to repress her unwanted emotions must be the result of what had occurred in Hank's office.

To keep her mind off Theuderic and his disturbing nearness, she made herself think about the computer that had caused her present predicament. She believed she knew what had happened to her. When she had accidentally hit the switch on the new component, a program Hank had left in the computer must have mixed itself up with the material she had been working on. The idea was fantastic, but her presence among a band of Frankish warriors was proof that there was validity to Hank's theory about space and time, so there was no point in questioning that much.

Now that she thought about it, she could remember exactly what part of Robert's notes had been displayed on the computer screen when the peach-colored light first appeared. She had been studying the events leading up to the famous military disaster at the mountain pass of Roncevaux in the Pyrenees on August eighteenth of the year 778. That terrible day had been celebrated in song and legend through all the centuries since the entire rearguard of the Frankish army, the very flower of youth and courage, had died during an ambush.

Marcion had mentioned Count Hrulund as if the man were still alive, favorably comparing Theuderic's bravery and battle skills to those of the count. Hrulund was known to later ages as Roland, the king's invincible champion and heroic leader of the rearguard at Roncevaux, and if he was still alive, then this was indeed a time before that fateful day.

India concentrated, trying to recall every bit of the information she had been reading. During the year 777, Charles, king of the Franks—the man known to the twentieth century as Charlemagne—had secured his eastern border against the Saxons, though occasional flare-ups still occurred. That would explain the skirmish she had intruded upon. She knew now, after listening to Theuderic's men talk, that it had been no real battle. Real battles, Marcion had told her, were larger and much worse.

After a little more thought, she decided that the year was probably 778, and from the weather and the unleafed trees, the month must be early to mid-March. Theuderic had said they were headed for Aachen, which in her own twentieth century was on the border between Belgium and Germany.

Now that she had worked out the approximate date and place, she did not feel quite so disoriented. She could do nothing about the fact that she had been forced to move from the spot where she had arrived in this time, but it was possible that Hank could find her anyway. She would keep her eyes and ears open for any indication that he was attempting to contact her. She told herself that all she had to do was stay alert and wait for his signal. And stay alive. That might be more difficult.

Beside her Theuderic stirred, moving closer. She did not have to lift her hand far to touch the hard links of his armor. So many circles of metal, hundreds of them, individually forged and linked together. And, she had read, so expensive were they during this period of history that only the richest nobles could afford chain mail. Her captor was no ordinary warrior then, but someone of importance. She touched the edge of his sleeve, feeling the smooth hardness of circle upon circle. His simple *brunia* was a work of art. It was heavy, yet he bore its weight easily. He could even sleep in it, a feat she could not imagine achieving herself, though on second thought, she wasn't certain Theuderic really was asleep. If an alarm were given, he would probably be on his feet, sword in hand, within a second or two. If she tried to get away from his camp, he would stop her escape before she had left the cover of his cloak, even if she were able to remove or cut through the rope that bound them together. The thought of what he might do then made her remove her hand from his sleeve. The damp of the earth had seeped through the cloak, chilling her. She trembled a bit in spite of her efforts to stop her reaction to the cold.

With a deep sigh, Theuderic moved again, stretching his arm across her waist. Was it for warmth, or just a way of reminding her not to try anything foolish? Smothering the tears she refused to shed, she turned toward him, seeking the heat of his sturdy body. Both of his arms enfolded her with surprising gentleness. Feeling oddly comforted, she snuggled her head into his shoulder and slept at last.

Marcion offered to carry her on his horse the next day, but Theuderic would not allow it.

"So long as I am your leader, this boy is my responsibility," he said.

When Marcion shrugged his shoulders and made no argument, India thought about Theuderic's leadership of his band. Marcion and Hugo were obviously his closest friends, but they all seemed to be on good terms, and no one showed the least shyness about expressing his opinion on any subject. Theuderic listened to each man, let them settle any personal disagreements among themselves, and gave direct orders only when necessary. It was a singularly democratic arrangement, yet when Theuderic barked out a command, it was instantly obeyed. Clearly he had the respect and trust of his men. Perhaps there was more to him than pure physical strength and steely determination. While she considered this possibility, Theuderic, mounted and with his shield slung across his back, leaned out of the saddle, extending a hand toward her.

"Put your foot on mine and give me your hand," he said. "I'll lift you up."

She was awkward about it, nearly falling before he caught her and sat her in front of him in the way she had ridden the day before.

"Stiff and sore, are you?" he asked, smiling a little. "It happens to everyone in the beginning. It will wear away as the day goes on, and as you grow more used to riding."

Once she had found her balance, he released her to take the reins in both hands, so that she was enclosed by his mail-clad arms. The temptation to sink back against his chest and rest her head on his shoulder was almost irresistible. Recalling how she had awakened that morning wrapped in his arms and his cloak, to find him watching her through eyes like silver water, and how he had sat up without a word, pulling aside his garments to unfasten the knot of the hide rope so he could rise and stride off through the forest, still without speaking to her, she wondered how she could survive another day so close to him.

"Wouldn't you be more comfortable if I rode behind you?" she asked, thinking that arrangement would be infinitely easier for her, too.

"I want you where I can see you," he replied. "If you vanish in an instant, in the same way you appeared, I want to know it at once."

"Is that how it seemed to you?" she asked.

"You arrived out of the air," he said. "One moment you were not there, and the next moment, you were. The others think you heard the sound of fighting and ran onto the field in confusion, while they were looking elsewhere. Only I saw the true manner of your coming."

"No wonder you don't trust me. I'm surprised you didn't kill me at once."

"I would have," he said, "but I saw the medallion."

"I am human," she told him, fearing what he might believe. "I am flesh and blood and bone, as you are. I should not be here, I will return to my own home as soon as I can, but while I am here, I mean no harm to you or your men, nor to anyone else."

"That may be true, but it is no explanation for your appearance among us. Your mere presence may cause harm, whether you mean it or not." He fell silent for a bit, as if considering something, then spoke again. "I have heard stories about odd-looking men who come to Francia in vessels that fly through the air. The stories say these men live in a land called Magonia. Is that your home?"

"No." She twisted around to look at him. "I have never heard of such a place, nor have I read or heard of that story."

"Where is your home?"

"I live in Cheswick." That was safe enough to admit. It would mean nothing to him.

"Where is this *Chess-veeck*? Did I say it properly?"

"You came very close." She smiled when he repeated the word. His hard face softened just a little, the corner of his mouth quirked upward in a half-smile, and there was real laughter in his eyes. She added, "Cheswick is far from here, a journey of many long years."

He studied her face, the laughter fading from his own. She was sorry to see it go.

"Once again you tell me the truth," he said, "and once again you evade speaking all of it. Why?"

"Sometimes the truth can be dangerous."

"To you or to me?"

"Not to you," she said, wishing she had kept her mouth shut.

"Can you be sure of that?" he asked. "Can I be sure of it?"

"Please don't ask me any more questions. I have told you what I can." She had been looking at him all this time. Now, unwilling to meet his steady eyes any longer, she turned her head forward again, and he fell silent without promising that he would make no further inquiries of her, leaving her to believe it was only a matter of time before his questions began once more. She thought a man like Theuderic would not give up until he had the information he sought.

They were traveling through a particularly thick section of the forest that covered vast stretches of the northeastern lands, and care was needed to be certain they did not lose their way. But though Theuderic did not speak to her again, she could not ignore him. With every step his horse took, his legs brushed against hers, and his arms on either side of her were like steel bars. If she moved so much as an inch, her back was pressed to his chest. She heard every breath he took. As the hours passed, she became more and more aware of him and more and more frightened of what she was feeling. She was greatly relieved when, some time after midday, Hugo created a diversion for her thoughts.

"A rabbit on a spit would taste good tonight," Hugo said. "I'm weary of bread and dried venison. If I remember this part of our path correctly, the trees should thin out in a little while. What do you say, Theu? Shall I lead a hunting party?"

"Can you hunt and not get lost?" Marcion put in, taking a thump of Hugo's great fist on his arm for the quip.

"Take Eudon and Osric with you," Theuderic agreed. "Marcion, you stay here with us."

"Ha! He thinks you'd be the one to get lost,

my friend," said Hugo to Marcion, laughing. He pulled his horse to one side, waiting while the others rode on. India looked back as the three Theuderic had designated moved into the trees at an angle to the path they were following.

"It would be easy enough to get lost here," she remarked.

"Not Hugo," Marcion told her. "I tease him, but he's a fine hunter. I can taste that rabbit already." He smacked his lips in a comical way.

"You aren't a Frank, are you?" asked India, regarding his close-cropped black curls and wiry frame. Perhaps conversation with this pleasant young man would help to take her mind off Theuderic's tantalizing nearness.

"I am a Lombard," Marcion told her. "I was brought to Francia five years ago after Charles conquered Lombardy and deposed King Desiderius. In the past, my father was one of Desiderius's most valued counselors, so I was made a hostage for the future good behavior of the rest of my family."

"You are a hostage?" India must have looked stunned by this information, because Marcion laughed and nodded his head in a reassuring way.

"It has been a most enjoyable time," he said. "I was immediately given into Theu's keeping, and we have become friends over the years. I have made many friends in Francia, not least of them Charles himself, and I have learned much from the Franks. Their king is a great man."

"How old are you, Marcion?"

"I will be twenty-one at the end of August," he said. "Then it will be time for me to cross the Alps and return to Lombardy. Charles has arranged a marriage for me with the daughter of one of his nobles. I will miss Francia, but it will be good to see my parents again and to show my home to my new bride."

While India was assimilating this agreeable picture of a hostage's existence, so different from the twentieth-century image of such a life, and trying to gather her nerve to ask Theuderic if he was married or betrothed, their progress through the forest was halted by shouts off to their left.

"Move behind me," Theuderic ordered her. "I can't fight with you sitting in my lap."

He started to swing her up and around, but before he could lift her, Osric burst out of the trees on a lathered horse.

"Theu, it's Eudon," Osric shouted. "He's been gored by a boar. Hugo said to come at once. He didn't want to leave Eudon alone."

"Lead us there." With those terse words Theuderic pushed India back in place in front of him and dug his heels into his horse's sides. He and the rest of his men followed Osric through the trees.

They found Hugo bending over his companion, who was lying on the cold earth. Theuderic leapt off his horse to go to them. India, left to her own devices, tumbled to the ground without assistance. Averting her eyes from the huge boar that lay a short distance away, impaled by Hugo's spear, she ran toward the wounded man.

"We never saw the beast till it attacked," Hugo told Theuderic. "Eudon and I had dismounted to track a pair of rabbits. Osric was keeping watch. He shouted as soon as he saw the boar, but it was too late. It charged out of the bushes and gored Eudon in his right buttock."

"Better his buttock than his belly," said Theuderic, bending to inspect the damage. "You were fortunate this day, my friend. This is just a grazing cut."

Coming up behind Theuderic, India saw that Eudon's wound was a slash along the side of his buttock.

"I thought boars always charged their prey head-on," she said, with images of pictures of medieval hunts in her mind.

"They do," Hugo told her. "This would have been a death blow had Eudon not turned aside when Osric shouted."

At this point Theuderic spared a glance for the boar, another for Hugo.

"A good, clean kill," he said appreciatively. "Neatly spitted."

"Now cook it," came Eudon's voice through gritted teeth. "I plan to eat its heart. Give the liver to Hugo; he's earned it."

"Before you eat anything," Theuderic told him, "we are going to cauterize that wound.

Osric, tell the others to find some dry wood and start a fire. Hugo, get the bandages."

"No," India protested. "That's barbaric. Can't you just wash it with wine, or with clean water?"

"If we had brought any wine with us," Theuderic said, "we'd have drunk it long ago. It's not a deep wound, but a boar roots up its food from the ground, so its tusks are dirty. If we don't cauterize it at once, Eudon will die of the poison that was on the tusks. If you don't want to see how we treat him, I suggest you keep out of the way. I'll assign someone to guard you."

"There must be something I can do for Eudon," she insisted. "I tended my master in his last illness, so I am accustomed to caring for the sick. Let me help."

"Eudon is not sick, and he's not dying. He has been wounded. There is a difference," Theuderic told her. "But perhaps you can be useful here. You don't look strong enough to hold him down when the moment comes, but you can help me to undress him." His face was perfectly serious, with no hint of humor, but India was certain that in his heart Theuderic was laughing at her, expecting her to dispute his suggestion with sudden modesty.

"Do you want everything off?" she asked coolly, telling herself that a man's body held no mystery for a woman who had been married.

"Just pull his tunic up and remove his breeches and underdrawers," Theuderic replied, watching her closely.

Determined not to betray her female status, India reached boldly forward to lift Eudon's tunic and undershirt so she could tug at the cord that held up his coarse woolen breeches. Removing them was an unpleasant process and took a while, for Eudon, though he tried to help her, was in considerable pain and was loath to move in any way that might cause more discomfort. Theuderic let her do the job by herself, waiting until she had the breeches down around the man's knees before he knelt to remove Eudon's cross-gartered stockings and unlace his shoes. Eudon wore linen underdrawers, torn and bloodstained like the breeches, and these India also removed, leaving him lying on his left side with his remaining garments hiked up to his waist, half naked in the cold dampness. Theuderic spread Eudon's own cloak, and he and Hugo moved the man onto it.

"Who'll hold his head?" asked Hugo.

"I will," India offered, sitting down and pulling Eudon's head onto her lap. Gently she smoothed back his tangled hair, brushing it off his face.

"Boy, are you strong enough?" Hugo demanded.

"I held Robert Baldwin when he was racked with pain," India replied, meeting Hugo's eyes squarely, but aware of Theuderic watching her every action. "I will do no less for this man."

"Let him stay where he is," urged Eudon. "His hands are gentle as any woman's on my brow."

"Do him no harm," Hugo warned India. "He's

my friend. You will answer to me if you hurt him."

"I only want to help," India assured him. To try to distract Eudon from the preparations for his coming ordeal, she asked him, "Have you a wife?"

"No," Eudon replied, "but there's a whore in Paderborn who likes me well. I pray I will be able to serve her in the future as I have in the past."

"If you satisfied her before," Hugo said, "she'll cry out in pleasure again when next you come together. This wounding won't affect your manhood, and you'll have a fine scar to show her as proof of your courage. Now, here's the cloth." He had been folding a piece of fabric as he spoke. This he placed between Eudon's teeth.

India saw Theuderic squatting by the fire holding a knife blade into the flames. Now Osric took one of Eudon's arms, Marcion took the other, a third and fourth man held his feet. Hugo knelt beside India, his hands on Eudon's shoulders.

"If you've never done this before," Hugo said to India in a low voice, "he'll buck and heave at first, and it will be hard to hold him. The cloth is to keep him from biting his tongue. Don't worry, Theu knows what he is doing, and he'll make it as quick and painless as possible."

"I understand." And she did, despite her initial protests and her horror at what must be done. This, after all, was not the familiar twentieth century, with hospitals and antibiotics readily available. Without cauterization of the wound, infection would soon set in and Eudon might well die. With it, he had a chance to heal and recover. In the faces of the men around Eudon, India saw the reflection of her own understanding of his condition—saw, too, their open and honest concern for him. Hardened warriors they might be, but the comradeship among them was a fine and heartwarming thing, and for those few minutes India was proud to be a part of it and determined to be worthy of their acceptance.

Theuderic rose from his place beside the fire, holding the heated knife. He came forward and knelt at Eudon's right side. India stared at the knife, then raised her eyes to Theuderic's face.

"Are you ready, Eudon?" Theuderic asked, but India felt as if he were asking her the question. When Eudon said something muffled by the cloth in his mouth and nodded his head, India gritted her teeth and nodded her own head.

"Hold him," Theuderic said in a quiet, calm voice, and a moment later laid the knife flat upon the open wound.

Eudon squealed in pain, his jaws clamped hard on the cloth. His body fought the searing heat, and it took the six of them to hold him on the ground. Theuderic kept the knife where it was. Eudon went limp.

"Well done," said Hugo, releasing Eudon's shoulders. The other men relaxed their grip and sat back. "You can move now, lad. We'll roll up his breeches and use them for his pillow."

India rose on unsteady legs, telling herself she dared not faint, because if she did they would all know she was a woman. Worse than that, she would be embarrassed before men she was beginning to respect. She took a few deep breaths to clear her head.

"He'll need bandaging," she said to Hugo. "I'll do it if you like."

"That's my job," Hugo said.

"Someone should sit with him."

"Osric and I will do it." Hugo was a big-boned bear of a man, but his massive hand was remarkably gentle when he patted India's shoulder. "I'm sorry I doubted you, lad. You did what you said you would, and I thank you for it. Eudon will be all right. Get yourself some food. There's fresh meat tonight."

She saw then what the rest of the men had been doing while seven of their number had been occupied with Eudon. Underbrush had been cleared away from the area around the fire, and the horses had been tethered nearby and their trappings removed. The boar had been skinned and cleaned, and the carcass was cooking on a heavy spit set over the fire. With branches stripped from the trees, the men had built several rough shelters for themselves, little more than flimsy lean-tos against wind and rain, and no protection at all against the cold. In one of these shelters a bed of pine needles had been prepared and onto it the men who had held Eudon were laying him under Hugo's supervision.

"I misjudged you," Theuderic said, very low. He had come silently to stand before her. "You are no coward. But I should have known that. No craven soul would be permitted to wear this." His right hand lightly touched the pendant that still hung from the chain around her neck. With his eyes holding hers, he moved his fingertips until they rested at the spot where one small, firm breast began to swell. Very gently, he pressed against the softness. The corner of his mouth began to turn upward. And then, amazingly, while India stood frozen, unable to react in any way, he removed his hand and turned from her to the fire.

"Come and eat," he said in his normal voice. "You've earned your slice of meat this day."

Chapter Five

They carved the boar by hacking off the outer-most pieces, which were burned on the outside and dripping red an inch or so inside, and they left the remains to continue cooking until the meat was more thoroughly done.

India sat on the bare ground between Theuderic and Marcion. The others were eating heartily, and she was hungry, too. She had a chunk of greasy meat in one hand, a crust of stale bread in the other, and a wooden cup of sour ale on the ground beside her. It was a wonderful, restorative feast. When she thought of the way she used to pick at her plain, non-fat yogurt and sip her decaffeinated coffee, she felt like laughing out loud. She had just survived two incredible days, she felt more alive than she had ever felt before, and she cared not at all if her present diet would be considered unhealthy by twentieth-century standards. Enormously grateful for the food, she swallowed the last bite of her meat and licked her fingers as Marcion was doing to his.

"Why did you build the shelters?" she asked Marcion. "We had none in the last place we stopped."

"Because we'll be here for two or three nights," he replied.

When she looked at Theuderic for confirmation of this, he nodded.

"I won't divide my band," Theuderic said. "Not while we're still east of the Rhine. We stay together, and we stay where we are until Eudon can travel again."

"How far is it to the Rhine?" she asked.

"Half a day's ride at the speed we were traveling. Had Eudon not been hurt, we would have reached it by tomorrow evening, and we would cross the next morning. As it is, we will wait." He said this with no sign of impatience or irritation, as if a definite schedule were unimportant. She thought that in a land where time was told by the rising or the setting of the sun and wristwatches had not yet been invented, perhaps the delay of a day or two did not matter. She found that a restful notion.

"Who's on first watch?" Marcion asked, smothering a yawn.

"Osric and Rollin," Theuderic decided. "Then you and Hugo. I'll take the dawn watch with one of the others. I'll ask for a volunteer."

"I'll do it," India said, feeling at one with the group around the fire and wanting to contribute to its collective welfare.

"Not you, India." Theuderic's look was warm. "Thank you for the offer, but we need a full-grown man, able to use sword and battle-axe if need be."

"Is it so unsafe here?"

"Probably not. This part of Saxony is well subdued, not like the area where you found us. Still, it's always wise to post a guard." He rose in a smooth, easy motion that showed her once again just how flexible and strong he was. "I'll see Eudon now, then we can bed down for the night," he said to her.

She went with him. They found Eudon slightly feverish, but conscious and alert.

"You'll feel better in the morning," Theuderic promised after checking the wound. "I'm sorry we have no wine or herbs to ease you into sleep. I see Hugo has been wiping your face with cool water. That will help."

"I'll be all right." Eudon actually managed to smile. "I'll be eating by next midday. Keep some of the boar for me."

"We're saving the best part," said Theuderic, laying one hand on Eudon's shoulder for a moment.

"You care so much for your men," India remarked as they walked away from the lean-to.

"How could I lead them if I did not?" Theuderic asked.

"You are so tough, so completely a warrior,

73

and yet you are kind, too. You are very different from the man I first thought you to be." When she realized that she was speaking even as the thoughts came into her mind, without censoring what she said, she fell silent, looking shyly at him. His returning glance was mild but penetrating.

"So are you different." From his neutral tone she could not tell exactly how he meant that remark, but after his earlier praises, she thought it might be a compliment.

They had reached one of the lean-tos, and she saw the pine that had been heaped into a bed. Next to it lay the hide rope. Theuderic threw his cloak over the pine and motioned to her to lie down.

"Please," she said, "don't tie me again. It's humiliating to be leashed like a dog."

"Have you never observed that unleashed dogs often wander from home?" His voice remained as quiet and his manner as nonconfrontational as before, which gave her the courage to insist, hoping to sway him.

"When I am bound, you are bound, too," she said. "If the Saxons should attack, you would waste precious time releasing me so you could fight them."

"Should the Saxons attack us tonight, I will do what I would have done last night," he replied, showing her the knife he had used on Eudon's wound. "After you slept, I kept this in my hand all night, so I could kill you quickly before you could be captured. The Saxons reserve special tortures for prisoners such as yourself. I will do my best to protect you from that horror."

"Dear God," she whispered, sinking down upon the fragrant pine. All her earlier sense of peace and safety had dissipated, his words having recalled her to her true situation. She was alone and frightened in a barbaric world. The trees surrounding their camp, which until then had seemed to her like the walls of a large room securely enclosing Theuderic and all his company, instead became in her imagination hiding places, behind which fierce and cruel Saxons or ravenous beasts might be skulking. Compared to either of those threats, Theuderic and his men, rough and unlettered warriors though they might be, represented all that existed of civilization, offering her the only protection she might hope to find. Meekly, she put out her right hand and let him knot the rope around her wrist.

"Surely there are dangers in your own country," he said, fastening the loose ends of rope around his waist.

"Terrible and violent ones, especially in certain parts of our cities," she admitted. "But they are known to me, and I can try to avoid them. Here, where I am a stranger, perils seem to lurk behind every tree."

"I understand. Doubtless I would feel as you do, were I to travel to your land."

They lay down together, and he pulled the cloak over them. Perhaps sensing the tenseness of her mood, he made no attempt to touch her. She did not sleep until it was almost dawn.

In the morning, six of the men organized a hunting party. Hugo and Osric remained in camp, hovering like anxious parents over Eudon, whose sunken eyes and flushed cheeks revealed the effects of fever and persistent pain. India sat with Eudon while his nurses went off to tend to their personal needs and break their fast, but they were soon back at Eudon's side, insisting there was no more she could do. Theuderic was nowhere to be seen, Marcion was cutting firewood, and she could see one or two other men standing guard over the camp.

Her fears of the previous night having eased somewhat with the rising of the sun, India decided to find a place where she could wash in private. She had been living with more than a dozen men for almost three days, and she wanted a few minutes alone. She would be careful, keeping her eyes open in case of danger, and she would not go so far from the camp that she could not return quickly.

She followed the trickling water that ran beside the campsite until it flowed into a small stream, then into a larger one. Springs and streams and little pools abounded in the forest, many of them fed by melting snow. India found a rock that had been dried by the sun and knelt on it, leaning over the stream to dip her hands into the water. She was not foolish enough to remove her tunic, though she wanted to. She longed for a hot bath and plenty of soap, for thick towels to dry with, and a comb for her hair and clean clothing when she had finished, but she would have to be content with using cold water and her hands. She splashed water onto her face, afterward raising an arm and bending into her sleeve to dry herself. Then she tried to scrub away the dirt that was ground into the knuckles of her hands and caked beneath her fingernails. Eagerly she searched for sand to use as a cleanser, but there was none. She saw only pebbles and brown leaves in the water and, a few feet downstream, a cluster of bright green leaves growing at the verge where muddy bank and stream met.

"Watercress!" Forgetting her distaste at her filthy condition, she went to investigate. Pulling a plant out by the roots, she tasted some of its leaves, closing her eyes in order to enjoy the experience more intensely. Crunchy, tangy green sensations delighted her tongue. "Oh, it's delicious." She reached for more.

"Why have you left camp?" She had not heard him come across the carpet of moss and moist dead leaves. He wore his iron helmet and carried a spear in his hand.

"Don't you ever take off your armor?" she asked rather defensively, for she had at once understood that he might just as easily have been a Saxon.

"I will remove it when we reach Aachen. You

77

know it is unsafe for you to wander about alone. Shall I tie you to my side during the day as well as at night?"

"I was only washing my face. What I've found makes up for leaving without your permission," she said, pointing to the watercress. "We can have salad tonight. It will be good for Eudon, too. Watercress is full of vitamin C, which is supposed to speed the healing of wounds."

"So your people use it as a healing herb." Theuderic smiled a little, as if he had caught her in an unintended confession. "To me, cress means that spring will come soon. Sometimes, during this cold winter, I wondered if it ever would."

"Does that mean you like greens?" She offered a branch of the plant she had been holding while they talked, the same plant she had tasted. It was a kind of peace offering, an apology for leaving camp. She thought he understood, for he took the cress and chewed on it, smiling more broadly at the fresh taste of it.

"Always the first greens of spring are welcome after a winter of dried or salted meat, of pickles and turnips and cabbage. The cress is strong, yet delicate, too. Like you. Here." He pulled off his helmet, offering it to her. "Fill this."

Laying down his spear, he squatted beside her, reaching into the clump of greenery to snip off stems with deft movements. India quickly added her contribution, heaping watercress into the helmet.

"Be careful," he told her. "Don't pull it out of

78

the mud that way. You must leave enough of root and leaf to allow it to grow again. Others coming this way may need the nourishment of these plants more than we do, and we, returning another year, may need it again."

"Just what I always wanted to meet," she muttered, trying to pick the watercress the way Theuderic did, "an eighth-century conservationist." It did not strike her as odd that he would care about leaving watercress roots to grow again. His concern for a simple plant fit into a pattern of behavior that was gradually revealing to her a complex and interesting man.

With the helmet full, Theuderic stood, reaching down a hand to help India to her feet. They faced each other, the brimming helmet between them.

"Even with the paint worn off your face by time and water," he said, "still your skin is smoother than that of any unbearded boy I have ever seen." The back of his hand brushed across her cheek in a gentle caress. He was looking at her mouth in a way that sent heat swirling through her.

"Theuderic?" She wanted to take his hand in hers and press it against her throbbing bosom. She wanted him to put his arms around her. She wanted. . .

"Ah, well," he said, "it's only a few more days till we reach Aachen. I can wait until then."

"What will happen in Aachen?" she asked.

"Why, then we can safely remove our armor," he said, in a way that made her wonder if he was teasing her. The hand that had touched her cheek dropped to her shoulder and then to her sleeve, where he rubbed the fabric of her tunic between his fingers. "Then, India, we will all remove our armor. Every bit of it, I promise you."

Eudon joined them for the evening meal and ate with a healthy appetite, devouring leftover cold boar meat, a fair-sized chunk of spit-roasted rabbit, and several handfuls of watercress. But when he tried to convince Theuderic that he would be able to travel the next morning, Theuderic decided to wait another day in order to be sure Eudon's wound was well on its way to healing.

There was some good-natured grumbling about the delay, several of the men complaining to Eudon that his injury was keeping them from the arms of their sweethearts. Marcion, who was as usual sitting beside India, gave vent to a long sigh.

"How I miss my little Bertille," he said. "It will be weeks yet before I see her again, and then her strict mother and the queen will take care that we do nothing more than kiss or hold hands. I will have to wait until summer ends before I can claim the prize I have desired since the moment I met her."

"It's a fortunate man who loves the wife chosen for him by his king," said Hugo, on Marcion's other side.

"Have you a wife, Hugo?" asked India, leaning forward to see him better.

"I have so little land that no woman would want me, and no parents would agree to give their daughter to me," Hugo replied. "You see, it is our Frankish custom to divide a parent's lands among all the children, including the daughters, so they will have dowries. Generations ago, my family held vast lands, but by the time I was born, my father had only a small estate to bequeath to me, and I owe part of it to my sister when she's old enough to marry. But I hope to earn a grant of land by my sword. Charles is generous to the men who fight for him. For now, being poor, I have only a widowed mother and a ten-year-old sister for female companionship."

"Don't listen to him," Osric called to India. "Hugo has plenty of women." This claim was greeted with laughter and a few raunchy comments about Hugo's successes with the ladies.

"If I had a good wife," Hugo said, his big, honest face sad, "I'd be faithful to her forever, and I'd do my best to make her happy."

"He would, too," Theuderic said, seating himself beside India. "Most of us know what a great treasure a good and gentle woman can be. Like Hugo, I'd protect such a lady with my very life and gladly give all I have into her keeping. But that is not to be my fate. Not now. It's too late for that."

"Then you have no wife, either?" Her heart

lightened at the realization. It would be appalling to learn that the man who filled her thoughts through every waking hour was another woman's husband. If Theuderic was unwed, if he loved no other woman, then—then what? She had known him for a little more than three days. How could she feel anything more for him than an overheated interest in his physical attractions? She watched him stare into the fire for a while before he spoke again.

"I was married for a year," he said. "She died giving birth to my son."

"I'm sorry. Did you love her?" She had not intended to say that, but the question was in her mind and it slipped out without conscious thought on her part. He did not take offense at her prying.

"Not at first," he said. "We met but once before the wedding, and she was ten years younger than I, only fourteen when we married. But she was sweet and kind-hearted, and she tried so hard to please me that soon I did love her. When she died, I thought my heart would break from the pain of my loss. I swore then that I would never again allow myself to love a woman, for to love again would mean risking a second and similar loss, and that would drive me mad or kill me."

"You do not appear to me to be the kind of man who will live an entirely chaste life," she said, angry with him and with herself because she was so hurt by his words.

"Few soldiers are entirely chaste," he said.

"Knowing that, for *her* gentle sake, I do not allow my men to rape following a battle, nor to harm our female captives."

"But you told me they would harm me!" India exclaimed. Only when Theuderic turned his head to regard her with a quizzical look did she realize what she had revealed.

"True enough," he drawled, "but a *boy*, traveling alone, is something different from a virtuous woman, is he not?"

"It is just possible," India declared hotly, "that such a boy would need the same protection a woman would."

"That is so," said Theuderic, very quietly, "which is why I have given you my protection. Boy or maid, I'd not see innocence ruined without trying to help."

"Theu." Marcion, who had been conversing with Hugo and Osric, now broke into his leader's speech. "If you prefer, India may share my shelter with me tonight. I sleep more soundly than you and would scarcely notice his presence."

Theuderic gave him a long, level look, during which it seemed to India that the two men shared an unspoken understanding.

"Thank you for your concern about my rest," Theuderic said dryly, "but the boy is my responsibility. He stays with me."

"As you wish." Marcion acceded with a graceful movement of his expressive hands. "Though you should know, Theu, that after the care he gave to Eudon, all of us consider India to be a

83

member of this band and therefore our joint responsibility."

"I'm glad to hear it," Theuderic said, adding, to India's consternation, "If I am killed, see that India is safely delivered to Charles."

"Killed?" India cried. "Do you anticipate having to fight before we reach Aachen?"

"I do not. But, as you saw in Eudon's case, unexpected events happen." His big, square hand rested on hers for the briefest of moments. "I want you kept safe. If I am not available, Charles will care for you."

Later, with her wrist bound to him for a third night, after both of them had lain stiffly for hours beneath his cloak, each trying not to touch the other, Theuderic turned to her with a muffled oath and took her into his arms, to hold her close so they could sleep at last.

When she wakened, he was gone—hunting, Eudon told her—and he did not return until the day was almost over. Eudon spent the better part of the day moving about the camp and exercising his right leg in preparation for the long ride to come.

"Riding will be painful for you," India warned. "It will be a while before that wound is fully healed."

"Theu has given me more time to recover than any other leader would have," Eudon returned. "I won't delay him any longer."

Theuderic took the first watch that night, so India retired alone to the lean-to they usually shared. She was glad of his absence, for it was becoming increasingly difficult to hide the way she felt about him. He had given her his cloak, saying he would be warm enough until he joined her later, but in the morning he was not in their lean-to. She found him stretched beside the dying fire.

"Why did you sleep on the bare ground when you might have had shelter with me?" she demanded.

"It doesn't matter." His abrupt manner suggested to her that he, too, was having trouble concealing his feelings. "Eat quickly. I want to leave at once."

By now, the bread the men carried with them was so stale and hard that it could only be eaten by soaking it in their ale first. It made a singularly unappetizing mess, but India did not complain. It was not long before she was mounted in front of Theuderic once more and they were back on the almost invisible track through the forest, traveling more slowly than before, to accommodate Eudon.

They reached the Rhine in mid-afternoon. Flowing smoothly along its course through dense forest and a few low hills, it was not as exciting a sight as India had expected. All the wild, romantic cliffs and rapids she had read about and seen pictures of lay upstream, to the south, and most of the famous castles that in her own time were the signatures of that great river, would not be built for several centuries.

On the western bank, across the sparkling clean, blue and silver water, lay the town the

Romans had originally named Colonia Agrippina, though the Franks referred to it simply as Köln. By squinting against the bright sun, India could make out a recently restored Roman wall around the town and what looked to her like a Romanesque church surrounded by smaller buildings.

Of more immediate interest to their party, on the eastern side of the river a few houses stood near the water, making the tiniest of villages. The flat barge that served as a ferry was tied to a wooden wharf. Set apart from the houses was also a large Roman building, its stone faded over the centuries into a warm, golden hue. Innumerable additions had been added to this edifice, its sprawling walls now housing the Frankish garrison kept there to guard the ferry crossing.

Theuderic led his men through the open gates, past a series of sentries, all of whom snapped to attention when Osric called out their identity, each syllable rolling off his tongue in a way that suggested this was his usual job and one he relished.

"He just called you count," India said. She was not especially surprised. She knew Theuderic had a large estate near Metz, for he had told her so himself, adding that his son, now three years old, lived there under Theuderic's mother's care. No man who wore chain mail and led a well-disciplined warband could be less than a nobleman. Still, she was impressed. In the realm of Charles the Great, only a few dukes and Charles himself ranked higher than a count.

"My grandfather fought the Saracens at Tours with Charles Martel," Theuderic responded to her comment with quiet pride. "My father was a close friend to King Pepin, and I am Charles's man. It was he who made me a count."

They were by now inside the courtyard of the garrison, and India could see that it was crowded with busy men and with horses. Apparently, the king of the Franks believed the Saxons were a danger serious enough to make him keep this outpost well staffed.

"Now for some decent food," said Hugo, smiling when he saw a portly man in a green tunic and jeweled sword belt coming toward them. "Savarec keeps a fine table. India, lad, we have returned to civilization at last."

Behind India, Theuderic moved, dismounting, and then he and Marcion, now on foot too, went forward to greet the garrison commander.

"My dear Count Theuderic, Lord Marcion, welcome, welcome." Savarec's ruddy face shone with pleasure. "I am pleased to see you return in good health and with your men uninjured. You must give us the news of your battles with the Saxons. Have you a report from Paderborn? Perhaps some news directed especially to me? With so many men stationed here, I would welcome the chance to let them work off their extra energy in a small battle." Still talking in a way that allowed no interruptions or even answers to his numerous questions, Savarec swept Theuderic and Marcion with him through the door of what appeared to be the main section of the garrison building.

"Enthusiastic, isn't he?" Hugo grinned at India, who still sat upon Theuderic's horse. He tilted his chin toward the doorway through which Theuderic and Marcion had vanished. "You'd better dismount, lad. I see a servant coming toward you with a look that suggests Theu was finally able to get a word in to tell Savarec we've a king's messenger among us."

"But I'm not," India protested.

"Don't tell Savarec that," Hugo advised kindly. "He'll treat you better if he thinks you are. He's a good man, and a brave one, but a bit too much in awe of rank and title."

Once on the ground, India faced a swarthy fellow who sported both a lush beard and a sweeping mustache.

"If you will be so good," the man said, almost stumbling over the words in his eagerness, "please come with me. Savarec regrets that he was not aware of your presence. This way, please, good sir." With what was apparently intended to be a bow, the man indicated that India should precede him into the building.

"Go on," said Hugo, his big face perfectly serious. "Don't worry about the rest of us. I'll see the men well billetted, and then I'll join you." By now India's guide was some distance ahead of her, and after a quick glance in the man's direction, Hugo gave her a long, slow wink. "Enjoy your exalted state, lad."

She knew as she entered the building that she was probably in serious danger of having her disguise penetrated in that place, but suddenly she felt like laughing. Hugo had looked so comical, and the other men had been openly grinning their encouragement. She followed Savarec's man with a jaunty step.

"My dear young man," exclaimed Savarec when she had been shown into the great hall, "I assure you, I intended no slight when I neglected to greet you as well as Count Theuderic and Lord Marcion. Come in, please, and join us."

India did as she was bidden, looking around with great interest at this first Frankish interior she had seen. The hall had a high roof and a long pit down the center of its stone floor, wherein burned several separate and rather smoky fires. Two rows of tables were arranged on either side of the firepit, confirming India's assumption that this was where the garrison assembled for meals. Theuderic, Marcion and their host stood together near the door. The only other people in the room were servants who were setting the tables with wooden plates and cups. From behind the door at the end of the hall wafted the smell of cooking meat and vegetables, particularly cabbage, which overlaid the even less pleasant indoor odors of damp wool and unwashed bodies.

Savarec himself looked reasonably clean, his

89

greying hair and mustache carefully combed, his clothing fresh and unspotted. He personally poured a cup of wine and gave it to India, his manner revealing no sign that he saw the woman beneath the boyish exterior. Offering up silent thanks to heaven for Savarec's acceptance of her, India took the cup from him with a polite bow of her head.

"Drink it slowly," warned Theuderic. "After the last few days, wine will be new to you."

On impulse, she lifted her cup, toasting him for an instant before she drank. She saw his eyes widen in surprise. At once, he returned the gesture with his own cup. The wine was slightly fizzy, and a little too sweet for her taste, but it was doubtless the safest liquid she could drink in that land.

"Excellent," she said to Savarec, as if she were a connoisseur. Savarec looked pleased.

"I hope you will find the evening meal to your liking also," he said, beaming at her. "I am curious to know more about your land of *Chess-veeck*, which Count Theuderic has been describing to me. Will you be good enough to tell me about it tonight?"

"Describing it? Theuderic?" India stared at that gentleman, but all she got in return was a bland, innocent look.

"We will talk more tonight," Savarec promised. "For now, let this servant escort you to your room while I oversee the details of our feast. I regret that we are so overcrowded that there is but one guest room available, and most of your men will have to sleep in the barracks. Until later, Count Theuderic, Lord Marcion, Lord India."

India nearly choked at that bestowal of an unearned title upon her, but went with her companions to the guest room that had been prepared for them on the second floor of the garrison building.

It was not large, and half the space was taken up by the bed that sat in one corner. This piece of furniture had railings at the head, foot, and one long side. It looked remarkably like a twentieth-century daybed. The similarity was increased when Marcion lifted the undyed woolen coverlet to pull out a trundle bed tucked underneath.

"Hugo and I can sleep on this," Marcion remarked, pushing the trundle back under the bed until it should be needed. "There will be plenty of room for all of us."

"What about Eudon?" India asked, more than a little shaken by Marcion's apparent assumption that she and Theuderic would be sleeping together in the larger bed. "Eudon really ought to have a comfortable place to stretch out his right leg tonight, or he'll be too stiff to ride tomorrow."

"I'll see to Eudon's comfort." Marcion's boyish grin was filled with pure mischief as a servant appeared with twin pitchers of steaming water, a second man following with a wooden basin, a bowl of soap, and a linen towel. "I'll check on the horses, too. My absence will give you both more room to move around while you wash. Hugo and I can take the second turn at the water, after you've finished."

There was a single window in the room, with a wooden table beneath it. The servants set the water pitchers and other supplies down on the table and withdrew. Marcion followed them, leaving Theuderic and India alone.

"Are we all really expected to sleep in here, together?" India asked nervously.

"Why not?" Folding his arms across his chest, Theuderic stood watching her as if to judge her every reaction and each word she spoke. "We have slept as closely together every night since you joined us."

"It's not the same. That was in the open. Here there are walls, a floor, a ceiling."

"It will certainly be more pleasant than the damp forest," he agreed, his eyes never leaving her face.

"And presumably safer," she added, believing it would not be safe at all to spend an entire night in the same bed with this man. "Will you still bind my wrist and tie me to you tonight?"

"If I thought you would fly out the window while I slept, I might well tie you again." He moved suddenly, the action surprising her. He stood so close to her that they were almost touching. "You would leave if you could," he accused her, his voice soft.

It was true. If Hank were to give her any indication that he had found a way to take her home again, she would go without a backward glance. Or would she? Looking at Theuderic's hard face, into his sharp grey eyes, she wondered if she had been driven mad by what had happened to her, because the thought of never seeing him again stabbed her like a knife in the heart.

"I don't know how to answer you," she whispered.

"It wasn't a question. But I'll show you how much I've grown to trust you. I'll leave you alone here for a while, to wash in private. There is a covered slop pot under the table if you need it." He paused with one hand on the door latch. "Of course, Hugo or Marcion might walk in at any time."

"Thank you."

"For granting the privacy, or for warning that others may intrude upon it? Surely you understand by now that it can be difficult to be alone for more than a moment or two." The familiar quirk of his mouth suggested to her that he was teasing. She felt absolutely certain that he had penetrated her disguise days before, yet most of the time he gave no indication that he knew the truth about her. Only occasionally, when no one else was present, did he let the barriers between them slip even a little. As he did now. Something remarkably close to a smile touched his lips, and his cool eyes turned gentle. "Later," he said, and left her.

It was Hugo who interrupted her, but not before she had washed her face and hands with the harsh soap and tried to straighten her hair with her fingers. When she heard a light knock on the door she went toward it, but Hugo came right in.

"Have you finished?" He gestured toward the water pitcher. "I'd like to wash myself."

"I'm not sure what to do with the dirty water in the basin," India confessed.

"You could pour it into the slop pot," Hugo said, "but we don't know how often it's emptied, and there's no point in filling the pot too soon. I'd say, toss the water out the window. I see a garden down there; you can sprinkle the flowers."

Stretching, India leaned across the table to peer out of the window. There were no flowers in bloom so early in the year, but she saw two feminine figures pacing along a gravel path.

"Someone's down there," she said. "I don't want to spill the water on them."

"It's easy enough to avoid." Hugo had stripped off his woolen tunic and undershirt. He came forward bare-chested, to stick his head out the window and shout, "Beware below!" Picking up the basin, he tossed the water through the open window with no further regard for anyone who might be splashed.

India saw the smaller of the two figures in the garden look up toward the window at Hugo's cry. She caught a glimpse of two long, silver-gilt braids and a pure, delicate face, before the second figure seized the girl's arm, turning her so her back was to the window.

"What a pretty girl," India said.

"Where?" Hugo had already poured fresh water into the basin and was lathering his hands. He craned his neck, trying to see better, but the two females in the garden were making their way toward a door set in one wall. Hugo shook his head in disappointment. "I'm sorry I missed seeing her. It must have been Savarec's mysterious daughter."

"Why is she mysterious?" India watched Hugo rub soapsuds onto his face. He had a barrel-like chest with lots of light brown hair on it and hard, bulging shoulder and arm muscles. He was thoroughly masculine, yet there was in him nothing to stir the combination of danger and attraction that underlay all her dealings with Theuderic. She could stay in the same room with bare-chested Hugo all the day long and still feel only a mild affection toward him.

"Ow!" Hugo bellowed suddenly. "I've got soap in my eyes."

"It's probably made with lye," she said, handing him the towel. "I'm sure it stings." She watched him wipe at his eyes, then rinse and dry his face.

"Tell me about Savarec's daughter," she said.

"There's not much to tell." After glancing out the window, Hugo threw away the water, then reached for his undershirt. "Because there are so many men moving in and out of this garrison

95

all the time, Savarec keeps her well guarded. I don't know of a single man who has ever seen her, to report on her looks. For all anyone knows, she could be a monster."

"She didn't look like a monster to me," India said. "If it's the girl I saw, she has blonde hair and a sweet face."

"Has she?" Hugo adjusted his tunic and took up his sword belt. "You've seen more than most, then. I wish I could see her, just once."

"It can't be a very agreeable life for a girl," India said. "Kept under close guard, not allowed to meet people of her own age—it sounds lonely to me."

"She goes to a convent school," Hugo revealed. "She will meet other girls there. I come through here fairly often. Sometimes she's here, visiting her father. Sometimes she's at school."

Marcion came in just then, with Theuderic close behind him, so the conversation about Savarec's daughter ended there, but the image of that upturned, delicate oval face stayed in India's thoughts.

Chapter Six

True to his reputation for setting a fine table, Savarec provided a bountiful feast to honor his guests. Fresh green vegetables were scarce at that time of year, but there were plenty of boiled turnips and several huge platters of cabbage stewed with herbs. There were dried apples and raisins for sweets and more than enough fresh-baked bread, but most of the meal consisted of meats. There was mutton boiled with onions and garlic, large trays of game birds of various kinds that had been cooked on spits over a fire, and half a roasted ox. There were pitchers of the sweet, lightly carbonated wine that made India think of cheap grape soda.

Theuderic, India, Marcion, and Hugo all sat at the head table along with Savarec and a few of the higher-ranking officers who helped him maintain the outpost meant to keep the river crossing safe from the Saxons so it would always be ready should the king of the Franks need to transport an army into his lands in Saxony. There were few women present, none at the high table, and no sign of Savarec's daughter, an absence that did not surprise India after what Hugo had said earlier. Most of the feminine shapes that India noticed were servants, though there were some painted ladies at the lower tables, whose function seemed fairly obvious.

At first, Savarec talked mostly to Theuderic and Marcion, asking each of them intelligent questions about conditions in Saxony.

"I was in Paderborn last summer for the annual assembly," Savarec said. "The Saxons who presented themselves to Charles there seemed peaceable enough. But I say, never trust a Saxon, even if he allows himself to be baptized. The Christian church means nothing to them. They are all pagans at heart."

"They have their own religion," Theuderic said mildly. "Converting them will take time."

"It would take less time," Savarec answered, "if so many fighting men were not being withdrawn from eastern Francia to take part in this summer's campaign."

"You don't seem to be lacking in men just now," Marcion put in, looking down the crowded hall, where every seat at the long tables was filled.

"Here I am well staffed," Savarec admitted,

"but I am worried about the lands farther east. If the Saxons take advantage of Charles's absence in Spain this summer, who can tell what will happen?"

"I share your concern," Theuderic said. "As for the campaign planned for this summer, I have no great liking for it myself. When next I see Charles, I will tell him what you have said. We won't change the arrangements he has already set in motion, but we might convince him to release a levy or two to help you and the others on the eastern frontier to hold back the Saxons should they rise while Charles is occupied in Spain."

"For that I thank you." Savarec now turned to India to ask her a few questions more penetrating than she would have liked about her home and her life there. "I would be pleased to lend you a horse, Lord India, to ride until you have reached Aachen. Enough people travel back and forth to allow it to be returned to me easily."

"Riding is not common in Lord India's country," Theuderic interrupted this generous offer. "It is safer if I keep India on my own horse, with me."

India believed this reluctance to let her have her own mount was the result of Theuderic's concern that she would disappear. She did not see how he could think she might try to run away from him. There was no place for her to go, and he surely knew it. Until Hank found her, she was safer with Theuderic than anywhere else—if spending yet another night beside him could be called safe.

"May I ask, Lord India," said Savarec, leaning closer to her as if to speak in confidence, "if you are wed or betrothed?"

She thought for a moment about how to answer him. She had a feeling that Theuderic, sitting on Savarec's other side, would be listening with great interest to whatever she might say to the garrison commander, so she kept her reply short and simple, telling Savarec only, "No, I am not."

"I have a daughter," Savarec said to her. "Innocent, well-schooled, a charming girl."

"I'm sure she is." By now she sensed that not only was Theuderic listening, he was surreptitiously watching her, too, and Marcion and Hugo as well had stopped eating to pay attention to the conversation between herself and their host.

"Like you, my Danise is not yet betrothed," Savarec said, and India could tell from his tone of voice that she would have to do some quick thinking.

"Sir, I believe I understand your meaning," she responded. "But you know nothing of my situation in my own land, nor of my prospects for the future." She said that last word with a bitter inflection that made Theuderic look sharply at her, but he said nothing to help her out of the quagmire in which she was foundering. She wondered wildly if real men ever felt this way when parents approached them about marriageable daughters. She knew she would have to extricate herself from this embarrassing and potentially dangerous situation without hurting Savarec's pride or in any way insulting his daughter, and she had to try to do it without revealing her gender.

"You can be nothing less than a noble," Savarec said. "You are well-spoken, though your accent is strange. The clothing you wear, travel-stained as it is, still is of the finest quality. And, of course, there is the medallion."

With her mind trained to late twentieth-century caution in social matters, she thought that for all he really knew of her, she could be a brutal axe murderer who would ravish and kill his daughter. For the briefest of moments she wondered how anyone with any claim to intelligence could be so gullible, or so careless about his own child's happiness. But after another moment's thought, she knew why. Arranged marriages among noble families were common at every period of history. As Theuderic and his men had judged and accepted her, so had Savarec. In appearance and speech, she seemed to them a foreign noble. Alone and unarmed, she presented no physical threat. And Savarec, according to Hugo overly concerned with status, would doubtless think it an honor to ally himself with a noble foreign house. He might even think it would raise him in his own king's estimation.

There was only one way she could think of to resolve the dilemma presented by Savarec's offer. It was a typically medieval way that would have been more effective in the later Middle Ages, after the idea of chivalry had been firmly established, but considering what she knew of Savarec's character, it just might work on him.

"Though I am neither married nor betrothed as yet," she said carefully, "still I am not free. My late master sent me upon a quest, which I must fulfill before I can think of my own life or what I might want."

"I see." Savarec received this information with perfect seriousness. "May I ask what this quest is?"

"That is the problem when it comes to responding to the remarkable proposition you have suggested to me," India confided, lowering her voice and taking great pleasure when she saw the unhelpful Theuderic tilt his head to hear her better. "I am sworn not to reveal the nature of the quest to anyone except the king of the Franks. When I have spoken with him, if he sets yet another task for me, I am then bound to obey him. So you will understand, Savarec, that though I respect you and honor your daughter because she is your child, I am unable to answer you in any way."

"I do understand," he said, and India began to breathe freely again. But there was one more matter about which she wanted to be certain.

"I have a request to make of you," she told Savarec, afraid the man might not give up so easily after all. "If it should happen that some suitable arrangement can be made for your Danise, I beg you to take advantage of it. Do not prevent your daughter from knowing the happiness of a wife and mother for the sake of one who may soon depart from this world."

"Nobly spoken," said Savarec. "I agree to your request. You have a generous heart, Lord India."

"Indeed yes," said Marcion from further along the table. "If Lord India speaks with as much wisdom and diplomacy to Charles as he has just spoken to you, Charles may well send him on a mission of peace to the king of the Saracens at Jerusalem."

There was laughter at that, and the conversation turned to other subjects. It was not until much later, when India and Theuderic were in their shared chamber with the door closed that he made reference to Savarec's offer.

"Do not imagine he's a foolish man for all his apparent willingness to give his daughter to an unknown noble," Theuderic said, his face serious in the light of the oil lamp that flickered in a dish upon the table. "Savarec has not lasted for more than ten years in this outpost by being careless. Had you shown any interest in his Danise, he would soon have discovered all there is to know about your past, your parentage and rank, and your prospects for the future before he finally agreed to give the girl to you."

"There is nothing for him to discover," India returned. "I said what I did in order to stop his suggestions without insulting him. After all, he is our host."

"You dealt with him most wisely," Theuderic conceded. "Tell me, do you really have a quest?"

"Only to return to my own home," she replied.

"I do confess," he said softly, "that I'd be sorry to see you go."

"I thought at first I would be unhappy here," she said, responding to his tone. "But it's not so. It's different here in Francia—how different you cannot imagine—but I am not unhappy. You and your men are good people, Theuderic. I like Savarec, too. I might even like Danise if I were to meet her." She stopped there, fearing he would misinterpret her words if she told him that she had been wondering what a Frankish girl's life was like. She needn't have worried. Theuderic wasn't thinking about Danise, or about Savarec's proposal. As soon as Marcion and Hugo appeared, eager to pull out the trundle bed and test its comfort, Theuderic threw himself down on the larger bed.

"Are you going to sleep in your armor even here?" India asked, incredulous. Theuderic did not open his eyes when he answered her.

"We are still east of the Rhine," he said.

"Savarec doesn't wear his armor," she noted.

"That is Savarec's affair. I do not remove mine until we reach Aachen." His words brought into her mind the picture of a misty late-winter forest, a stream, and an iron helmet filled with watercress. "That is my quest," he added quietly.

Marcion burst into irreverent laughter at his leader's announcement.

"I will also sleep without undressing," Marcion declared. "That way, I'll be ready to leave at dawn."

"Me, too," said Hugo. He removed his sword belt and boots, then fell onto the trundle bed fully clothed, his great weight making it creak and sway alarmingly. Once it had steadied again, Marcion lowered himself more carefully to the mattress and pulled up the quilt.

India looked down at them, at Marcion curled on one side of the bed with the quilt around his shoulders, at Hugo trying to wrestle his fair share of the quilt away from his friend, and at Theuderic on the other bed, stretched out with his hands behind his head and his legs crossed at the ankles. And she *knew*, absolutely and certainly knew, that all three of them were fully aware of what she was. They were going to sleep with their clothing on in order to spare her, and themselves, from any embarrassment. How dear and kind they were. She wished she dared hug each of them. Well, perhaps not all three of them. . . .

"Put out the lamp and come to bed," said Theuderic, watching her through half-closed eyes.

She did as he ordered, the open shutters allowing enough light through the window for her to find her way to the bed.

"You will have to move over," she told Theuderic.

105

"Ah, no," he replied. "If you are not to be tied to me this night, then you will have to sleep between me and the wall."

"But—" she began.

"I'm weary," he said. "I've not rested in a bed for weeks. If you are wise, you'll let me sleep and not test my mood."

Bending over, she removed her boots, then tried to crawl across his legs to get to her allotted portion of the bed. She paused, kneeling on his shins while she fumbled with the covers. She heard him swear under his breath just before he sat up, caught her around the waist, and flipped her onto her back. Somehow she was beneath the covers with Theuderic's mail-clad form on top of the quilt making a wall to keep her from escaping.

"Good night, Lord India," said Marcion in a perfect imitation of Savarec's voice. Hugo emitted a long, relaxed snore, then complete silence fell upon the room.

India began to laugh. She was quiet about it, but she could not help herself. It was all too funny—Savarec trying to marry her off to his daughter sight unseen, the three men with her surely aware that she was a woman but no one admitting it, herself forced to lie in bed next to Theuderic without being allowed to touch him as she wanted to, her very presence in that time and place—all of it was absolutely, completely ridiculous. She knew she was close to hysteria, but she could not stop the laughter that demanded release. She began to shake. In another moment howls of laughter combined with floods of tears would pour out of her and she would not be able to stop.

Two of Theuderic's fingers came down firmly across her lips, pressing hard, trapping her laughter.

"If you make a sound, I'll strangle you," he murmured into her ear. "I swear I will."

She put her own hand over his and did what she wanted to do. She kissed his fingers. She heard him catch his breath, and then her hand was held against his lips, and she felt the moist fire of his tongue across her palm. In a way she did not understand, that gesture calmed her, bringing her back from the brink of lunacy to the realization that she could not give way to her feelings. Not here, not yet. All she could do for the moment was trust Theuderic to get them through to some other place, some later day, when they could resolve what lay between them. For the first time since coming to Francia, she found herself hoping that Hank would not be able to locate her soon.

She fell asleep with her hand still clasped tightly in Theuderic's.

They were all up well before the sun, and as soon as it was light they loaded the horses onto the barge that served as a ferry. India and most of Theuderic's band also went aboard, but Theuderic, Marcion, and Hugo waited on the shore with the two ferrymen.

"Why the delay?" India asked Osric, who was

helping her to make Eudon comfortable on some bales that had been stacked near where the horses were tethered.

"There are more passengers to come," Osric replied. "That's all I've been told. But, see, there they are now."

Having finished tucking Eudon's cloak beneath him in a way that would help to support his injured hip, India turned to look at the building that dominated the little village. The gates of the garrison were open, and out of them rode Savarec in a green cloak. Behind him came two horses, each bearing a woman who was sitting sidesaddle and, last in the group, a young man whose horse also carried a sturdy middle-aged woman riding pillion behind him.

While those on the barge watched with considerable interest, this procession made its way to the wharf, there to be greeted by Theuderic and his lieutenants. Eager to learn what was happening, India moved toward the gangplank.

"I give my daughter Danise into your safe-keeping," Savarec was saying to Theuderic. "Deliver her to Aachen, and from there she will be escorted back to school at Chelles."

India knew the abbey of Chelles near Paris maintained a famous school for noblewomen. The king's own sister resided there, and she would in time become its most famous abbess. It was perfectly reasonable for Savarec to ask Theuderic to see his daughter safely as far as Aachen, but after the previous evening, India could not help wondering if the garrison commander had some ulterior motive for the arrangement.

Of Danise herself, little could be seen. She was completely covered by a hooded brown mantle. India guessed that the tall thin woman in black robes would be the nun who was her companion,and the middle-aged woman was doubtless a servant. The young man would be a groom sent with them to care for the horses.

With the respect owed to a woman sworn to the religious life, Theuderic politely gave his arm to the nun to help her cross the gangplank, and Hugo, at a word from his leader, extended his own arm to Danise. Having delivered his daughter to Theuderic, Savarec started back toward his headquarters.

With neither the nun nor her father watching her, Danise pushed her hood off, revealing the pale gold braids and oval face that India had seen in the garden the day before. As she put her hand on the waiting Hugo's forearm, Danise looked up to meet his eyes and smile at him. Hugo's face reddened. Danise appeared a bit startled, but then an expression of wonder and joy crossed her features, making her radiantly beautiful. Hugo smiled down at her.

It happened in the time between two breaths, but India, watching the scene, knew that Hugo had just found the love for which he longed. From Danise's entranced expression, she did not doubt that Hugo's feelings were returned.

How she envied them. How she wished that she, too, could allow herself just to feel without analyzing her emotions and without fearing them. Deeply moved by what she had witnessed, she watched Danise glance one last time toward her departing father, watched Hugo leading her onto the barge, saw them exchange a few words. As though in a dream, India wove romantic predictions about the pair until a footstep beside her caught her attention. With her expression unguarded and all her feelings open to him, she looked into Theuderic's eyes. The longing she saw there made her tremble with a rush of sweet desire.

With the additional horses and people now brought aboard, the barge was more crowded than ever. Someone brushed against Theuderic, making him take a few steps forward. India put out her hands, resting them on his chest, on links and links of chain mail. His lips parted, his eyes devoured her. She felt his right hand at her waist. She could not breathe.

"Count Theuderic!" The nun tapped him on the shoulder as if he were a servant. "The lady Danise and I expect more attention from you. I see no provisions to make us comfortable or to keep us sheltered from the sun. Lord Savarec assumed that you would provide the necessary amenities for ladies of our rank."

"Dear Sister Gertrude, don't fret." Danise had arrived on board, with Hugo beside her. "I am quite content with the arrangements made for us."

"Danise, put up your hood at once," snapped the nun. "You know your father's orders. Do not

110

display your face for all these common men to see. Oh, what are we to do? There is not even a decent place for us to sit. This is shameful treatment, shameful. The next time I see your mother, Count Theuderic, I will complain to her about this."

"You could sit with Eudon," Hugo offered helpfully. "Some of those bales are soft as pillows."

"Bales?" Sister Gertrude was outraged. "Do you mean we shall have to sit upon cargo?"

"Please, Sister Gertrude," came Danise's patiently respectful voice, "I don't mind standing. Indeed, I would enjoy it, so that I can see everything better. Perhaps, Lord Hugo, you would show us a place where we won't be in the way."

"It would be my greatest pleasure." Hugo wisely offered his arm to the nun rather than to Danise. With surprising grace for a man so large, he led the ladies across the now moving barge toward the port railing.

"I will speak to you more strongly later, Count Theuderic," said Sister Gertrude. Over her head, Theuderic smiled at India.

"I am at your service, Sister Gertrude," he said with perfect manners.

India watched the nun try to pull Danise's hood forward, but as soon as Sister Gertrude's hand left the fabric, Danise swept the hood off again. Then she smiled into Hugo's eyes.

"Does Sister Gertrude really know your mother?" India asked Theuderic.

"It is entirely possible. She looks to be about

forty years, which is my mother's age. My mother was schooled at Chelles, so they might have been girls together. But my mother is nothing like that nun, I assure you."

At the moment, the nun seemed to be concerned by all the horses on board, watching them with a wary eye instead of guarding her young charge. Standing at the railing, Hugo bent his head toward Danise.

"Hugo loves her," India murmured.

"Who, Sister Gertrude?" She was familiar enough with Theuderic by now to be able to see the way he tried to keep his mouth firm and hard, but the corner that always betrayed his sense of humor turned upward in spite of his best efforts.

"That would be a remarkable match," said India, trying not to laugh. "No, I mean Hugo and Danise. I saw it happen. It was beautiful."

"Love is a foolish thing. It always ends in grief."

Somehow she knew he did not speak only of Hugo and Danise.

"Theu." She had never before called him by the familiar nickname his men used so freely.

"India." He said her name in the slow, accented way that always stopped her breath. His eyes held hers, and in their silver-grey depths she saw the answer to the question in her heart. Her throat closed, preventing any sound. Her breasts tingled. Why, oh, why, would he not touch her? Why did he keep his arms so stiffly at his sides instead of putting them around her? She ached for some physical contact with him.

"It's madness." At first she wasn't sure whether she had spoken or if he had, because the same thought lay in her own mind. But it was Theuderic, with his firm sense of reality, who guided her away from the paralyzing, overwhelming desire that would have exposed them both to scandal. "We cannot give way to feelings. See to Eudon's comfort. Consider that an order and leave me, please India, for at this moment I have not the strength to leave you, and we are attracting Sister Gertrude's notice."

"Yes, sir." It was fearfully hard to break contact with his eyes, but she did. Bowing her head, she went to Eudon, and at his side she stayed until they reached the western bank of the Rhine. By then it was mid-morning, and the sunny sky had been replaced by rolling clouds. India was glad to leave the dampness of the river for Eudon's sake as well as for her own.

"We will need to rest here for several hours," Sister Gertrude said to Theuderic as soon as they were all ashore at Köln, "to recuperate from the rigors of the crossing."

"Sister, if I may suggest," said Theuderic, all politeness, "there is a guesthouse but a few hours' ride from here, where I plan to spend the night. If we leave at once, we can easily be there before dark and, I believe, without tiring you or the lady Danise too badly."

"The lady Danise's health will not permit an

immediate departure." Sister Gertrude was adamant.

"But I am perfectly well," Danise declared, laughing at the nun's concern. "I want to ride on. Besides, those clouds will bring rain soon. Perhaps we can reach the guesthouse before the weather breaks."

"I believe it will snow," Theuderic said to her, "but you are quite correct about reaching the guesthouse. Sister Gertrude, I have an injured man in my company. I would like to see all of you properly sheltered tonight."

"Yes," said Danise. "Our duty of charity toward the sick requires that we not inconvenience poor Eudon, who I am told is in great pain. Lord Hugo, if you will help me to mount, I am prepared to ride."

With no excuses left, Sister Gertrude was helped to her own horse. When she saw India mounted with Theuderic she found more cause for complaint.

"That boy ought to ride behind you," she insisted. "Or better yet, put him with someone else. The leader of a troop of the king's men ought to display his rank by riding alone, at the head of his men. Why didn't you require a mount for him from Savarec?"

"Sister Gertrude," Danise protested, "surely Count Theuderic knows more about military matters than we women do. We must allow him to distribute his men as he sees fit. Come now, ride beside me, for I do enjoy your company."

"That's a good girl," Theuderic noted, after the two women had fallen back to ride behind the first group of his men. "She's worthy of Hugo."

"Do you believe he has a chance to win her?" India asked.

"I think so, if he seriously wants her. He has little land now, but his family is a good one, and Charles likes him. Hugo could win an estate with his sword and then ask for Danise. Other men have won their wives that way."

"I hope it happens," India said fervently. "I like Hugo. He deserves to be happy."

"Most men do, but few men are," he retorted. "Happiness is not the only goal of life. Loyalty to the king, personal honor, the welfare of one's family—all are more important than one man's feelings."

"But you cannot always control feelings," India said. "Love comes unbidden."

"Yes." His voice was quiet. "It comes."

She turned around to look at him, and if he had moved his head by a fraction of an inch their lips would have met. But he seemed to have an infinite amount of self-control.

"I was right," he said. "Look, it's snowing."

Fat flakes drifted slowly downward, melting when they touched the ground, but collecting on tree branches. Once more, as she had done so often on this apparently endless journey, India sought shelter in Theuderic's cloak and warmth from his solid body. She leaned back against his chest. His left arm came around her waist, his face was in her hair, she felt his breath on her brow. Then he was pushing her away.

"Don't," he said. "Sit up and away from me, or by heaven, I'll make you ride pillion behind Sister Gertrude."

"A fate worse than death," she said, straightening her spine as he had demanded. She heard him chuckle, low in his throat, and a great tenderness rose in her. She was still a bit unsure of her feelings for him, but she knew now that it was something more than mere physical attraction.

Because of the heavy clouds and the steadily falling snow, it grew dark early on that day, and by the time they reached their goal, they were all glad to seek warmth and light and hot food. The guesthouse was a large hall with a firepit in the middle of the earth floor. There were shelves down each long side of the hall, where travelers could sleep. There was a separate kitchen building with quarters for the caretaker and his family, a stable, a small chapel, and a tiny, windowless room off one end of the hall, which Sister Gertrude immediately appropriated for herself, Danise, and their serving woman.

"You are far more accustomed to rough conditions than ladies are," she said to Theuderic. "You won't mind sleeping with your men. When the evening meal is ready, you may send it to our room."

"That's the rudest nun I ever met," remarked

Hugo, looking wistfully after Danise, who was being shepherded toward the separate room.

"She gives holiness a bad name," India agreed. Hugo let out a loud whoop of laughter at that, slapping India on the back so hard she almost fell to the floor.

"Aye, lad, that she does. A bad name indeed." He went off to tell the other men what India had said.

The caretaker brought food for them, a stew of salted fish, turnips, and cabbage, tasty dark brown bread, cheese and apples, and a jug of ale. All of this was placed on a trestle table at one end of the hall. India noticed that Eudon was not eating much.

"He looks feverish to me," she said to Theuderic.

"The best thing we can do for him," Theuderic replied, "is get him to Aachen and let him rest there until he has completely recovered."

With the meal over, India left the hall in search of the latrine, which the caretaker had told her was on the far side of the guesthouse compound. She was glad of the snow, for it outlined buildings and well-trodden paths with white, making it possible for her to find the hut she sought. Inside, it was foul-smelling, and the wick burning in the dish of oil that the caretaker had given her provided little light.

When she came out again, she noticed a series of footprints around the hut that she had not seen before. Apparently someone else had come into the night after her, but had not returned to the hall. She started back along the path, pausing when a skinny figure appeared out of the gloom.

"Hello, boy," said an unfamiliar voice. "You know me, don't you? Lady Danise's groom. I followed you here to speak with you alone."

"Is something wrong?" India asked. "Does Lady Danise need help?"

"No, but I do," the groom said. "There's a part of me that's burning for your help. Come into the stable with me, boy."

"I cannot. Count Theuderic expects me." Uneasy now, and fearing the groom had realized she was not a boy at all, India began to walk toward the hall again. The groom stepped in front of her, barring her way, his sharp features illuminated by the oil lamp she still held.

"I've seen you cuddling up to him," the groom said, adding with a sneer, "I know what you are, boy, and I want some for myself."

"Some what?"

Her question was answered when the groom made a grab for her crotch. With a cry of dismay, she struck his hand aside. She dropped the oil lamp, the flame quickly sizzling out in the snow, leaving her with no light except that reflected off the thin layer of snow on the ground. The groom stood between her and the hall, and the door was closed. No one would hear if she called for help.

"Let me pass," she demanded, trying to sound brave, though she was shaking.

"Not till you come into the stable with me," the groom said, reaching for her again. India stepped backward. He followed her, beginning to whine as he spoke. "Come on, it'll only take a little while. I won't hurt you, boy, but I have to have it now. Count Theuderic will never know."

"He already knows."

The groom spun around, as startled by Theuderic's appearance as India was. But not for long.

"This boy accosted me," the groom declared, having recovered his earlier boldness. "He wanted to stick his thing up my arse and got mad when I told him no."

"Get back to the stable where you belong," Theuderic said, "and count yourself lucky if I do not report this incident to Sister Gertrude."

"You do, and I'll tell her the boy belongs to you," warned the groom defiantly.

"Get out of my sight!" Theuderic's hand rested on his sword hilt. The groom needed no further convincing, but faded into the night.

"Are you hurt?" Theuderic asked India.

"I'm fine." She was surprised to hear how frightened she sounded. "It didn't happen the way he said."

"I know." He laid his palm against her cheek and she reveled in his touch. She leaned toward him, giving in to the irresistible attraction that drew her.

"India." She loved the way he said her name.

"He is still there, in the shadows, watching

119

us," Theuderic said, so softly she could just hear the words. "If I kiss you now, he will believe that what he suggested about us is the truth."

"Isn't it?" Her voice was as soft as his had been, but he heard it, and he dropped his hand.

"Go inside," he said. "I'll follow in a little while. If anyone asks for me, say our paths crossed coming and going from the latrine."

"Don't send me away."

"Go now. Leave me or I'll take you here in the snow and not care if the groom watches us. Sleep next to Eudon tonight."

"Theu—"

"Go!" There was such passion, and so much pain in that one word, that she fled from him into the hall, to smoky warmth and masculine laughter and at least the semblance of safety.

Chapter Seven

The king of the Franks would not begin to build his famous palace and chapel at Aachen for another two years, but he often visited there to enjoy his favorite sport of hunting amidst the beauty of Aachen's wooded hills and its lake. An accomplished swimmer and firm believer in personal cleanliness, he also delighted in the many hot springs in the area. In fact, the springs had been popular since Roman times for their health-restoring properties, and there were still a few picturesque ruined stone buildings of ancient origin scattered about the landscape. There was also a good-sized lodge, along with other wooden dwellings erected to accommodate Charles and his nobles when they came to hunt.

It was mid-afternoon when India first saw

these rustic beginnings of what would one day be the capital city of the Frankish empire. The late-season snow had stopped during the previous night and had melted as the day progressed, so their journey had not been delayed. After leaving the guesthouse in the early morning they had forded a river and then had made their way southwestward through miles of thick forest.

Theuderic reined in his horse on a slight rise, waiting there for the rest of his company to catch up with him, and India saw before them a wide swath of meadow. Here and there a patch of snow still showed, but during the midday hours the air had become so warm that a mist was rising from the ground, making the settlement look as if it lay within some fairy enchantment. The sky was milky blue, nearby trees were bursting with early buds, and Charles's hunting lodge rose out of the mist like a magical construction.

"It's lovely," she breathed.

"Look there," Theuderic whispered, touching her arm. A few feet away a doe stood gazing at them with soft brown eyes. They sat in silent delight upon Theuderic's horse watching the deer until it moved off through the trees.

"Aachen seems deserted," India said, looking again at the misty scene just below them.

"It's not. There are always clerics and servants and plenty of men-at-arms, in case Charles arrives with little notice," Theuderic told her.

"He's not here now," India said. "If he were,

his nobles would be living in tents all over that field, and we would have been challenged to explain our presence long before this."

"You are right." He nodded his approval of her observation. "Charles has taken the court southward. He left shortly after Christmas and plans to spend Easter along the way. The levies are to gather at Agen, and Charles will meet them there soon after Easter."

India felt a cold chill in spite of the spring-like air. She knew what his words meant.

"Levies for the Spanish campaign," she said.

"So you've been listening to the men talk. Yes, as you heard Savarec say, last summer our yearly gathering was held at Paderborn, not far from where you and I met. A delegation of Saracens appeared there to invite Charles to take his army into Spain. They want him to resolve the dispute between two would-be rulers of their country. In return, they have promised to turn over several of their great cities to him. Charles is not blind to the glory and the wealth he will garner in Spain, but most of all, he hopes to convert the Saracens who live in that land to the True Faith."

"What do you think of the expedition?" she asked. "You told Savarec you weren't too pleased with the idea."

"I'm not," he said. "I wonder if the infidels can be trusted, and I question whether any man who rules a city will willingly turn it over to another man without a fight. We are unfamiliar with Spain, and once we have entered it, there will be a tall mountain range blocking the way between us and Francia, with only a few passes we can use to bring our army home again. Count Hrulund and a few others are less cautious than I, and eager to do battle with the Saracens."

"But you won't have to go there, will you?" she said. "You are stationed here, in the north."

"I have sent my levy on ahead," he told her. "My orders from Charles were to ride into Saxony, put down the small revolt that had begun there, and return to Aachen to make a report, which will be sent to him by rapid messenger. After a few days' rest, the men with me and I are to ride south to join Charles and the rest of my levy at Agen."

"Do you mean that you will march with him on the Spanish campaign?" A sudden fear for him made her choke out the words.

"We're all here," interrupted Hugo's cheerful voice from just behind them.

After a curious look at India's frightened face, Theuderic raised his right arm to signal that all should follow him. He led them down the hill and into Aachen with Osric once again riding beside his leader and shouting out Theuderic's name and title, clearly savoring every moment of his own performance.

Upon their arrival, they were at once surrounded by an efficient bustle of servants and grooms. After gracious thanks to Theuderic and a sweet, slightly tearful farewell to Hugo, Danise and her serving woman were borne away on the wings of Sister Gertrude's chronic irritation. Eudon was taken to the infirmary to be examined by a physician, with Osric in attendance; Hugo was put in charge of the horses; and Marcion went to see the men billetted. Theuderic ordered the loot that had been taken after the battle with the Saxons turned over to the clerics, who would make an inventory of the goods, set aside the king's share, and then disperse the remainder among the men and Theuderic. Within half an hour of their arrival, Theuderic and India stood alone before the entrance to Charles's hunting lodge.

"I'll take you to my quarters," he said. "You can rest there while I dictate my report to the clerics. Afterward, we will talk."

"I am absolutely filthy after our long ride," she said, irrationally irritated by his matter-of-fact attitude. Ever since he had rescued her from the groom on the previous night and sent her away so sternly, he had shown no emotion toward her at all. She had never known a man who could so completely hide his feelings. She could not conceal her own emotions nearly as well, so when she spoke she sounded waspish. "I want a hot bath."

"That will be simple enough. Follow me."

To her surprise, his quarters were not in the lodge as she had expected. He had a small wooden house set beneath an oak tree that grew near one of the hot springs. Old Roman masonry, cracked and damaged after eight centuries of use, formed an oblong pool. Through the steam rising from the surface of the water India glimpsed a mosaic fish design at the bottom of the pool.

"Soap and rinse yourself first," Theuderic instructed her. "Then bathe. That way, the water stays clean."

He showed her his house, a single room with a firepit, furnished with a table and bench, two wooden chairs with cushions on the seats, a couple of chests for clothing, and a typical Frankish bed with rails around three sides, its long side pushed against the wall. Pillows and a bright blue coverlet made the bed into seating space during the day. In one corner of the room sat a square wooden box with a large wooden tray on top of it.

After lighting a fire and stacking a few extra logs nearby in case she needed more, Theuderic found a covered wooden bowl of soap and a small linen towel for her to use.

"I will need a bucket," she said.

"It's in the shed at the back of the house, along with a stool you may want to use."

"And something to wear while I wash my clothes. Then something clean to put on after I bathe."

He gave her a long, searching look. From the twitch at the corner of his mouth, she was sure he was secretly laughing at her demands. At least he did not accuse her of being unreasonable.

"No one will disturb you. Don't wear anything while you do your laundry. I don't when I am at the bath, nor do any of the other men." He searched through one of the wooden chests, pulling out a shirt. "You may use this while your clothing dries."

"How long will you be gone?" she asked, watching him head toward the door.

"I don't know. It depends on how many questions the clerics ask me. Some of them will be about you." His amused look faded to seriousness. "I leave you untied. The rope that once bound us together is gone."

"Yes," she whispered, shaken by the sudden burning intensity in his eyes. She was not certain whether his next words were a plea or an order.

"Don't desert me now, India. Be here when I return."

She washed her tunic and trousers first, using some of her precious supply of soap and wringing the garments out as best she could. She spread them over a nearby bush, dumped out the dirty rinse water and filled the bucket again so she could remove and wash her underwear. Never having been naked in the open air before, she found the experience a bit frightening, but exciting too.

Next it was time to work on herself, and she went at the job with enthusiasm. Counting the time since she had arrived in the eighth century, she discovered with a mixture of laughter and horror that it had been seven days since she had bathed or washed her hair. It was wonderful to be clean once more. She cast the contents of the last bucket of soapy water in the general direction of the forest, vowing never again to feel superior to the supposedly dirty folk who had lived in earlier times than her own. Without readily available hot running water, getting clean and staying that way was strenuous work.

After using the bucket once more to rinse away the soap left on her body, she went to the pool and sat down on the ancient stones, dangling her feet in the water for a while before she jumped in and began to swim. The water was almost too hot to be comfortable, but the combination of the heat with the moist cool air was so relaxing that after a few minutes she turned onto her back and just floated, letting aching muscles unknot, allowing her thoughts to drift like the swirling mist above her.

She nearly fell asleep there in the pool, until she heard unfamiliar masculine voices a short distance away. Not wanting to have to explain her presence at Theuderic's pool to strangers, she left the water, gathered up her scattered clothing, and retreated indoors. There, finding no place to hang anything, she took the cushions off the chairs, used the backs and arms as drying racks for her garments, and pushed the chairs close to the fire. She put on the shirt Theuderic had given her, a heavy linen garment, knee length, with a round neck and long sleeves that she had to push up to free her hands. She discovered that he had left a comb with the shirt, and this she used to remove a week's worth of tangles and snarls from her hair. Then, unable to fight off sleep any longer, she pulled aside the coverlet and crawled into Theuderic's bed.

She wakened with a start, aware that someone was in the room with her. Quiet voices murmured words she could not distinguish. More than one person then, Theuderic and someone else. She heard the soft chink of rings upon rings of metal moving against each other.

"Thank you. Put the food there," she heard Theuderic say.

The door opened and closed, and she was alone again. Sitting up, she looked around. A lighted oil lamp sat on the table, where bread, cheese, a wine jar with two cups, and a covered dish now rested. A pile of folded fabric lay on the bench. In the corner, in the wooden tray atop the square box, was Theuderic's chain mail *brunia*. Propped against the wall at the head of the bed was his sword.

She heard sounds coming from the direction of the spring and pool. Rising, she opened the door to peer outside. There was no one in sight, but she heard the sounds again and she knew what they were. She rounded the corner of the house just as Theuderic lifted a bucket of water into the air and poured its contents over his head. In the rose-gold light of early evening, the water sparkled as it ran down his body.

India stopped, her eyes wide. He had not seen her yet, so she had time to feast her sight upon him. She had never seen a man so strongly muscled. His shoulders and upper arms were massive, no doubt the result of years of hefting sword and battle-axe and spear. He reached toward the bubbling spring to refill the bucket and she noted the ripple of muscles along his magnificent haunches and calves. When he raised his hands above his head to dump the water over himself again, she could see that he had his share of warrior's scars, a particularly nasty one running along his left side, but nothing could detract from the image he projected of robust health and steely strength.

Setting down the bucket, he stepped to the edge of the pool, paused for an instant, then dove into the water with a smooth, easy perfection that raised barely a splash. She saw his dark head surface, and he began to swim, not in the modern Australian crawl she had used, but in a kind of breaststroke.

India walked to the spot where he had stood, and waited there. He saw her almost at once, pausing with his head and shoulders out of the water.

"Is that you? For a moment I thought you were a ghost, in that white shirt and with the mist and steam around you." He swam to the side and pulled himself out, using his powerful shoulder and arm muscles. He stood before her glittering with moisture and narrowing his eyes against the setting sun behind her. He was so close to her that, as the water streamed from him, droplets splashed onto the shirt she wore.

He had been to the barber. Seeing him clean-shaven for the first time, with his wet hair plastered against his finely molded head, his eyelashes stuck together by water, and the sun full on his face, he looked younger to her, boyish almost, and defenseless. She wanted to put her arms around him and draw his head down onto her shoulder—or to her bosom. She reached toward him. He caught her wrists in cool, moist hands, holding her away from him.

"Not yet," he said. "Not until you tell me who and what you are, and how you came to me, there in Saxony." He dropped her hands and stepped away from her. That he desired her must have been as painfully undeniable to him as it was obvious to her, or to anyone who might have looked at him just then. He turned to pull his towel off the bush where earlier she had draped her underwear, and stood with his back to her rubbing at his hair and then his face and arms. Finally, holding the inadequately sized towel across his loins, he headed toward his house.

India followed him, frightened by the thought of what his reaction might be to what she would have to tell him.

Inside the house he drew on a blue woolen tunic, fashioned much like her own linen shirt, and gave his hair one last swipe with the towel.

"There's food," he said, glancing at the table, "but I think we should talk first."

"I don't know how to explain," she began.

"But explain you must. I cannot trust you

131

otherwise. I will know everything, and I will know it now. What have you been hiding from me?" He was so stern, so determined, that she knew it would be useless to try to resist giving him the information he wanted. While she sought for the right words, he walked to one of the chairs and picked up her bra.

"One question I had about you was answered when I first took you up before me on my horse," he said, stretching out the filmy, gold-colored lace. "This garment only confirms what I already knew. No boy would ever wear such a thing. And this other piece of clothing, with a texture like finest silk when I draw it through my fingers. What possible purpose could there be for apparel such as this, if not seduction? Are you a demon, sent to steal my soul from me?"

"I am human," she cried, frightened by his suggestion. "I told you that before. I'm not supposed to be here. It was an accident."

"Explain to me how this accident occurred."

"How can I, when I don't understand it myself?"

"Then begin with this." Tossing her underwear back onto the chair, he picked up her necklace from the table where she had put it before bathing. He held it out toward her, the pendant dangling, the chain wrapped in his fingers so she could not take it from him. "Who gave you this?"

"Robert Baldwin gave it to me."

"And who is this *Robair Baudoin*? How did

he acquire the sign of a royal messenger?" Trying to decide how to answer him without telling an actual lie, she did not speak at once. When she was silent too long, he asked another question. "He was not your master, was he?"

Another pause. Theuderic frowned, watching her closely. She knew she could put off speaking the truth no longer.

"Robert Baldwin was my husband," she said.

"Husband." He took a deep breath. "Where is he now?"

"He is dead, as I told you that first day, of a long and painful illness."

"What illness? Did you poison him?"

"Why would I do that? I loved him!" She was deeply shocked by the idea, and she hoped it showed. He looked at her long and hard before nodding.

"I believe this answer. You have always spoken of him with respect and affection."

"It was more than that. He was a decent, honest man, and a fine scholar. I was his assistant. We worked together every day. He became vitally important to me. He was a large part of my heart. When he died, I thought the world had ended."

"I understand," he said. "It was that way for me, too, when my wife died. Now tell me why he gave you the medallion."

"It was a gift. It isn't real, Theuderic. It's what we call a museum reproduction, a copy, made because the object is beautiful to us."

"I believe Charles would consider it a criminal offense to make such a copy." He held up the necklace again.

"Here, in your time, that may be so," she cried, desperate to make him understand that she was not lying to him, "but in my time it is intended as a compliment, an honor."

"Your time? My time?" He had seized upon the important element in her declaration. "What do you mean?"

"Theuderic." She had to tell him. He would not stop questioning her until he knew the whole truth, and she could not bear to lie to him. She wanted him to understand what had happened to her, and then to tell her that he still desired her. His eyes were sharp on her face, searching for any sign of falsehood. She restarted her explanation. "I was born in a land far from here, more than twelve hundred years from now, in the future. A friend of mine has a machine, which malfunctioned and sent me back in time."

"What are you saying? Are you mad?" His face looked frozen; his voice was a harsh whisper.

"It should not have happened. It was an accident," she said again.

"The battle," he decided. "That began the madness. You told me you had never seen bloodshed before. Then Eudon's accident, the long trek through the forest fearing a Saxon attack at every step, the way I treated you when I tied you to me at night—this is my doing. It's my fault you've lost your wits."

"I am not mad," she stated as firmly as she could. "I am occasionally confused because I am in the wrong time, but I am not mad, nor am I bewitched. Nor are you. Please don't blame yourself for anything. It's not your fault in any way."

"More than twelve hundred years," he said, shaking his head. "So long a time. Yet you are here, and you did appear out of the air, in the blinking of my eye. Perhaps it is true. There might be such a magic, though whether it would be for good or evil, I cannot tell. I want to believe you, India, but this is such a strange story."

"I'm not at all surprised if you find it hard to accept," she told him, much encouraged that he was at least considering what she had said. "I could scarcely believe it myself at first, when my only hope was that Hank would find me quickly and take me home again."

"Who is *Ahnk*?" he demanded.

"It was his machine," India said.

"A man? Is he your lover?" He tossed the medallion onto the table and came toward her with a purposeful step.

"Of course not. Hank is in love with my best friend." She stopped talking when he took her shoulders between his hands with a roughness he had never displayed toward her before. Realization dawned on her, and with it a deep joy that canceled her fear that he would reject her if he knew everything. "Are you jealous?"

"Of everyone who looks at you or speaks to

135

you," he grated, pulling her toward him. "I am jealous of Marcion, of Hugo, and poor Eudon, and of Osric. I am even jealous of Sister Gertrude. Most of all, I despise this *Ahnk*, who, from what you say, may take you away from me at any time. India, I want you more than I have ever wanted any woman before, including my dear wife. My passion for you at this moment, when I am not certain whether you are witch or spirit or human as you claim to be, shames me as much as my desire shamed me when I first looked into your eyes and wanted you, even though I thought you were a boy. You cannot know," he added ruefully, "how relieved I was to mount my horse and put my arm around you and discover you are a woman."

"All those nights lying beside you," she said, remembering each of them, "all those long days, so close together on your horse."

"A penance for my many sins," he murmured, touching his lips to the curve of her throat. "A penance, too, was my decision to wear my chain mail day and night as a barrier between us, until I could ascertain exactly what you are. Without that armor to keep us separated, I would have made you mine the first night we lay together."

"Oh, Theuderic." She could not decide whether to laugh or to cry. She pushed at his chest until he loosened his hold on her and raised his head. She wanted to look into his eyes when he answered her next question. "Do you believe me?"

"I may be bewitched," he said. "Or we may

both be mad. I could be risking my immortal soul. But yes, I do believe your story, perhaps because I want so very much to believe that you would not lie to me."

"Theu, I swear to you I am telling the truth. There is no witchcraft involved in my being here, and no madness."

He held her eyes with a deep and steady gaze for a moment before he nodded.

"Then I have only one more question to ask you tonight," he said, his voice almost a whisper. With a firm pressure on her shoulders, with one hand sliding down to her hips to guide them forward, he drew her to him. She felt his hard masculine need, as she had seen it earlier by the pool.

"The answer is yes," she said, putting her arms around him at last, after so many days of wanting to hold him.

Once he had her assent, he wasted not a second, immediately taking complete possession of her lips. She had never been kissed like that before. She could not have freed herself from his embrace, even if she had wanted to be free. His arms encircled her, holding her so tightly that she could barely breathe, while his mouth demanded her response.

Overwhelmed by his desire and her own, she reacted with hungry abandon to a kiss that seared her soul and branded her as his, and his alone. Afterward, she hung fainting in his arms while he kissed her throat and ears and cheeks, until he found her mouth again. There he drank greedily, while her lips and face and neck flamed from his touch, and the tightening of her arms around his neck brought her into ever closer contact with his body. He tugged at the linen shirt she wore, lifting it upward until it was at her waist.

"Ah, sweet lady, this is what I need." He stroked her hips, his callused hands against the smooth softness of her skin. One hand slid down between them, across her abdomen and downward, downward. . . .

With a soft cry of consent, she moved a little to let him feel the moist heat that would tell him how much she wanted him. He lingered there, probing, testing her readiness, driving her half mad with rising desire until she cried and begged him to stop—and, when he obeyed her, begged him not to stop.

He understood what her nearly incoherent babbling meant. With one long motion he pushed her shirt up and over her head, then tossed it onto the bench. Looking at the expanse of pale skin now revealed to him, he expelled a soft breath of admiration.

"Exquisite." He placed a hand over each of her breasts, his fingers cupping the high, round firmness. "So delicate, so fragile, and yet you are so strong. See how your breasts stand up hard and proud at my touch. Oh, India, India." He lowered his mouth to first one and then the other breast, and she began to shake with violent tremors. She clutched at his shoulders for support.

He knew she could stand no longer. He must have known, without her telling him, for he lifted her as if she weighed nothing at all and carried her to his bed. When he laid her upon it, his hands caressed the length of her body right down to her toes, then upward again, along the inside of both legs, over thigh and hip and upward to her breasts, where he paused for a breath-stopping moment before continuing onward to cup her face in his hands and hold her steady for a sweet, deep kiss. Then he straightened to strip off his tunic and throw it aside. He knelt above her, and although she believed he would not hurt her, she involuntarily, with the concern of a woman who has not known a man for long, empty years, shrank away from his size and his strength.

"Don't fear me," he said. "I only want you to feel as I do."

"I'm not afraid." To prove it to him, she touched his cheek, then laced her fingers through his hair. "I want you so much. Come to me, Theu. Come to me now." With those words she let one hand trail across his chest, along the fine brown hair that grew there, downward across his taut belly, and lower still, into a tangled mass of brown curls. Her eyes never leaving his, she touched him, deliberately, provocatively. His surprised gasp filled her with delight. She reached farther, deeper into the mat of hair to stroke a smaller, rounded warmth, then slowly drew her fingers out again, stroking, always stroking. He closed his eyes and moaned. Daring to look where her hand caressed, she watched him grow larger and harder. The heat inside her was rapidly becoming unbearable, and only he could quench it.

"Theu, please." He opened his eyes again.

"Never have I received such an invitation," he said in a broken whisper.

"Accept it," she begged, "before I die of wanting you."

"If you die, I die too," he told her, his hands separating her legs. With wry humor he added, "Shall we die together?"

After that she could not utter anything but gasps and moans and, occasionally, his name.

This was like no lovemaking she had seen in the movies or on television, nor was it in any way similar to what she had experienced in her marriage. Where her husband had always been almost deferential with her, Theu's loving was a fierce, vigorous assertion of his imperative masculine need, and it was not entirely gentle. Yet there was a tenderness in his actions, as if he assumed that whatever gave him pleasure would please her also.

He entered her with a swift, hard thrust that shattered her senses, and so strong and urgent was his hunger for her that she wondered if she would survive to rise from his bed when he was done with her. His passionate attack tore her breath from her throat and nearly stopped her heart. Her gasp of amazement when his great size filled her completely made him pause for just an instant.

"Don't fight," he groaned, his eyes silver-pale with passion about to be forcefully unleashed. "Come with me. I want you with me."

She was incapable of speech, nor could she move, because she was fastened to the bed by the weight of his body, impaled on the hot hardness of his desire. There was only one way she could answer him. She lifted her head an inch or so to place her lips on his and gently, delicately, let her tongue slide between his teeth to touch his tongue with the tip of her own.

With a wild cry, he tore his mouth from hers to renew his passionate onslaught. For an instant she feared he would split her body in two, but then something within her, some deep atavistic longing, awoke to match his fierceness with her own. Urging him onward, she rode the crest of passion with him, wrapping her legs around him to draw him ever deeper into her aching, throbbing center, laughing and crying at once, calling out his name over and over again, *Theu, Theu, Theu* . . . until tears and laughter and passion mingled in an explosion that forged them into one ecstatic, rapturous being.

Nor would he leave her. He stayed within her, moving more gently now, kissing and caressing her with tender hands and mouth, whispering sweet, endearing lover's nonsense until she had completely recovered her senses. Only then, when she could answer him like a reasoning person again, did he withdraw to lie beside her, gazing at her with deep affection. In the half light of the oil lamp, he was handsome beyond belief, and his hard warrior's body was a source of wonder to her. He had aroused in her emotions she had never imagined she could feel, and her tenderness toward him was tinged with gratitude for that gift.

"Never," she began. He stopped her with a single finger against her lips.

"Don't speak," he whispered. "What lies between us is too strong, too profound for words. And I am a man of action, not a scholar. Let my body speak for me, let my behavior be whatever proof you need of what I feel."

She took his hand from her mouth, held it between hers, and kissed each finger and his palm and inner wrist. When she had finished, she laid his hand upon her breast. He pressed downward, his palm against her nipple, and she felt the hardening from the immediate physical contact—felt also, far down in her pelvis, a quickening throb. Even now, when she was completely satisfied by his loving, still, newly awakened passion lay waiting to blossom into heat and beauty once more. He bent his head to suck at her hard nipple, and the inner throb grew stronger.

He lay back, pulling her across his chest. He drew up the bedclothes, confining them under the down-filled quilt and blue coverlet, holding her against his heart, rubbing her shoulder affectionately and kissing her brow, and she snuggled against him in warmth and contentment, the fire within her banked, waiting, not yet extinguished. Believing he had fallen asleep, she rested her cheek and one hand on the hair on his chest, waiting till he wakened. She began to drift toward sleep herself.

"Are you hungry?" he asked.

"Hmmm." She did not want to move, unless it was to make love again.

"The stew will be cold, but we can reheat it by the fire." He stood up, lifting her with him and setting her on her feet. He took the covered bowl from the table and put it into the ashes, then added more wood to the fire, pushing the smoldering logs around until the flame burst forth and caught the new timber. When he straightened, looking across the flames at her with simmering passion in his eyes once more, she tried to cover herself with her hands. "Don't be shy, India. Your body is beautiful. Let me see you. All of you."

"I'm not used to anyone looking at me like this. I feel safer with my clothes on."

"Do you want to be safe from me?" He appeared to be disappointed. With a quirk of his mouth, quickly repressed, he scooped her bra and teddy off the chair and held them out to her. "If you wish to cover yourself, wear these. And wear the stockings, too. They are like black cobwebs, so fine that my rough hands would tear them to shreds if I touched them. But at least they will veil your lovely ankles and your beautiful feet from my sight."

"I didn't mean—" she began, but he stopped her, taking the bra out of her hand and holding it up to peer through the lace.

"I would so like to see this garment stretched across your breasts. But I think if your pretty nipples were hidden from me, I would surely rip the offending cloth away."

"Don't talk like that. It's embarrassing."

"Why should it be, after what we have done together?" He stopped, watching her, as if a surprising thought had just struck him. "Tell me, India, how old was your husband?"

"He was nineteen years older than I," she replied, startled by the question.

"That explains much. You are, what? Eighteen? Twenty?"

"Twenty-six," she said.

"You look younger. And you have never until now known a young man's passion." He took the teddy from her, as he had taken the bra. "Later, I will ask you to wear these for me, because I want to see you covered and yet revealed in them. But for this moment, come back to bed and know a warrior's love once more. You cannot deny the evidence of your eyes, that I want you again. Touch me now as you did before." He took her hand, placing it on himself.

Whimpering with quickly rising desire, she did what he asked, watching him spring into arrogant fullness as she caressed and stroked. She stood only a step or two away from the bed, so when he pushed her backward, she sprawled onto it, her legs falling apart. He flung himself on top of her, covering and penetrating her at the same instant. She was more than ready for his first bold thrust. Passion, never entirely gone since their initial coming together, flared in her again, wild and sweet and blazing hot. His mouth was on hers, he was deep inside her, and she was whirled away into pure sensation and pulsating pleasure.

When, after a long time, she came to herself again, his full weight was on her and the pair of them were slowly, inevitably, sliding off the bed and onto the beaten earth floor. The downward motion of her hips as she fell off the side of the bed pulled them apart.

"Theu!" She was sitting on the floor. He had a knee on each side of her hips, her head was forced backward onto the edge of the bed, and he was kissing her throat. "You are breaking my neck. And my legs!"

He roared with laughter, pulling her to her feet to hug her and kiss her again.

"You are wonderful, glorious." Another long kiss interrupted his description of how remarkable a lover she was. "And thanks to you, I am starving." He swept her up in his arms to lay her on the bed again, tucking the quilt in around her. "Stay there. I will feed you."

He retrieved the stew from the firepit, cursing when he burned his fingers on the pot, and set it on the table. He ladled the mixture into a smaller bowl, the fragrant odors of meat and vegetables making India's stomach growl in hunger. He dragged the bench over to the bed and set stew, bread, and cheese on it. Picking up the only spoon, he began to feed her, with alternate spoonfuls for himself. She took the knife he had left on the bench to slice the bread and cheese so she could feed them to him. They drank the wine later, with Theuderic lying beside her and filling the cup at intervals.

"Theu, we do need to talk more." She was struggling with her desire to tell him what she knew about the Spanish campaign, while at the same time fearing that if she did, her action could alter history in frightening and unimaginable ways. While she sought for the right words with which to warn him without revealing too much, he spoke.

"You need not say it," he told her, misconstruing her intent and distracting her from the speech she wanted to make. "I understand from what you have already told me. At any moment your friend *Ahnk* may repair his machine, so that he is able to return you to your home. When that happens, we will be separated for all time."

"Oh, Theu." She wanted to cry. "When I first came here, getting home was all I thought about. But when I'm with you, I'm not sure I want to return home at all."

"Then stay with me," he said. "I am powerful enough to make certain that in Francia you will be treated with honor, and your life would not be unpleasant."

"I know Hank well enough to know he won't stop trying to get me back. I have no way to contact him, so when the moment comes, I don't think I'll have anything to say about it. I will simply go, in an instant."

"You will vanish, as I feared you would when I tried to keep you with me by tying you to my side? There will be no time to say farewell, no moment for a last kiss, no clasp of hands? Even marching into battle is not so dreadful as that. When we part from our womenfolk, we take proper leave of them. This *Ahnk* of yours is a heartless man."

"He may not know where I am. He may think I am drifting somewhere, lost in time, and that if he does not find me I will die. I told you, I don't understand exactly what happened to me."

"If he does not know where you are, he may never find you." Theuderic looked more cheerful. "Since this is so, we will go on as if you are to stay with me permanently, but we will treasure each moment we have together, knowing it could be our last."

"In my time," she told him, smiling, "that attitude is considered the best philosophy of life."

"No philosopher, no scholar am I," he said. "Not like Alcuin or Adelbert or the others in Charles's employ. But for as long as you want, or as long as you can stay with me, I freely offer you a place by my side."

Chapter Eight

"There, that should do it." Wiping the perspiration off his face, Hank dropped into the chair next to the computer. "Let's see how this configuration works."

"It had better work," came an angry voice from directly behind him.

"Willi, I don't think you fully appreciate what a significant scientific breakthrough this could be," Hank said. "If I can bring India back in one piece and then duplicate what happened when she hit the wrong button, my name will go down in history. I just hope she can remember exactly what she did." He broke off as a slender hand tipped with brilliant red fingernails grabbed his hair, pulling his head back hard against a black leather belt.

"I don't care one damned bit about your place

in history," Willi ground out between set teeth. "This is my best friend we are talking about. How can you be so cold-blooded? I'd like to wring your neck for setting up a program that would allow this to happen."

"Hurting me won't help India," Hank gasped. "Come on, now, you know I want this to work even more than you do. It's *my* program and if she—if she—aw, Willi, I'm sorry."

"You have tried to get her back five times in the thirty minutes since she disappeared," Willi snapped in the same angry tone she had used before. "What if she's someplace where she can't breathe? What if she's bleeding? *Get her back now!*"

"You're hysterical. I can't do anything for India until you let go of my hair," Hank yelled, jerking his head away at the same instant that Willi's fingers suddenly relaxed their grip. Hank's forward motion nearly propelled him into a collision with the computer screen. Recovering himself, he smoothed down his hair. "I had no idea you could be this violent," he said, glancing over his shoulder at her with an injured expression.

"I'll give you violent if you don't correct your stupid mistake," Willi replied.

"It's not entirely my mistake." Hank was deeply affronted by this suggestion. "I explained before that India did something to my program. But I'm trying to make it right, really I am. I feel at least half responsible for what happened.

I just hope she hasn't forgotten exactly what she did—oh, jeez, Willi, don't be mad at me." Hank uttered this plea when Willi shook one finger at him in a menacing way. "I promise I won't think any more about publishing a paper on this until after it's over."

"I'm not interested in your career path, and I don't want to hear any more excuses. Push those buttons, damn it! And make sure they're the right ones this time."

But before Hank could begin, there was a tap at the office door. Without waiting for an answer, a white-haired man walked in.

"Professor Moore," Willi exclaimed, "what are you doing here on a Sunday?"

"Looking for my secretary," he said.

"India's not here," declared Hank.

"I can see that," replied the chairman of the Department of History and Political Science. "This is most irregular. When I saw Mrs. Baldwin yesterday afternoon, she told me she would be here today."

"She stepped out for a minute," Hank said. "She should be back soon. We'll tell her you were looking for her."

"Yes. Yes." Professor Moore looked a bit befuddled. "Do that. I have some last-minute typing for her to do. I'm retiring next week, you know, and with final exams and the holiday coming and all, well, I can't seem to get anything finished." With that, he dropped the manila folders he had been holding, the papers scattering out of the folders and across the floor.

"Here, let me help you," Willi offered, bending to pick up the sheets and hand them to him. "Hank, can you get the papers that went under the computer?"

"Yeah, sure." Hank reached down. "Hey, look at this. Maybe this is the problem." His attention on the wires leading out of the computer, he absent-mindedly handed the papers to Willi, who passed them on to Professor Moore.

"You know, in my time," said the professor, "we tried to find romantic places to make out. Isn't that what you young people call it nowadays? But you really shouldn't be doing it in here. Anyone could walk in. I just did, didn't I, and interrupted you?"

"You sure did," said Hank, who was trying to move a section of the computer out from the wall.

"Now, I would suggest a walk in the woods," said the professor, "or a romantic movie. I courted my wife at the movies."

"Thank you for the suggestions," said Willi, handing him the last of his papers and gently steering him toward the door. "You've been very helpful."

"Yes, well, I do try to be broad-minded. Though I must say, some of the activities young people get up to today are scandalous. Now, you will tell Mrs. Baldwin that I'll need her to do this typing?"

"I'll tell her the minute she comes back," Willi promised. She closed the door behind him and leaned on it, blowing out a long breath of relief.

"It's a good thing he's retiring," Hank said from in back of the computer section he had moved. "That old coot can barely remember his own name."

"Don't be so disrespectful," Willi responded with some heat. "He's a nice man. India likes him very much."

"Yeah, well, the new chairman will probably work her butt off," said Hank. "At least the old guy did some good. When I bent down to get his papers, I noticed something I hadn't seen before."

"What?" asked Willi.

"Just watch. And stand back," Hank warned, resuming his chair and reaching for the switch. "If you see a bright glow beginning, get out of the room fast. I don't want you getting lost in there, too. You'd probably mess things up so completely that I'd never find either of you."

He flipped the switch on and began to work at the keyboard. The computer screen slowly brightened until the room was filled with light. Disregarding Hank's advice, Willi stayed where she was, right behind his chair.

"Now here," Hank said, "just at this place in Robert Baldwin's notes, is where India was working when it happened."

Inside the light dim shapes formed, flickered, and reformed.

"There!" Willi cried, pointing. "Do you see it?"

"I see." Hank continued to push keys. "That's India. Oh, my God, there's a guy with a sword!"

"India!" Willi shouted. "India, can you hear me?"

With a loud popping noise, the entire computer shut down. Hank and Willi groaned in unison.

"What happened this time?" Willi asked, her eyes still glued to the dark screen.

"The computer has a built-in surge protector that shuts down the machine if too much power enters the co-processor—and it's a good thing," Hank said, "because if anything happened to the co-processor, we'd never get India back."

"I don't want to hear another one of your confusing explanations of what that means." Willi fixed the back of Hank's head with a stare that ought to have frozen him into total immobility. "Just tell me what we do now."

"Now," he responded wearily, "we start all over. We try again. But, hey, we almost found her. We might have brought her back. That's a step in the right direction."

"Great." With barely controlled rage and the beginning of real dislike, Willi regarded the man she had until that day believed she loved.

"Get back to work," she ordered.

Chapter Nine

Theu had fallen asleep before the light began to glow inside his house, so it was India, lying awake beside him, who saw it first. It began in the corner where the tray containing his *brunia* sat atop the wooden box, and her immediate thought was that if something inside the box was on fire, the valuable *brunia* would be ruined. Fearing she might have to run into the night if the fire spread, she pulled the coverlet off the bed and wrapped it around herself in haste, then went to investigate.

"What is that?" By this time Theu was awake. India heard the bed creak when he leapt out of it and immediately afterward heard the soft swishing sound of a sword being drawn from its scabbard. Moving swiftly, Theu strode forward to place himself between her and whatever danger had invaded their retreat.

"Innndiaaa!" The distorted voice came from the very center of the light.

"Demon, show yourself," Theu challenged, brandishing his sword. "Come out and fight." He was crouched in a warrior's stance, his naked, heavily muscled form outlined in peach-gold by the eerie glow. Intent, wary, poised for instantaneous action, he waited, scarcely breathing. The only response from the light was another long cry.

"Innndiaaa!"

Theu took a cautious step forward, lifting his sword a little higher, obviously intending to attack before he and India could be assaulted.

"Wait." Her emotions in turmoil, India caught at his arm. "I recognize that peach color. I think Hank has found me."

"So soon?" Still holding his sword out to fend off whatever was in the corner of his house, never taking his eyes away from the pulsing light, Theu straightened to put a protective left arm around her. "How can I let you go to him?"

Torn between conflicting desires, she could not speak. She leaned against him, drawing courage from his unflinching strength.

"Don't go. Stay with me," he urged.

Before she could answer him, a fearful movement tore through the single-roomed house like an earthquake, the vibration rattling the walls and the door and almost knocking them off their feet. The house went dark except for the glimmering oil lamp on the table and the fading embers in the firepit. Remarkably, there seemed to be no damage, only an echoing silence when the long tremor was over.

"What has happened here?" Releasing her, Theu took a step toward the corner where the mysterious light had been. He moved his sword about, reaching here and there into the corner with it, as if he expected to encounter some obstacle unseeable by human eyes.

"I believe Hank's attempt at rescue has failed," India said, unsure whether she was happy or sad about it. Not dropping his sword by even a fraction of an inch, Theu withdrew his gaze from the corner to send a fierce glance in her direction.

"You need no rescue from me."

"Hank doesn't know that." Her voice trembled and she felt distinctly shaky, as if she were being pulled in several directions at once. She thought it was more than an emotional reaction on her part. Aware of a strong physical aspect to what she felt, she surmised that Hank had come very close to actually retrieving her.

"He will try again," Theu said. "I would, if I thought you were in danger. I would not stop trying until I had you safe beside me once more." With a final searching look around the house to be sure no perils waited in the shadows, he turned aside to lay his sword upon the table, where it would be within easy reach should he need it. India, still staring at the place where the light had been, did not see him stand

157

with bowed head and clenched fists, keeping his back toward her while he exerted all his will to contain his rage against Hank and his fear of losing her.

"I wonder why the light appeared in that particular corner," India said. "Theu, what is in the box?"

He did not answer for a moment or two. She started to ask the question again, but he came toward her, his face composed and hard, not looking directly at her.

"Clean sand," he said.

"Sand?" she repeated. "Are you serious?"

"To clean the *brunia*. I put sand in the tray and rub the links through it to scour away blood or rust or any other dirt." He paused, then added, "If you are still here tomorrow, I will show you how it's done."

Hearing the pain in his voice, she laid one hand upon his arm. He moved out of her reach, shaking off the touch she had meant to be comforting.

"Well, if it's sand and nothing more," she said, determined not to give way to the tears of confusion now threatening to destroy her fragile composure, "then there can't be any specific reason why the light appeared in that corner. But I should have known that. If location had anything to do with it, the light wouldn't have appeared here at all, but in Saxony, where I first landed in this time."

"You want to return," he accused her. "You want to go back to him."

"Not to *him*," India responded."I do not love Hank. You believe the rest of my story—believe that, too. Actually, I would like to see Willi again and tell her everything that has happened to me and hear her comments about it all. But except for Willi, there is no one and nothing to draw me back to the twentieth century."

"Then stay in this time."

"I don't know if I can. And even if I can, I don't know if I should. Can I move from one time to another, blindly changing the course of history in ways I can't even begin to understand, and not pay some terrible price? Or possibly cause people in my own time, or in this time, or in the intervening centuries to pay the price for me?" She watched him shake his head at that, and knew he had no more answers than she had. He was silent and thoughtful for so long that she began to fear he was angry with her.

"Would you tell your story to someone else?" he asked, the proposal startling her by its suddenness. "Before you answer, consider that there is a benefit to this night's unpleasant incident. Before it occurred, I believed you because I wanted to believe you. Now I *know* that you are telling the truth, having seen with my own eyes what happened here, and I can bear witness to your honesty, should any person question it. There are those who would blame that light we saw on witchcraft, but I know one who would at least consider your explanation of it."

"It's possible that the more people who know

159

what has happened to me, the more damage will be done," she said, wrestling with philosophical and mathematical concepts far beyond her training. "Who is this person?"

"Alcuin. I know him well enough to ask for his time and his opinion."

"The famous scholar?"

"Charles has ordered him to reform the palace school," Theu said. "Thus, Alcuin must follow the court, though he hates to travel. We will find him at Agen, with Charles."

"He will succeed with the school," she told him, almost forgetting her own problems in sheer excitement at the possibility of meeting one of the most remarkable men of the period. "More than that, Alcuin will sponsor a style of writing that is so easy to read and write that it will be the basis for handwriting and for machine printing for centuries to come. He'll invent punctuation, too, and write a prayer that is still used in the churches of my day. I learned it when I was a child—'Oh, God, to whom all hearts are open, all desires known, and from whom no secrets are hid,'" she quoted.

"He will be happy to know this," Theu said when she paused for breath.

"I can't tell him," she responded sadly. "I shouldn't be telling you. Theu, I never considered it before, but can you read and write?"

"A little. It's difficult to do."

"I'm sure it is. I've seen pictures of the old script—lots of strokes above and below the line, and no punctuation at all. It's a wonder anyone ever became literate. It never occurred to me that you would be."

"For the most part, I choose to remember the information I need," he told her, his words making her once again reassess this man whom she had at first thought was a purely physical creature. "Memorization is easier than writing words down, and parchment can be lost or destroyed. What is in my thoughts remains there. India, will you tell Alcuin your story?"

"I would like very much to meet him, because I admire him enormously," she said slowly, thinking over the idea. "After we have talked, then I will decide whether or not to tell him. Does this mean I can go to Agen with you?"

"There was never any doubt of it. You will have to see Charles because I had to tell him about you in order to make a full report on my foray into Saxony."

"Then I'll meet Charles and Alcuin both," she said, awed by the prospect.

"If you are not elsewhere by the time I reach Agen." He amended her statement in a quiet, matter-of-fact way, but she heard the sadness behind his words and went to him to put her arms around his waist and lay her head upon his broad chest. This time he did not reject her effort to provide comfort, nor did he hide his feelings.

"How can I live if you are gone?" he asked, folding her in his embrace. "Suppose *Ahnk* comes again today or later tonight? Will you believe it is your duty to go with him?"

"I'm not sure I'll have any choice when the time comes," she said. "But I have a feeling that whatever will happen, won't happen immediately. I suspect that Hank has blown a fuse, and possibly burnt out a new component or two. If that is so, it will take a while for him to make the necessary repairs."

Theu had found women's clothing for India to wear. That was the pile of folded fabric he had brought to his house the previous night and which he shook out for her inspection in the early morning. A coarse linen shift, a faded blue wool gown with rounded neck and short loose sleeves, a belt made of twisted and knotted fibers, and a square of grey wool that could serve as a shawl or short cloak, depending on how it was folded and draped, made up her new wardrobe.

"It's a serving woman's clothing," he told her, "since there are no noblewomen here from whom I could borrow a gown. I am sorry that I cannot offer you silk or fine wool in some beautiful color. You deserve better than this, but at least it is clean."

"So you really did know I wasn't a boy before you saw me without my clothes," she said, fingering the gown.

"How could any true man not know?" he replied. Winding his hand through her hair, he pulled her close to kiss her. She responded with eagerness and relief.

After the mysterious light had vanished during the night, he had held her possessively for a time, as if to reassure himself that she would not leave him. But when she felt his body begin to stir into passionate arousal, he left the bed to dress himself and sit in one of the chairs, remaining on guard while she tried to sleep. She thought his sudden reserve was caused by a concern that while they were in the midst of lovemaking, Hank might try again to get her back. This belief was reinforced by the carefully controlled way in which Theu set her aside now. Sighing, she slipped the linen shift over her head and reached for the gown. In silence, Theu cut a wedge of leftover bread and a chunk of cheese and handed the food to her.

"Talk to me," she begged. "Tell me what you're thinking."

"Only that I must visit Eudon this morning," he said, "and later begin to make arrangements for horses and supplies for our journey to Agen. Then I ought to speak to the clerics to be certain my report is on its way to Charles."

"That isn't what I meant," she protested.

"It will have to do for now." Picking up the grey wool square, he wrapped it around her shoulders. "You should have a brooch to hold this together. Most noblewomen do. I'll find one for you as soon as I can. If you are still here."

While arranging the grey folds at the back of her neck, his fingers brushed against the chain holding her medallion, which she had tucked

163

beneath her clothing. He pushed aside a lock of her hair that had become entangled in the chain.

"How can we talk about what has happened when we know so little?" he asked. "All I am certain of is that what is between us will be of short duration, for you will leave me, whether you want to or not. All we have is now. This day, this hour, this moment. And in every day there is duty as well as pleasure. While I may wish to lie with you again, to bury myself in your sweetness, I have obligations I cannot deny."

She would have reminded him that each day's duties had an end, that when nightfall came they could be together once more in the privacy of his house, but she knew he was right. When evening arrived, she might be gone. In his firm restraint, in his determination to do what duty required of him for the benefit of his king and his men, she found strength.

"Tell me how I can help you this day," she said and saw in his eyes his warm response to her offer.

She went with him to see Eudon, who lay on a pallet placed upon the floor of the narrow, barracks-like building where the men-at-arms slept. Hugo was with him.

"We've just come back from the bath that's famous for healing wounds," Hugo informed them. "In the hot water Eudon was able to move his leg and hip freely again. The stiffness he suffered after riding is completely gone."

After the last few days of riding and occasional bouts of fever, India had expected Eudon to develop an infection in his wound and probably die of it, since the only treatment available after the cauterization Theu had done was application of herbal poultices. To her surprise, he appeared to be recovering.

"I'll be fit to ride again in a day or two," he informed Theu. "I'll not miss the coming campaign."

"You will have several days to regain your strength before we can leave," Theu said.

"Don't go without me." Then Eudon smiled at India. "I always knew you were a girl. You have hands too gentle for a boy."

"Are we still to call you India?" Hugo asked, looking at her feminine garb.

"It is my real name," she replied.

"It's a relief to me not to have to pretend anymore that you are a boy," Hugo told her. "I'm not good at pretending."

"Did everyone know?" she asked him.

"All of us." He grinned at her. "You couldn't fool the most stupid of us for very long, but we went along with your disguise because Theu said to, in case you were a Saxon spy or perhaps a criminal running from justice. But we soon saw you were no ordinary woman when you did not complain at the pace of our travel or the lack of dainty food. Then, after you helped Eudon, you were like one of us."

"How fond I am of you," she said, looking at Hugo and then down at Eudon. "Of all of you."

"Be warned, Marcion will surely tease you about wearing boy's clothes." Hugo's pale blue eyes twinkled at the prospect. "Answer him boldly."

"I shall." Changing the subject, she asked, "Hugo, do you know if the lady Danise has left Aachen yet? If not, I would like to visit with her."

"Sister Gertrude is resting after her travels, and keeps Danise by her side." Hugo's smile disappeared. "I had hoped to see her again before she's carried off to Chelles, but I begin to fear that won't be possible. If you see her, and if you can do so without Sister Gertrude overhearing, will you tell Danise she is in my thoughts?"

With Eudon napping, Theu and Hugo went off on some masculine business having to do with the trip to Agen. India decided she would try to see Danise. After asking directions of a servant she located the guest chamber allotted to the nun and her charge, which was on the second level of the lodge. Danise herself opened the door at India's knock.

"Yes?" She looked at India politely but blankly, not recognizing her at first. Then her face changed. "Oh, my. It is you, isn't it? I was right. I thought you weren't a boy."

"It seems that everyone I met knew," India said dryly.

"Not Sister Gertrude. She said the most awful things about you and Count Theuderic." Danise began to blush. Laying one finger across her lips to caution silence, she leaned backward into the room, speaking in a whisper. "Clothilde, sit with Sister Gertrude while she naps. I won't be long, I promise. If she wakens, tell her I've gone to the kitchen to try to coax a treat for her from the cook."

"Perhaps that is what we ought to do," India said after the door was closed. "Then you won't be guilty of an untruth."

"An excellent idea," Danise agreed. "I know the way."

She was a clever girl. It did not take her long to convince the cook to fill a flat basket with apples, nuts, and several kinds of dried fruit intended for Sister Gertrude. The cook added two still-warm sweet buns, sticky with honey, for the young women, then shooed them out of the kitchen, saying she had much work to do before the midday meal was ready.

Leaving the kitchen, India and Danise found a towering oak tree and sat leaning against its trunk while they ate their buns.

"Do you like the school at Chelles?" India asked, wondering exactly what would interest a Frankish girl who looked to be no more than fifteen or so.

"It's confining," Danise said. "There are so many rules to follow. I try to be good, but secretly I wish I could be free. How I envy you, dressing in boy's clothes and traveling through Saxony."

"Only a day or two ago, I was envying you," India told her.

"Why?" asked Danise, licking honey off her fingers.

"Because of Hugo."

Danise grew very still, clasping her hands in her lap.

"You don't want Hugo," she said. "You love Count Theuderic. Even Sister Gertrude saw it. That's why she said what she did, thinking you were a boy and that you and he—. I should not be saying such terrible things. I shouldn't even know about them. My father would be horrified to know how the girls at school talk sometimes."

"Your father tried to arrange a marriage between you and me," India said, believing it was best to warn the girl, in case Savarec should raise the matter again. Danise burst into laughter.

"Poor Papa. He is a wonderful military commander, you know, but where I am concerned, he can sometimes be amazingly foolish."

"Perhaps I shouldn't interfere," India said, "but I think Hugo would be interested in the arrangement for you that I was forced to refuse." She then relayed Hugo's message.

"I hoped it was so." Danise's pretty face shone with pleasure. "Thank you for telling me. He is often in my thoughts, too. When next I see my father, I will mention Lord Hugo to him in the most discreet way. Perhaps by then Hugo will have made a famous name for himself in the coming campaign."

They talked on, India asking most of the questions, for she was genuinely interested in Danise's life, and she also did not want to reveal too much about herself. Even with that self-imposed constraint, it was good to talk to another woman after being so long in the company of men.

"I ought to return to my room," Danise said after a while. "If Sister Gertrude wakens from her nap and finds me gone, she will punish poor Clothilde as well as me. I hope we can talk again, Lady India." Taking up the basket intended for the nun, she headed toward the lodge.

Left to her own devices, India wandered about Aachen, trying to resolve the ethical problem brought back to her mind by Danise's words about Hugo earning fame in the summer campaign. She wanted to explain to Theu that the Spanish campaign would be a disaster that might prove fatal to him and to his men. But ought she to remain silent about what she knew, and let history take its appointed course? The question unsettled her, for if she did what her heart demanded—if she warned Theu about the dangers he would face in Spain—would his actions then change history, possibly disrupting the lives of uncounted people right down to her own day? Or was Hank right in his theory that over many centuries any changes would be corrected? Thinking about these questions made her head ache, and she walked about unseeing for a long time.

Only gradually did the peaceful somnolence of a royal residence when king and court were elsewhere begin to impress itself on her consciousness. She felt remarkably safe. The few men or women she met nodded to her politely or exchanged a word or two of greeting if she spoke first, but no one accosted her. With a quickening of interest, she explored the lodge itself, looked into the stables, and inspected the area around the royal baths, which were suitably larger than the small spring and pool by Theu's house. Later she re-entered the kitchen, where she was informed by the friendly cook that the main meal of the day would be served almost at once, and it would be a simple dinner of stewed fish and vegetables because it was a fast day. Following the cook's directions, she made her way to the great hall. Theu and several of his men were there before her.

"I have found a horse for you," Theu told her when they were seated at the long trestle table and enjoying the stew, brown bread, and wine the servants passed around. "She's a gentle mount, since you aren't used to riding."

"Will you ride sidesaddle now that you are a lady again?" teased Marcion from the opposite side of the table.

"I've heard that it's difficult to do," she returned, laughing back at him. "I would much prefer to wear my old clothing and ride astride."

"You could always mount yourself with Theu again," said Marcion, still teasing. "I doubt he'd mind if you did."

"We will travel faster if you do ride astride," said Theu thoughtfully, rising from the table and pulling India up with him. "You can practice this afternoon. Meet me at the stable after you have changed into your boy's clothing."

Her tunic and trousers were still a bit damp, but she put them on after first donning her lace bra and teddy. From the searching look Theu gave her when she found him holding both his grey stallion and a smaller chestnut mare, she thought he might be wondering what she wore beneath the wrinkled green outer layer of clothing. But he said nothing, confining himself to a serious explanation of what she would need to know to enable her to travel at the pace he wanted to set. At last he allowed her to mount, and together they rode across open meadows and into the forest, finally stopping beside the lake.

"We leave the day after tomorrow," Theu said.

"Will Eudon be ready to travel again so soon?"

"Eudon will. Will you?"

"Certainly. I'm no weakling."

"You sound offended. Perhaps you don't understand how hard the journey will be."

"I won't delay you," she returned with some annoyance. "Did I slow you on the way here from Saxony?"

When he did not answer, but sat frowning at the lake, she repressed the sharp comment she had been about to make, choosing instead to show him how much she had learned about riding. Pulling her horse around, she dug her

171

heels into its sides and took off in the direction of the stable. She bent low over the animal's back, feeling the rhythm of its muscles and the wind in her hair, hearing Theu's shout and then the sound of his horse's hooves in pursuit of her. She was laughing when she came to a stop in the stableyard, proud that she had stayed on the horse's back and delighted to know she had won the impromptu race by a second or two.

"Get off!" Theu blazed at her, grabbing the reins out of her hands. "Dismount before I throw you off!"

Too surprised to object, she slid to the ground while he gave the lathered horses over to the groom, who had hurried out of the stable to see what the commotion was.

"Tend them well, especially the mare. She's been ridden too hard," Theu said to the groom. Turning to India in a fury, he added, "You fool! How dare you use a valuable animal in that way? You aren't skilled enough yet to ride safely at such a speed, nor do you know the paths around Aachen. The horse could have been injured so badly it might have had to be killed. You might have been thrown. You could have broken your neck. Did you stop to think of that?" Catching her arm, he dragged her away from the astonished groom, pulling her in the direction of his house.

"Theu, let go of me!" Too late, she remembered the other name his men had applied to him on the day of her arrival in Francia. *Fire-*

brand, for his temper and his fury on the battle-field. "I will not be treated like this!"

But he did not release her, nor did he speak again until they had reached his door. He wrenched it open, forced her into the house with rough hands, and slammed the door shut behind them.

"I ought to beat you," he said, breathing hard. "Have you no sense at all? You could have been killed."

"But I wasn't," she responded boldly. "Besides, I thought it was the horse you were so worried about." Her display of courage quickly evaporated before his anger.

"Theu, no. No, please." Not certain what he might do, she backed away from him. He followed, stalking her across the room until she stood with the back of her legs pressed against the table. She put both hands on the tabletop behind her, to keep herself from falling onto it.

"Are you determined to drive me mad?" he demanded. "You burst into my life, destroying my hard-earned peace, making me want you until I am half blind with passion, and then you do foolish, thoughtless things that make me fear for your life. Any other man would beat you, would starve you into humble submission, would lock you away and forget about you." He caught her hair in both hands, stopping her backward motion across the table. "But I will never be able to forget you, though you leave me now and I never see you after this moment.

173

Your hair, your glorious gold-brown eyes, your skin smooth as silk. *India.*" His mouth bruised hers, his hands kept her head where he wanted it so he could plunge his tongue into her, ravishing her mouth with such terrifying insistence that when he let her go, her knees buckled and she did fall onto the table. He straddled her legs, bending over her, his hands on her shoulders to hold her there.

"I ought to take you here and now," he said, "without tenderness, without warming your heart or your body first, to show you how angry I am and how much I want you. Would that convince you that I care what happens to you?"

"It would convince me that you are a brute," she replied. "And considering how vigorous you were last night, the table would probably collapse before you had any satisfaction at all."

He glared at her for a long, breathless moment, during which she was uncertain whether he would hit her or take her by force as he had threatened. Because she was quivering with tension after his display of dominant maleness, she saw only his hard grey eyes, missing the sudden upward tilt at the corner of his mouth. She did not know what to expect when he hauled her upright with one hand.

"Take off your clothes," he ordered.

"Theu, please." She was shaking, but it wasn't with fear; it was because of a growing excitement. Every line of his body exuded a barely controlled passion that was directed entirely at her. And she welcomed it—she rejoiced in it.

"If you do not want to resew the seams before we set out for Agen," he told her, "then remove those garments or I will tear them from you."

She kicked off her boots, then unfastened her trousers, letting them fall to the earth floor. With his eyes still on her, she lifted the tunic over her head, laying it and her necklace on the table.

With one strong arm he raised her off her feet, so he could press his face into the silky fabric of her teddy and kiss her breasts. When he began to circle one nipple with his tongue, the fiery heat of his mouth through the lace made her pulses pound. She leaned backward, away from him, trying to catch her breath. He took immediate advantage of the slight distance she had put between them. Still holding her with one arm, with his free hand he explored the curve of her abdomen, then moved downward to the sloping valley that led to the aching spot between her thighs. There he pushed aside lace and fabric with so purposeful a motion that she thought he would tear the teddy off her. His fingers stroked into her, the intimate touch threatening to drive her mad with longing.

"Please," she whispered, steadying herself with both hands on his shoulders. "Please." She had no doubt about what it was she was begging for, nor any doubt at all that he would soon provide it. Taking his hand away, disregarding her distraught protest at the painful deprivation, he set her on her feet once more.

"If *Ahnk* comes for you now," he muttered,

reaching to catch the straps of her flimsy garment and pull them off her shoulders, "I will slay him without a moment's thought."

Half fainting with desire, she could make no answer. She could only stand unresisting while he removed her teddy, leaving her clad only in lacy black knee-high stockings and equally lacy gold bra. Swaying on her feet, she watched him tear off his own clothing, shamelessly exposing his need for her. She whimpered when he caught her at the waist, lifting her off her feet again, thrusting at her as he did so. Instinctively, she wrapped her arms around his neck. Then she screamed with surprise and swiftly mounting passion when he pulled her legs up and around his waist at the same instant that he entered her with a hard, jabbing movement.

It was there again, filling her mind and her every breath, that aching, primitive desire he roused in her each time they made love. It was beyond rational control; it overcame her with terrifying speed, leaving her incapable of thought. Driven half to delirium by a need she could not, and did not want, to fight, she gave in to the demands of her passion for him. She moaned when Theu carried her toward the bed, the motion of his powerful thighs pushing him deeper into her with every step. The force of their joined fall onto the bed drove him deeper still, his manhood piercing her body and her heart with a sweet, sharp joy as thrust followed vigorous thrust until her overwhelmed senses could endure no more and with a final, ecstatic cry she soared with him into rapturous completion.

When darkness fell, Theu sat at the table with the tray of sand and his *brunia* before him. India had lit a second oil lamp, and the fire in the firepit burned brightly, so there were few shadows in the little house. She poured a cup of wine and pushed it toward him, being careful not to spill any on the armor. He did not take his eyes off the *brunia*. Working on a sleeve, he pushed a handful of sand through the chain mail, rubbing, rubbing, then lifted more sand and began again.

"Is it ever finished?" India asked, taking up a portion of the other sleeve, which he had not cleaned yet.

"When I finish, I begin again," he said. "Though sometimes when I am on campaign, I am unable to clean it for a week or more."

"So many links." She looked more closely at the mail. "Each forged separately, each fastened into a circle with a tiny rivet. Every ring linked to four others."

"As a warrior is linked to God, to his king, to his friends. And to his love." Theu's eyes met hers. "If one ring is broken, the wearer becomes vulnerable to wounding and death. All the rings are necessary to the integrity of the whole armor. Men are the same. Each person is necessary to all the others in his world."

"The fabric of life," she said, scrunching up a portion of the sleeve she held, feeling the crisp, cool metal in her hands before she smoothed it out upon the table. "You would make a fine philosopher, Theu."

"Not I." He laughed, his eyes on his work again, his strong hands manipulating sand and metal. "If you want philosophy, or an explanation of man's proper place in this world and the next, speak to Alcuin and his friends."

"I will."

He stopped working. He looked into her eyes and put his hand over hers where it rested on top of his chain mail. They sat that way for a long time.

Chapter Ten

Because he was busy with the preparations for their departure from Aachen, Theu asked Marcion to ride with India on the following day.

"See that you obey his orders on the handling of your mount," Theu told her sternly. "I want to hear of no incident like yesterday's, when you spent your horse unnecessarily."

It seemed to India that the look he gave her was cool. Recalling that he had once told her he would never love again, she wondered if he was concerned that they were growing too close. Perhaps he had decided to put some emotional distance between them. Or perhaps the revelations of the past two days had damaged the fragile connection that bound them together. Watching him go off with Hugo, she wanted to run after him, seeking reassurance that what he felt for her was more than just a particularly intense variety of sexual desire.

"Are you coming?" Marcion waited, observing her with laughing yet shrewd eyes. "Will you tell me what punishment Theu meted out to you for mistreating your horse? I tried his patience in the same way once, when I was new to Francia, before he knew me well. He sent me to muck out his stables for three days. After that, I had a new appreciation of his intent to be obeyed when he gives an order."

"I wasn't sent to the stables," she said, thinking about the passionate night just passed, "but I know what you mean. I have seldom seen anyone so angry."

Alone with her, Marcion proved to be the same as he had been in the midst of Theu's warband—an amusing companion, a man with whom she could relax because the tension of physical attraction was absent between them. He was also knowledgeable about horses and patient with her ignorance of them. But, in her continuing insecurity about her place in Theu's life and how long she would be able to remain with him, she would rather have been with Theu, and she was happy to return to his house in late afternoon.

He had a visitor. India and Marcion met the man about to leave Theu's house just as they were entering it. India recognized him at once by his swarthy complexion and his thick black beard and mustache. He was Guntram, one of Savarec's messangers.

"I hope nothing is amiss with Savarec," she said, fearing the rebellious Saxons might have done some harm to Danise's father.

"Not at all, Lord India," Guntram replied. "Savarec is in excellent health and sends his greetings to you. Count Theuderic will tell you about the rest of my message."

"You will be certain to take the groom back with you," Theuderic said in a commanding voice, "and tell Savarec what I have reported about him. I will not have him in my party all the way to Agen."

"I have no doubt that he will soon be sent to fight Saxons," Guntram replied. "Fare you well, my friends. I return to Savarec at once."

When he had gone, Marcion looked at Theu with raised eyebrows.

"What now?" he asked. "More trouble with the Saxons?"

"Not this time," Theu replied. "Savarec has received an invitation from Charles, or to be more specific, from Hildegarde. The queen has invited Danise and a female companion to visit the court for the summer. Savarec has asked me to escort her there."

"Hugo will be delighted," said Marcion, adding in a joking voice and with a wink at India, "Do you think Savarec still hopes to wed his daughter to Lord India? Is that his reason for this request?"

"His message did not specifically mention India," Theu said, casting an amused glance at her, "but he may intend that they grow fond of

181

each other along the way. If that is his plan, he will be greatly disappointed." He looked as if he might laugh, but sobered at Marcion's next words.

"The additional women will slow us," Marcion noted. "And we know who the female companion will be. Where Danise goes, Sister Gertrude goes, too."

"I am not looking forward to her company," Theu admitted. "But Savarec was my father's friend and has always been mine. I could not in friendship say no to him."

"Well, then, it's settled," said Marcion.

Apparently, Sister Gertrude did not think the matter was settled at all. With Danise in tow, she swept up to Theu and India just as the evening meal was ending. She spared a piercing glance for India, who was wearing her woolen gown and shawl.

"It is a great relief to me to discover that Count Theuderic is not consorting with boys," the nun remarked in acid tones. Turning the full force of her tongue on Theu, she added, "However, I am most displeased with your actions. You have sent away the groom Savarec lent to us," Sister Gertrude scolded Theu. "You had no right to interfere in our affairs in that way. How is our servant Clothilde to travel without a horse to ride? Who will care for our horses during the journey? Answer me, Count Theuderic!"

"I assume from your words that Savarec's

messenger found you." Theu did not mention what the dismissed groom had tried to do to India, and he showed no sign of annoyance at being verbally attacked before his own men and the residents of Aachen.

"Found me and delivered his message," the nun snapped. "I am not happy about these new arrangements. A royal court is no place for an innocent young girl."

"Hildegarde is the most responsible of queens." Marcion's declaration drew Sister Gertrude's attention from Theu to himself. "My own betrothed, the lady Bertille, resides at court. I do assure you, she has suffered no loss of innocence there. In fact, I am scarcely allowed to see her."

"Which is very proper in the case of a young maiden," said Sister Gertrude. "But what about the journey to Agen? The company of coarse men, the dangers upon the road—I cannot understand why Savarec would allow his daughter to make such a journey."

"Because the queen invited her," Theu said patiently. "No doubt Savarec was thinking of Danise's future, of the ladies she will meet and make friends with at court."

"But what are we to do for a groom?" cried Sister Gertrude, returning to her original complaint.

"I will care for your horses along with my own," offered Hugo. "As for your servant, she can ride behind any of the men she chooses."

"Lord Hugo, you are most kind to help us,"

said Danise, who had remained silent through Sister Gertrude's protests. She sent a charming smile Hugo's way, which Sister Gertrude did not notice because she was again scolding Theu over the loss of her groom and the change in plans and whatever other lament came to her tongue.

"What a delightful journey this will be," said Marcion sarcastically to India while Theu listened to Sister Gertrude with remarkable politeness.

"But at journey's end you will meet your Bertille once more," India reminded him. She was not really thinking about Marcion and his betrothed. She was thinking about Theu. For a warrior noted for his ferocity, for a man with the kind of temper he had displayed on several occasions, he was peculiarly polite to women. She could not imagine any twentieth-century man she knew enduring Sister Gertrude's attacks without making a rude response. Theu merely listened, agreed with the nun when possible, or made some statement aimed at calming her ire.

Nor had he been rude to India—occasionally rough, or frustrated, the day before furiously angry when she was plainly at fault in the way she had used her horse, but never deliberately rude. A firm respect for women showed in all his dealings with them. It was yet another aspect of the character that continued to intrigue and entice her—and to frighten her, too, for the better she knew him, the more terrible the thought of separation from him became.

During their final day and a half at Aachen, India scarcely saw Theu. He came to bed late, after she was asleep, and contented himself with a quick kiss and a hug before he closed his eyes in weariness. In the morning he left before she wakened. Knowing that he was busy and that his duty was vitally important to him, she did not complain when she did see him, and she tried to occupy herself with her own preparations for the coming trip.

Inspired by Theu's sense of responsibility and not wanting to have to depend on Hugo or one of the other men to do her work for her as Sister Gertrude would do, she enlisted one of the stableboys to instruct her in the proper care of her horse while they were traveling. With Marcion's help, she acquired from an itinerant peddler a long woolen cloak and a brooch to fasten it. She planned to wear the cloak with the tunic, trousers, and boots in which she had come to the eighth century. She was unable to use a sword to bolster her traveling disguise as a young man, finding the weight of the broad, two-edged Frankish weapon difficult to lift, and having no skill at all in its application, but Hugo gave her a long knife and a belt to hold it.

"If you stay with Theu or one of us at all times," he advised, "you will be safe enough. There are men who take only a knife and a spear and axe when they go off to join the army, so the lack of a sword won't make you especially noticeable, but it would look strange if you had no weapon at all."

On Theu's orders, Hugo also found saddle-bags for her. She was fascinated to learn from Hugo that each man in the Frankish army was expected to carry his own food supplies, enough for three months. He told her that these were usually bread to eat at first, coarsely ground flour to make more when the bread was gone, a slab of bacon or some dried meat, and wine or ale to drink, this last item to be replenished along the way.

"Though Charles is so strongly opposed to drunkenness that any man found guilty of it is condemned to drink only water until the campaign is over. And we all know how unhealthy water is," Hugo said with great seriousness. "It will kill a man as fast as any enemy, sometimes faster."

Considering the probable sources of water available to a large army on the march, India could believe this was no joking matter. She fastened a filled wineskin to the saddlebags she had packed with food and rolled up her woman's clothing to squeeze into the remaining space in the bags.

On the night before they were to leave, her personal preparations were complete. Knowing that it would be a long time before she could again enjoy the luxury of a hot bath or a shampoo, she took soap and towel to the spring next to Theu's house. In the light of the rising full moon, she soaped hair and body, then rinsed and rinsed again. There was just enough moist chill in the air to make her look forward with eagerness to the moment when she would immerse herself in the hot water of the pool. With a pleasant expectant shiver, she moved toward the edge, watching the steam that drifted upward from the surface of the water. Balancing on one foot, she cautiously dipped in a toe.

"There's no need to test it," said Theu from behind her. "The heat is always the same." He caught her hand, spinning her around like a dancer and wrapping their locked arms across her back to draw her against him. He had removed his clothing before coming to the pool, so her bare wet skin was pressed against his dry warmth. Desire for him, never far from her consciousness, blossomed at the contact, but she kept her voice under control.

"Have you also come to take your last bath before we leave?"

"I have neglected you these past two days," he said, acknowledging her attempt at coolness. "I'll remedy that tonight. Perhaps you'd be willing to help me clean away the day's dirt and sweat."

"I might be." Leaving his arms, she moved toward the spot where she had left the bowl of soap and the bucket. He followed her.

"There will be a reward for your assistance," he promised, drawing aside her wet hair to kiss the back of her neck.

"A good deed is its own reward, needing no other recompense," she murmured, relishing his appreciative chuckle.

"In that case, dearest lady, I will not delay your act of charity. Begin whenever you wish."

She answered him by pushing him down onto the low wooden stool that sat next to the spring and then pouring a bucket of hot water over his head. The soap in the bowl was not quite solid. She scooped a little of the gelatinous substance into one hand and began to wash his hair.

"Be careful," he warned. "If it gets into my eyes and stings, I will be angry."

"It seems to me," she told him, "that you ought to be grateful for my help instead of sounding like Sister Gertrude."

At that, he seized her right hand and began kissing her wrist and fingers in spite of the unpleasant taste of the soapsuds adorning her skin.

"Let me go," she whispered, all her senses stirred by the touch of his mouth on the pulse point at her wrist, "or I won't be able to wash your back."

When he released her hand, she gathered up more soap and began to massage his back while he leaned forward on the stool.

"Now your chest," she told him, moving around to kneel facing him.

"No." He caught her hands. "I'll do the rest myself. If you touch me once more, I won't be able to wait. I want this night to be a feast of love for both of us, not just for me."

He rose, pulling her up with him. They stood in hazy moonlight, wanting each other yet delaying what they knew would soon happen, drawing out the desire and the fulfillment they would find in each other.

"Our idyll here is coming to a close." He was still holding her hands, lacing his fingers through hers. "Once we are traveling again, there will be few occasions to make love as freely as we do in this private place. But whether you sleep in my arms or not, never doubt my longing for you. Never imagine I have ceased to want you, though I may not show my desire as your woman's heart might hope. And when at last our journey ends, then you and I—" He stopped, dropping her hands and moving toward the pool. When he spoke again, she had the impression that he was fighting against an almost unbearable grief.

"I sometimes forget," he said in a choked whisper, "that you may not always be with me. I begin to plan a long and happy time together, and then I remember, and it is as though you are already gone from me."

"The truth is," she told him, "that we can't be certain Hank will ever be able to remove me from this time. I have been here for eleven days now, and he has been able to make just one unsuccessful attempt. It is entirely possible that I will be stranded here for the rest of my life."

"I wish it were so," he said.

The thought of never going back to her own time ought to have made her unhappy, but

Theu's quietly spoken words filled her with a joy that blotted out regret for whatever she might have lost in the twentieth century. Though he had not mentioned love, he had made clear how much he wanted her. Considering how uncertain the future was for both of them, perhaps it was better if they never spoke of love.

"I begin to think you are in more danger of leaving me than I am of leaving you," she said. "Theu, I am afraid of what will happen in Spain."

"Do you know something about the Spanish campaign?" he asked. "You have mentioned it before, and I have seen your face when Hugo or Marcion speak of it."

"It will end in disaster," she began, but he raised his hand in a gesture that stopped the words she dreaded to say but had to speak if he was to be warned.

"Not now," he said. "Don't spoil this beautiful evening with what you know of the future. For this one brief night, I want to think of nothing but you. Tell me later what you think I ought to hear. And if there is no later for us, if you are taken from me before you can speak what I believe will be sad words, then I will do what I would have done before ever you came to this time. I will obey my king and lead my men into battle—and try to bring as many of them home again as I can. The only difference will be that if you are not waiting for me, it won't matter to me whether I live or die.

"And now, we have talked so long that the fever that was in my blood has cooled enough to let you finish washing me after all."

She moved toward him, lifting soap-filled hands which she laid on his chest. But it was soon evident that the fever he had spoken of had not abated. He reached for the soap bowl himself, just as her hands slid downward along his flanks and around to his groin. He froze in mid-motion.

"Get into the pool," he said. "Unhand me now or this lovemaking will end too soon."

"I'm not sure I want to unhand you," she replied, stroking the inside of his thighs.

"Take your hands away or I'll throw you into the water."

"You always threaten violence," she murmured, still touching him.

"I may threaten, but I could never hurt you." Since she would not do as he ordered, he pulled her hands from his lower body and held them against his chest. She took full advantage of the opportunity thus offered to her, moving close to his soapy, glistening strength. Stretching upward, she kissed him full on the mouth. He pulled back, turned her around, and pushed her toward the water.

"While I may never hurt you," he said sweetly, "I *will* teach you to obey me."

It seemed the gentlest of touches between her shoulder blades, but she was by then standing at the very edge of the pool. She fell into the water, sinking to the bottom before she was able to overcome her shock at this treatment. With a hard kick against the mosaic tiles she turned herself right side up and rose to the top again, sputtering and coughing when she finally reached the air. Theu stood watching her in the pose so typical of him, with his legs apart, fists on hips. Something in the bold self-assurance of his stance brought out an unexpected wildness in her.

"Don't you dare laugh at me!" she cried, grabbing at his ankle and pulling hard. It was entirely satisfying to see him do a slow cartwheel out over the water before he landed with an awful *whack* that must have knocked the air right out of his lungs.

"Why, Theu," she said, displaying not the least bit of sympathy when he finally surfaced, "you forgot to rinse first."

"I'll have my revenge for your foul deed," he told her, flashing a wicked grin before he vanished into the steam.

For the next few minutes it was like being in the pool with a playful sea creature. Theu dove again and again to touch her beneath the water, stroking and patting her legs and breasts and buttocks, tickling her feet and the backs of her knees, once even pulling her under to kiss her until her ears began to ring from loss of air. After that she hung by one hand from the stones at the side of the pool, wiping her streaming hair out of her eyes and wondering where he would strike next. Suddenly he was in front of her, pinning her against the stone with a hand beside each of her shoulders and his full length pressing on her.

"Do you know now who is your master?" he asked, kissing her throat.

"I'll never surrender," she gasped.

"Oh, but you will, in just a moment or two." With no apparent effort at all he lifted her out of the water, sitting her on the stone edging. She tried to get to her feet, intending to run away from him, but he was too fast for her. He knelt beside her, the moonlight shining on him, and she knew she did not want to run away after all. With laughter and a deep, sweet yearning, she opened her arms to him.

He was wet and cold and warm, all at the same time. He was a shaft of ice inside her that melted and boiled and nearly destroyed her with his furious heat. He was a gentle spring rain that nourished and renewed her when the first madness of his passion was spent.

They did not sleep at all that night. They loved again by the pool, then bathed once more before they retired to his house to latch the door against the world. In the intervals between the loving, they talked. He told her of his boyhood spent learning to be a warrior, of the father he adored and wished to emulate, who had been killed while fighting in Aquitaine for Charles's father, King Pepin. He spoke of Charles and his deep affection for that finest of kings, and talked with gentle love about his wife who had died too young, and of the infant son she had left him, his great hope for the continuation of his family line. In return, she told him about her parents' death by accident, of her husband's long illness, and then described her years of friendship with Willi. As morning came, they loved one last time, a sweet, slow, and ultimately tearful passion on her part, permeated by the belief that this could be their final coming together.

When the sun rose, they left Aachen, India riding beside him in her twentieth-century tunic and trousers, with her eighth-century brown cloak thrown over her shoulders, love and worry filling her heart and the weight of future events pressing upon her. It was evident to her that if she wanted to protect Theu from almost certain harm, she would have to tell him what she knew about the Spanish campaign. After what he had said during the night, from the kind of man she knew him to be, she had an awful feeling that when he was aware of the terrible dangers to him and all of the Frankish army, the knowledge would not change his determination to follow his king into Spain, or even to die for Charles if it were necessary.

Chapter Eleven

Sister Gertrude surprised them all. Once they were on their way, she seemed to accept the change in plans that had been imposed upon her and her charge. She did not lessen her fierce protectiveness of Danise, keeping the girl separate from Theu's men as much as she could, but she stopped scolding Theu, and she proved to be a resilient traveler. While India and the still-recovering Eudon walked about slowly each morning, bending and stretching and rubbing at aching muscles, trying to ease the previous day's saddle stiffness before they had to mount once more, Sister Gertrude was always ready on time, prepared to ride and showing no sign of physical distress, though she was the oldest member of their party.

She also began to moderate her disapproval

of India. On the day after they left Aachen, she took advantage of a time when Theu was riding with Hugo and Marcion and was so well occupied in talking to them that he would be unlikely to overhear her comments.

"You are a foolish young woman," the nun said, urging her horse closer to India's. "Do you imagine that wearing men's clothing and riding like a man will endear you to Count Theuderic?"

"In my country," India replied, "women often wear this kind of clothing. And they decide for themselves how they will ride." She half expected a sour retort to her attempt at self-defense, but Sister Gertrude fell silent, apparently thinking about what India had said.

"I met a Byzantine woman once," Sister Gertrude remarked a little later, "who told me that in a place far to the east of Byzantium, the women wear such garments as yours, made of silk. If that is the case, and if that distant land is your home, then I will not criticize you for following your own customs. But you must realize that in Francia we do things differently. You cannot attend court in such attire."

"I will remember your sensible advice," India responded, surprised yet again by the adaptability of a woman who had supposedly spent her life sheltered from the world. She began to look at the nun with a new respect.

From then on, Sister Gertrude became more friendly toward India, often asking penetrating questions about her life that India found difficult to answer as truthfully as she would have liked. However, Sister Gertrude never missed an opportunity to comment unfavorably upon the actions of the men, until India came to the conclusion that the nun heartily disliked all those who belonged to the male gender.

India found this new journey much different from the earlier trek through Saxony. Their route once more wound through dense woodlands, but Theu's band no longer camped in the forest, rolling themselves into their cloaks at night. Instead, they slept in abbey guesthouses or in the houses of nobles, their often crowded accommodations allowing little opportunity for either lovemaking or serious conversations.

At first, believing they would pause for a day or so in Noyon to allow people and horses to rest, India planned to speak to Theu there about the horrors awaiting the Frankish army in Spain. But at Noyon, where they stayed in the royal residence, Theu spent the better part of the night in talk with the noble who headed the household in Charles's absence, and they rode forth again at first light. Two days after that, they crossed the River Seine in a drenching downpour. Sister Gertrude sent a long look and a sigh in the general direction of Chelles, but she said nothing, and they continued on without pausing.

A day later, they were housed again in an abbey, this one south and west of Paris, and still India had not revealed to Theu what she knew. She decided she would not go to bed that night until she had spoken to him. She had discarded her earlier concerns about what effect her revelations of the future might have upon the history of centuries to come. She had been given more than enough time in which to recognize and deal with her feelings for Theu. Loving him with a deep and reckless passion unlike anything she had ever known before, she wanted only to save his life.

It was Hugo who gave her the opportunity for which she was hoping. After the light evening meal of bread and cheese, she excused herself to Sister Gertrude and Danise, then hurried to catch up with Theu as he left the refectory. Encountering Hugo and Theu speaking together at the doorway, she paused, waiting until they had finished.

"Would you like me to speak to Charles on your behalf?" She heard Theu ask Hugo. "Or to Hildegarde? If either of them were to mention you favorably to Savarec, he might be more willing to give his daughter to you."

"You know my problem," Hugo responded. "I have nothing to offer a noble lady. I have only the small estate where my mother and sister live, and if my sister is ever to marry I will have to give up part of those lands in order to provide a dowry for her. Danise deserves much more than I possess, and Savarec will surely tell me so."

"Look to Spain," said Theu. "Knowing the kind of fighting man you are, I think it likely that you could make your fortune there."

"Where the sun shines every day," Hugo said,

a dreamy look on his plain, honest face. "Where every castle has a beautiful garden with a fountain and a flowering almond tree. And oranges, ready to drop into a man's hands—or a lady's. I think Danise would like that. She should live in a fine castle on a hilltop in Spain, with servants to obey her every wish. I swear to you, Theu, I'll win it all for her with my sword."

"Before we leave for Spain, I will speak to Charles about arranging a marriage between you," Theu promised, sending Hugo away to bed with a smile and a friendly clap on his shoulder.

"If Hugo depends upon Spanish treasure to win himself a bride, he'll never marry Danise," India remarked, making Theu look sharply at her in the shadows of the refectory entrance.

"It's time we talked about this," he said. "Come with me."

He did not take her to the tiny guest's cell he had been given for his own use that night, nor to the smaller cell where India would sleep. He led her to the scriptorium where, even at this late hour between Vespers and the final devotional service of the day at Compline, a pair of monks still labored, copying manuscripts by the light of candle stubs burned too short to be used in the chapel any longer.

"They won't overhear us," Theu said, choosing a carrel and a bench at some distance from the monks, who did not raise their heads at this intrusion. "They are too intent upon their work."

He straddled the bench, leaned one elbow on the writing shelf of the carrel, and motioned to India to join him.

"Now tell me why every mention of the Spanish campaign fills you with dread," he ordered as soon as she had seated herself.

"You said once that you do not entirely trust the Saracens who have invited the Frankish king into their country, offering to turn over cities and treasure to him," she began. "Your concern is well placed, though it's not so much that the Saracens are untrustworthy, but rather that their affairs are so confused. The Saracen lords of Spain are fighting each other, and they are involved in complicated intrigues among themselves. Loyalties shift from day to day. The situation is really a civil war. I'm not sure you understand that term as I do, but anyone who involves himself in Spanish politics will soon regret his decision."

"Charles is aware of all of this," Theu told her. "While most of his nobles enthusiastically favor the campaign, there are a few, myself included, who feel it is unwise to entangle ourselves in quarrels best left for the Saracens to settle among themselves. So what you have just told me is nothing that I and others have not already discussed with Charles."

"But he is going anyway." There was despair in her voice, and a black, desperate fear for Theu clutching at her heart. "And you will go with him."

"The decision was made last autumn," he

said. "Nothing will change it now. I pledged my loyalty to Charles years ago. I will follow where he leads."

"What will you do when the Spanish Christians turn from Charles to join their Saracen countrymen and fight the Franks together?" She had to make him understand the terrible risk in going to Spain. If she could not prevent his going, at least she would try to convince him to be on his guard at all times. "How will you deal with the Gascons and the Basques who live in the mountains and the rough country between Francia and Spain, who will harry you along the way, who will lie in ambush for your return?" She stopped, choking with terror, knowing yet not caring that she had said too much, for she was gripped by a dreadful premonition. His response was exactly what she had feared it would be. She had not known him for long, but she knew him very well.

"What would you have me do?" he asked. "Shall I play the coward and beg to remain on this side of the Pyrenees? Desert my king when he needs me and my men? If I and every man of my levy are destined to die for Charles in Spain, which is what you are suggesting, then so be it. I will not defect from my duty. If I did, I would be less than a man and unworthy of your affections. Unworthy, too, of my son's honor and a disappointment of all my parents' hopes for their descendants."

"Charles will eventually give up the campaign, having gained little at the cost of many lives," she said, casting aside all remaining caution, determined to tell him everything she knew. "On your return through the Pyrenees, the rearguard will be ambushed in a mountain pass—not by Saracens, but by Christians."

"*Stop.*" In the shadowy light he looked frozen, hard, a man of steel and stone. "There is something evil in this foreknowledge of the future. I will listen to no more."

"I am trying to save your life!" she hissed. Mindful of the monks on the other side of the room, she lowered her voice when she tried again. Her throat was dry with fear, and she felt close to tears. "For me it isn't the future, it's the past—it's history. I know I shouldn't be telling you any of this, but Theu, I'm so worried about you, so afraid you'll be badly wounded or even killed."

"All men die," he said, "and warriors sooner than most. As I do before every campaign, I have made my peace with the possibility that I will not survive the coming battles. If you are my true friend, you will do the same. You will take pride in my courage and let that pride sustain you through whatever happens to me in these next months."

"I'm not like you," she whispered. "I'm not used to constant warfare."

"Yet you have more courage than most women." After a quick glance toward the monks, he leaned forward to touch her cheek and rest his hand upon her shoulder. "Were our positions reversed, were I by some magic sent to your century, I think I would go mad with the horror of what had happened to me. But you, finding yourself in my time, have displayed a bravery worthy of any warrior. India, I want you to forget what I said at Aachen about speaking to Alcuin. Give me the answer to only one question more, and then I want you to seal up your knowledge of the future in your heart and never speak of it again, not to me or to anyone else, for it seems to me that such knowledge is dangerous beyond our reckoning. It could change our actions in this time and thus affect the lives heaven has intended for all those who come after us."

"Hank has some strange theories and complicated mathematical formulas to explain that sort of thing," she told him, "but you have said it more simply and more truly than he ever could. Theu, I meant no harm and certainly no insult to your honor by telling you all of this. I only wanted to warn you, because I—because I worry about you."

She had almost said she loved him, but the words had been stopped in her throat by the way he had called her *friend*. If she was to him no more than a friend, then the last fragments of her shattered pride would prevent her from admitting that she loved a man who could not love her. But was she wrong about that? His fingers gripped her shoulder more tightly for a moment, as if he would convey to her a message he could not allow himself to speak aloud.

"I understand and I thank you for caring

about my welfare," he said. "Now answer my only question. Will Charles survive and continue to rule the Franks?"

"He will become one of the most famous of kings," she responded. "His memory is still honored and respected in my own day. Men will call him Charlemagne—Charles the Great."

"I am content." He stood, holding out his hand to her. "Let the future happen as it must. We will speak no more of what you know."

But now you know, too, she thought. *Surely that knowledge will change your actions, just as you said it would. Remembering what I have told you, you may live to return from Spain.*

They went out of the scriptorium hand in hand, nor did he release her when they entered the hall where visitors were received. There they found a dark-haired stranger.

"Count Theuderic." There was no respectful bow from the newcomer and no smile of greeting, only an abrupt dip of his head before he resumed his previous rigid stance. By his appearance, he was a person of some importance, for beneath his dust-streaked brown cloak he wore expensive chain mail and he carried a rounded metal helmet in the crook of his left arm. A long puckered scar slashed across his left cheek and chin, and his ice-blue eyes were cold when they rested on Theu. "I have been searching for you."

"Autar of Chalons." Theu spoke pleasantly enough, but India was aware of the sudden tensing of his strong frame beside her, and his hand tightened on hers. She saw Autar glance toward their hands, then back to Theu's face. "I assume you have some message for me," Theu said.

"Count Hrulund, the Warden of the Breton March, has commanded me to greet you in his name," responded Autar, "and to invite you to join him at Tours. From there you will travel together to Agen."

"There are women in my party," Theu said. "I am not certain if Hrulund will want to travel with us when he learns of their presence."

"There is a convent at Tours, where the women may stay while you are there," Autar replied. "Count Hrulund expects you. Let him decide how you will travel from Tours to Agen."

"Will you ride with us?" Theu seemed not at all offended by Autar's cold manner.

"I will join you in the morning." With another abrupt little dip of his head, which was his only gesture of politeness or of acknowledgment of Theu's superior rank, Autar turned his back on them and marched away toward the dormitory.

"I do not like that man," India said.

"He is a fine warrior, one of Hrulund's best," Theu informed her. As he spoke, he released her hand, and when he did she felt abandoned, as if he had already gone off to war with his men and Hrulund and the rest of the Frankish army.

They left the abbey the next morning with India no longer riding beside Theuderic. Her former position was taken by Autar. She did not protest the change. By the look Theu sent her way, with his eyebrows raised and his face serious, she understood that, for whatever reasons of his own, he wanted her to keep away from Autar. From then on, she rode between Marcion and Hugo. From their talk, she learned that while Hugo called Hrulund the second greatest of all warriors next to Theuderic, Marcion had little admiration for him and less for Autar.

"Hrulund's men are all like that," Marcion said in response to a question from India, "cold-hearted and brutal. They kill for the pleasure of shedding blood and inflicting pain."

"And don't you?" she asked. "After all, you are a warrior, too."

"Most men fight out of loyalty to their king, or to protect their homes and families," Marcion replied, "and some fight to win lands or a great title, but most respect a brave enemy and regret the need to kill him in order to remain alive themselves. But as for Hrulund, I think he does not care whether he lives or dies, nor does he care for anyone else's pain. I believe Hrulund cares for only two things in this life—his own glory and Charles's friendship."

"Is he jealous of Theu's friendship with Charles?" asked India.

"I think so," Marcion said. "It's my opinion that Hrulund hates Theu. We will have to be very careful in Tours."

Chapter Twelve

The building into which they were ushered by Autar was made of stone, its low ceiling supported by wide pillars that ended in curved arches. There was no carving on the pillars, no decoration at all to lighten the weight of the pale, heavy stone. Nor was there any furniture, nor a fire in the cave-like hall where Autar led them. Here it was gloomy, cold, and damp, a place created for warriors who cared nothing for comfort or warmth. There was not the slightest hint of anything feminine in it.

Walking between Marcion and Hugo, India shivered, oppressed by the atmosphere and almost wishing she had stayed at the convent with Danise and Sister Gertrude as they had wanted her to do. But she had insisted on going with Theu, and he had agreed. Just ahead of her, Theu walked with Autar by his side as he had been for days, the two of them approaching the golden glow of a single candle set upon a man-sized brass stand. Within the fragile circle of candlelight, at a spot where the stone floor was raised like a dais above a wide, shallow step, two men awaited them.

The shorter, rather stout man was clothed in the glittering scarlet and gold vestments of a bishop just come from a religious service. As for the other man, India thought she would have recognized him even if she had come into the hall unaware that he would be present. Half a head taller than Theu, with close-cropped blond hair and blue eyes, he was the person who several centuries later would inspire one of the greatest romances of the Middle Ages, the hero in whose memory songs would be sung, about whose life and death legends would be woven. The man later ages would call Roland wore a simple, undyed woolen tunic. At his side hung an unusually long sword, the famous Durendàl.

"My lord Turpin," said Theu, bowing to the man in red.

"Welcome, my son." Bishop Turpin extended his hand so Theu could kiss the episcopal ring he wore. "We have eagerly expected your coming."

"Count Hrulund." Theu made a slight bow to the taller man.

"Well met, Firebrand." There was little warmth in Hrulund's manner. "Since I see you alive and uninjured, it seems you were able to put down that *very minor* rebellion in Saxony, as Charles *ordered* you to do."

At this insult, which implied that Theu had been unwilling to do his duty voluntarily, India heard Marcion murmuring an impolite comment about the great warrior's parentage.

"I see you still have your Lombard puppy with you." Hrulund looked at Marcion as if Marcion were beneath contempt. "And your landless companion, too," Hrulund added, sparing a cold glance for Hugo.

"They are my valued friends," Theu began, but what he would have said next was interrupted by Bishop Turpin.

"Of course they are, my dear Count Theuderic, and as your friends, they are every bit as welcome as you are yourself. As are all of your men," said Turpin.

From behind her, India heard Eudon grunt in discomfort and sensed him shifting position. She thought his injured right buttock was probably bothering him. It usually happened at the end of a long day's ride. She wished there were a place where Eudon could sit or lie down to stretch out his leg. For that matter, she would like to see a bed and a decent meal herself.

Hrulund had noticed Eudon's movement. With a sharp, intense look that reminded India of some bird of prey discovering a convenient victim, Hrulund came down the steps toward Eudon.

"Have you brought the halt and the lame to fight for you?" Hrulund asked Theu, speaking over his shoulder. "This man is wounded. Tell me, fellow, how did you come by your injury? Was it earned while fighting Saxons? If so, you are to be commended, though you should not be here in this condition."

"It is but a minor wound, and soon healed," Eudon said. "I was gored by a boar."

"Were you, indeed? So you had time enough for hunting. Not a Saxon in the forest, eh?" sneered the famous hero. "And where is that boar now? Still roaming through Saxony?"

"We ate him for dinner." It was Hugo who responded, deliberately drawing Hrulund's attention away from the unfortunate Eudon. Taking full advantage of his superior height, Hrulund stepped nearer, obviously bound on intimidating Hugo. But Hugo did not retreat by a single step.

"I see," said Hrulund, a faint glimmer of respect creeping into his voice and his eyes at Hugo's display of quiet courage. "If you feasted on the carcass, then the day was not entirely wasted."

"Let us not stray from the matter at hand, Count Hrulund," Turpin urged from his position on the dais. "We have much to discuss with Count Theuderic, and with our friend Autar."

Hrulund nodded at that, and took a step away from Hugo, heading back toward the bishop and the two men standing with him. His cold blue gaze passed casually across India's face, moved on, paused, then returned to her. Before she could blink an eye or protest his action, Hrulund's hand shot out to catch her chin and turn her face toward the light so he could see her better.

"By all that's holy!" Hrulund snatched his hand away as if India's flesh had scorched him. "Theuderic, how dare you bring a woman into this place?"

"A woman?" echoed Bishop Turpin, looking startled.

"Indeed, my friends," said Autar from his place beside Theu. "That was part of the information I have been waiting to report to you. This most unusual woman has been traveling with Count Theuderic since well before I joined his party."

"This is disgraceful." It was Hrulund, not the bishop, who looked from India to Theu with an expression of disgust on his face. "It is a sorry enough state of affairs if you cannot restrain your basest desires, but to dress your concubine in boy's clothing is even more shameful."

"I am no man's concubine." India stepped forward, approaching Turpin, who looked her over with an eye clearly appreciative of feminine charms.

"India," said Theu in a tense voice, "be silent."

"Women only obey orders when it pleases them," Hrulund remarked scornfully.

India almost bit her tongue to keep herself

from asking him how any man who apparently disliked and avoided women could possibly know that for sure.

"Why do you call her unusual?" Turpin asked Autar.

"You have heard her speak," Autar answered, "so you know she cannot be a Frankish woman, yet no one knows the name of her country."

"You mean, none of Theu's men would gossip about her," Hugo put in. "If you wanted information, Autar, why didn't you ask Theu—or India herself?"

"That would be too easy," murmured Marcion, but loud enough for Autar to hear him. "It is so much more entertaining to gather facts by stealth."

"India comes from a land far away." Theu spoke just in time to avert some hostile action on the part of Autar, who had begun to unsheathe his sword while taking a menacing step in Marcion's direction. Theu then added the half-truth he had once believed himself. "India carries a private message for Charles, and she wears the medallion of a royal messenger."

"Why would anyone use a woman to carry a message?" asked Hrulund. "Everyone knows women are deceitful and untrustworthy."

"Nevertheless, if she has the medallion, we must make her welcome," Turpin said. "If there is falsity in her, Charles will see it and punish her as she deserves."

"Very well." Hrulund gave in at the mention of his beloved king. "We will leave the woman to Charles, who is wiser than any of us. But I ask you, Turpin, to send her away now, so we men can discuss serious matters without female interruptions."

"I will have her conducted to a private chamber, where she can rest after her long ride," Turpin said smoothly. "One of my own men will guard her safety. As for your people, Count Theuderic, allow me to house and feed them while you remain at Tours." He raised one white hand, and out of the shadows at the side of the hall appeared several armed guards.

"We stay right where we are," Marcion declared, his hand straying toward his sword. "We won't leave you, Theu."

"What admirable loyalty," noted Bishop Turpin.

"There's no cause for concern, Marcion." Theu's tone was mild, and he smiled as he spoke, but India was aware of the tension in him. Like Marcion, she wanted to remain within sight of Theu, who now turned to Turpin and bowed. "I am certain that in my lord bishop's care we are all completely safe until it is time for us to resume the journey to our king."

"You have my word on it," responded Turpin.

"This way," said the burly armed man who during this exchange had moved to stand next to India. She glanced toward Theu. He nodded, indicating that she should go with the man. With a growing sense of fear that she tried her best to conceal, India let the guard escort her out of the hall into a smaller chamber. There he took a torch from a wall sconce and used it to light their way down a long flight of stone steps. At the bottom of the steps, they entered a shadowy corridor. India was sure they were by now well below ground level. They passed several stout wooden doors before the guard stopped at one. He pushed it open.

"In here." He was not rude or threatening, just completely uninterested in her as a person.

"Do you call this a guest chamber?" While the guard lit an oil lamp, India looked around in disbelief at a thin pallet upon the stone floor and a three-legged stool. In one corner sat a covered pot, the smell coming from that area leaving no doubt as to its purpose. There was nothing else in the room, and the only light came through a narrow slit high in one wall. "I would like hot water and a towel so I can wash." She had no real hope that her request would be granted, but she voiced it anyway, as the only protest she dared make against what was clearly imprisonment.

"Food will be brought to you in the morning," the guard said. He set the oil lamp on the stool, where it did little to relieve the general gloom.

"Why are you treating me like a prisoner when I haven't done anything wrong?" she demanded.

"I'm only following the orders I've been given," the guard said, not unkindly. "I will be outside your chamber door so you won't be disturbed during the night, but I warn you, I am not permitted to enter this room once I have left it—at least not until the bishop sends for you—so spare your breath and your knuckles if you think to cry out or pound on the door until someone else comes to release you."

"Who gave you those orders? I never heard them," India began, but the guard only shook his head and went out. A moment later, she heard a bar slide across the door on the outer side.

Left alone in that cold and stony cell, she knew real terror. She had been afraid since her arrival in that unfamiliar time, and had experienced one or two flashes of near panic, but always Theu had been with her on those occasions, usually with Marcion and Hugo close by to offer additional aid if it were needed. Now, for the first time, she was completely alone, bewildered by what had happened and so frightened that her legs would not support her. She fell to her knees on the pallet, quickly discovering that it was padded with the thinnest possible layer of scratchy straw, inadequate to fend off the damp chill of the floor. Leaning back against the wall, she stretched out her legs, trying to overcome her fear, trying to think calmly and clearly, if only to stop the urge to weep or scream.

Theu had said they were all safe under Turpin's care, and the guard had shown no animosity toward her, which suggested that she was not in any immediate physical danger. But who had given the guard his orders?

After considering the question for a while,

she concluded that the arrangements must have been made in advance, before Autar had set out to intercept Theu and his party. If this was so, then it was possible that cells like hers had been prepared for each of Theu's men. They wouldn't even have to be disarmed, they could just be locked into their rooms, alone, with a dependable guard posted outside each one. Which meant that Theu, alone with Turpin, Hrulund, and their men, could be in danger. That was the most frightening thought of all, for there was nothing she could do to help Theu.

Time crept slowly by. The light coming through the too-small window slit faded and disappeared. India was thirsty, hungry, dirty, cold, and tired—and most of all, frightened for herself and Theu and their friends. No sounds came from the other side of the door. If the guard really was still there, he was being remarkably quiet. She believed hours had passed. Her shoulders stiff and sore from leaning against the stone wall, she lay down at last on the pallet. After a while she fell into an uneasy doze.

She wakened to total blackness and the sound of the bar being drawn back across the door. The sudden glare of a torch nearly blinded her.

"Come along," said the guard, motioning to her to pass through the door.

"Where am I to go?" India sat up, rubbing her eyes, but she did not move off the pallet. "What time is it?"

"Past midnight. Bishop Turpin wants to see you." Again she noted the guard's curious indifference to her, but at least he was not threatening. India got to her feet.

"I hardly look presentable enough to see a bishop," she said, wondering what the man's reaction would be. "Could I have some hot water and soap?"

"If Turpin wants you clean, he'll provide the water," the guard said. "Don't keep him waiting."

Deciding that it was probably best not to annoy either the guard or Turpin by further delay, India went with the man. He took her to the far end of the corridor, to a narrow, winding stone staircase that led upward past the landings for two other floors before he stopped her at the third level. They passed through a small anteroom, bare and cold as the rest of that forbidding building, to a door on the other side. The guard knocked, and India heard Turpin's voice bidding him enter.

The chamber into which she was now conducted was so different from anything she had so far seen in Francia that it made India catch her breath in surprise. There was a brazier burning charcoal to warm the room and enough tall, thick, beeswax candles to light and scent it. The Frankish bed pushed against the wall to India's left was covered in glowing red silk and well padded with silk cushions in many colors. The floors were strewn with patterned Arabic rugs over a layer of dried herbs and rushes. A swath of more red silk had been draped across part of the wall opposite the bed, covering what India assumed was a window. At a table sat a scribe, using a quill pen to write upon a narrow parchment scroll.

In the center of the room, facing the door, stood Bishop Turpin. He had discarded his scarlet vestments in favor of a bleached white linen cassock, cinched around his thick waist with a knotted cord.

"Wait outside," Turpin said to the guard. To the scribe he gestured with one smooth white hand. "You, too. Leave us."

When they were alone, Turpin motioned to India to come forward. He was a good two inches shorter than she, and there was about him a facile, almost oily manner that she found repulsive. His hands, now folded before him at waist height, were plump, with tapered fingers ending in clean, shining nails, as if they had recently been manicured and polished. The amethyst ring of his rank gleamed in the candle-light.

"From what heathen country do you come, that you do not bow to a bishop?" Turpin demanded.

"A country where all men and women stand upright and address each other with respect," she answered. "A land where people are not thrown into cold prison cells without just cause or any explanation."

"The room where you are housed is no prison cell," Turpin told her. "Hrulund's own men sleep in such rooms and do not consider it a hardship."

"Yet in Francia there are men who indulge in luxuries." India looked pointedly around the bishop's own room. She expected some scathing retort from Turpin, but instead he smiled at her.

"Well said. Not all of us wish to endure the rigors of a warrior's life. Please be seated, Lady India."

"I'll stand." The only places to sit were the bed or the stool the scribe had been using, and Turpin was blocking her way to the stool.

"I insist that you sit." There was steel beneath the bishop's mellifluous tone and his eyes were hard. "Let me offer you wine."

"You gave Theu your word that we would be unharmed," India reminded him.

"Have I harmed you, sweet lady?" His eyes still hard, Turpin spread his plump hands. "I have merely invited you to sit."

Unwillingly, India perched on the very edge of the bed, watching Turpin pour out the wine. She wanted to refuse it, but thought it would be unwise to anger him. She took the gold-and jewel-decorated glass he offered, and barely touched her lips to the wine.

"What do you want of me?" she asked.

"To know you better." Turpin sat down beside her. India tried to move away from him, but the railing at the foot of the bed prevented her from going far.

"Why should you be interested in me?"

"Autar knows little of women, but he judged you rightly when he called you unusual. You are a fascinating mystery. You are also lovely." Turpin leaned nearer. "I believe you and I could easily become close friends—perhaps even allies."

Turpin reached across India to place one hand on the footrail of the bed. Since she wanted to avoid physical contact with him, his movement forced her backward until her head came to rest on one of the silk pillows. She was now reclining, with Turpin bending over her. India seriously considered tossing into his face the contents of the wineglass she still held. What stopped her was the thought of Theu and his men. She would not do anything to put them into any greater danger than they were in already. Still, she had no wish to be assaulted by this too-slick man who was looking at her in the same way a cat regards a cornered mouse. She almost expected to see Turpin's tongue come out and lick his lips in anticipation. She tried to think of a way to avoid him without angering him. Then she recalled the manner in which he had used the name of the king of the Franks to stop Hrulund at a tense moment. Perhaps the same invocation would make Turpin pause, too.

"Sir," she said, pressing yet further into the pillows to avoid touching him, "I do not know exactly what you expect of me, but I must remind you that you may not harm one who wears the royal medallion while carrying a message to Charles."

Turpin drew back until he was again sitting upright on the side of the bed. India began to breathe more easily, but almost at once she wished she had not spoken.

"Ah, yes, the message." All the intimate suggestiveness was gone. Suddenly, Turpin was alert, sharp-eyed, and determined to have the information he desired. "I am one of Charles's closest confidantes. You may therefore give the message to me."

"I can't do that. Surely you understand the need for discretion in such a matter. I cannot believe that you, Bishop, would ever want me to betray either your king or my master, who made me swear to deliver the message to Charles's ears only." The thought of how many falsehoods were in that declaration nearly took India's breath away. She wasn't used to lying so profusely, and she wasn't sure Turpin would accept what she said. He was frowning at her, looking as if he would make some irritated rebuttal, when the door flew open and Hrulund walked into the room. Turpin leapt to his feet.

"Well?" Hrulund demanded. "Have you got it out of her yet? What is this message she claims to be carrying? Is there any message at all, or is she lying, like every other woman?"

"Turpin, you were trying to entrap me," India exclaimed, more to see how Hrulund would respond than out of genuine surprise. She had understood perfectly well what Turpin was trying to do. She stood and approached the two men, her fists clenched as if she were angry.

221

She should have expected Hrulund's reaction. His disdainful gaze touched her face, then moved to the wrinkled coverlet and the disarranged pillows.

"You were trying to seduce Bishop Turpin," he accused her.

"Don't you see what a wily, cunning man he is?" she cried. When Hrulund just stared at her as if she were some disgusting insect, she answered her own question. "No, of course you don't. You can't see beyond the tip of your sword. Hrulund, I ask you to believe this much—even a woman would not violate the confidence of a message sent to Charles. I will not betray your king. Even a mere woman and a foreigner would keep faith with so great a man as Charles." Seizing the medallion, she held it up so he could see it clearly. She felt no shame at all in piling lie upon lie, not when dealing with these two men. Thinking she saw a faint warming in the twin glaciers that were Hrulund's eyes, she decided to press whatever advantage she had won with him by her passionate declaration of loyalty to his king.

"For Charles's sake, can't you put aside your feud with Theu?" she asked. "You would each be more valuable to Charles if you could work together instead of quarreling like jealous brothers."

"He does not love Charles as purely as I do. No one does." Hrulund's eyes were totally icy once more. "Theuderic and I were born to hate each other." Going to the door, Hrulund called in the guard.

"Take this woman back to her room," he commanded.

India was glad to go. When the guard looked at her and jerked his head toward the anteroom, she instantly obeyed the unspoken order. But behind her, Hrulund did not shut the door quickly enough. As she followed the guard across the anteroom and started down the stairs, India could hear Hrulund arguing with Turpin.

"It is shameful," Hrulund declared, "to allow your lustful impulses to dictate your actions. You wanted to bed her!"

"What about your impulses?" Turpin replied. "You could not restrain your impatience, so you came in too soon. If you had given me just a little longer with her, she would have told me everything we want to know."

The door closed then, cutting off whatever else the two men said to each other. India went down the staircase shaking her head in wonder at her own escape from Turpin's room and feeling grateful to Hrulund for bursting in when he had. It was not until she was once more alone in her cell—for that was what it was, no matter what Turpin called it—that she began to shiver in delayed reaction to danger. She might have been killed by either man, and she knew it.

Her fear for Theu and for the rest of their friends almost choked her. She slept no more that night.

Chapter Thirteen

"So, the oil lamp went out at last, did it?" asked her guard, pushing across the floor in her direction a wooden plate on which lay a chunk of bread and a little cheese. "It doesn't matter. It will be daylight soon enough."

"Isn't there anything for me to drink?" she asked.

"Hrulund is right," the guard said. "Women do nothing but complain and make foolish demands on a man." But he placed a jug of water beside the plate of food, and before he left her and secured the door, he added a new lighted oil lamp so that she could see to eat.

Alone once more, India managed to swallow the stale bread and part of the moldy cheese, but, remembering Hugo's remarks about the dangers of water, she drank nothing in spite of her thirst. Instead, she used the vile-smelling pot in the corner of her cell, then used the water to wash her face and hands as best as she could. By this time a feeble light was coming in the window slit, and she could hear church bells in the distance. She began to walk back and forth across the cell to warm herself. Much later, when she had begun to give way to a new fear—that she would remain where she was indefinitely—she heard a muffled noise outside her door. It sounded suspiciously like a scuffle followed by a smothered cry. She backed against the wall, wondering what would happen next. When the door swung open, Marcion appeared, followed by Eudon.

"Thank heaven." India sagged in relief.

"Time to go," Marcion said.

Upon leaving the cell, India was immediately surrounded by four of Theu's men, all of them holding their swords at the ready. She was so glad to see them that she almost started to cry. She controlled herself, knowing that they would think her weak if she gave way to tears.

"Where is Theu?" she asked, as calmly as she could.

"Above. Hugo and the others will have joined him by now. No doubt he'll apologize for not being able to rescue you himself." Marcion led the way to the long staircase.

"Have they hurt him? Or anyone else?" They were moving so fast up the steps that she was breathless.

"Not yet." Marcion grinned at her. "There's

nothing to worry about. Everything will be all right."

"Don't be so sure of that," she replied, looking around as they entered the large hall where the day before they had first met Hrulund. Theu and the rest of his men were there, swords drawn, facing Count Hrulund and two dozen or so tough-looking warriors, each with his weapon in hand. Only Bishop Turpin was unarmed. He stood by the single candle, his red robes glittering when he moved, turning first toward Theu and his men on one side of the hall, then to Hrulund and his companions on the other side. From the tension among the men, India had the impression that she had walked into the beginning of a swordfight.

"There is no need for this," Turpin said just as India and her escort joined Theu. "Hrulund, you would be better advised to wait until you can spill Spanish blood. Leave Theuderic and his men to fight for Charles in Spain."

"But he has opposed the campaign," said Hrulund, taking a menacing step toward Theu, who raised his sword and waited, his eyes never leaving Hrulund's face. "It is not right for Theuderic to disagree with Charles."

"A difference of opinion does not constitute disloyalty," said the bishop. Hrulund's response to this remark was to scowl and shake his head as if he found it difficult to understand the concept of loyal disagreement.

"If you want to fight," said Theu, "I am willing."

"It would greatly please me to end your life," Hrulund replied.

"Charles will not like this," cautioned Bishop Turpin.

"I will tell him I have killed a pack of traitors," said Hrulund, moving his sword to include all of Theu's men in the threat.

"Enough talk," growled Theu, crouching in readiness. "If you cannot believe my word when I say I am loyal to my king, then I will prove it by force of arms."

"You," returned Hrulund, baring his teeth in a fierce grin of anticipation, "will die, here and now."

India was so frightened she could not speak or move. Nor, it appeared, could anyone else in that hall do anything to stop the bloodshed that surely would follow Hrulund's words. Everyone was staring at the two men facing each other, all of them waiting for the first strike. It was not long in coming. Suddenly Hrulund leapt forward, both hands on the hilt of his sword, aiming a mighty slash at Theu. Their swords clashed together. India heard the sound of metal sliding against metal as Theu parried the blow, forcing Hrulund backward by a couple of steps.

"Put up your weapons!" So intent upon the swordplay was everyone that at first the angry female voice did not penetrate their concentration. It was not until Sister Gertrude spoke again that she was given any attention at all.

"You foolish and ignorant men, do you know of no way to settle your differences except to kill each other? My lord bishop, how can you allow this disgraceful display?"

"I would prevent it if I could," said Turpin. "I'd rather see them killing Saracens than other Franks."

"Well, I *can* prevent it." Showing no evidence of concern for her personal safety, Sister Gertrude walked forward between the two groups of armed men. She was followed by Danise, by the serving woman Clothilde, and by a young man in dusty clothing who looked about with great interest. Having reached the place where Theu and Hrulund still stood glaring at each other with their swords ready for further action, Sister Gertrude stopped. She put out a hand to Theu's wrist and pushed his arm down to his side. She would have done the same to Hrulund, but he leapt backward, not allowing her to touch him, lowering his sword without her pressure.

"Garnar, come here," called Sister Gertrude, and the young man with her came forward at once. Sister Gertrude pointed. "That is Count Theuderic."

"Aye, I know him by sight," said Garnar. "Count, I have a letter from Charles." He pulled a folded and sealed square of parchment from a pouch hung at his belt. This he handed to Theu who, after examining the seal, broke it and read. The men in the hall shifted about,

229

the tension among them easing a bit. Marcion looked at India and smiled. Hugo's eyes were on Danise.

"Since Hrulund cannot read," Theu said, handing the parchment to Bishop Turpin, "I would ask you to read this letter aloud so that he, and all the others assembled here, will know its contents. I want no one to accuse me of cowardice for ending this day's fight."

Turpin took the letter, made a little ceremony of holding it close to the candle to better see the royal seal, and then unfolded it.

" 'Charles, by the grace of God king of the Franks and the Lombards and patrician of the Romans, to Count Theuderic of Metz,' " Turpin read. " 'Having received your report of your recent activities in Saxony, we do hereby order you to bring the woman called India to Agen at once. Escort her yourself, for we would meet her before we leave for Spain.' This is Charles's signature. You will know it, Hrulund, for as usual he has written it in the form of a cross." Turpin held the letter up so all could see the royal name.

"Hrulund, our present dispute must be set aside," Theu said when Turpin had refolded the letter and returned it to him. "I know you would not have me disobey Charles. I and all my men will leave here at once." The note of challenge in his voice made Hrulund frown uneasily. Turpin sent a cautionary glance in Hrulund's direction, as if to quiet any possible protests over this decision.

"I quite agree," said Turpin, adding, "You must learn to support the coming campaign with your whole heart and soul, Theuderic, for it is right and necessary and the best thing for all Franks."

"No," India cried out, "it is not." At a flashing look from Theu, she fell quiet again, but not before Hrulund had turned his gaze from Theu to India and then to Sister Gertrude.

"So, Firebrand," sneered Hrulund, "this explains your sudden distaste for warfare. You have been listening to foolish women."

"I was opposed to the Spanish campaign before I ever met any of these ladies," Theu returned hotly. "As I told you last night, I will say what I think to Charles if he asks my opinion, but I will follow wherever he leads. I can do no more without violating my conscience."

"Pah! It's not your conscience at all, it's the women's doing." With a swift movement Hrulund lifted his sword, holding it up by the blade, the heavy gold pommel uppermost, the flaring gold quillons where pommel and blade were joined giving the weapon the appearance of a cross. He went down on one knee, still holding the sword up before his face. In the candlelight, his face took on a burning purity, an ecstatic quality that silenced any objections to his action among the onlookers and stilled all movement in the hall.

"I swear now as I have done in the past, upon my sword, upon the tooth of St. Peter and the drop of St. Basil's blood sealed within its pommel—upon these sacred relics I do most solemnly swear that for all my life I will love only Charles and the warfare that does him honor. I would rather sleep with this sharp-edged blade than with any woman, for I know my beloved Durendal will never betray me. For God, for Charles, and for Francia!" With that cry, Hrulund kissed the place on his sword where hilt and blade met, gazing at the weapon with luminous eyes. A moment of profound silence followed his oathtaking, until he rose. Sword hilt in his hand now, he lifted the weapon high again, its blade gleaming silver-blue in the light when he moved it. "I call upon you all to pledge yourselves anew to Charles and his noble cause. Swear now, good men, upon your knees, with hearts untainted by earthly desires. Promise your sword arms and your lives to aid Charles in carrying the True Faith across the Pyrenees to free Spain from the wicked Saracens!"

India looked toward Theu's men. A few of them had partially lifted their swords at Hrulund's words, and every face save Marcion's was alight with the same glow that lit Hrulund's features. In another moment, they would all be on their knees as he had bidden them. In that instant India understood the dreadful glamour of the man, and knew why he was called a hero.

"We have sworn to Charles before this," Theu said, apparently immune to Hrulund's charismatic personality. "There is no need to pledge ourselves again." At his words, his own men released their weapons, putting them away and turning from Hrulund. The charmed moment was over.

"Theuderic," Hrulund said, "you have gone soft from too much love. Women drain a man's energy and blunt his vital force when he ought to keep himself free to think only of the service he owes his king on the battlefield. Women make a man weak because he wants to return to his love instead of desiring a glorious death in battle."

"Perhaps," Theu said softly, "you are too willing to do battle and think too little of living in peace."

"Peace is for cowards and weaklings," Hrulund returned. "I care only for serving my king, as you should do."

"I honor your courage," Theu replied, "and I respect the great love you bear to Charles. But in this matter of the Spanish campaign, Hrulund, you are wrong."

"Unsay that insult, Firebrand, or I'll cut you into pieces! I am *not* wrong!" His eyes fierce, his face hard, Hrulund took a step toward Theu, brandishing Durendal in his hand.

"If you kill him," came Sister Gertrude's sharp voice, "how will you explain to Charles that you ignored his expressly stated desire to meet with Theuderic?"

That stopped Hrulund. He lowered his sword.

"For Charles's sake only, I'll let you live, Firebrand," he said. "And I will pray that you regain your courage in time to prove yourself in battle in Spain."

India let out the breath she had been holding, but when Hrulund spoke again, she was filled with dismay.

"Turpin, we cannot let Theuderic and these women go to Agen unescorted, and we will not be able to leave for another day or so. Let me send my man Autar with them."

"While I feel certain that Count Theuderic and his men are capable of protecting the ladies," Turpin replied, "still, Autar has served me well as a messenger in the past. With your kind permission, Hrulund, he will do so again, for I ought to write to Charles."

"We will have to set out at once," Theu objected.

"By the time your horses are ready and your men have mounted," Turpin promised, "the letter will be written and Autar will join you. There will be no delay." He left the hall, Autar following him.

"You," Hrulund said to Theu, "will pay for your refusal to pledge yourself to Charles."

"It is meaningless for a man to repeat an oath he has already taken," Theu responded. "Charles heard my oath when he was elected king, and he knows I will keep it until I die."

"God willing, that will be soon." With a look at Theu that would have driven a lesser man to his knees in terror, Hrulund turned on his heel and motioned to his men to follow him out of the hall.

"Garnar," said Theu, "will you ride to Agen with me?"

"I have other letters to be delivered in Paris and Noyon," Garnar replied. "I am only grateful that Sister Gertrude heard me inquiring at the convent if any knew of your passage through Tours. Otherwise, our paths might have crossed without our knowledge."

"Then we must thank Sister Gertrude," said Theu, with a look at the nun that suggested he might want to thank her for more than delivery of a royal letter.

"Did they lock all of you in barren cells as they did me?" India asked. It was Hugo who answered her.

"Each of us was put into a cell with a guard, so we could not talk to each other or aid Theu if he needed us. It was Marcion who was clever enough to overpower the guard who brought his morning food. He knocked my guard unconscious, too, and together we released the other men. I am sorely disappointed in Count Hrulund, and in Bishop Turpin, over this affair." Hugo added, "I think we ought to protest their ungracious treatment of us to Charles."

"Charles has enough to occupy his thoughts just now without his nobles coming to him with their quarrels, like squabbling children to a parent," Theu responded.

"You haven't told us yet how Turpin and Hrulund treated you last night," Marcion said to Theu.

"They fed me an inadequate dinner while trying to convince me to give up all my objections to the campaign," Theu replied with a casualness that made India look hard at him and wonder exactly what *had* happened. She wanted to tell Theu about her own interview with Turpin, but she could not do it there in the hall. If she did, Theu might well decide to go in search of Turpin and Hrulund and begin a new fight with them.

"I am sorry I missed hearing Hrulund's attempts to argue with reason," Marcion said to Theu. He laughed at the idea. "Only that thick-headed ox would think to bully you into submission. The man is so single-minded he can talk of nothing but weapons and battle."

"And how much he distrusts women," India added. "Was he ever actually betrayed by a woman, or does he just fear it might happen?"

"Those around him would be a lot happier if Hrulund could love some other human being besides Charles," Theu answered, giving India a strange, lingering look that left her breathless. "Hrulund is betrothed, but he pays no attention to the poor girl. He even convinced her brother to take her away from court to keep her safe from frivolous influences, though many think he only wanted to avoid her."

"The gossips claim he has never lain with any woman," Marcion told India, "and I half believe the tale."

"He's a hard man," Hugo said, still disturbed by the events of the day and night just passed. "A great warrior, but not a friend I would want."

"No," India said. "He's a saintly man, a fanatic who can carry others along with him. When he knelt with that sword in his hands, I felt a stirring of battle fever myself, and I ought to be completely immune to that kind of thing. There is a terrifying purity about Hrulund that makes him dangerous."

"From what I've seen of him," Sister Gertrude put in, "I think India understands Hrulund well. Now, Count Theuderic, I would like to suggest to you that we depart from this hall before Hrulund changes his mind about letting us go. I have no taste for the bloodshed that will surely result if he tries to stop us."

"You are right. Hugo, see to the lady Danise," Theu ordered. "Marcion, give Sister Gertrude your arm. Eudon, Osric, see to the horses. The rest of you help them. India, come with me."

No one made any attempt to prevent their going when Theu led them toward the courtyard. Just behind her, India overheard Marcion speaking to Sister Gertrude.

"Lady," Marcion said, "like Theu, I thank you for your timely arrival. I could kiss you for your good sense."

"I pray you will not," said Sister Gertrude with all her accustomed sharpness. "It was to escape the kisses of brutish men that I first entered a convent. I have no wish at my age to endure such embraces now."

"Then I will confine myself to eternal, chaste devotion to you," teased Marcion.

India saw Danise look at Hugo just then, with laughter in her eyes. At least Danise did not feel the same way about men that Sister Gertrude did, although, after meeting Hrulund, India could understand why a Frankish woman might prefer not to marry.

"You did not need to look so frightened back there," Theu said to India, capturing her attention away from Hugo and Danise. "There was no real danger."

"You might have been killed!" she exclaimed. "And I was terrified in that cell they put me into. I had no idea what would happen to me, or to you and your people. Didn't you think about me and wonder if I was all right?"

"I had Turpin's word that you would come to no harm," he said with great reasonableness. "Do you not believe the promises made by the bishops in your own country? You were kept in that room to protect Hrulund's men from you, lest you stir lustful thoughts in them. Hrulund does not allow his men to take women. He is right when he says it is best not to love women, for they do weaken a man's purpose. It was foolish of me to let you come here. You should have stayed at the convent with Sister Gertrude and Danise, as I wanted you to do."

"You don't care about me at all, do you?" she cried, furious with him for being so unconcerned when she had been badly frightened—and angry with herself for loving him so much. He had warned her soon after they met that he would never love again. She ought to have believed him.

"I care whether or not you reach Agen safely, because Charles wants to see you," he told her, giving her another peculiar look and sounding as if he were trying to convince himself. But she was too hurt and too angry with him to pay any attention to what he might be feeling.

"You could have been killed back there," she said again as they emerged into the courtyard. "We all could have been killed."

He stared at her, looking so disturbed and unhappy that she finally forgot her own rage long enough to wonder what was wrong with him.

"I cannot," he said, as if arguing with himself. "I swore I would not, not ever again. I will not allow myself to feel this way."

"Theu, what is it? What's the matter?"

He did not answer her. He only shrugged his shoulders and headed toward his horse, which Eudon was holding.

"Mount, all of you," he called over his shoulder. He took care not to look in India's direction. "Let us be gone from here."

"Oh!" Renewed fury boiled up in India. She could not remember ever being so hurt and angry. She turned to address the nun standing beside Marcion. "Sister Gertrude, I think you are absolutely right. It is better for a woman to live in a convent than to subject herself to the whims and the indifference of a man."

"I told you so," said Sister Gertrude.

Chapter Fourteen

They headed south from Tours, the weather growing steadily warmer as they traveled along a road that cut through yet more forest. In fact, most of Francia was wooded, though here and there farmland had been cleared and planted, and in the infrequent open meadows cattle grazed. These southern lands were lush and green with all the freshness of early spring. Showers were frequent but brief and caused no inconvenience. As soon as the sun came out again, their clothing dried, so there was no need to seek shelter from the rain.

India estimated that it was by now the end of March or early April, and probably close to four weeks since Eudon had been wounded by the boar. He claimed to be completely healed. Certainly he had borne up well during their travels and seemed to be less stiff each morning. India herself was growing used to riding all day, the exercise and fresh air combining to make her feel remarkably healthy. But physical well-being was not everything, and her heart was in turmoil.

Unable to deal with what she saw as his lack of concern for her feelings or her safety, she avoided Theu as much as possible and spent her days riding with Danise and Sister Gertrude, willingly sharing a room and frequently a bed with the two of them at night. It hurt her deeply that Theu did not seem to notice or care.

"Never rely on a man for your happiness," Sister Gertrude said to her one evening while Theu sat with his men and their host. All of the men ignored the women when they left the great hall to seek the guest room. "Even Hugo does not spare a glance for Danise. Men think nothing of destroying a woman's peace and contentment."

Having seen Danise and India into bed, Sister Gertrude made them promise to remain there, then took herself off to the chapel, saying she had neglected her prayers of late. India and Danise lay beneath a feather-filled quilt, India trying not to weep. She wished she could put her head under the pillow and cry herself to sleep, but she had no privacy, and so she had to keep her feelings bottled up inside herself.

"Sister Gertrude does not like men," came Danise's soft voice out of the darkness.

"I had noticed," India replied dryly.

"She will not speak of her youth at all," Danise went on, "so I cannot say for certain, but I have heard gossip about her at Chelles that makes me believe she was disappointed in a man while she was just a girl. One story the students tell about her youth claims that a man she loved and hoped to marry was killed in battle. As a result, the story goes, Sister Gertrude hates everything to do with warfare and the use of weapons, and she refuses to trust any man. You have seen how carefully she guards me from Count Theuderic's men."

"To Hugo's great sorrow," India said, making Danise giggle.

"And now to Count Theuderic's sorrow also," Danise responded, still laughing a little, "since Sister Gertrude protects you from him."

"Theuderic has his own sad past," India replied. "It is no secret that he has sworn never to love again in order to avoid being hurt a second time as he was when his wife died."

"While my mother was still alive," Danise said, "my father looked at her as if his heart would melt at the very sight of her. Count Theuderic looks at you in the same way. I think you have touched his heart, whether he wanted it or not. He may be struggling against himself, but I think he will not long deny what he feels. From what I have seen of the warriors under my father's command, I believe they seize the moments of happiness granted to them, for they above all men know how short life can be."

243

"You are remarkably wise for so young a girl," India said.

"Perhaps not so wise as you think," Danise responded. "I am nearly seventeen and should have been married years ago except that my father could not bear to lose me after my mother died."

India began to think about what Danise had said about the way Theu looked at her. She thought, too, about her anger toward him. She was still not sure exactly what had happened to him at Tours during the time when she was locked in her cold, unfurnished cell, nor why Theu had treated her with such marked indifference since that day. It was possible that Danise was right and Theu was struggling with emotions he did not want to have. One thing was certain—he would soon go to Spain, where he would be in terrible danger. Whenever she thought about what could happen to him there, fear clutched at her heart. It was fear that kept her from hearing Danise's next remarks, until the girl repeated her question.

"Would you help me?" Danise asked. "I want so much to speak privately with Hugo, but Sister Gertrude would never allow it."

"I shouldn't allow it, either," India said, unwilling to be drawn into whatever romantic plot Danise might be formulating. "Sister Gertrude would have my head if she discovered I had let you meet Hugo."

"But you are a widow, which makes you an acceptable guardian for me. I only want you to stand a little aside so you can't hear what we say. It would only be for a few moments, just so I can let him know I will think of him often while he is in Spain. Once we arrive at Agen, I may not have another chance to tell him what is in my heart before he goes away."

"To Spain." India said the word as if it were a curse. "Always Spain. Yes, I'll help you."

Sister Gertrude returned just then, heralded by the light of the oil lamp she carried, and the two younger women broke off their talk. India moved over to make room in the bed for the nun. Soon Sister Gertrude began to snore, while on India's other side Danise's quieter breathing indicated that she, too, was asleep. But India lay awake thinking about Hugo and Danise, and then about Theu and what Danise had said of the way he looked at her.

At mid-morning of the following day India reined in her horse beside Hugo.

"Do you know where we are to stay tonight?" she asked.

"There is a manor house, where the lord will have left for Agen by now, but his lady will give us a meal and a bed." Puzzled, Hugo gave her a searching look. "Why didn't you ask Theu?"

"Have you been to the house before?"

"Once or twice." Again he sent a questioning look her way.

"Is there any place where a young girl and a man might have a private conversation? Nothing too secluded, you understand, in case they

245

are discovered. We don't want a scandal, do we?" Seeing the smile that had begun to spread across his face, she quickly put out a hand to touch his arm. "No, don't look at her. You don't want to arouse anyone's suspicion. If you can think of a good place now, or if you find one after we arrive, speak to me, not to Danise. And, Hugo" —here her hand tightened on his arm— "I will be there, too, to protect her reputation. I don't want unpleasant gossip attached to her name."

"Nor do I," said Hugo. "But, if she will allow it, may I kiss her on the cheek? It might be my only chance."

"If you ask her," India said, "she may feel obligated to say no."

"Then I'll be a thief and steal the kiss I want." He laughed aloud at the prospect, then sobered almost immediately. "I'm going to ride with Eudon for a while, because that cursed Autar is watching us. Marcion and I believe the message he carries is just an excuse, and he was really sent to spy on all of us—which means I'll have to think of a way to keep him well occupied this evening."

The manor house in which they rested that night was small, and at first India thought there would be no opportunity for Danise and Hugo to meet. But the lady of the manor was a pious woman of about Sister Gertrude's age, a famous needlewoman who was currently engaged in embroidering an altarcloth for the local church, and soon the lady, the nun, and the servant

Clothilde decided to retire to the lady's chamber to spread the cloth out upon the bed in order to examine it more thoroughly away from the hall and the possibility of spotting from food or wine.

"Be sure you and Danise stay together," Sister Gertrude said to India. "I leave her in your care."

"I'll see that she comes to no harm," India promised.

When the older women had gone, she looked around the hall, but could not find Hugo.

"Where is he?" Danise whispered nervously. "Perhaps he has changed his mind. India, did he speak to you at all?"

"What he said," Marcion remarked, passing behind India on his way to where Theu and Autar were talking, "was that Lombards like me are skilled at intrigue and therefore I am to whisper to you of the beauty of the herb garden at twilight. For myself, I would much prefer a candlelit room, but the Franks have their own peculiar customs." With a teasing smile for both of them, Marcion moved on.

"But where would the herb garden be?" India asked.

"I can find it." Her pretty face alight with expectation, Danise headed for a door at one end of the hall.

"Wait, not so fast. We don't want to be noticed," India told her, following as rapidly as she dared. "You aren't going anywhere without me. I promised Sister Gertrude."

The herb garden was long and narrow, set within stone walls, with a path down the length of it and an old apple tree at the far end. There were only a few delicate new shoots on the plants and no flowers in bloom yet, but India recognized savory, rue, and sage, a patch of mint peeking up in a sheltered corner, a rose-bush that would in early summer produce five-petaled, single flowers, and some green leaves that looked like lilies pushing up out of the damp soil. Hugo stood next to a sundial at the halfway point on the path, waiting for them.

"My dear lady." He went to one knee, seizing Danise's hands to kiss them both.

"Hugo, you must behave yourself," India cautioned. "And I cannot leave you alone."

"There's a bench under the apple tree," Hugo said. "If Danise and I sit there, you could walk and look at the plants."

"And not hear what you are saying?" Feeling like an elderly aunt, and suddenly understanding at least some of Sister Gertrude's responsibilities, India waved them away. "Go on, but remember I will be nearby, and don't stay too long. If we are caught, we will all be punished by an outraged nun and you may never be allowed to speak to each other again."

She watched them hurry down the path before she turned her back to give them some privacy. She tried to interest herself in the herbs, and then in the pink and gold sunset that lit the sky. From the direction of the apple tree came the sound of Hugo's low-pitched voice

248

and Danise's gentle laughter. The evening air was soft and mild, and it was so quiet that India whirled at the sound of a foot on the grass. She looked anxiously toward the garden entrance, fearing the approach of Sister Gertrude.

But it was Theu who came through the arched opening in the garden wall. He stood watching the couple at the other end of the path, while India wondered how to explain why she had permitted their meeting and tried to think of a way to convince him not to tell Sister Gertrude about it. Then, as she had done, he turned his back toward Hugo and Danise and stood beside her, looking down at the patch of mint.

"Did you plan it?" he asked. "Or did she?"

"We planned it together," she answered. "Actually, Hugo found the place, and Marcion delivered the message. You might say we all contributed."

"At the moment, Marcion is plying Autar with wine. I suppose that is part of your scheme, too—to keep Autar occupied? Or did Marcion or Hugo think of that? It's how I knew. Marcion never drinks so much unless he has a good reason for it. Then I noticed that the three of you had disappeared. Finding you was easy."

"There's no harm," she began.

"Especially not with two of us to watch them." His hand rested on her shoulder in the gesture that had become familiar to her. "Are you still angry? Still disappointed in me?"

"Yes." She was curious about his response to

such an answer, but she refused to disguise what she felt.

"So am I angry," he said, "and disappointed, too, for I thought you would trust me. I thought you'd know I would never let any harm come to you."

"I believe you mean that," she said, "but if you had been killed at Tours, Hrulund would have killed me along with the rest of your people."

"Turpin would not have allowed my death," Theu said. "He knew that if Hrulund killed me, Charles would have seen both of them executed for the murder."

"Theu, what was the purpose of that strange meeting?" India asked. "Why did they send Autar to meet us, and to make certain we stopped at Tours?"

"They weren't interested in you and the others," Theu said. "I am the one they hoped to intimidate. The evening I spent with Turpin and Hrulund was unpleasant as well as pointless. Turpin, at least, must have known from the first that he could not change my opinion of this summer's campaign. Hrulund was there solely for the pleasure of insulting me to my face. I cannot pretend to understand the workings of Turpin's mind, but Hrulund is easy enough to read."

"I think Turpin had another purpose once you told him I was carrying a message to Charles," India said. Quickly, choosing her words carefully so as not to further inflame his wrath against either Turpin or Hrulund, she described her midnight interview with the bishop.

"Turpin may have hoped to make you reveal some secret he could use to his own advantage." Theu looked hard at her. "Did he harm you in any way?"

"He did not." Her answer was as assertive and positive as she could make it. "Turpin's fingertips barely touched mine when he offered me a glass of wine. I believed then, and still do, that he meant to frighten me by hinting that he wanted me, but what he was really interested in was the content of my nonexistent message to Charles. It was all unspoken threat."

"And all Turpin's doing," Theu added. "Hrulund would have tied you up and held his precious Durendal at your throat while he openly demanded the answers he wanted. Turpin is more subtle—and more clever. If you were to complain of what he did, he would doubtless say he only offered you wine and conversation and meant nothing more. He would claim you misunderstood his intent, because you are a stranger in Francia and unfamiliar with our ways."

She could tell he was angry, and she was glad she had said nothing about her meeting with Turpin until they were well away from Tours.

"Promise me you won't quarrel with Turpin about this when you meet at Agen," she begged. "He could be a dangerous man."

"Danger would not stop me," he replied. "But

I will not carry a personal quarrel into the royal court, where Charles would hear of it. No, I'll say nothing to Turpin, but neither will I forget what he has done to you—and to me."

"Perhaps you ought to thank Hrulund," she said lightly, trying to counter the cold anger she heard in his voice. "It was he who stopped whatever Turpin had planned for me, by coming into the room too soon. Theu, is there no way for you to call a truce with Hrulund?"

"I would be willing to engage in a friendly competition for Charles's favor. Such a contest would sharpen our skills and make us both better warriors," Theu told her. "Unfortunately, Hrulund has not the wits to understand that Charles's heart is big enough to love all his friends. Hrulund wants to be his only friend."

"Marcion was right," she said. "Hrulund is jealous of you. Theu, about Spain—"

"We agreed not to speak of what you know," he reminded her.

"But it's about Hrulund," she persisted. "He was—will be—responsible for—"

"It seems," he said, "that where the subject of Spain is concerned, there is only one way I can silence you."

He caught her face between his hands and kissed her hard. She pushed at his chest, wanting to finish her warning about Hrulund, but it was like pushing against the stone garden wall. He was immovable. His lips caressed hers, and he wrapped his arms around her, holding her tightly while his tongue sent moist flame across her mouth before he plunged it into her, tormenting her with a highly erotic rhythm. Her anger at the way he had treated her since leaving Tours evaporated. She forgot everything but her love for him. She put her arms around his waist and kissed him back until they were both breathless.

"Too many nights I've slept alone," he said when he had loosened his grip on her. "I suppose tonight will be no exception. I think you are as well guarded as Danise."

"We are to sleep in our hostess's own chamber," India told him, "Sister Gertrude with the lady in her bed, Danise and me on the trundle, and Clothilde on a pallet on the floor."

"I can have no hope of abducting you from that army of watchful Amazons," he said between a groan and a laugh. "But I will find a way soon, I promise you."

"I hope so," she confessed. "I've missed you, too."

"Trust me. Please. It's all I ask of you." His eyes held hers while he awaited her response, his arms still around her.

"I do. I will," she said. She caught her breath, remembering the meaning of those words in her own time and knowing she had just pledged herself to him, though he was unaware of it.

"Now that the roaring in my brain has lessened a bit," he said, smiling, "I think I can hear Sister Gertrude's sweet voice. We had better rescue those children before she catches them together. Hsst! Hugo! Come here."

To Hugo's credit, he obeyed at once. Danise was not far behind him on the path.

"We'll go," Theu said to India. "You walk with Danise and exchange girlish confidences. I will find a way for us to talk again soon." He paused to kiss her quickly, then, after peering out of the garden entrance to be sure their way was clear, he and Hugo left.

He had been right, for from somewhere close by, India could hear Sister Gertrude talking to their hostess. India linked her arm through Danise's, drawing the girl back along the garden walk.

"Thank you for what you did," Danise whispered. "I am so happy. Hugo says he will return from Spain a wealthy man, and when he does, he will ask my father to let us marry."

"I'm glad you are happy," India said, her heart a bitter lump in her bosom, for she feared Hugo's plans would never become reality.

"How good of Count Theuderic not to give us away," Danise went on. "I saw him kiss you. You see, I was not mistaken—he does care for you. Would you marry him, if he asks for you?"

India was spared the need to answer this question by the appearance of Sister Gertrude and the lady of the manor.

"What are you doing out in the cold night air?" asked the nun. "You know it is unhealthy."

"It was still daylight when we first came out to the garden," Danise replied. "We were talking and didn't notice how dark it has grown."

"At least you removed yourselves from the company of the men in the hall," Sister Gertrude conceded. Still talking while she led her charges away from the garden, she did not notice the amused looks India and Danise exchanged, nor hear Danise's quickly smothered giggle.

They were well into Aquitaine, according to Theu only a day or two from Agen, before he and India were able to circumvent both Autar's constant watchfulness of Theu and Sister Gertrude's sharp eye for India's every action. After a long morning in the saddle, they stopped beside a lake to rest and water their horses and to eat a midday meal of the usual bread and cheese washed down with wine grown slightly vinegary during their travels. A little apart from the men, Sister Gertrude was arguing with Clothilde about something and had drawn Danise into the discussion.

Having allowed her mount to drink its fill, India led it away from the water, looping the reins around the branches of a bush so the horse could enjoy cropping the new grass without wandering off while India ate. She had become fond of the chestnut mare Theu had chosen for her and was patting its neck and talking to it when Marcion came up to her. Behind him she saw Autar looking annoyed, possibly because Theu had suddenly disappeared. Marcion leaned one hand on her horse's flank as if to examine the animal's legs, bending his head so Autar could not see or hear him speak to her.

"Walk straight into the trees, then on to the clearing," he said softly.

"Autar," called Hugo from some distance away, "come here a moment, will you? I'd like your opinion."

"Go now," said Marcion, dropping his hand and stepping away from the horse. He went to Autar, took him by the arm, and began to lead him toward the waiting Hugo. Beyond the men, Sister Gertrude still held forth to Danise and Clothilde.

India wasted no time in following Marcion's directions. She plunged into the trees, which grew so thickly and with so much underbrush that for a while she feared she would be permanently lost. But she pressed forward, sensing a thinning of growth ahead, and before much longer she emerged from the trees into an open space that contained a tumbledown shack set in an overgrown field long unfarmed.

As she had expected, Theu was waiting for her. Forgetting everything except that she loved him, she flew into his arms, letting him crush her against his chain mail, not caring if his embrace bruised her. All that mattered was his mouth on hers, his warm strength surrounding her.

"I've missed you, missed you," she cried, moaning when he bent to kiss her throat and put his hands on her breasts.

"We haven't much time," he said, pulling away from her. "I told Marcion and Hugo that I wanted to talk with you in private. They will keep Autar occupied for as long as they can, but he's remarkably single-minded and he'll soon begin to search for us. India, wait, I can't let you go now that I have you to myself." He drew her back into his arms, kissing her cheek and her forehead.

"Should we be doing this if Autar is likely to appear? Or Sister Gertrude?" she asked in a breathless voice.

"I need to hold you for just a while, because I can't bear to look at you without touching you," he said, his arms tightening about her, "and because I must tell you what I began to understand at Tours, when Hrulund spoke so slightingly of women. As I listened to his cold words, I knew that I could never close my heart as he has done. I have broken the oath I once made to myself. I swore I would never love again, but you have found a place in my heart and I cannot remove you, no matter how I try. Our quarrel over what happened at Tours, and our separation for so many nights, have proven to me how much I love you. Once I swore never to say those words again, but now I cannot help myself. Whatever happens, to you or to me, know that I will love you through all time."

"Oh, my love." Almost in tears from the joy his declaration brought her, she touched his face with both her hands, caressing his strong bones, outlining his fine mouth with tender fingers. "I remember the odd way you looked at me at Tours. I thought you were angry." Winding her arms around his neck, she kissed him. "Make love to me, Theu."

"Truly, my dearest, I meant only to talk to you, to tell you what is in my heart. I would not hurt you, so I cannot lie on you while I'm wearing chain mail. Once, in Saxony, I wore it as a barrier between us, to keep myself safe from you. Now it prevents me from holding you as I would wish." But even as he spoke he was drawing her downward.

"It need not keep us apart. I will lie on you," she told him, sinking to her knees with him, watching him unbuckle the belt that held his sword so he could lay the weapon aside.

They knelt together on the soft spring grass, arms around each other during a long, deep kiss. His tongue probed the depths of her mouth while his hands searched beneath her tunic, releasing the fastening of her trousers so he could push them away and touch the smooth skin of her thighs.

"You can't stop now," she whispered.

"This isn't the way I want you," he groaned, though he continued to stroke her back and her hips. "Not half clothed and hurried, as if we were doing something wrong. I want you to lie beside me all night, with nothing between us, just your sweet skin against mine, and all the time we need to find our deepest joy."

"If this is all the time we have," she told him with remarkable logic considering the pounding of her heart and the way heat was sweeping along her body in response to the constant motion of his hands on her, "then I'll accept this kind of lovemaking and be grateful for it and not ask for more. So long as it is you who holds me, who enters me and drives me wild with love and longing, I will be happy."

Giving him no time to argue the sanity of what they were doing when they might be discovered at any moment, she kicked off her boots and tossed aside her trousers.

"How can I resist you when your need is as great as mine?" he asked, pulling at the cord that fastened his own trousers. He pushed them downward in a swift motion, then lay back on the grass, lifting his tunic and chain mail up to his waist, exposing himself for her. He reached out to pull her to him, but she was already kneeling at his side. In the warm early April sunshine she bent to kiss the upward-flaring evidence of his need for her and ran her tongue around its velvet-soft tip.

"No, wait, my dear love. You'll drive me mad." He caught her shoulders, forcing her to lie across his chest so he could kiss her mouth with all the frustrated, yearning passion of all the nights since their last night together at Aachen. Even now, even constrained by lack of time and the fear that they might be discovered, his male pride would not allow her to be the dominant partner. Not yet, not until the last possible moment. His hands moved over her hips and thighs, swiftly, urgently, and from the gathering

259

storm inside herself, she knew he could not wait much longer. His fingers brushed between her thighs. Involuntarily she moved against him, then realized he was only unfastening the bottom of her teddy so he could move the fabric out of his way. He held her face tight for one more near-violent kiss, then tore his mouth from hers.

"Now," he gasped. "Right now. This moment."

His strong hands grasped her hips, lifting her, then sitting her on top of him so that he entered her in the hard, quick motion she had learned to anticipate with delight.

And then it was her turn. She felt him dig his heels into the ground to push his hips upward. He had finally relinquished control of their lovemaking to her, and she relished her position. She drew her hands along his body, enjoying the contrasting sensations of cold chain mail and hot skin. She leaned over him, kissing him on the mouth once more just before she began to ride him like a great, beautiful animal, riding harder and harder. He filled her with his bold masculine strength, filled her more completely with each movement of their bodies until she cried out her wild, exultant passion and then bit her lips together lest someone should hear and interrupt them, for she knew she would die if they were separated now. And at the end, when he had groaned and called her name over and over through an aching, prolonged ecstasy, when her head was spinning and her eyes were unfocused, he half sat up to wind his hands into her hair, to hold her close and kiss her and cradle her head on his shoulder until the tremors convulsing her had ceased and she collapsed, gasping and sobbing, against him, feeling him relax against the earth.

She lay with her cheek on the hard links of chain mail covering his chest, listening to his heart beat and loving him with all that was in her. When she felt him move and opened her eyes to see what he was doing, he offered her a handful of tiny flowers he had pulled out of the grass next to the spot where they rested. She took the flowers from him, lifting them first to her nose to inhale their soft fragrance, and then to her lips.

"White violets," she murmured. "So delicate and so short-lived."

"Not at all," he said. "They survive the snows of winter and the harsh summer sun and heat. They only look delicate." His hand smoothed down her disordered hair in a gesture so tender she almost wept at his touch.

From a branch on a nearby tree a bird called, and received an answer from another direction.

"I hear it's mating season," Theu said, laughing. "For the birds as well as for you and me. I wish we could stay here all day in this peaceful place and watch the stars come out when it's evening, but we ought to go now. The others will be waiting for us."

She got to her knees again, still holding the flowers, lowering her face to them once more.

"I can't throw them away," she said, and slipped them carefully into the pocket of her tunic.

Theu was already on his feet, adjusting his clothing, then reaching for her trousers. When she had them on and fastened, he knelt to help her with her boots. Sitting now, she brushed his straight brown hair back with a gentle hand. He looked up into her eyes, laughing again.

"What joy you've given me," he said. "How much I love you."

It was then that Autar found them. He came marching out of the forest to the meadow, blinking in the sudden sunlight, and stopped short when he saw Theu kneeling before India.

With admirable calmness, Theu finished sliding India's boot onto her foot, then rose, one hand on her arm to help her up, his other hand holding his belt and sword. As if to send a deliberate message to Autar, Theu kissed India full on the mouth, taking his time about it, and she saw a glint of humor in his eyes just before she closed her own to better savor the sweet taste of his lips.

When Theu let her go and began to buckle his sword belt about his waist as if he had not a care nor an enemy in the world, India noticed Marcion and Hugo approaching with purposeful tread. But Autar had begun to move again toward the couple in the field, and Marcion and Hugo followed him.

"This is activity unworthy of a great lord

when he is soon to ride into Spain to kill the infidels," Autar declared. "How can heaven speed our course or grant us victory if Charles's counts dally with worthless women in this way?"

"Come now, Autar," said Marcion, laughing, "do you really imagine none of Charles's nobles will lie with a woman from now until we return from Spain? That's asking too much of mere men."

"Not too much for Count Hrulund—or for me and the rest of his men," Autar answered before accusing Theu again. "You ordered these two to occupy me so you could bring your concubine to this field unnoticed and lie with her like a rutting animal." He would have said more on the subject had not the look on Theu's face stopped his tongue.

"If I do not use my sword on you here and now," Theu said in a quiet, deadly voice, "it is only because you carry Bishop Turpin's message to Charles. But I tell you, Autar, if you ever again say anything insulting about India, I will kill you within the hour."

"Theu, I'll be there as your witness," said Marcion.

"And I," Hugo added.

"You will regret this," Autar promised, looking from man to man. "All of you will." After a glance at India that plainly showed what he thought of her, Autar turned his back on them and stalked away.

"I am so sorry," India said to Theu. "I seem to cause you constant embarrassment. My very presence makes enemies for you."

"Those who are my enemies," Theu responded, taking her hand, "would be my enemies whether you are beside me or far away. To Autar, or to Hrulund and Turpin, you are but an excuse. Lacking you, they would soon find some other reason to voice their enmity toward me.

"What lies between us," he went on, looking into her eyes, "is no light or casual thing. I think you know I would wed you at once, if you would only agree."

"I'm glad to hear you say that," Hugo told him. "I had begun to wonder what your intentions toward India might be. I feel toward her almost as tenderly as toward my own sister, and I'd not like to see her hurt."

"Will you marry him?" Marcion grinned at her. "You owe him an answer, after he has asked you before witnesses."

"I wish I could say yes." India's eyes were still on Theu's. "But I cannot, for a reason Theu understands."

"What reason?" asked Marcion. "Widows are free to marry where they please, unless the man is totally unsuitable, which Theu is not. If it's a dowry you need, I'll be happy to provide one for you once I return to Lombardy. I can give you a small estate in the hills, with a nice little manor house. . . ."

"Or if you need someone killed so you can be free to wed," Hugo offered, "I'll do the job for you. If there's more than one person to finish, I'm sure Eudon will be glad to help."

"We've seen Theu through a long and lonely time," Marcion added. "I, for one, would like to leave him with a good wife when I go home this autumn."

Caught between laughter and tears, India looked from Theu to his friends.

"You make me wish I could stay in Francia forever," she said. "But I may have to go home myself, and quite suddenly, too. It wouldn't be fair to Theu to marry him and then leave him."

"That makes sense," Hugo agreed. "Husbands and wives should not be separated, except when the husband goes to war."

So saying, Hugo headed toward the trees into which Autar had vanished. Marcion followed him, with Theu and India, still hand in hand, trailing behind them.

"If it should happen that you find you can remain with us after all," Marcion said, looking back at India as he spoke, "then you could still marry him, you know."

"Thank you, Marcion," said Theu in a dry tone of voice. "If India's circumstances should change, I will ask her again myself, with no help from you or Hugo."

Marcion, still looking backward, was about to make some laughing reply, but he stopped walking instead, his eyes going wide at something he had seen in the open field behind them. India and Theu both turned to see what had caught his attention.

In the field, hanging just above the place where they had lain together, a globe of brilliant orange light was steadily expanding. India edged closer to Theu's side.

"No," she whispered, "I don't want to leave you."

Releasing the hand he had been holding, Theu set her behind him and began to pull his sword from its scabbard. She heard the whisper of Marcion's blade being freed, too.

With a loud clap, the orange light disappeared, leaving the field as empty as it had been a few minutes before.

"What in the name of all the saints was that?" With his naked sword in his hand, Marcion took a tentative step onto the field. At the same moment, Hugo came crashing out of the trees with his own blade drawn.

"What happened?" Hugo demanded. "It wasn't Autar—I heard him well ahead of me. What made that noise?"

"Lightning and thunder," Theu replied, sheathing his weapon. "I recognize it now."

"Out of a cloudless sky?" Marcion looked as though he could not believe this explanation. "I have never seen lightning like that."

"I have," Theu said, looking at India, speaking as if to relieve her trembling fear. "I've seen it before. It causes no harm unless it actually strikes someone. There is no danger now. It's over and won't come again for a while. But let us gather everyone together and be away from this place as quickly as we can."

For all his brave words, he put an arm across India's shoulders, holding her tightly while they made their way back through the trees, holding her as if he would never let her go.

Chapter Fifteen

"Which circuit did you blow out that time?" An emotionally exhausted Willi leaned back against the office wall. After this latest unsuccessful attempt, she could no longer hide from herself the possibility that India was gone forever.

"No problem," said Hank. "I can easily get the stuff I need from the storeroom. The repairs won't take long."

His complete self-confidence set Willi's teeth on edge. Since India's disappearance, she had learned entirely too much about Hank's character. She was sorely disappointed in him—and in herself for not realizing sooner what kind of person he was. And she blamed herself for suggesting that he should give computer lessons to India.

"You can't get anything from the storeroom

today," she pointed out. "It's Sunday. No one will be in the office. Besides that, you need a requisition, properly filled out and signed by your department head. That's the way we get supplies for the Art History Department. All of which means that you will have to wait until tomorrow to get what you need. But tomorrow may be too late for India," she finished bitterly.

"Not to worry. I know how to bypass all that administrative red tape." Digging one hand into his trousers pocket, Hank brought out a well-filled key ring. Having selected the key he wanted, he held it up for her to see. "Clever, yes?"

"How did you get that?" she asked, appalled by his sheer nerve. She did not really want an answer to her question. She knew in advance that she wouldn't like his explanation, and she could easily imagine what he would say if she reminded him that he could be fired for possessing a departmental key he wasn't supposed to have.

"The janitor is never around when I need him," Hank's voice broke into Willi's thoughts, "so I had my own key made. Crooks do it all the time—why shouldn't I? Don't let anyone into this room. I won't be gone long."

After the door had closed behind him, Willi sank into the only chair, burying her face in her hands. She had just seen yet another side of Hank that she had refused to acknowledge before, and she knew she had to think about her relationship with him at once, whether she wanted to or not.

"I could have loved you forever," she whispered, badly shaken and uncertain what to do about Hank's appropriation of university property without a requisition, which had apparently been going on for some time, or his cavalier attitude toward breaking and entering, which was what his use of the illicit key was. "You aren't the honest man I believed you were. I think I always knew you cared more for your experiments than for any human being, including me, but now I find you've been stealing heaven-knows-what from the university to improve this computer they let you use. Improve? That's a joke! Whatever you've done to it has destroyed India." The thought of her dearest friend dead because of Hank's actions brought Willi to tears.

"Oh, poor India," she sobbed. "This is all my fault. I wish I had never asked Hank to help you. Oh, I wish I were dead, too."

"Excuse me, do you know where I could find the janitor?"

At the sound of an unfamiliar masculine voice, Willi sniffed and began to wipe the tears off her cheeks.

"I knocked, but I guess you didn't hear me. I'm sorry to interrupt your work, but I was supposed to deliver some personal property to the History Department office and I can't find anyone to open the door for me."

"It's Sunday afternoon," Willi said with another sniff, still keeping her back toward the speaker because she had just realized that her makeup must be a mess after all the crying she had done. "Actually, it's almost Sunday evening."

"I know, but my brother promised there would be someone here. Do you think you could help me?"

After wiping her cheeks one last time, Willi stood up to face the intruder, a slender young man with dark curly hair and dark blue eyes. He had a charming, slightly mischievous smile that faded as soon as he saw her face.

"You're crying." He pulled a spotless white handkerchief out of his pocket and handed it to her.

"Good guess." Willi blew her nose rather noisily into the handkerchief. "What did you say you wanted?"

"The key to the History Department office," he repeated very distinctly.

"I'm not supposed to leave here," she informed him, waving a hand toward the computer. "There is an experiment going on, and it had better work soon or there will be murder done in this room. But Hank should be back before long, and he seems to have the keys to every blessed door in this building."

"I take it you aren't too fond of Hank," the stranger said, watching her reaction.

"I used to be." Willi blew her nose again. "But I just discovered how dishonest he is. And he lost my best friend."

"Now, that's what I call bad policy, mislaying a friend." The stranger smiled at her, once again suggesting mischief and abundant charm. "I'm sure your friend will turn up soon."

"If she doesn't," Willi said, "I'll go to Campus

Security and tell them everything I know. If they can't help, I'll go to the police, maybe even the FBI."

"You're serious, aren't you?" The man's smile vanished. He took a step into the room, his eyes on Hank's machinery. "What's really going on here? And what the devil are all those extra components attached to the computer?"

"Don't answer that." Hank came through the open door carrying a large box in his arms. "Willi, I thought I told you not to open the door to anyone. Who the hell is this guy?"

"This *gentleman*," Willi told him, "needs the history office key."

"What makes you think I have it?"

"Haven't you? Along with all the other keys?" Her voice was tart. Hank set down the box, looking at her as if he would like to throttle her for revealing anything about his activities, but she stared back at him until he relented.

"Okay, Okay. Come on, mister, I'll open the door for you. Willi, don't let anyone else in here."

"Are you sure you'll be all right?" The stranger looked concerned until Willi nodded.

"I'll be fine." She tried to give him back his handkerchief, but he pressed it into her hand, folding her fingers around it.

"Keep it. I have others. I hope you find your friend."

After he and Hank had gone out, Willi looked more closely at the handkerchief she was holding. It was real linen with the initial *B* embroidered at one corner.

"Elegant," she said. "Most people use Kleenex. He must be rich." When Hank reappeared, she stuffed the handkerchief into her pocket and promptly dismissed it from her mind because Hank was fuming.

"What did you say to him?" Hank demanded.

"About what?" Willi tried to recall everything she and the stranger had talked about, but she had been so upset that she couldn't remember all of it. "Why are you asking?"

"He told me not to be so rude to you. Said you are a lady and I ought to treat you better."

"Did he?" In spite of her fears for India's sake, Willi almost smiled. "Gosh, that's nice."

"Who is he, anyway?" Hank began to pull his supplies out of the box he had brought.

"I don't know. I never saw him before and will probably never see him again." She experienced a pang of regret at the thought. Men didn't call her a lady very often. She came on too strong for that. But she found she liked the idea. She had a momentary vision of herself with her hair grown longer, wearing a soft floating dress in pale green, with matching shoes and pretty earrings, dancing with the unknown man. She sighed, thinking it would never happen to her. Then she forgot all about the mysterious stranger when Hank started to work on the computer and the screen began to glow once more, renewing her hope that they just might be able to find India after all.

Chapter Sixteen

"I did not come so long a distance to Agen," snapped Sister Gertrude, "to be housed in a tent among crude warriors."

"It was kind of Count Theuderic to let us use his tent," Danise said in her most soothing tones, "and to say he would not mind bathing and dressing in Lord Marcion's tent. After all, dear Sister Gertrude, it's only until we are presented. You said yourself we could not appear before the queen unbathed and travel-stained."

"Danise, this gown is lovely," India put in, hoping to stop the annoyed retort she could see coming from Sister Gertrude, who had recovered all of her old acerbity now that their journey was over. "Thank you so much for lending it to me."

"It is the very finest Frisian wool." Sister Gertrude tugged at the skirt to settle it more gracefully over India's hips. She stepped back, casting a critical eye at India. "If only your hair weren't so short, you could braid it, or pin it up. The last time I was at court, most of the ladies were wearing topknots with jeweled ornaments. It was such a pretty style and would become you better than just letting your hair hang loose."

"It will grow, in time." India wished she had a mirror so that she could see herself. The borrowed gown was a lovely shade of deep blue, with a round neck and loose sleeves that ended halfway between elbow and wrist. She wore beneath it a fine white linen shift, the edges of which showed at the neckline and sleeves, and a loose gold belt rested upon her hips. Her only jewelry was the medallion on its gold chain, the multicolored enamels glowing against the dark color of her gown. For all that she was not used to wearing dresses that fell to her ankles, India found this clothing remarkably comfortable and not the least bit constricting.

"Now, both of you turn around for me just once more," Sister Gertrude ordered. "Yes, you look very nice. Danise, that green silk is most becoming. Are you ready? Good. It's time to go."

When they reached the building that was serving as a temporary palace while the court was at Agen, Danise and Sister Gertrude were called into the reception room first. While India was wondering whether to join them without being announced, Theu and Marcion appeared.

"Wait," Marcion called, running to catch and stop her before she could follow her companions through the door.

"I hardly recognized you," she said, surveying his wine-red silk tunic trimmed in gold and his jeweled belt, the luxurious clothing a startling reminder to her that her humorous friend on the long journey from Saxony was in fact a wealthy Lombard nobleman.

"We always dress well at court, just to impress the ladies," Marcion told her, joking as usual. Flinging out a hand in Theu's direction he added, "Behold now our mighty leader, freshly bathed and clean shaven. Does his magnificence take your breath away? I hope so, for that is what he planned, and it took him so long to dress that we are almost late."

"Theu always takes my breath away," India murmured, regarding the man who now arrived at the entrance to the reception room at a more dignified pace than Marcion had used.

Theu's tunic was made of silver-grey silk the exact color of his eyes, and his bright blue cloak was of a wool even finer than India's gown, fastened at his shoulder by a gold brooch set with pearls and rubies. He wore several rings on each hand, and the gilded belt holding his sword was one India had not seen before. But all the finery could not disguise the tough, battle-ready man beneath it, who yet had a softer side for his friends and for the woman he loved. He laughed at Marcion's teasing, and the smile he gave India erased any nervousness on her part about meeting the king and queen. If she went into the royal reception room with him, there was no need to be concerned that she might slip up and say or do something improper.

"How beautiful you are," he said, clasping her hand. "We are to see Charles in private before you are presented to the queen. Come this way."

He and Marcion took her to a door that led to a chamber directly behind the reception room. The single guard outside threw open the door at their approach, and she walked between Theu and Marcion into the presence of the king of the Franks.

Except for Hrulund, all of the men India had met since coming to Francia had been her own height or at most an inch or two taller than she was. Towering almost six and a half feet, Charles looked like a giant, an impression enhanced by his heavy bone structure and remarkably well-developed muscles for a man of thirty-five, which in his time was well into middle age. A narrow gold circlet sat atop his pale gold hair, and he sported a sweeping Frankish mustache. He had the bluest, most piercing eyes India had ever encountered. Even in the plain woolen tunic that was his habitual costume, there was no mistaking him for anything but a king.

By contrast, the two black-robed clerics standing near him made at first almost no impression on India. She could not stop looking at Charles, who was welcoming Theu and Marcion back to his court as if he considered them among his dearest friends. Then his eye fell on India, measuring her worth, watching her reaction to him with interest and curiosity. Overcome at meeting the great man against whom all future European kings would be measured, India sank into a deep curtsy, a gesture she had learned in dancing class as a girl. Charles took both her hands in his, raising her.

"Seldom have I been so gracefully acknowledged by one who pretends to be a boy," he said, his blue eyes dancing with laughter, making her laugh back at him. "You are welcome at my court, India.

"Now," Charles instructed, "be seated, all of you, and tell me of your adventures. Alcuin, come sit beside me. Adelbert, take your place at the table there and write down all that is said. It promises to be an entertaining tale."

As the two clerics came forward, India looked at the famous scholar. Alcuin said nothing, merely favoring her with a polite nod before he bent his tall, stoop-shouldered form to sit on a bench beside his king. His shorter companion headed toward the table Charles had indicated, and now India looked closely at this man for the first time.

"Hank!" she cried, reaching toward him to clutch at his arm. "Hank, what are you doing here?"

They were all staring at her. Theu's hand had strayed toward his sword, though he had not yet drawn it. Charles watched her with some amusement, still laughing a little. Marcion looked puzzled. Alcuin sat with raised eyebrows and an interested expression, looking from India to the cleric.

"Lady, I do not know you," said the cleric. "My name is Adelbert, not what you called me."

"Do you think he is *Ahnk*?" Theu asked India, his right hand still hovering near his sword hilt. "If there is a chance he might harm Charles, or you, I had best kill him at once."

At this the cleric gave a terrified squawk and hurried to put the table between himself and Theu.

"Adelbert has been my assistant for three years now," said Alcuin calmly. "I know him well. What, or who, is *Ahnk*?"

"He is the man who is responsible for my being here in Francia," India said, having recovered somewhat from her first shock. "He looks much like this man, but I see now that I was mistaken. This cannot possibly be Hank." Still, the resemblance was remarkable. Adelbert had the same untidy dark blond hair and pale eyes as Hank, and the same sharp, curious way of looking about him, as if he did not quite trust his surroundings.

"I apologize. I didn't mean to startle you," India said, feeling uneasy when Adelbert met her eyes. She sat down across the room from him, next to Marcion. After sending a threatening look toward the cleric, Theu sat on her other side.

"Alcuin and I have read your thorough report

on events in Saxony," Charles said to Theu. "Tell us now anything you did not write in the report and then describe what happened after you left Aachen."

Theu took care not to mention India's origin in the future, or Hank's attempts to return her to her own time. Otherwise, he left out nothing. As for the episode at Tours, he told the story without comment, giving only the facts as they had occurred. When he had finished, Charles turned his attention from his friend to India.

"The only thing I do not understand from Theu's account," he said, "is where you have come from and what your message to me is."

"My home is far away, many long years' journey from here," she replied, conscious of Theu's eyes on her and knowing he had not changed his opinion since the night when they had talked in the abbey outside Paris. He still believed it would be wrong for her to tell Charles the entire truth. Having thought often and seriously about the possible results if she were to reveal that she had come to Francia from a future time, she knew Theu was right. Even so, she had to try to warn Charles, for Theu and his friends, who had become her friends too, might well be among the men killed in Spain or while returning to Francia. Taking up the enameled medallion, she lifted the chain over her head and gave the necklace to Charles. He examined it carefully, then handed it to Alcuin.

"It appears to be real," Charles said, "though there is something not quite right about it. Theu said your husband told you to give the medallion to me, and that he also sent a message."

There was no way to avoid saying something that would serve as the promised message. With Charles and Alcuin looking at her expectantly, and Adelbert's pen poised to write down whatever she said, India knew this was likely to be the only chance she would ever have to voice her fears to Charles. She had seen the bustling activity when they rode into Agen earlier that day. She had listened while Theu heard from one of the officers of his principal levy that three days previously Charles had sent half of his army under the command of his uncle, Duke Bernard, southward into Spain by the pass at Puigerda, then on to Barcelona to receive the prearranged surrender of that city. The other half of the army, including Theu and his men, would follow Charles along the old Roman imperial road through the pass of Somport and then down onto the Spanish plains near Saragossa, where the army would reunite before the walls of the second city the Saracens had promised to turn over to the Franks.

"What is this message from your husband?" Charles prompted her with a friendly look. "Was it that he recommended you to my care? If so, I will gladly take you into my household and find a new husband for you if you want."

"My lord." She paused, searching for the right words. She saw Theu looking at her intently and imagined that he was willing her not to reveal what she knew. But she had to try. She could not live with herself if she did not, for her words might save not only Theu's life but the lives of countless others as well. "My husband was a great scholar in our land, who studied the many ways of waging war. He knew of your plans for the Spanish campaign and begged me to tell you it would be dangerous and costly."

"All wars are dangerous, and scholars like them not at all," Charles said. "Just ask my friend Alcuin here. He is most unhappy about my latest plans."

"It's the traveling I detest," said Alcuin. "I dislike rattling my aged bones over bad roads in every kind of weather. I would rather be studying."

"There, you see? That's why I'm leaving him here at Agen." Charles appeared to be much amused by Alcuin's response. "I'll wager your scholar husband was no different in his complaints."

"I know it is too late to stop you from going to Spain," she said, beginning to feel desperate. "I have been told that half your army has left already. But I beg you, take the greatest care, especially on your return journey, and please—oh, please—beware of Hrulund's mad desire for glory. If you do not control him, he will cause much grief."

"Did Hrulund not desire glory, he would not be half so fine a warrior," said Charles, adding in a stern voice, "Have you warned me about him because of the way you were treated at Tours?"

"Because of what I saw in him there," she answered.

"Or is it that you would rather I prefer Theu over Hrulund?" Charles asked. "You must be aware of the feud between them."

"That's not it at all," she cried, frustrated by her inability to make him understand.

"Women as well as scholars dislike war," Charles said. "Who can blame them? Their gentle hearts break at the damage warfare inflicts. Let me warn *you* now, India. Do not interfere in the work of warriors. Nothing you can say or do will stop this campaign or make me conduct it differently than I would have if you had not spoken."

His tone and his commanding presence defeated her. There was no way to convince him of what she knew, except to tell him a truth he would never believe. He would think she was a madwoman. She did not know what they did with insane people in Francia. She might be locked away for the rest of her life. Away from Theu. She bowed her head, accepting her failure.

"As you wish, my lord," she said.

"Good." His blue eyes looked kindly on her again. He smiled, pleased by her apparent meekness, and put out one giant hand. "Come, I'll present you to Hildegarde myself."

She placed her hand in his and let him escort her into the reception room next door, where his queen sat among her ladies upon a well-cushioned chair placed next to a much larger chair that could only have been intended for this unusually tall man.

Hildegarde was twenty-one years old and had been married to Charles for seven years. A sweet-faced woman with soft grey eyes and light brown hair, her body was swollen with her fifth pregnancy. She rose a bit clumsily when Charles appeared, leaning hard on the arms of her chair for leverage.

"No, my love, don't disturb yourself," Charles said, leaving India to hurry across the room and place a supporting arm around his wife. "Hildegarde, sit down, please. The midwives have advised you to rest."

"I would rather walk. It eases the pain in my back," she said.

With one arm still around Hildegarde, Charles waved his free hand toward India. She came forward at once to curtsy again, though not so deeply as she had for Charles.

"This is the lady India," Charles told Hildegarde, "come from a great distance to visit us for a while."

"You are welcome to join my ladies." Hildegarde smiled at India, then smiled more broadly when Theu and Marcion greeted her, each man kissing her upon both cheeks. "Here are my brave warriors, returned to me at last. But where is Hugo?"

"He's busy with preparations for our leaving," Marcion answered her. "He will join us tonight. Lady, may I speak to my betrothed?"

"I knew that would be your first request of

me." Laughing now, Hildegarde called out, "Come here, Bertille, and greet Lord Marcion with a friendly kiss."

Marcion's love obeyed the queen, detaching herself from the other women to walk quickly to where he was. She placed her hands on Marcion's shoulders, reaching upward to kiss him lightly on one cheek. Marcion's hands moved to encircle her waist, his attitude giving India the distinct impression that he would have liked nothing better than to pull her close and kiss her full on the mouth.

"Welcome, my lord," said Bertille, the sound of her voice catching India's complete attention.

At first she could see nothing of Bertille but smooth dark hair worked into two long braids and her dainty back encased in light blue silk. But when Marcion released her and she turned to greet Theu, India gave a shocked, hastily smothered gasp. She knew that short, well-rounded figure, recognized the sparkling eyes and the impish face with its pert, upturned nose. It was Willi—and yet it was not Willi. The features were not identical and there was a further shade of difference—a lightheartedness where sadness always lingered on Willi's face even when she laughed. Bertille had no sadness in her at all.

Bertille greeted Theu with great charm and a bright smile, then looked toward India. And India, wanting no second fuss like the one she had created earlier over Adelbert's resemblance to Hank, said nothing, waiting until Marcion had formally presented the girl to her.

"I think my mother will agree," said Bertille, "that you as well as Danise may stay with us in our chamber."

"An excellent idea," said the queen, now re-seating herself with some awkwardness. While Charles leaned over her, murmuring softly, Theu stepped to India's side.

"About Adelbert," he began, glancing toward where the cleric stood with Alcuin.

"It's worse than you think," she said. "It isn't just Adelbert. Bertille is enough like Willi to be her sister."

"I have known Bertille since she was a small child," he informed her. "She has not come here from another time."

"If you remember, Alcuin said something similar about having known Adelbert for years." She shook her head, as confused and upset as she had been on her first day in Francia. "I don't understand this."

"Children often resemble their parents," Theu said. "Is it possible that the people you know are descendants of Bertille and of Adelbert?"

"Could they look so much alike with so many generations separating them?" she asked. "I don't know. All I *do* know is that I can't say anything to them about the way they look. Theu, I don't want to stay in the women's quarters. I'd be uncomfortable there, seeing Bertille all the time, and I want to be with you every minute. We have so little time before you must leave."

"I promise I will see you often," he said, shaking his head at her, "but for now, stay with the ladies, I beg you, and set me free to make the necessary preparations for Spain."

"Very well, Charles." Hildegarde's patient voice cut across India's further protest. "Since you insist, I will retire to my chamber and rest. But, please my dear, go somewhere else and busy yourself with manly concerns. I cannot sleep if you constantly ask me whether I feel well or not. I have done this before, I know how to bear a child. Let me attend to the welfare of this dear baby, and you take care of your army. Sister Gertrude, my dear old friend, I would have you with me, and Lady Remilda also. The rest of you, girls and women, need not attend me until this evening." Hildegarde left the reception room with Sister Gertrude and a stately lady.

"Lady Remilda is Bertille's mother," Theu said to India, "and here comes Bertille with Danise. Go with them. I'll see you this evening."

He and Marcion joined Charles, who upon his wife's departure had gathered a group of men about himself. The women began drifting out of the room in small groups. Bertille and Danise stopped to speak with Alcuin and the cleric Adelbert. When Charles called to the two men, Adelbert delayed, wistfully watching Bertille cross the room toward India, until a word from Alcuin recalled him to his duties.

India soon discovered that Bertille and Danise had met the summer before, when the court was at Paderborn and Danise's father had taken her there. By the time they reached the chamber allotted to Bertille and her mother, the two girls were chattering to each other like old friends, discussing fashions in gowns and hairstyles, the most recent marriages and betrothals among the nobility and—their principal topic of interest—the handsome warriors gathered at Agen, especially the manly attributes of Marcion and Hugo. India felt a bit left out until she realized that she had been expecting Bertille to treat her with the same intimacy she had always enjoyed with Willi. She told herself again that Bertille was *not* Willi, that she, India, was at least ten years older and infinitely more experienced than these innocent girls in their mid-teens. However, out of all the mysteries bedeviling her, there was one question to which she could have an answer.

"Bertille," India asked when the girls had fallen silent for a moment, "I saw you speaking to Adelbert. Is he a special friend of yours?"

"Adelbert? No, he's only a cleric," Bertille answered.

"From the way he looked at you, I thought he might be fond of you."

"It would not matter if he were," Bertille replied, openly shocked by this suggestion. "I have given him no cause to think I find him interesting. Even if I were not already betrothed, a cleric is an unsuitable object for a noblewoman's affections. Adelbert is soon to take his final holy orders. I will be no priest's wife, and certainly not concubine to one. Do not think I care for Adelbert, or that he would dare to love me. We have talked occasionally, that is all. I *want* to marry Lord Marcion. He is the right man for me. My parents think so, and so do I."

"I see," India said weakly, more confused than ever.

Despite the distraction provided by the girl's chatter and her own disturbing thoughts, India could not forget Theu for a moment. Having grown used to his presence for the greater part of every day, she sorely missed being with him constantly. Nor could she let go of her fear for him, which grew stronger with each hour that passed. She tried to think of something, anything, she might do that would set a different course for the events soon to begin unfolding. Having revealed to Charles as much as she dared, and having been told in effect to be a good girl, stop worrying, and let the men get on with their primary business of warfare, she decided that the only thing left for her to do was speak to an influential man who had no interest in war. She would do what Theu had originally suggested to her at Aachen, and had later urged her not to do. She would talk to Alcuin.

Chapter Seventeen

There was no large feast that first night of India's stay in Agen, just a light, informal meal of roasted game birds, bread, and cheese. There was wine, but no one drank much because Charles had such an aversion to drunkenness that he had almost single-handedly transformed the drinking habits of the previously bibulous Franks. Nor, so Bertille informed India, did Charles like long, formal banquets unless there was a special reason for them.

"He says we will feast and make merry once the army is victoriously returned to Francia," Bertille added. "For these last few nights before his departure, he wants quiet evenings."

Charles and Hildegarde sat together at the head table with their three surviving children. Six-year-old Charles, called Charlot, was a sturdy, flaxen-haired boy who wore his own miniature sword and freely climbed upon his father's knees, thus displacing his three-year-old sister Rotrud, who howled at this treatment until Charles took one child in each arm and bade them behave or go early to bed. Baby Carloman gurgled happily in his nurse's arms while Hildegarde cooed at him and offered a crust of bread for him to chew in place of his thumb. It was a pleasant domestic scene, with the lords and ladies of the court relaxed and talking with familiar ease to both king and queen, but for India the earlier half of the evening was spoiled by the absence of Theu and his friends.

Still, Alcuin was present, sitting at a table with Adelbert and another cleric. Leaving Bertille and Danise talking together, India approached the scholar. He stood as soon as he saw her.

"May I speak with you about something very important?" she asked.

"Please join me here." He indicated the bench from which he had risen. As soon as India was seated, he took his place again, glancing backward once to be certain his shoulders would screen them from the notice of the other clerics. "You may speak freely. I perceive that you are worried."

"I know I cannot prevent the army from going to Spain," she said, "but can you tell me any way that I might convince Charles to take extra precautions, especially on his return?"

"Charles has taken all the advice he will hear

on the subject of Spain," Alcuin replied, closely watching her reaction to his words. "He will conduct the campaign in the way he thinks is best. I can tell you that he never risks the lives of his men unnecessarily, which is one reason why they follow him so willingly. I see my answer does not comfort you."

"I know that something terrible is going to happen," she said. "I have to try to prevent it."

"Your concern is for Count Theuderic. It is natural for a woman to fear for the man she loves. My advice will be the same as Charles's was. Women and clerics both must learn this difficult lesson. Do not interfere in matters on which no man will listen to you. You cannot change what will happen."

"That's just the trouble," she cried. "I have to change it. I have to!" Her voice rose on those last words, and a nearby couple turned to stare at her. She knew she would have to get herself under control before she attracted more attention. She fought back her tears and the ever-present fear that gnawed at her. While she struggled, Alcuin never took his steady gaze from her face.

"Tell me," he asked, once she had regained her composure, "is your homeland truly so far away? Many long years' journey, you said."

"It's true."

"Then how is it that your husband knew about the Spanish campaign before he died? Charles did not decide upon it until last autumn, yet you claim to have been traveling for years to warn us against it." He gave her such a concentrated, direct look that she could not move or in any way escape his next questions. "Was your husband a magician? Did he foresee the future?"

Here was the danger she had feared if she said too much. She knew she would have to answer Alcuin truthfully but very carefully. He was too intelligent to be fooled for long by lies or evasions, yet evasion and half-lies were all she dared to give him. She hated the need to do so, wishing she could tell this wise and obviously good-hearted man everything that had happened to her.

"Robert Baldwin was not a magician; he was a scholar," she said. "I was only his secretary and now am but the carrier of his message. His knowledge and his intelligence were far greater than mine."

"I have known women who outdistanced many men in both, Charles's mother and sister among them, and a few ladies of this court also. Whatever your full story may be, I sense in you no evil intent, only the desire to protect those you love. India, I beg you, take my advice for which you asked." His ink-stained right hand covered hers, the touch imparting a genuine solicitude for her. "During the short time remaining to you, do not torment yourself or Theuderic with your fears for him, nor press him to change what he will do in battle. Love him, give him all your heart, and the day after tomorrow send him away with a smile. When he is gone, pray constantly for his safe return. Weep then, if weep you must, but not now—not while he is still with you."

She was saved from making an impatient answer to advice she did not want to hear by the sudden appearance of Bishop Turpin, Count Hrulund, and Autar. Turpin, in full bishop's regalia, greeted Charles and Hildegarde with severe dignity. Hrulund fell on both knees before Charles, bowing his head so low that India half believed he would touch his forehead to the floor.

"My lord king," Hrulund proclaimed in a loud voice, "I come before you prepared to give my life in your service."

"Let us hope that won't be necessary," said Charles, shifting little Rotrud a bit higher against his shoulder so he could motion to Hrulund to rise.

"I will perform any task you set me, dare any danger, and count it nothing for your sake," Hrulund replied.

"It would please me," Charles told him, "if you would have a care for your life and the lives of your men."

"I can think of no greater glory than to die in your name while killing black-hearted Saracens," said Hrulund. He went on in this way, passionately vowing the complete extermination of every unbeliever in Spain.

"Alcuin," India said, still watching Hrulund's posturing, "*he* is the most dangerous man in Charles's army."

"Charles understands him well and uses the man to his own advantage," Alcuin told her, patting her hand again. "You need not concern yourself about Hrulund, my dear."

Upon hearing those words, she understood at last that no one would take her fears seriously. There was no way for her to prove that she had come to Francia from the future or that she knew what would happen in Spain. It was a miracle that Theu believed her. No one else would. If what had happened to her was beyond her own comprehension, how could she expect Charles and his friends to understand it? Her conversation with Alcuin had frightened her, for his searching questions had almost led her into saying more than she should. With a long sigh, she admitted that Theu was right. The only thing for her to do was keep quiet, let history take its course, and pray that Theu and all his band of friends would survive the coming warfare.

At that point in her thoughts, she saw Theu, Marcion, and Hugo enter the room. They went at once to Charles, who was still listening to Hrulund.

"Theu," cried little Charlot, not caring that he interrupted Hrulund's latest boast, "look at my new sword. Will you practice with me?" He jumped down from his father's lap and ran to Theu, who stooped to admire the wooden blade. Hrulund looked about angrily, but Charles only smiled.

"He'll be a fine warrior in a few years," Charles said to Theu, pride in his son sounding in every word. He glanced around the room. "This is what I like best. It's good to have my family and my dearest friends near me. The memory of this evening will cheer my heart until we are all together again."

"Some of those friends are impure and unworthy of you," declared Hrulund in his most arrogant tone. "Count Theuderic found a strange woman in Saxony and has taken her as his concubine. Autar can testify to that."

"Indeed I can," Autar spoke up. "One day, while we journeyed here from Tours, I discovered him alone in a field with the woman India, kneeling before her, replacing her boots. From his tender manner toward her, it was clear to me what they had been doing."

"My lord," Theuderic began to protest, but Charles held up a hand, silencing him. Setting Rotrud down with a gentle hug, he rose, and when he looked up from his tiny daughter to his friends he was laughing.

"In a field, eh?" he said. "I've done the same myself more than once. So long as the lady is willing—and a widow, not an innocent maiden—and the weather is dry, where's the harm? Now, Hrulund, Autar, understand this— not all men can maintain your unblemished purity, my friends. Keep a little charity in your hearts and do not chastise the rest of us for loving our women often and well."

India saw Hildegarde blushing at her husband's words and could feel her own face flaming.

"Well, Theu," said Charles, grinning broadly, "what have you to say to this accusation? I will listen now."

"When we return from Spain," Theu responded, smiling back at his king, "I will marry India, if she will have me. Since she has no male relatives in Francia, I have already spoken directly to her."

"And I, my lord," spoke up Hugo, seizing the opportunity to make a request dear to his heart, "will also ask for a lady's hand when I return. Perhaps one day my children and Theu's will further cement our long friendship by intermarrying. And all of our children, I know, will gladly follow your heirs when we three have gone from this world."

"Theu has mentioned your hopes to me, Hugo," said Charles. "I approve of your choice. You need only win an estate large enough to satisfy the lady's father. I think it will not be a difficult task for you."

Hugo rightly took these words to mean that he was assured of a substantial reward once the Spanish campaign was completed. He could not keep himself from looking at Danise, who gazed back at him with shining eyes, so that everyone present saw the happiness and the bright dream that lay between them. India saw something else in addition. She saw Hrulund looking at Theu as if he would like to run him through on the spot. An instant later, Charles began to talk to someone else, and Hrulund was forced to move aside. Theu came to where India still sat beside Alcuin. The two men exchanged a few friendly words.

"Excuse me," Alcuin said to them. "I believe Charles wants me."

No sooner had Alcuin left them than Bishop Turpin approached.

"Lady India, what a pleasure to meet you again." Turpin smiled at her. Before he could say anything more, Theu stepped in front of India.

"If you touch her," Theu said to Turpin with barely suppressed violence, "if you threaten her again, or frighten her in any way, or lay one hand on her, I will forget who you are and punish you as you ought to be punished. Harm India, and your priestly robes will no longer protect you."

"If I were you, I would not be so hasty." Turpin's fixed smile did not reach his eyes. "Were I you, I would never forget that a bishop is not without his own power. Nor would I trust a woman about whom nothing is known." Turpin's smile vanished. With a chilling glance at India, he moved on to speak to someone else.

"I hope you were not embarrassed," Theu said when they were as alone as two people could be in that crowded room. "I thought it best to warn Turpin."

"I think you should not have angered him," she responded, "but I thank you for trying to protect me. I also appreciate what you said to Charles."

"I meant every word," he assured her. "I begin to hope you may be able to remain with me. After all, *Ahnk* has attempted twice to take you back, and he has failed both times. As for Autar's accusations, no one here will think less of you for lying with me. Widows are free to love where they choose, especially those who do not have great estates to consider."

"I want to spend tonight with you," she told him, "and every moment until you leave."

"It cannot be tonight. Charles will keep us up late, talking and planning. He loves to work at night, when others are abed. But at mid-morning, put on your riding clothes and join me at my tent."

"Theu," called Charles, "we are going to the council chamber." Most of the warriors present, along with Alcuin, Adelbert, and a few other clerics, left the room with him.

Hildegarde headed toward the women's quarters, holding Rotrud by one hand, Charlot by the other, and followed by the nurse with the baby. Danise and Bertille were talking to Bertille's mother. No one noticed when Theu put his arm around India's waist and drew her near for a swift, hard kiss.

"Until tomorrow," he said. "When I finally sleep this night, I will dream of you." He was gone, leaving her to look after him with a resurgence of her earlier fear, yet with an odd renewal of hope. If he was right and Hank could not take her home, if he returned safe and whole from Spain, they might have a future together after all.

She shared a bed with Danise again that night, and found herself bound to listen to Danise's girlish happiness.

"What good fortune for us that Charles likes Hugo," Danise whispered. "I am sure he will return to me a wealthy man, and then, since we have the king's approval, my father cannot object to our marriage."

"There are still many battles to be fought before that day comes," India reminded her, hoping to calm the girl so they both could sleep.

"I know it," Danise whispered back, "and I will pray for him every day that he is gone."

In the morning the ladies all went to chapel, then broke their fast with bread and a little wine. Hildegarde was not feeling well and had asked for Sister Gertrude and Bertille's mother Lady Remilda to attend her, so there was no one to object when India changed from the borrowed blue gown to her own tunic, trousers, and boots. Nor did anyone stop her when she left the palace and made her way from the town to the outlying fields where Theu's tent was pitched among dozens of others in what had become an auxiliary town.

He was waiting for her with her horse and his own. In the midst of that military encampment, with his men all about, he gave her only a brief, unemotional greeting before he helped her to mount. They rode out of the camp, away from all the noise and the bustle of packing and loading baggage carts, past smoky cooking fires and the smell of roasting meat and boiling cabbage, past itinerant merchants who hoped to dispose of their wares to the soldiers, and past the inevitable camp followers in tawdry rags who would trail after the army into Spain, taking with them their pimps, their children, and occasionally their aged parents.

Soon they had left the camp behind. Agen was built in a pleasant spot between the protection of the wide River Garonne and a high hill that guarded its back. Theu headed toward the hill, keeping the horses at a walk. As they climbed higher, more of the landscape came into view. Below them rolled the Garonne, joined near Agen by the sleepy River Gers, which flowed into it.

"The army will cross there," Theu said, pointing to an ancient stone bridge, "and take the Roman road into the mountains."

She could see the foothills, green with spring, the leaves fresh and new on oak trees and birch and chestnut, and in the far distance, beyond the first rippling rise of land, the darker shades of evergreens. And then came the Pyrenees themselves—white-capped, rocky, stretching all across the southern horizon.

"And beyond the mountains, Spain," she said, noting the now-familiar knot at her heart. There were other words on the tip of her tongue— words of warning, begging, pleading words—

but she remembered Alcuin's advice and did not speak them.

She was rewarded for her reticence when Theu leaned across the space between their horses to kiss her, his tongue teasing along her lips, one of his hands brushing deliberately across her breasts. The tight feeling in her chest eased, replaced by the warmth his touch always roused in her. If she did not know yet where he was taking her, she was certain of what they would do when they got there. A heavy, sweet ache began far inside her.

Theu found a spot where they were sheltered by trees but still could look out upon the scenery below. He spread his cloak for them to sit on, and brought out bread and cheese and a small jug of wine from his saddlebags.

"We won't be disturbed here," he said, drawing her down to sit beside him and putting his arms around her.

"The food," she began, but he stopped her half-hearted protest with his mouth.

"We will eat later," he informed her in his commanding way. "I want you now. And you want me, or you would not be here."

He was not wearing chain mail, not on this occasion, and he made short work of removing his clothes. India had her outer garments off and was pulling at the straps of her teddy when he put his hands on top of hers.

"Let me," he said, and pulled the teddy downward in rough haste. He had barely removed it before he was on top of her, his mouth searing hers, one hand in her hair, the other holding her face still for his kiss, and all his weight on her, fastening her to the earth. The ache that had been growing inside her suddenly became an all-consuming need. Caught in a delirious surge of passion, she shifted her legs, allowing him to fit between her thighs. In one swift, determined thrust he was inside her, where she wanted him to be, and her clamoring emptiness was filled. She clutched at him, raking her nails across his back in her urgent desire to be closer, ever closer to him, to make herself one with him. It was a hard and fierce joining—and a brief one, for their mutual climax was almost instantaneous and it caught her like a whirlwind, tearing thought from her mind and breath from her lungs. She heard a woman scream and a man cry out, and then she knew nothing except her body's violent throbbing.

When she again became aware of her surroundings, Theu was stroking her breasts, which were still covered by her bra, for he had not given her time to remove it.

"This gossamer fabric is like cobwebs," he whispered, setting his tongue against one nipple. India squirmed in pleasure. Seeing her reaction, he transferred his attention to her other breast.

"This can't be happening again," she moaned. "Not so soon."

"Why not, if we want it to happen? I wish we had loved more often. It's my only regret about our time together. So many days I have ridden southward with you, watching you while my desire for you grew and grew, wondering if we would come together again or if you would disappear forever. Now we have so little time left before I have to leave you. For this afternoon we will enjoy each other without waiting, and without concern for how often. Nor will I ever repent what we do. I love you too well to feel guilt."

"In that case . . ." Boldly she touched him, delighting in his immediate response and in the pleasure he displayed at her actions.

"You are like wine in my veins," he said. "I am drunk on you. I reel with happiness each time you accept me into your lovely body. But I would not have you think I am only a rough warrior. I can be gentle."

"I have no objection to your fierceness," she murmured, acknowledging a renewed sensation of aching emptiness as his hands and his mouth began to arouse her to fever pitch. She reciprocated his every caress, growing more and more shameless in what she did to him, until he begged her to stop lest he lose all control. Obeying his harsh whisper, she lay back on his cloak and let him do with her what he would.

She thought he would never stop stroking or kissing her, thought she would die of wanting him inside her, and believed he would burst from his need of her, before slowly, tenderly, he entered her once more. Then, with infinite care and patience, he showed her what his kind of gentleness meant, and she wept with the beauty of it and gave him all of her heart without reservation.

"I love you," she whispered, tears upon her cheeks.

"I have longed to hear you say it," he replied, "for though I once swore never to love again, you have conquered my heart. Know now the proof of my love." His mouth covered hers, he moved still deeper into her, and together they dissolved into a long, breathless kiss.

"I will love you forever," he whispered. "Forever."

She lay beside him with the sun shining down upon them, a soft golden warmth on her closed lids. He was sleeping. She could hear his peaceful breathing. They had eaten and talked and slept. She knew he would waken soon and love her again.

She was completely relaxed, her body pleasured beyond anything she had imagined possible in her earlier life. The physical component of the love between herself and Theu was so strong and so explosive that at times it overwhelmed her. Yet even during the height of their passion there was always something more than the joining of two bodies. There was a spiritual joining, too, a combining of their souls and hearts in which each took what was needed, each gave completely to the other, and both emerged stronger and more firmly bound together. Fierce and gentle, valiant warrior and tender lover, staunch friend and loyal follower of his king, Theu was all she could ever want in a man. She felt him move beside her and knew he was watching her.

"Lying naked in the sun, you will burn your fair skin," he warned.

"It's your back that will be burned," she teased, not opening her eyes just yet. "You have been sheltering me all afternoon."

"I would shelter you for the rest of your life if I could." His lips touched her eyelids, each in turn, then her cheeks, and finally her lips. She raised languid arms to encircle his shoulders, not because she feared he would draw away— she knew he would not—but because she wanted to touch him, to caress and hold him, as evidence of her love.

"I'll love you once more," he whispered, nibbling at her earlobe, "and then we ought to leave. It will be dark before long, and the path down this hill will be difficult for the horses."

"Does that mean you have brought other women here? Is that how you discovered the tricky path?"

"What an insult!" That he was not insulted at all she could tell from his laugh. In an abrupt movement, he broke from her embrace to straddle her, holding her wrists at either side of her head. He lowered himself slowly, trying to look angry and not succeeding because of the love in his eyes. "I rode this way yesterday, seeking a safe place to bring you. That is why I know the path." His mouth was by now only a fraction of an inch away from hers.

"We do seem to spend a fair amount of time making love in the open air," she said, longing for his kiss. Her lips parted, she looked straight into his silvery eyes.

"There is no place more private than the out-of-doors. I love to watch the sun on your face and your hair, and it turns your eyes to amber-gold. My love." His lips touched hers lightly, stirring warmth and deep tenderness in her. Her mouth was still open, so his tongue slid into her, touching her own tongue with silky heat. Between them, where their bodies were pressed together, she felt his manhood surge into powerful hardness yet again. He laughed softly, the sound of strong, confident masculinity.

"You have that effect on me," he whispered.

"As you have on me, though it doesn't show so obviously."

"I can see it in your eyes. I always can."

This was a long, slow, highly emotional, and ultimately tearful fusing of their separate beings into one, and when it was over she lay exhausted and trembling, still weeping, watching him dress and buckle on his ever-present sword.

"Come, India, we must go. The sun is near to setting." The golden shafts of light illuminated his face, turning his skin to the marble translucence of a heroic statue, catching the moisture remaining on his own lashes and making them sparkle. She caught her breath at the beauty and the grandeur of the man she loved. "Come, my dear girl, my beloved woman. I don't want to go, either, but I have obligations I cannot forget."

She pulled on the tunic and trousers she had worn for so many days, and stamped her feet into her boots. While he went to release the horses from the tree where he had tied them, she shook out and refolded his cloak. Hearing him behind her, she turned to smile at him, standing with her back to the slowly setting sun. He dropped the horses' reins and came toward her.

"The sun on your hair is like rosy gold," he said. "How I love you."

She leaned against him, wanting one last kiss before they ended the perfect afternoon.

His arm was about her waist when the peach-gold light surrounded them.

Chapter Eighteen

"I got her!" Hank shouted. "Stand back, Willi. Here she comes!"

The light was so vivid that it made Willi shut her eyes, but she could still hear the machinery humming and throbbing.

"All right! Way to go!" But Hank's cry of triumph was cut short. "Oh, my God! I got somebody else too!"

Willi's eyes flew open again. There, still within the boundaries of the shining peach-gold globe of light, stood India, her hair oddly longer than it had been when Willi had seen her last just the day before, her tunic wrinkled, but she was alive and apparently healthy. Beside her was a man unlike any man Willi had ever seen before, a creature with such a hard toughness about him that Willi stopped her welcoming forward motion toward India and stood gaping as the man drew a gleaming sword and threatened Hank with it.

"*Ahnk,*" the man shouted and launched into a long sentence Willi could not understand.

"Willi," India cried, "Willi, I'm all right. Don't worry—"

There was a roar from the computer, a vibration that rattled the office door, and India and the man with the sword vanished.

"No!" Now Willi did run forward, to pound on the computer in unbearable frustration before she turned on Hank. He backed away from her, looking frightened. Willi raised a fist at him. "Get her back!"

"I can't. I keep blowing that damned—oh, what's the use? You wouldn't understand." Hank ran a hand through his hair, leaving it more disheveled than it already was. His own frustration at the failure of his repeated efforts in India's behalf boiled over into shrill anger with Willi as his target. "You, Wilhemina, are overly emotional and intellectually incapable of comprehending the historic and technological significance of my work. I have single-handedly achieved a major breakthrough here."

"Don't go looking for a Nobel Prize," she told him sourly, "because, come tomorrow morning, I'm going to see your job on the line unless you succeed in reversing your experiment."

"If you would stop screeching at me like a

banshee, maybe I could get some work done," Hank shouted.

"I do not screech. I am a lady," Willi said, lifting her chin and drawing herself up to her full height of five feet, three inches. "A *gentleman* told me so."

"Ha! Not you," Hank declared, still angry. "You are a witch, a shrew, a termagant, a pain in the neck, and just plain stupid, but never a lady. You are also interfering with my work."

Willi never had a chance to tell Hank how unjust she thought his accusations were. Without even a knock this time, Professor Moore entered and bore down on Hank with a fearsome glare in his eyes and rage written all over his elderly face.

"Young Mr. Brant tells me you have a key to my department office," the professor said. "Hand it over, Mr. Marsh."

"I don't know any Mr. Brant," Hank declared.

"I believe you let him into my office earlier while I was not there."

"Oh, him," said Hank. "Who is he, anyway?"

"He is the younger brother of the gentleman who will replace me on January first," Professor Moore responded. Putting out his hand, he added, "The key, if you please, Mr. Marsh."

"Oh, all right." Hank pulled out his key ring and began to search for the correct key.

"You have a remarkable collection there." Professor Moore looked shocked. "Do you have a key for every door in this university?"

"Not quite." Hank gave up the history department key. The professor frowned at it, then at him.

"I am sorry to have to say this, Mr. Marsh, but I am going to have to report you to the head of Campus Security first thing tomorrow morning. In the meantime, I want you out of this office."

"This isn't your department. You have no right," Hank began.

"I have every right to stop dishonesty when I encounter it," Professor Moore responded. "I assume the disreputable jacket on the floor is yours. Pick it up and leave at once."

"Wait!" Willi cried. "Professor Moore, you don't understand. Hank is in the middle of an important experiment. If he stops now, he will have to begin all over again, at the beginning, and that will cost the university a lot of money. Just let him stay here and finish what he started. It won't take much longer."

"It was my impression," said the professor, "that you two were not working at all. You have been in here smooching, haven't you?"

"Absolutely not," Willi declared with great feeling. "I have no desire whatsoever to 'smooch' Hank—er, Mr. Marsh. I just want to help him finish his work successfully. Please, Professor Moore, it's terribly important."

"You do seem dedicated." He appeared to be softening.

"I am," Willi said, struggling against the panic she felt at the prospect of Hank's being stopped before he could retrieve India. "Please, just give us until the university workday begins tomorrow morning."

"I ought to save university funds whenever I can," the professor said thoughtfully. "Very well, let the experiment continue." He added, with a look at Willi, "I always did have a soft spot for a pretty girl."

"Thank you," Willi said. "You won't be sorry."

"I will still report Mr. Marsh in the morning. Now, are you certain Mrs. Baldwin will return today? She has been gone for a remarkably long time, and I do have that typing waiting for her. You haven't said where she went."

"I expect to see her back in this office any time now," Willi assured him. "I will remind her about the typing."

"Thank you." With a last severe look at Hank, Professor Moore allowed Willi to see him out of the office.

"Okay, Hank," Willi said, "you may think I'm stupid, but I just bought you all the additional time you are going to get. Start using it."

But Hank was too upset to go back to the computer immediately.

"What are all these people doing, wandering around the building on the Sunday before Christmas?" he demanded in an offended voice. "First that Brant guy, now old Moore comes in here for the second time. Why don't they stay home and decorate their trees? If I have one more interruption while I am trying to think, I swear I'll—"

"Mr. Marsh, is everything all right?" asked

315

the janitor, opening the door and poking his head into the office. "You just blew another circuit down in the basement."

"We're fine. Just fix it—and fast," said Willi, pushing the door shut again.

"—give up," Hank finished, throwing his hands into the air in disgust.

"No, you will not. I won't *let* you give up." Knowing he needed encouragement, Willi faced him with a smile, trying her best to hide the cold anger she felt toward him. For India's sake, she would be nice to Hank for a while longer. "You almost succeeded on this last try. You only need one more attempt, Hank. Just one more. Come on, you can do it. You know you can."

Chapter Nineteen

In a blast of peach-colored light, India and Theu stood once more upon a hillside near Agen. The first thing India became aware of after realizing where she was, was the sound of frightened horses. Dropping his sword and letting go of her, Theu leapt to the animals to catch their reins before they could bolt.

India watched him wrestling with the horses, unable to do anything to help him because she felt too slow-witted and clumsy to move. By the time Theu had tied the horses to a tree and returned to her, she was swaying on her feet.

"Sit down until you are steadier," he ordered.

"No." She leaned against him. "Don't let me go. Hold me." His arms were reassuring, providing stability and a measure of safety.

"Did it make you sick, too?" she asked.

"I was only dizzy for a moment," he replied. "India, I saw your time. I caught a glimpse of the world in which you once lived. There was a room with pale walls and glowing white boxes."

"That was Hank's office." She was feeling a little better with his arms around her.

"It was an ugly place," he said. "Everything was smooth, with no decoration, and so little color."

"Did you see my friend, Willi? She was there, too."

"I saw a girl who looked like Bertille." He took a deep breath. "I could never live in that world, India."

"I know." She burrowed into his chest, clinging to his strength. "I don't think I could live there either now. Not after knowing you."

They rode back to Agen in the way they had originally begun their travels together, with India seated in front of Theu on his horse. Her own horse was tied to Theu's saddle and ambled along behind them. India lay against Theu's chest, still feeling unsettled and ill after her brief trip to the twentieth century and back.

"Theu," she said as they neared Agen, "let me go into Spain with you. Let me be with you for as long as I can."

"It is impossible, and you know it." His mouth was hard, and it seemed to her that her words had broken their earlier closeness, driving him away from her. "When I am on campaign, all my thoughts must be on my men and on the coming battles. Your presence would distract me from the things I have to do. Nor would I put you into the danger you would surely face along the way and when our battles are fought."

"Please," she begged, thinking with fear of their coming separation.

"I cannot allow it. Do not ask again."

But she did ask again, not of Theu, who she knew would be immovable on the subject, but she could ask Marcion and she did, during her second evening spent with Charles and his family and friends.

It was a quieter night than the previous one. Hrulund, apparently preoccupied by thoughts of the march that was to begin on the morrow, and perhaps by thoughts of the hard days to come after the morrow, confined himself to only a few mild boasts and then sat talking with Autar and Turpin. Hildegarde was plainly unwell, but did her valiant best to appear cheerful before her husband and his companions. Around the reception room, friends gathered in small groups to say their farewells. Men and women stood together holding hands or arm-in-arm, and a few overwrought young girls burst into tears throughout the course of the evening. While Theu spoke to Charles, India sought out Marcion.

"I want to go, too," she said. "I can ride well now, and I would find ways to be helpful."

"Under no circumstances would Theu allow it," Marcion replied with uncharacteristic seriousness. "You would only be in the way. We would have to worry about you, perhaps even rescue you from the Saracens. The conditions on the march and in our nightly camps would not be suitable for you. A woman does not belong in a military campaign."

"In my country, women are soldiers, too," she cried. "And what about the women who follow the army?"

"You are not one of *them*." Marcion was horrified. "Do not bother Theu with this foolish plan. He would never agree to it. Let him think of you safe here, with the queen and the other ladies. Give him that peace of mind, so he can devote himself to warfare."

"You don't understand."

"I do." His mood turning gentler, he became once more the friend she had known since Saxony. "You love him and you do not want to part from him. It's natural enough. No one can blame you for what you are feeling, but give up this foolish idea. India, Lady Remilda has said that I may have a few moments alone with Bertille, and she is beckoning to me. I must leave you."

Nor did she have any better luck with Hugo.

"You can't do it," Hugo said bluntly. "Not one of Theu's men would help you, and rightly so. There would be no point in trying to disguise yourself, either, because then you would have to stay away from Theu to keep your identity hidden, and that would defeat your purpose. If Theu discovered you along the way, he would only send you back here to Agen, and that would mean wasting men who would have to ride with you to give you protection. Do as Theu wants. Stay here. Don't risk his anger or your life. Not every man in the army is as good-hearted as those in our band who brought you here from Saxony. Charles keeps the army on a tight rein, so there is not as much rape or killing of women and children as you would find in other armies, but still, a woman alone is easy prey. Be sensible. Don't do it." He left her then to seek Danise's company, leaving her with the impression that he was nearly as angry with her as Theu would have been if he had heard their conversation.

India felt utterly defeated. She could not make anyone understand her warnings, and she would not be allowed to travel into Spain with Theu. But there was one thing she could still do for him before they parted. When he returned to her side, she approached him directly.

"Take me to your tent tonight," she said.

"That would not be wise," he began, but she cut him off. In this at least she would not be thwarted.

"Wise or not, I will find my way into your bed tonight," she said, adding with great daring, "unless, of course, you are too weak and weary after today's activities?"

"Never!" Fierce male pride blazed in his eyes at the implied insult to his virility. It was quickly followed by laughter and tenderness as he relented. "If you do not come to me, I think I will invade the women's quarters and drag you off by your hair," he said. He paused, looking

around the room. "Nor do I imagine that anyone would notice your absence, for on this night
all lovers will want to be together."

The evening ended early, with Charles and
Hildegarde taking their children and retiring
for an hour or two of family privacy before the
little ones were sent to bed. Once they were
gone and the rest of the company had begun to
leave too, Bertille came to India and linked
arms with her. India pulled away.

"I will be sleeping elsewhere tonight," she
said, not certain what Bertille's response would
be. So far, there had been remarkably little con-
demnation of her publicly announced relationship with Theu. Sister Gertrude had made a
few expected pungent remarks, but the other
women, including Bertille's mother, the strict
Lady Remilda, seemed to feel that since India
was a widow, it was her own business if she had
a lover. Bertille accepted her statement with
casual ease.

"I'm not surprised," Bertille said, kissing her.
"I wish my mother would let me go to Marcion
tonight."

"Your mother is wise to protect you." India
thought of unplanned pregnancies and men
who did not return from war.

"She says our time will come," Bertille went
on, "and that when it does, I will understand
why the waiting was necessary."

They parted after a few more words, India
silently wondering if Bertille and Marcion
would ever know a time when they could be

together as lovers. Then she saw Theu waiting for her by the door, and she forgot everyone and everything but him.

Outside the town, among the tents, the horses, the piled-up supplies, and the heavy wooden baggage carts, the campfires were ablaze, lighting the figures of men hastening to finish loading the carts or packing their saddle-bags. For those who had completed their preparations and who did not have their own women at Agen, the camp followers were busily plying their trade.

Amid all the bustle and the coming and going, Theu's tent was a place of quiet. It was sparsely furnished, containing a table, a chair, and a bed—all of which could be easily folded up—a traveling clothes chest and a small box of sand to clean his armor.

"We'll make room for both of us," he said, seeing her looking at the bed.

"It's such a small place to be your home for months at a time," she remarked, touching the undyed wool wall of the tent.

"It is often crowded, too. Marcion has his own tent that he brought with him from Lombardy, but when the weather is bad, I invite Hugo to share mine with me."

"What about those who are sick or injured?"

"There is always a tent for the worst cases. We take along barber-surgeons, and several baggage carts filled with bandages and other medical supplies."

The ever-present knot in her chest tightened,

and suddenly India did not want to hear another word on that subject.

"Love me," she whispered, believing that if she could hold him close enough she would be able to convince herself that he might return to her in spite of all her fears.

"I intend to," he said, reaching for her. "All night long, until the trumpet blows at dawn."

"Don't talk of trumpets. Don't talk of anything but love." She put her arms around him and gave him her lips.

"Knowing our time together is brief makes each moment all the sweeter," he said. "Believe me, India, and listen well, lest I have no time to say it later. Until the last breath leaves my body, I will not stop thinking of you or wanting you. If I die in this campaign, I will die wanting you in my arms just once more, wanting your lips on mine for one last kiss."

"Don't talk of dying, either," she cried, clutching him as tightly as she could. "I can't bear it."

"I promise I will do all I can to return to you, and I pray that when I see Agen again, you will still be here, waiting for me."

"I will be." The words tumbled out, spurred by fear and love. "I'll refuse to go with Hank. I'll find a way. I will wait for you, Theu. I promise I'll wait."

His mouth was on hers, urgent, demanding. They tore at each other's clothes, and when they were naked, fell onto his cot for a wild and passionate coupling that rocked the inadequately sized bed until India thought it would collapse.

Oddly, they made love only once more that night. It seemed more important to talk. She asked endless questions, wanting to know every detail of his life up to the moment of their meeting in Saxony.

"Did you really think I was a boy and still want me?" she asked, amused by the idea of her passionate and intensely masculine lover caught in such an imaginary predicament. It was hard for her to think back to that time, when she had believed Theu was nothing but a bloodthirsty warrior.

"My heart knew you at once for what you are," he told her. "You are the one who has brought joy and love back into my life."

Toward dawn, all talking done and knowing there was not much time left to them, they came together again in a joining that was exquisitely sad, yet happy too, and above all, deeply reverent, as though they were sealing the bond that made their hearts one.

"You are my wife as surely as if there were a marriage contract between us," Theu said, kissing her tenderly, "or a priest blessing us when the contract has been read. Never think for a moment that anything we have done together is wrong. You and I were meant to love, and even time could not keep us apart."

Too soon came the moment when the trumpet blew to rouse the men.

"I'll help you arm," she said, pulling on her borrowed blue gown in some haste, in case someone should come to speak to him. She vowed that she would keep her rising terror under control, but her hands began to tremble.

He had his tunic on when Osric appeared to help him with the heavy chain mail *brunia*, and India was glad for the intrusion, knowing she would have been of little use to Theu by then. But she did buckle on his sword belt, then picked up his metal helmet.

"If I do not return," he began, and caught her face, making her look at him when she winced at the thought and would have turned away to hide her tears. "No, India, listen to me. You are to go on as bravely as you have done since first you came to me. You are the bravest woman I have ever known. Who else could do what you have done? Take pride in your courage.

"If I do not return, I ask you not to forget me. Let my memorial be in your heart. But if I should return and you are not here, if *Ahnk* finds you and, despite your best efforts, you have not been able to wait for me, then in that far-distant place where I cannot follow you, remember that you are in my heart also. I will never forget you. Never. If it is possible to continue loving even after death, then I will love you through all eternity."

"Oh, Theu." She could say no more. Tears poured down her cheeks.

"I beg you not to cry," he said. "If you do, I will not be able to leave you, and my weakness will dishonor me before my king and my men. You don't want Hrulund to mock me, do you?"

"Beware of Hrulund," she said, wiping away the tears and trying to keep her voice steady while she warned him one last time. "His jealousy, his blind arrogance and thirst for glory—"

"I care nothing for Hrulund." He enfolded her in his arms. "Let him become a great hero, let poets sing of his deeds down all the ages. I hold in my arms now more joy and greater glory than he will ever know. I have your love."

His lips were firm and sure upon hers, and his embrace gave her the strength she needed. When his men came to fold up and remove the furniture for packing and to strike the tent, she stood calmly at his side, watching them work.

Then it was time to bid farewell to Marcion, Hugo, Eudon, Osric, and all the others she had come to know as friends. In the confusion of leave-taking, Bertille suddenly appeared to throw herself into Marcion's arms and beg him to return safely to her. An instant later Danise, having gotten free of Sister Gertrude's surveillance, arrived to wish Hugo good fortune. Casting aside all maidenly modesty, she put her arms around his neck and kissed him hard, to the cheers of Hugo's friends.

"Here," Danise said, blushing prettily, "I brought this for you, so you won't forget me." She handed him her scarf of green silk woven with a pattern of gold threads.

"I'll take it gladly," Hugo said, "though nothing will make me forget you." With Danise's help, he wrapped and tied the scarf around his right arm above the elbow.

"To strengthen my sword arm," he said, making bold to kiss her again.

The trumpets sounded once more, warning that it was time to mount. Most of the tents had been taken down by now and the campfires extinguished. Hrulund's levy was already mounted. They clattered by on their way to meet Charles.

"You had best make haste, Firebrand," Hrulund called to Theu. "If you and your men dally much longer with your women, by the time you reach Spain, there won't be any Saracens left for you to kill."

"Good luck to you," Theu called back, refusing to take offense.

Beside Hrulund rode Bishop Turpin in chain mail and metal helmet, a metal-studded mace fastened to his belt in place of a sword.

"A priest in armor?" exclaimed India. "Will he fight too?"

"He's a mighty warrior," Theu told her, "but he won't use a sword because clergymen shouldn't shed blood. He does enough damage for two men with that mace."

All around Theu, his men were mounting. Osric brought Theu's horse to him. Theu looked hard at India, as if he were memorizing her features, and she knew there was no time left to them.

"Take Bertille and Danise back to the palace," he said. "Keep them from weeping if you can.

And do not weep yourself. I have no regrets. Have you?"

"None at all." That was not entirely true. She regretted that she could not stop his going, but he wanted her to be brave and she would not disgrace herself, or him, by crying in public, not even when he gave her a quick last kiss.

"Fare you well, India."

"And you. I love you."

"I love you. For all eternity." His hand touched her cheek lightly, and then he sprang onto his horse. He raised his right arm in a signal, and his men began to fall into position around him.

"Bertille, Danise," India called, "we are to go now. We can watch them leave from the palace, with the other ladies."

The field was muddy, the grass churned up by the feet of men and by horses' hooves. All around them were companies mounting up. Men hurried to their horses, orders were shouted, and lines of foot soldiers formed. The baggage carts creaked and groaned and began to roll out to the road. As she and the girls approached the palace, India saw Charles emerge from the main entrance with Alcuin. An instant later, Charles vaulted to the back of his horse with the energy of a much younger man. Noticing India and her two companions, he waved to them before wheeling his horse to ride toward the campground.

"The ladies are all gathered on the upper floor," Alcuin said when they reached him. "You ought to join them. There will be much noise and disturbance in the street when the army comes through."

They hurried into the palace and up the narrow staircase to the upper room where Hildegarde stood at the window, waiting to wave farewell to her husband. There, to India's surprise, neither Bertille nor Danise was scolded for leaving the palace, nor did anyone say a word to India about her night-long absence.

"Come here, child," said Lady Remilda, and put her arm around Bertille's shoulder, holding her daughter by her side in a comforting way.

"If you stand here," Sister Gertrude told Danise, moving her into position, "you will be able to see better."

"Thank you for not being harsh with her," India said softly to the nun. "She's close to tears."

"As are you," Sister Gertrude replied crisply. "I am not completely heartless where either of you is concerned. I only wish Danise did not love that young man. Her life would be much less painful if she were content to remain at Chelles with me and the rest of our good sisters."

Having heard this, Lady Remilda murmured to India, "We all understand how important it is to hearten the men going off to war. Sister Gertrude may seem hard at times, but she knows it, too."

"Here they come," cried Bertille, breaking away from her mother's embrace to lean out of the window. All of the ladies pushed closer, some rising on tiptoe to see better.

"India," Danise called, "come and stand beside me at the other window, where there are not so many trying to look out."

With arms about each other, they watched the spectacular scene below. Charles came first, wearing his gold circlet on his pale hair instead of his helmet, his shoulders covered by a blue cloak. When he drew level with the window, he paused to wave and blow a kiss to Hildegarde, who blew one back to him. On Charles's right hand rode Theu with Marcion, on his left Hrulund and Bishop Turpin. Immediately behind them came the other important men of the court, some of whom India had met during her time there. She saw the seneschal Eggihard, Anselm the Count of the Palace, and others.

Theu looked up and waved, but she did not think he could see her among so many other women. She kept her eyes on him until he was so far down the road that she could distinguish nothing but the glimmer of sunlight on his polished helmet.

"But where is Hugo?" cried Danise.

"Theu's levy hasn't passed yet," India said. "Hugo will be leading it."

"There! There he is. Hugo! Hugo!" Danise leaned so far over the windowsill that India grabbed her by the waist to prevent her from falling to the street below.

Hugo heard her. He looked up, his broad face creased into a grin beneath his helmet, and lifted his right arm in salute to Danise, so that the ends of her green-and-gold scarf floated out like a happy banner in the spring breeze.

Most of Theu's troop were looking at the window now. Bending forward, India waved along with Danise, bidding a final farewell to the men with whom she had ridden and lived for weeks. When they were gone, other ladies pressed toward the window, wanting to bid their own men good-bye, and India drew Danise away to make room for them.

"He looked so handsome," Danise said, tears in her eyes. "So brave and handsome. I am so proud of him."

It took several hours for the army to pass below. The women came and went, depending on which company was departing at any particular moment, but through it all, Hildegarde remained in her place, waving to leaders and common soldiers alike, cheering them on their way, her only concession to her condition being her acceptance of a chair so that she could sit for a while. Food was brought and served, but India took only a little wine, as did the queen.

When the last of the foot soldiers and the final groups of late stragglers had gone by, Hildegarde rose from her chair, took a few steps, and sank into a near faint.

"My lady, you are exhausted," cried Lady Remilda, catching her before she hit the floor. "Sister Gertrude, help me. Let us take her to her bed." She called upon one or two of the older ladies to go with them, and together they bore the queen off to her own chamber, where she remained in bed for several days.

Then began the long time of waiting, of days which stretched into weeks, then became a month, two months, three months, four. Once the novelty of living at a royal court had worn off, India became bored. To help pass the time, she attempted the delicate needlework with which many of the ladies employed themselves, but she was not good at it and soon gave up trying. She could not concentrate on anything for very long, not when she was constantly haunted by thoughts of Theu in danger.

In the increasing summer heat, the queen was often unwell, which meant that picnics or other outdoor activities were curtailed. India was occasionally able to get permission to take Danise and Bertille riding, but on those excursions she never approached the hill where she and Theu had spent their last day together. It would have been too painful, and she had an irrational fear that if she went to the spot where they had made love, Hank might be able to reach her. She did not want to chance having to return to her own time—at least, not yet. She had to stay at Agen until the army returned, whether Theu came with them or not. She had promised him she would wait, and she would keep her promise.

The court now consisted largely of women, the only men being those Charles had left behind to guard the safety of the queen and her ladies—and of course, the clerics who followed the court everywhere.

India saw Alcuin every day. Her original awe and respect of the great scholar remained, but were soon softened by a growing affection. The man had a gift for friendship. Even the queen, who had no intellectual interests and could neither read nor write, loved him, as did her children and everyone in Agen who was or ever had been his student. Each evening Alcuin sat in the reception room with the other clerics, his current students both male and female, and whichever ladies cared to join them, and there he raised subjects to be discussed or asked questions until a lively dispute arose. Then he would sit back, wine goblet in hand, a half smile on his face, and let others talk.

"That is your secret," India said to him one night. "You listen well."

"It's the best way to learn," he said. "I live in order to learn and to teach."

He invited India to join his group, which she did, hoping thus to distract herself from her constant worry for Theu's sake. She listened in fascination to the discussions, but she contributed little, partly because she feared she might reveal too much about her origins, and partly because she felt inferior to Alcuin's friends. They were all remarkably learned, including the women, and they talked about astronomy, philosophy, logic, religion, and a myriad of other subjects.

Among the clerics, Adelbert was always present, usually with quill pen, parchment, and pottery ink jar set before him so he could write down anything interesting that was said. India caught him watching Bertille so often that at last she decided to speak to him about his badly concealed interest in the girl.

"She's pretty, isn't she?" India said to Adelbert one night when his look followed Bertille to the door leading to the women's quarters and then lingered on the spot where she had disappeared. Adelbert jerked his head to one side in a clumsy attempt to hide what he had been doing.

"Any man would find her charming," India persisted, sitting down on the bench across the table from him. She kept her gaze on him until he was forced to look directly at her. In his poorly disguised irritation with her, she saw a nearer resemblance to Hank and wondered again at the similarity between them.

"There is nothing I could give the lady Bertille that Lord Marcion could not double," Adelbert said, not pretending to misunderstand her. "For all her sweet nature, she is as frivolous as most women are. She will want rank, jewels, a fine home with servants, a high title."

"Then you do care for her." India began to feel a bit sorry for him, until Adelbert quashed that sentiment.

"There is no woman who has ever been able to keep me from this." Using the feather end of his quill pen, he tapped the parchment spread before him. "Given a choice, I prefer my work

335

to a woman's fickle heart. I mean no disrespect to you, Lady India, but I would like to return to what I was doing."

"Forgive me for interrupting you," she said, rising from the bench. He did not appear to hear her, nor did he speak to her again. He bent his head, dipped his pen into the ink, and began to write. In so doing, he reminded her even more sharply of the work-obsessed Hank.

When she mentioned Adelbert to Bertille later, the girl at once became annoyed with her.

"I have told you, Adelbert is a nice enough man, but it is Marcion I want." Bertille's eyes filled with tears. "It's Marcion I miss every day, Marcion I fear for constantly and long to see again."

So there the matter of Adelbert's interest in Bertille rested, though it tugged at India's thoughts whenever she saw him. It was as if something needed to be set right, but she was not sure whether what was wrong was in the eighth century or in her own.

In early August, Hildegarde gave birth to twin sons.

"That explains why she was so large and so uncomfortable," said Bertille, sounding like the most experienced of midwives.

"Both the babies are small and will have a struggle if they are to live," Lady Remilda told India. "And the queen is very sick. She will be in bed for many days yet."

After the excitement of the royal births had

died down, summer heat and torpor once more descended upon Agen, relieved only by frequent heavy thunderstorms. Now India began to count the days. Exhausted riders sent by Charles brought occasional messages, along with their own accounts of what was happening on the other side of the Pyrenees. The tales were always what India, with her foreknowledge of the campaign, expected to hear. The Saracens were too busy fighting among themselves to provide the support they had promised to the Franks. The Christian Spaniards had joined forces with those Saracens who opposed the presence of the Franks in their land, and together they were resisting the invaders. The commander of Saragossa, who was to have opened its gates to Charles on his arrival there, instead bolted them against him, and the city had been under siege for months. There had been battles, but the Franks had gained little. They would return to Agen by the end of August.

There were women who went about the court in mourning now, more of them each time a courier brought news of new deaths. There was no word of Theu and his men. India, Danise, and Bertille grew ever closer, the differences in their ages forgotten in mutual concern and constant worry.

Chapter Twenty

With evening falling on another day of warfare, Charles, king of the Franks, sat in a wooden chair in front of the entrance to his tent, listening to the reports of his war leaders. Around him stood his closest companions, every man battle-weary and sweaty, some bearing wounds, all tight-mouthed and unhappy at the disappointing end to what should have been a glorious and fruitful campaign. Only the man facing Charles looked fresh and untouched by the events of the past few months.

"We took no prisoners." Hrulund finished his report with flashing eyes and the ring of pride in his loud voice. He swept one arm in the direction of the blazing ruins a mile or so south of the camp, inviting Charles to gaze once more on what the Franks had wrought there. "Pamplona is razed to the ground. Thus we need not concern ourselves about pursuit from either Saracens or those treacherous Spanish Christians during our return to Francia." Hrulund smiled happily at Charles's nod of approval.

"And you, Theu?" Charles asked the man standing next to Hrulund. "What have you to report?"

"We took fifty prisoners," Theu responded. "Ten of them are officers, whom I turned over to Eggihard the seneschal to hold for ransom. We disarmed the ordinary soldiers and set them free. They are too disheartened by the destruction of their city to cause any trouble until we are long departed from the vicinity of Pamplona."

"You set them free?" Hrulund's long-standing anger against Theu rose anew. "You fool! You should have killed them all, even the officers. *I* never take prisoners!"

"I know," Theu said, staying calm in the face of Hrulund's ire. "But I see no reason for senseless killing."

"There is nothing senseless about destroying Charles's enemies!"

"The more you kill after a battle is over, the more enemies you make for Charles, from the families and friends of the dead men, whereas mercy often results in compliance among the defeated."

"Why should we care about that? We are returning to Francia tomorrow, and won't have to deal with the survivors. It's your love of women that leads you to this foolish weakness. That's what's wrong with you. *Women*." Hrulund spat out the word with deep contempt.

"Be still, both of you." Charles spoke with unaccustomed sharpness. "I grow weary of the need to intervene in your constant quarrels. I have more important concerns on my mind."

"My lord." Hrulund was on his knees before Charles. "I ask a favor of you. On our journey through the mountains, allow me to lead the rear guard. Should the Saracens dare to follow us, no one will defend you more valiantly than I and my men."

"I thought you just claimed that thanks to you, there would be no pursuit," Theu began, but stopped at a warning glance from Charles.

What Hrulund had just asked for was an important command. The man who led the rear-guard would not only be responsible for protecting the vanguard of the army against attacks from the rear, but would also be in charge of protecting the baggage carts laden with the plunder accumulated in Spain. The value of this loot was less than the Franks had hoped it would be, but it was still enough to be tempting to marauders.

Then there were the people who would not be able to keep pace with the rest of the army. Those too badly wounded to ride horses or to walk would have to be carried in the baggage carts. These men, along with the camp followers, their children, and the few merchants who accompanied the army would all need protection, and many of them would in addition need compassionate help if they were to traverse the mountains and reach Francia alive. In battle, few could surpass Hrulund, but Theu did not think he was the man for a task requiring humane qualities of character.

While Hrulund talked on, trying to convince Charles, Theu thought about the repeated warnings India had given him. He thought about Hrulund's arrogance, his lack of concern for human life, including his own life, and his mad desire for glory. It would be just like Hrulund to leave the last of the army to struggle through the pass at Roncevaux on its own so that he could ride back onto the plain to engage in battle any warband his scouts might notice. But if Theu and his best men were among the rearguard, their mere presence might make Hrulund adhere to a duty that would require more patience than he usually showed. Thus, Theu and his loyal men might avert the tragedy India had foreseen.

"Very well," Charles said, raising a hand to stop the flow of Hrulund's impassioned words. "I give you command of the rear guard. Take as many men as you think you will need."

"My lord, I thank you with all my heart. I will not fail you," Hrulund said, rising from his knees. "I will choose from among my own men."

"My lord." Theu stepped forward. "Allow me to go with Hrulund."

"I don't need your levy, Firebrand," Hrulund told him rudely.

"Not my levy," Theu replied quietly. "There are too many of them for such a duty. I have my own personal warband of twelve men besides Marcion and myself. My lord, I volunteer to place myself under Hrulund's orders, and I swear to obey him until we reach Francia again. Allow me to add my strength to his so that we may all pass safely through the mountains and return our wounded to their loved ones."

"A noble gesture, to put yourself under the command of one who is not your friend," said Charles. "Is it perhaps intended to end this long and unpleasant feud between you and Hrulund?"

"My lord, if it has that result in addition to seeing all of your army home again with no further losses, then I will be happy, for I know my disagreements with Hrulund trouble you," Theu told him.

"Well said, my friend. You may go with Hrulund."

There had been much murmuring among Charles's companions during this exchange, and now several other nobles came forward, with Bishop Turpin leading them.

"Please," said Anselm the Count of the Palace, who stood with his friend Eggihard the seneschal. "Let us join Hrulund, too."

"I also would ride with my friend Hrulund," declared Bishop Turpin.

"If you all go with him, who will accompany

me?" asked Charles, hiding a smile. He knew well the respect his nobles had for Hrulund's prowess in battle—knew, too, of the friendship among Theu and many of the men now standing before him. He pointed to a few of these men. "Turpin, I know you too well to think I can prevent you from doing what you will. Go, then. Anselm, Eggihard, you may go, but not you, Marcion."

"I have ridden with Theu since I came to Francia," Marcion protested, dropping to his knees in much the same way that Hrulund had done. "Do not shame me before the Franks, my lord. Let me go, too—let me show what a good and loyal Lombard can do in service to his king."

"I said, no." Charles's voice was kind, but firm in the way his friends knew meant he would not change his mind. Softening his refusal with a smile, he added, "No one doubts your loyalty, Marcion, but I would keep my favorite hostage safe rather than chance another war with Lombardy immediately after this hard campaign. You will stay in the vanguard next to me."

"It doesn't really matter," Theu said, clapping Marcion on the shoulder. "This march across the mountains is no great thing, and it won't be for long. We will meet again tomorrow evening, in Francia." They clasped hands and parted, Theu going off to find Hugo and the rest of his men, leaving Marcion to look after him with a worried light in his eyes.

"Without me," Marcion murmured, "there will be thirteen in your band." He crossed himself several times to ward off the evil of that unlucky number.

At some distance from the royal tent, Theu fell into step beside Hrulund.

"Since we came into Spain by another route," he said pleasantly, "I have sent out several men to reconnoiter the pass at Roncevaux. They returned yesterday with some reliable advice on where it would be best to post scouts along the way. We will need to guard our flanks."

"Will you break your promise to Charles so soon?" Hrulund shouted at him. "I am in command. You are to obey me until the entire army has passed into Francia. Only Charles may countermand my orders. Remember that, Firebrand."

"I only thought you might be glad of useful recent information," Theu replied as mildly as he could manage in the face of Hrulund's belligerence. "You are welcome to speak to my scouts without my presence, if that is what you wish."

"What I wish is for you not to advise me," Hrulund declared. "I, and I alone, will decide what is useful information. You thought to ingratiate yourself with Charles by putting yourself under my command. Now obey me. Find your men and tell them to assemble before dawn. And do not question my decisions or presume to advise me again!"

Oh, India, Theu thought, watching Hrulund

stride away toward his own campsite, *you were right. Now God help us all and make our arms strong.*

On the morning of the eighteenth of August, India remained in the chapel after the service was over and the other women had gone. There was nothing she could do for Theu on that fateful day except pray. She tried to clear her mind so that she could sense any thoughts he might be sending her way, but the oppressive weight of her fear overpowered her until it shut out all else. She thought her heart would break; she thought her life would end before that day was over, and there was no one in whom she could confide. She alone, out of all those in Agen, knew what was happening in the pass at Roncevaux. Barely able to breathe from terror for Theu's sake, she prayed over and over that he would not be among those with Hrulund, or, if he were with Hrulund, that he would somehow survive to return to her unscathed.

"I told you she would be here." Bertille's voice came to India from a great distance. She felt two pairs of hands lifting her.

"Why are you lying on the stone floor? You will be sick." Danise sounded worried. "India, speak to us."

Between them, they set her on her feet. With both of them supporting her, they half carried her out of the chapel.

"Have you been there all day?" asked Bertille. "Look, the sun is setting."

"Then it's over," India rasped, her voice hoarse. Her head ached, making her close her eyes against the reddish glare of the sun. She let her friends take her toward the women's quarters. "Whatever has happened, is finished now." She began to shiver.

"Where did you find her?" asked Sister Gertrude. "The foolish creature has obviously taken a chill. Danise, help me get her into bed. Bertille, find your mother and ask her to give you a cup of the same heated wine she keeps for the queen."

Not caring what they did, India let them undress her and tuck her beneath the covers. When Bertille returned with the wine, she forced herself to drink it all, knowing they were trying to be kind to her, knowing, too, that they could not understand what was really wrong with her.

When they left her alone to sleep, and even later, after Danise had crawled into the bed they shared and had whispered good night and kissed her cold cheek, India lay dry-eyed and numb, staring into the darkness.

Chapter Twenty-One

In the high mountains, the clang of metal on metal was silenced at last. The cries of the dying had ceased. Even the reverberating echoes were stilled. Within the confines of the narrow, rocky pass, the boulders the Basques had rolled down from the heights onto the rear guard were surrounded by the smaller rocks and stones that had been hurled at the Franks after that first attack. The hand-to-hand combat had come later, under the searing August sun, with the survivors of the initial ambush sweating in heavy chain mail and the horses rearing and screaming in fright, their hooves causing as much damage as any sword to friend or foe without discrimination. It was all finished now, and there was no more sound in that place except the whine of the wind. Far above the dreadful scene, the intensely blue sky arched, pure and cloudless, while the burning sun sank toward the simmering heat of the Spanish plain.

Theuderic of Metz lay on his back, staring up at the blueness while his life seeped slowly away into the earth beneath him. A piece of gold-threaded green silk blew across his line of vision, revealing a rusty-red stain on the brightness of the scarf. Theu was too weak to turn his head, but he knew from where the silk had come. Hugo lay beside him, already stiff and cold, like the rest of his men scattered nearby. Hrulund and Turpin and their men were dead, too, along with Eggihard the seneschal and Anselm the Count of the Palace, all of them slain by their fellow Christians, just as India had warned.

India . . .

The weight of the chain mail on his chest made it difficult to breathe. His armor had never felt so heavy before. But he had never been so weak before. Theu thought about his son, growing up safe in his mother's care, and knew Charles and his mother together would see to it that the boy fared well. No cause for worry there, only sadness that he would not see his son again.

India . . .

She had loved him so willingly, and now she would know for the second time in her short life the heartbreaking loss of a man she loved, and she would have to go on without him. He was the more fortunate one, for the pain of knowing he would never see her again would be brief . . . only a few minutes more, an hour at most.

He was too weak to pray aloud, but he found the words in his mind, one by one, forming them carefully, fighting the weariness that made thought increasingly difficult.

Please send India home. Don't leave her in this time. Send her home . . . and please . . . please . . . send someone to love her. . . .

The blue sky seemed nearer now. It was surprisingly painless to die in this way, on a mountainside, with the heavens so close.

India . . . love . . . The blue enveloped him, drawing him upward, into a profound and blessed peace.

"Love never dies. Love lives on."

He did not have time to think about who had spoken those words. He only knew they were the last ones he would ever hear in his present life. It no longer mattered that in this lifetime he would never meet India again, because though his eyes were now blind to earthly sights, the blue surrounding him rolled back, so that the endless ages were revealed to him, century upon century, before him and behind him . . . eternity . . . and he understood . . . and smiled . . . and gave himself gladly to what awaited him.

"Love never dies. Love lives on."

Chapter Twenty-Two

Marcion returned to Agen with the courier who bore the terrible news. They entered the reception room unannounced. India, Bertille, and Danise were sitting together, the other two trying to make India laugh by telling silly jokes. When she first saw Marcion, India felt a glimmer of hope that eased the numbness of the past few days. She half expected to see Theu come in behind him.

"Marcion!" Bertille sprang to her feet and ran to him, throwing her arms around him. And Marcion, not caring who saw them or whether Bertille's mother had given permission or not, set down the heavy bundle he was carrying so that he could lift his betrothed off her feet and kiss her hard. Something in the desperate way he held Bertille quenched India's brief hope and must have touched Danise, too, for when India rose to go to Marcion, Danise was right behind her.

"The queen?" asked the courier, looking about the room.

"She's in the women's quarters," India said, pointing. "Through that door. She will want to receive you at once." She did not ask what news he carried. His message was for the queen's ears first. They would all know what it was soon enough, and suddenly India did not want to hear it.

Marcion set Bertille on her feet again, looking at her sadly before he released her. His eyes met India's. He did not have to say anything. She knew—*knew*—and she experienced a sensation of drifting in empty space unanchored by any attachments.

"India." Marcion's hand was on her arm. In his tear-filled eyes and on his face she saw all the pain he was feeling.

"India, you are pale as a ghost." Bertille took her hands and began to rub them. Danise clutched at India's elbow.

"I think I have known since Theu left Agen," India said, "that I would never see him again. Not in this world. Still, I could not stop hoping."

There came a long, despairing wail from the direction of the women's quarters, followed by the sounds of several women weeping.

"Not Charles?" cried Danise, wide-eyed and frightened-looking.

"Charles is well enough," said Marcion, "though he mourns deeply and blames himself for what has happened. He says now that he should never have gone into Spain."

They were joined at that point by Sister Gertrude, who at the courier's first word of disaster had left the queen's side to find Danise. They stood together before Marcion, Bertille still holding both of India's hands, Danise clinging to her arm, Sister Gertrude looking fierce, ready to defend the younger women if she could. But even she could not protect them from the news Marcion brought.

"Tell us everything," said Sister Gertrude. "It is better to know than to wonder in ignorance."

Obeying her, Marcion described first the bitter end of the Spanish campaign and how Theu had volunteered to serve under Hrulund, before he went on to tell the women what Charles and his companions, including himself, had found when they returned to Roncevaux to discover why the rear guard had failed to appear at their rendezvous.

"From the lack of our dead along the heights of all that long and winding pass, Charles has concluded that Hrulund foolishly posted no scouts to watch for attack upon his flanks," Marcion said. "Worse still, from the positions of the bodies, we could tell that when the attack came, the rear guard was riding in front of the baggage train, not along its sides and behind it as they should have been deployed if they were going to guard it properly. Only a few men were at the very end of all the carts and the stragglers."

India thought she understood why Theu had gone with Hrulund. She had given him knowledge of the future, and that knowledge had changed his actions, as he had said it could. By adding his best men to Hrulund's force he had doubtless hoped to prevent or to fight off the ambush she had warned him of. Her own thoughts having become intolerably painful at this point, she began to listen to Marcion again.

"Hrulund and Bishop Turpin, Eggihard and Anselm." Marcion recited the list of the dead, including the men of Theu's band. At each name, India recalled a face and remembered seeing that man ride off with Charles. When Marcion said Hugo's name, Danise cried out as if she had been stabbed.

"Theu's band was the group at the very end, exactly where the rearguard ought to be," Marcion said, his voice breaking. "I should have been there, too, but Charles insisted on keeping me with him."

"Danise, you have heard enough. Come away," said Sister Gertrude, "come to our room and weep in private. Bertille, help me with her, she may faint on the way. India, you come too."

"Later," India said, and gave all her attention to Marcion, whose pain she could feel in her own heart.

"After I was taken from my family and brought from Lombardy to Francia," he told her, "there were those who called Theu my jailer or my keeper, but he was never that to me. He was like an older brother, and he and Hugo became my dearest friends. Now they are gone. I should have been with them, to help them at the last." His shoulders began to shake. India drew his head down onto her own shoulder and held him while he shuddered with tears for the men they both loved.

They were not alone in their grief. The news had spread rapidly, so that everyone in the palace knew it within a few minutes after the courier had told the story to the queen. All the routine daily activities stopped at once, and a mournful silence fell over the palace, broken only by the sound of weeping.

"Why don't you cry, too?" Marcion asked, dashing the last traces of tears from his eyes and straightening his shoulders.

"I have cried all my tears already," she said, her voice dull and lifeless, "every day and every night of these last months. I have no tears left."

She had a deeper grief than Marcion knew, for added to her sense of loss was guilt. If she had not warned Theu about the ambush and about Hrulund's foolhardiness, might Hugo have survived to marry Danise and sire children who would have made their own impact upon the world? And what of Eudon, who had recovered from a boar wound in Saxony only to die in Spain? What of Osric, who would never again ride through some city gate or fortified outpost entrance calling out Theu's name and title with youthful pride and pleasure? And all the rest of that brave band—she knew and loved every man of them, and now she felt as though it was her fault they had died so young. And Theu most of all, who had listened to her warnings and taken them to heart and tried to do something about them—and who had died as a result. She stood bowed by regret and grief and guilt, until Marcion spoke again.

"I brought Theu's armor back." He picked up the bundle he had dropped on the floor when Bertille embraced him, and set it on the table. Opening it, he pulled out the chain mail. "They stole everything worth the taking, including all the swords, but Theu's *brunia* was so badly damaged they didn't bother with it. Still, I think a good armorer might be able to repair it. Charles said to send it to his son."

India touched the cold metal links, spreading the body of the *brunia* out on the table until she could see the tear through which Theu's life had drained. At the very edge of the tear there was one rivet that had been pulled half out of its link by what must have been a powerful thrust, too strong for any mortal to withstand. She touched the tear in the *brunia*, putting her finger over the damaged link where the head of the tiny rivet had been snapped off.

"The fabric of life," she whispered, thinking of a spring evening in Aachen.

She could not cry. The tears were there, inside her, but she could not let them out. She rocked back and forth, holding the edges of the

tear together as if her fingers alone could re-
store the damage, could make the *brunia* whole
again and bring Theu back, too, alive once
more, strong and loving.

"Give it back to me, India. I should not have
shown it to you." Marcion took the *brunia* from
her. "Charles has asked me to pack up the rest
of Theu's belongings and send them to his
mother. If there is anything of his you want, I'm
sure she wouldn't mind."

She looked at him from pain-filled eyes, still
rocking back and forth, though her hands were
empty now—hands and arms, both empty.

"I have my memories," she said. "I don't need
anything else."

"You are welcome to go to Lombardy with
me." The *brunia* folded away, Marcion sat down
beside her. "Bertille and I would be happy to
have you live with us, in our home."

"Two men," she said, as if she had not heard
him. "Two fine men. My husband first, then
Theu. Both died too soon, and all my efforts to
save them could not help either. Why? Why?"

"I don't know why one man lives and another
dies. Why was I with Charles and not with Theu
when he needed me?" Taking a ragged breath,
Marcion put his arm around her and pulled her
head onto his shoulder, holding her as she had
held him earlier. Only when she felt his tears
falling on her cheek did the knot that had lain
in her chest for so long begin to loosen, and she
was able to cry at last.

* * *

Charles came back to Agen two days later, leading a sorrowful army. He would not speak publicly about what had happened, leaving it to Alcuin to announce that there would be a memorial mass for the dead on the next day, after which the entire court was to move eastward at once, traveling far across Francia, to Auxerre in Burgundy.

"He may think the farther he is from the Spanish border, the easier it will be for him and for us, but that's not so," Bertille said. "There's no forgetting what has happened. India, he has ordered Marcion and me to hold our wedding as planned, saying we need to turn our thoughts to a happy occasion, and so we will be married in Auxerre. Will you be there?"

"I don't know," India replied. "I have the oddest feeling of being suspended between two places, two times. I can't explain it."

"I think I understand." Bertille put her arms around India, and it was as though Willi were hugging her, freely offering her vitality and affection to India. "My mother told Danise this morning that all grief eases with time, so please believe that yours will, too."

"Never," India whispered. "Never."

At India's insistence, Marcion went with her to the chapel where Theu's body lay next to Hugo's. Most of the dead had been buried at Roncevaux. Only a few had been brought back to Agen. Marcion had made certain that Theu and Hugo were among them.

"Hugo's coffin is closed already," India said.

Marcion did not respond to the question in her voice, nor did he look at her.

"You said you identified him." It sounded like a challenge.

"I recognized him by the scarf Danise gave him. He always wore it wrapped around his right arm," Marcion told her gruffly, then would say no more on the subject.

"I'm sorry." She made her voice softer, so he would know she was not angry with him. "How difficult that task must have been for you."

Stepping to the side of Theu's still-open coffin, she made herself look at the pale, cold face of the man she loved. He was so still in his white shroud, all the life and warmth, all the strength and humor gone out of him. Gone out of her, too. Gently she touched his shoulder as if to comfort him.

"I kept my promise, Theu. I waited for your return," she said to him. "Now it's over, all the loving and the joy and the sweet promises. Now I think it's time for me to go home."

"What are you saying?" Marcion asked.

"Don't look so worried. I'm not going to do anything foolish. It's just that I have had the strangest feeling since Theu died, as though I am meant to be somewhere else, and now I think I'm being summoned." Quickly she kissed him on the cheek. "Take good care of Bertille. She will love you all her life if you will let her. You have been such a good friend, to Theu, and Hugo, and to me. You have nothing to reproach

361

yourself with, Marcion." She kissed him again, but when he tried to hold on to her, she slipped out of his grasp.

"You are saying good-bye, aren't you?" he exclaimed. It wasn't really a question.

"I think so," she said. "I am going to miss you and Bertille."

"Where are you going?"

"Back to my own country, if I can find the way."

"But the memorial service," he protested. "You ought to be there."

"Theu will understand."

She was out of the chapel before he could stop her, heading for the palace and the women's quarters, driven by an inexplicable need for haste. Marcion followed her and stood by the chapel door watching her as she crossed the courtyard, but he made no attempt to stop her.

India hurried to the room Bertille's mother had so graciously shared with three strangers. There she found Danise sitting upon one of the beds with Sister Gertrude. When they had first arrived in Agen, Danise had made space in her small wooden clothing chest so that India could store her scanty belongings there. India knelt beside the chest, throwing open the lid and pulling out her tunic, trousers, and twentieth-century underwear.

"I hope you are planning to dispose of those men's garments," said Sister Gertrude. "The gown you wear now is more becoming and much more suitable. India, what are you doing?" This question was voiced as India lifted the blue gown and drew it over her head.

"I have to go," India replied, removing the rest of the borrowed clothing and donning her own, oblivious to the stares of Sister Gertrude and Danise. When she was dressed, India knelt beside Danise and took her hand. "I am going home. I am sorry to leave you while you are so unhappy, but I believe that I have no choice."

"Neither have I," said Danise in a low, sad voice. "Not with Hugo gone."

"Thus did it happen to me when I was young," Sister Gertrude told India. "I hope now to convince Danise to return to Chelles and stay there. The cloister provides a far happier life for a woman than marriage to a warrior."

"Don't force her," India begged. "She is so distressed right now that she can't know what she really wants."

"Danise will find peace and gentle comfort at Chelles," Sister Gertrude replied. "She will not be forced, but all of the sisters will rejoice if she freely decides to remain with us."

"Thank you. I know you will take good care of her." Impulsively, India kissed the nun's cheek and was surprised to have the kiss returned. She kissed Danise, too, and smoothed the pale hair that hung loose down her back. Danise burst into tears and clung to her until Sister Gertrude took the girl into her own arms.

"Go at once," Sister Gertrude said to India. "I will stay with Danise, and I will make your farewells to Charles and Hildegarde, and to Lady Remilda."

India met Bertille at the door of the women's quarters.

"Marcion told me," Bertille said. "Weren't you going to say farewell to me?"

"Of course I was. I came here a stranger, and now I have so many friends. I count you among them. You cannot know how hard this leave-taking is," India said to her. "I will never see any of you again."

"If we had known each other longer, I feel certain we would have become like sisters," Bertille said.

"In another time, and another place, we will be," India responded, knowing Bertille would not understand what she meant, but certain in her heart that she spoke the truth.

"I wish you a safe journey." Bertille hugged her. "Don't forget me."

"Not in twelve hundred years," India told her, laughing to hide her sudden desire to cry. "Will you see to Danise? She needs a friend near her own age right now."

There was only one other good-bye left to say. India found Alcuin in the reception room. Unusually for him, he was not reading, writing, or engaged in conversation. This most gregarious of scholars was sitting alone at one of the trestle tables, an untouched cup of wine before him, staring at his hands. When he heard her step, the eyes he raised to India's face were reddened. He looked tired and drawn, as if he had not slept for days. He regarded her costume with no hint of surprise.

"I am going home, dear friend," she said.

"So I gathered, from the manner of your dress," he replied.

"I wish I could tell you what I know about your work and what it will mean to those who come after you. I think the knowledge would lighten your sorrow today. But I know better now than to speak of such things, after making the mistake of revealing too much to Theu and thus costing him and his men their lives."

"Do not blame yourself for what has happened," Alcuin said. "There is seldom one single cause for any event. This is an axiom even more true during warfare, when so many men and innumerable opposing motives are combined. Charles would take all the blame on himself. Others fault Hrulund. Some call Roncevaux a defeat more glorious than many a victory and believe Hrulund was a great hero. Others say he was guilty of dereliction of duty for neglecting to post scouts to watch his flanks. After listening to so many conflicting versions of what happened, I doubt if your remarks to Theu could have made any difference to the outcome of that ambush. No, not even if you had complete foreknowledge of the future."

Startled, she looked directly into his eyes,

seeing there compassion mixed with something more—an understanding that far transcended the minds of most other men of his time.

"What happened at Roncevaux was meant to happen in exactly the way it did happen," said Alcuin. "It was part of heaven's plan, which our earthbound, human minds are too limited to comprehend. Perhaps we will understand it more fully in the next world." Rising, he took her by the shoulders and kissed her on each cheek.

"Go in peace, India. Remember me in that far land of yours."

"Always, dear friend." She could say nothing more. Her throat was too constricted to allow speech, but her heart was a little lighter. Though he was only a deacon and not an ordained priest, yet she felt as if Alcuin had absolved her of her aching, heavy guilt.

Leaving the reception room, she made her way to the stable, where the chestnut mare Theu had given her was kept since he had gone to Spain. She knew how to saddle it with no help from anyone. She had learned how to do it in these past months. She had learned so much in Francia. How to love again. How to rejoice in life, brief though it might be. And now, thanks to Alcuin, she had begun to accept both pain and loss, and she could give up her feeling that Theu's death was all her fault.

The present encampment outside Agen was smaller than the one in the spring of that year.

Aside from the absence of those who had died in battle or from disease, some of the levies had already left for home, and a few companies had been posted to citadels along the Spanish March, to keep the border secure against both Saracens and Basques. No one spoke to India or tried to stop her when she guided her mount across the field. Her hair had grown to just below her shoulders, longer than Frankish men wore theirs, but a casual glance at her would still have shown a young man in the saddle, without baggage or fine clothing, no one of interest to any soldier.

She had to search a while to find the path she and Theu had taken in the spring. The hillside looked different with almost five months of growth upon it. The leaves of the trees had the slightly dry, dusty look that comes toward summer's end, and as India's horse climbed higher along the path, she saw gleaming red or purple berries on many bushes. When she reached the place where she and Theu had picnicked and made love on their last day together, she found it overgrown with weeds and wildflowers. Here and there a few poppies showed bright red, like gouts of blood, and at the spot where India and Theu had lain together, a cluster of blue flowers grew, as if the dye from Theu's cloak had stained them.

India dismounted and looked about her. The scene from the hill was overlaid by a soft golden haze of heat and dust. Below, the Garonne flowed peacefully toward the sea, its smooth surface a ribbon of polished brass. High in a pine tree a bird twittered, but there was no other sound. There was not even a breeze to make the leaves rustle.

"Good-bye, friend," India said to her horse, fastening reins to saddle so they would not snag and thus bind the animal to some tree or bush along the way. "You go home, too. Marcion will be looking for you."

She slapped the horse on its rump and watched it wander away until it was lost to sight on the downward path. Then she went to the patch of blue flowers.

"It was right here that Hank found me the last time," she said aloud. "I will wait here."

Sitting down, she put one hand on the flowers. The unsettled feeling she had experienced ever since learning of Theu's death grew stronger. Having lost the one person who had held her securely in the past, she now felt suspended somewhere in disconnected time, between the eighth and the twentieth centuries. If Hank were still searching for her after so many months had passed, she believed it would be easier for him to locate and retrieve her while she was in this odd, floating state. She thought she might make Hank's task easier still by returning to a location he had touched once before.

And so she sat upon the long August grass while the afternoon waned and the sun slipped closer to the horizon. Around her a peculiar silence slowly grew. The single noisy bird stopped twittering. The sun sank lower still, and now a peach-gold ray of light shone full upon India's face. When she looked into it, she thought she saw movement—dark shapes forming and reforming and, finally, the shadows of human figures.

"Hank?" She scrambled to her feet. Raising her voice, she called, "Hank? Is it you?"

Gradually, the ray of light became a pulsating globe. India took a step toward it. Inside the globe, in the very center of the light, appeared a tunnel of darkness that drew her to it with an inexorable force. She had no desire to resist that force. She took another step, another....

"Innndiaaa!"

"Willi? Hank?"

The dark tunnel was closer, but its edges had begun to waver, and the darkness looked somehow fragile to her, as if it would not last long.

"Innndiaaa!"

She believed this would be her last chance to return to the time where she belonged, and she sensed that if she was to go, it had to be then, that moment, for the whole apparition of peach-gold light and the darkness at its center was changing, fluctuating, even as she peered into it.

Suddenly India did not care if it was death she would embrace within that light, or life in her own time. Opening her arms, she ran through the light and directly into the central darkness....

. . . Where nausea assailed her and complicated mathematical equations flashed before her eyes, where shapes and patterns formed and reformed . . .

Where she was falling, falling, through black, empty space and time . . .

Chapter Twenty-Three

The blackness enveloping her ended abruptly, and India found herself standing next to the computer in Hank's office.

"Am I glad to see you!" cried a familiar voice.

"Bertille?" India blinked once, then, seeing more clearly said, "Willi. Oh, Willi."

"Hang on, kid. Don't faint on me now. Here, sit down." Willi pushed the chair toward India, who immediately took advantage of it. "If you feel dizzy, put your head down."

"I'm all right." Looking around, India saw Hank watching her. "I knew you would keep trying to reach me, even after more than five months, even after failing the first three times."

"Five months? Do you mean that much time has passed for you?" Hank's serious face was transformed by a huge smile. "This is wonderful! You've confirmed my theory about time passing at different speeds—India, I want to know exactly when you were aware of my attempts to get you back. Wait a minute, I have to find some paper so I can write down everything you say. I wish I had a tape recorder."

"You wait a minute," Willi told him, shoving him on the chest to push him away from India. "Look at her, she's worn out. She's had a miserable day. Give her a break, Hank."

"What day is it now?" India was beginning to absorb the fact that time had passed very differently for her than for Willi and Hank.

"This is December twenty-second. It's still the same day," Willi answered. "At least, I think it is. It must be close to midnight by now, so it could be the twenty-third. Hank says you disappeared at noon, just before I got here. That would mean you were gone about twelve hours. India, what happened to you? Why is your hair so long? You just had it cut a couple of days ago."

"Exactly where were you?" Hank grabbed the notebook India had left next to the computer. Flipping the cover back, he picked up a pencil, then gave India an expectant look. When she did not answer him, he followed his first question with several more. "Do you know how long you were there by local time? Who did you meet? Did you have trouble digesting the food? What about the language? Could you understand it? Were you ever sick? I want every detail you can remember."

"Okay," Willi said, taking the notebook and pencil out of his hands. "That's enough. We both have to let up on the questions."

"If I don't debrief her immediately," Hank protested, "she might begin to forget what happened to her. Then how would I get the information I need to try again? After all, I can't stop now. Given all the possibilities of the space-time continuum—"

"Adelbert," India interrupted him, "you have no idea what you are saying. I never want to hear another word about your space-time continuum."

Adelbert? Hank mouthed to Willi. Aloud, he asked, "Did you tell her my middle name?"

"Never mind that." Willi was growing impatient. Pointing to the computer, she ordered, "Shut that thing down. Do it now, and do it permanently."

"I can't do that," Hank sputtered.

"If you don't," Willi told him, "I will report you for taking material from the storeroom without a requisition. I will back up the complaint Professor Moore is going to make to Campus Security. I'll tell everything I know about the keys you have that you shouldn't have on that key ring of yours. And I will talk, loud and clear to anyone who will listen, about what happened here today."

"You're talking about taking away my chance at a Nobel Prize for Science," Hank declared with great indignation.

"No." Willi was so angry her voice cracked. "I

am talking about getting you fired, which will mean you no longer have access to this room."

"But my experiments—my theories—you can't mean this!"

"I am talking," Willi said, speaking right over Hank's words, "about my best friend's life, for which you seem to have no concern. You self-absorbed lunatic, India could have died because of you and your experiments."

"But she didn't die!" Hank yelled. "Don't you realize how important my work is?"

"Indeed, I do." A bit calmer after having vented some of her rage, Willi gave him a cold, assessing look. "You care more for your work than for India's life, or for me. In fact, your work is all you really do care about."

This accusation was followed by a long moment of silence. Hank drew in a deep breath and let it out again.

"You're right, Willi," he said. "It's a relief to admit it. It's true. I love my computer and my theories too much ever to have enough free time to make any woman happy."

"You do understand, what happened here today means you and I are through," Willi said.

"Yeah," Hank replied. "I guess it does."

India had been watching and listening to this bickering in a bemused state, while her thoughts and all her sensibilities gradually became reoriented to the twentieth century. She would never have expected Willi to give up Hank so easily, but Willi seemed almost indifferent to the end of their relationship.

In Hank's remarks, India heard an echo of Adelbert's voice from long ago, saying something similar. She was not at all surprised. If it had been wrong for Adelbert and Bertille to be lovers in the eighth century, then it was equally wrong for Willi and Hank to have a romantic relationship in the twentieth century. Souls not meant for each other could never be happy together; souls intended to be together would always find each other.

That idea jolted India, but at the moment, she was still too confused and queasy to give it the consideration it deserved. She sat rubbing at her forehead and wishing her stomach would settle down, when suddenly the office door opened. When she saw the slender, curly-haired man who entered, the world tilted crazily on its axis once more.

"Marcion?" India stood up a little unsteadily.

"No, Mark Brant," the man said, holding out a hand. "Are you the lost friend, come home at last?"

"Something like that," she replied weakly. While shaking his hand, she became aware of the differences as well as the similarities between this man and Marcion. His eyes were blue and his nose not quite so high-bridged as Marcion's had been. His chin was wider, too. But Marcion's laughter and warm heart were in him, and it was those qualities she had recognized at once.

"What are you doing here so late?" Willi asked Mark.

"I couldn't get you out of my mind," he told her, "or your friend, either. I was worried about both of you, so I came back. Are you sure you're all right?" He asked the question of India, but at once returned his gaze to Willi. The way Willi looked back at him had a wonderfully steadying effect on India's nerves.

"Of course," India murmured. "Marcion and Bertille. Willi and Mark. That's the way it was always meant to be." Again the earth shifted a little beneath her feet, before it began to spin once more in its preordained motion.

"Hank," India said, "if you won't listen to Willi, then listen to me. You have to shut down this machine and destroy your program. You cannot imagine how much harm that program has caused. I believe everything is back in place now, but only because you were lucky. Only because I am here and not there."

"What is she talking about?" asked Mark Brant. An instant later, he caught India when she put one hand to her head and went limp. "Careful, there. Are you dizzy?"

"It's getting better." India leaned against him as if he were a dear and familiar friend. Which he was, though he did not know it.

"Kid, you look awful," Willi said. "You've had enough excitement for one day. Come on, I'm going to drive you home."

"No, you are not," declared Mark Brant. Willi had picked up India's pocketbook and was searching for her car keys. As soon as she found them, Mark took them out of her hand. "I am driving. It's too late for you to be out alone. If your friend here faints, how are you going to carry her from the car to her house?"

"Do as he says," India advised. "Just for tonight, let him take care of us."

"Sensible woman. I think I'm going to like you." Mark gave her an approving look. "Can you walk, or shall I carry you?"

"I'll walk. But before we leave, there are a couple of things I have to do. Hank, give me my floppy disks."

"Here." He handed her the disk that was lying on the table beside the keyboard.

"I want the other one, too."

"Aw, India—" Hank's protest was cut off when India brushed aside Mark's supporting arm to stand alone. She took a menacing step toward Hank, frowning at him.

"*Give me the disk.*" Never had she been so determined. Behind her, she heard Mark emit a soft whistle of surprise. Reluctantly, Hank slowly removed the second floppy disk from the computer. "The notebook, too," India said.

"I'm keeping the notes I just made. They're mine." Hank tore the last two pages out of the notebook. "These were blank when I used them."

"Just one more thing." India took back the second floppy disk and the notebook, putting them into her purse. "Don't bother asking me any more questions, Hank, because I won't answer them. I will not tell you what happened to me, or help you to confirm your theories in any

377

way. Just believe me when I say you must never use that program again."

"I can't use that particular one," he replied. "You stopped me from doing that when you took the disk. Without it, there is no way I can ever replicate what happened here."

"I hope that's true. Good-bye, Hank." It was India who closed the office door. Out in the hall, Mark Brant winked at her, and Willi looked amazed.

"Wow," Willi said, "good for you, kid. I never heard you talk tough like that before."

"My brother is going to love you," said Mark.

"I beg your pardon?" India stared at him.

"He's your new boss, as of the first of the year. But you already knew that, didn't you? Theodore Brant, chairman of the Department of History and Political Science. Sounds impressive, doesn't it?"

"Theodore? Oh, yes, I remember now." India could not take her eyes off Mark's expressive face.

"An old family name, traditional to the eldest son since time began," he said, laughing. "Most people call him Ted, but I've always had my own nickname for him. It's more poetic. Theo. Hey, watch out! It's all right, I've got you. Willi, pick up the stuff she dropped, will you please? I told you she'd faint and someone would have to carry her. . . ."

Chapter Twenty-Four

"Hello again."

"Mr. Brant." Willi pulled her old flannel bathrobe closer about her throat. "What are you doing here? What time is it?"

"Six-thirty. I wanted to see you before you left for work."

"Oh. Sure." Willi wasn't fully awake yet. She was finding it hard to think, especially with an indescribably handsome man leaning against her door frame and smiling at her. In his navy blue peacoat over a cream wool cableknit sweater and tight jeans, Mark Brant looked like a British sailor out of an old World War II movie—and just about as rakish, too. Willi had never seen a smile quite so devastating, or so mischievous.

"Are you going to let me in?" he asked. "Or

would you rather I wait out here until you get dressed?"

For a moment she wished he would leave. She knew she looked awful. She had been sound asleep when the doorbell rang. She hadn't taken time to splash water on her face, hadn't combed her hair or brushed her teeth, and she wasn't wearing any makeup.

"I woke you up, didn't I?" Mark Brant straightened from his relaxed position. "I'm sorry. I shouldn't have come so early, but I need to talk to you."

"It's all right." Suddenly she was afraid he *would* leave and she would never see him again. She pulled the door wider. "Come in, Mr. Brant."

"Mark," he said. "I told you last night to call me Mark."

"Would you like some coffee?" Willi headed toward the stove.

"Why don't I take you out to breakfast? It's the least I can do after waking you so early, and we have plenty of time before you have to be at work."

Willi did not ask him how he knew what time she started work. She just watched while he picked up the afghan from the couch and folded it, laying it across the back of the couch. He did not appear to be at all disdainful of the place where she lived—in fact he looked right at home there—but Willi was embarrassed.

It was all she could afford, a one-room apartment with a couch that opened into a bed, a miniature kitchen built into one wall and hidden by a folding door, and a bathroom Willi could barely turn around in. Usually she was proud of the way she kept it neat and cheerful with lots of plants in the window, but now she thought it looked shabby. At least she hadn't opened the couch, so her unexpected guest wasn't confronted by rumpled bedding. She had been so tired the night before that she had just pulled off her clothes, wrapped up in her bathrobe, and dropped onto the couch with the afghan for a blanket.

"After everything you did for India, I should make breakfast for you," she said to Mark.

"Not a chance. I want a big meal, and I don't want you so preoccupied with cooking that you can't talk to me. What about the Blue Ridge Coffee House?" Willi was standing next to the kitchen wall, and Mark was at the far side of the room, but when his brilliant blue eyes met hers, she felt as if he was caressing her.

"You look softer today than you did last night," he murmured. "What a remarkably pretty woman you are. If it weren't such a tired line, I'd ask you if we've ever met before."

She was startled by his words because she felt the same sense of familiarity. But she knew they had never met before yesterday. There was no way she would ever have forgotten a man like Mark Brant.

"I'll get dressed." Willi broke the disturbing eye contact and took a step toward the bathroom. She paused. "Just so you know, I've sworn off men for a while. After what happened with Hank, I need a breather, to get my head together."

"It's only breakfast," he said, smiling. As she began to close the bathroom door, Willi heard him add, "Breakfast and a few dozen questions."

Willi didn't go to the Blue Ridge Coffee Shop very often and had never been there in early morning. Among all the tweedy academic types and the conservative businessmen in dark suits and neckties who were apparently holding serious meetings over breakfast, Willi felt unusually conspicuous in her black leather outfit and maroon turtleneck. She also felt slightly naked without her usual heavy mask of makeup. Mark's comment that she was pretty, coming when her face was completely bare, had led her to apply only a dusting of powder, a smudge of dark eyeshadow, and a single coat of mascara. Her bloodred lipstick she had blotted until it was no more than a rosy tint on her lips. The look Mark had given her as they left her apartment convinced her she had done the right thing in toning down the makeup, but she wasn't used to going out that way. Heavy makeup and black leather were her armor against the snubs of an uncaring world. Now part of her armor was missing, and she was beginning to think she needed it because, while plying her with a huge breakfast, Mark was grilling her like the sausages on his plate.

"I think you have just learned everything there is to know about me," she protested. "All these questions make me uneasy. I don't usually talk about myself or my life, except to India."

"About India," he said, watching her with probing eyes.

"It's your turn now. Tell me about yourself," Willi said quickly, to intercept the questions she saw coming on the subject of her best friend. "What do you do? Are you a college professor like your brother? You don't look solemn enough for that."

"I can be serious when the subject demands it." He certainly looked serious enough right now. "I'm an astrophysicist."

"Oh, dear God, not another one!" Willi nearly choked on her French toast.

"What do you mean, 'another one?'" His voice had taken on a strangely cold timbre.

"Hank was always involved with numbers and complicated formulas, too," Willi said. "I was hoping maybe you taught English literature, or Romance languages, or possibly you might be an artist. I would love to meet someone with a job I could understand."

"Would it sound simpler if I told you I have worked on the space program?" He watched her sip her coffee. "The caffeine doesn't seem to be doing much good. You still look depressed. Willi, I want to know what Hank was doing yesterday."

"He was just fooling around, playing games with the computer." Willi's gaze dropped to the cup in her hand. She set it down very carefully, bracing herself for more questions.

"A man in my line of work knows more than most people about computers, and about what they can do." Mark's hand covered hers. His voice was compelling. "Willi, look at me."

Reluctantly, she met his bright blue eyes. Having done so, she found she could not look away.

"Tell me what Hank was doing."

"I honestly don't understand it," she said.

"Was he trying to break into some other system?"

"You mean, is he a hacker? No, I'm sure he's not. Hank is too independent to get involved in someone else's work. I think he wants to be the sole author of any discoveries he makes. He was talking about a Nobel Prize."

"Was he? That suggests something more than an idle game. Willi, I am serious about this. I want you to tell me anything you know about Hank's work. Professor Moore told me you were with Hank all day yesterday and that he has often seen you in Hank's office in the past. You are too intelligent not to have noticed the changes Hank made to that computer. Why did he add those components?" When she sat silent, staring down at his hand over hers, Mark said, "*Talk*, Willi."

"Did you join the CIA after you left NASA?" she asked.

"Don't ask silly questions." His voice was

stern. "I haven't said anything about either organization. And stop putting me off."

"Maybe you worked for the Spanish Inquisition."

"Willi." Now he sounded thoroughly exasperated.

"Okay, I give up." Willi did not want Mark Brant to be angry with her. She wanted him to like her and to speak to her in a kinder voice. "Hank always made me promise to keep quiet about anything I saw or heard in his office. But I don't know why I should still be loyal to him. He never really cared about me. I was just a convenience to him. He admitted as much last night. And after what he did to India—"

"What did he do to India? Where was she when you said Hank had 'lost' her? Why was she missing for so long? Why did she look sick and nearly faint when I walked in on you?"

"Why are you asking all these questions? Who are you?"

"Just call me a curious scientist." His blue eyes were almost hypnotic in their intensity. His voice was low and gentle, coaxing her. "Tell me what you know."

"Hank has some crazy theories about space and time. He's trying to prove the theories are right."

"Go on." The blue eyes did not waver. "How did India get involved? Was she working with him?"

"No. It was my fault." Quickly, she explained

how she had asked Hank to give India computer lessons. "According to Hank, he arrived at his office just as something unexpected was happening. He claimed that India had vanished into the computer."

"So the first time I walked in on you, during the afternoon, Hank was trying to get her back?" Mark did not seem at all surprised by what Willi had told him. Nor did he question whether it had actually happened. "How long did this episode last?"

Willi told him everything she knew, including the brief, mysterious appearance of a man with a sword. Upon hearing that piece of information, Mark's face went white and tense, and he made her repeat what she had said.

"Have you finished your meal?" he asked with just the slightest hint of impatience.

"I couldn't possibly eat anything else." His persistent questioning was making her more than nervous. She was beginning to be frightened.

"Let's go, then." Mark was on his feet, reaching out to help her up from the table. Willi was used to taking care of herself, but it was nice to have a man's hand on her back, guiding her toward the door.

"Where are we going?" she asked.

"To the university," he replied. "I just hope we aren't too late."

"Damn it! I should have taken care of this last night." Mark looked around Hank's office in disgusted frustration. "I should have expected him to dismantle everything after we left."

"What you should have done was call me right away," said the chief of Campus Security, who had let them into the office. "You say Professor Moore is planning to file an official complaint about Marsh's activities? That will be a help, but let's see if we can speed up the investigation. Can you tell me what's missing in here?"

"Nothing that belongs to the university is gone." It was Willi who answered him. She picked up a heavy electrical cable that had been disconnected, then neatly coiled and left on top of the table. "Every piece of equipment Hank was using is still here, but the room has been completely rearranged. I'm sorry, but I don't remember exactly how the components were connected." Sighing, she put the cable down again.

"Are you saying that he didn't steal anything?" The security chief looked offended.

"He did take away his papers," Willi said. "I'd be willing to bet he took any floppy disks he had, along with all the written information about his programs."

"If there hasn't been a theft," said the security chief, "then I don't think the local police will be interested in this. The university may want to sue him to recover the information on his project, but that will be up to Administration. I will have the lock on this door changed, just in case he plans to come back and remove any of this stuff. That's about all I can do here." He locked the door with his master key, then went off muttering about having to write up a report.

"Thanks for your help," Mark said to Willi. "You don't want to be late for work. I have to make a few phone calls."

"You can't dismiss me that easily," she declared. "I have answered every question you put to me. Now I have some questions for you."

"I'm sure you have, and I'll answer them as soon as I can. Willi, you said earlier that you were going to call India during your lunch break. When you do, will you ask her if she'll talk to me in the next day or so? It's important. And if you should see Hank, be careful."

"He wouldn't hurt me," Willi said. "Hank isn't a violent man."

"Not in the way you mean, no. But he could put you into the same danger India was in. I don't want anything unpleasant to happen to you." Mark placed one finger beneath Willi's chin, tipping her face upward. For a fraction of a second, for not even the length of a heartbeat, his lips brushed hers. Then he was gone, striding down the hall toward the main entrance. He had said nothing about seeing her again, but Willi knew he would be back.

Late that afternoon, a pale, wan India opened her door to Willi.

"How are you feeling?" Willi stepped over the loudly purring Charlemagne and followed India into the living room.

"I have never been so tired." India dropped

into a chair. At once, Charlemagne jumped onto her lap, rubbing against her. Absently, India scratched his ears. She wasn't actually paying attention to the cat, and Willi had the feeling that India didn't really see *her*, either. India appeared to be somewhere else.

"Professor Moore said you called in sick this morning," Willi remarked with deceptive casualness. "Okay, kid, here's what we'll do. We'll tell everyone you have a bad case of the flu. That'll give you at least a few days to stay home and pull yourself together, and people won't bother you for fear of catching whatever you have and being sick over the holidays themselves."

"I guess so." India sounded so indecisive that Willi began to be seriously concerned about her condition.

"India, can you tell me what happened to you yesterday? Do you *know* what happened?"

"I can't talk about it." India sounded on the verge of tears.

"In that case, I have just one more question for you, kid." Willi tried to sound enthusiastic because she wanted a positive response. "Am I still invited for Christmas dinner?" To her dismay, India looked at her blankly as if she had forgotten what time of year it was.

"Christmas dinner will probably be boiled potatoes or tomato soup," India said at last. "That's all the food I have in the house, and I don't think I can bear to go to the grocery store. But if you don't mind the menu, yes, please come. I don't think I want to be alone on Christmas Day."

"Just leave the menu to me, kid." Willi smiled at India, trying to hide her growing concern. "You supply the working stove, and I'll take care of everything else."

When Mark called Willi late that evening, she bit back the exclamation of relief that came to her lips. Nor did she tell him she had been waiting by the telephone for hours.

"I never asked India if she would talk to you," Willi said. "She's so sad, Mark, almost as if she's in mourning. She was like this after Robert died, but I thought she was starting to come out of it." When she told him about the Christmas dinner she was planning to cook for India, Mark broke in.

"Could I crash your party?"

"I'm not sure. India doesn't know you."

"Yes, she does. I'm the man who carried her upstairs to bed last night after she almost fainted again," he reminded her.

"Well," Willi said slowly, "if someone else is there, she might try to cheer up. She might even eat." Willi did not add that she wanted Mark to be present for her own sake.

"Good thinking." The rich sound of his voice cut through her worry over India, warming her. "We'll do it together, Willi. The university closes for the holiday at noon tomorrow, doesn't it? I'll pick you up at your office and we'll go shopping."

Willi hung up the telephone and sat back on the couch, staring at the ceiling but not seeing it. What was it about Mark Brant that touched her so deeply? She sensed that he was in some way different from other men she had known, but she could not decide exactly what the difference was—just that underlying feeling of warm familiarity, of closeness, as if they had known each other long ago. . . .

They bought food and decorations and a small tree for India, and stored it all in Willi's apartment. Mark also bought a table-sized tree for Willi, and a string of tiny white lights to decorate it. She brought out the few ornaments that had survived since her childhood and hung them on the tree, and Mark topped it with a new silver star. Watching his intent face and his fine, sensitive hands while he worked, Willi's eyes misted over until everything in her apartment was seen in soft focus. With Mark there, somehow the single room took on a romantic appearance. She resisted a sudden desire to touch him.

"Do you ever look at the stars?" he asked, taking his hands away from the one on the tree.

"Not since I was little. I'm not sure I could find the Big Dipper anymore."

"Then it's time to start again. I propose a Christmas Eve picnic."

She did not object that it was a cold night. When he looked at her and smiled, she knew she would willingly go anywhere with him.

He bought hamburgers and french fries and soda at the local take-out store, then drove her to a hilltop well away from the lights of Cheswick. There he spread a blanket and they sat upon it, eating while he pointed out the stars to her and named the constellations and told her about his work.

Willi expected him to try to make love to her, but he did not. When he pulled a second blanket over their shoulders, wrapping them together in a cozy cocoon, it wasn't so he could fumble and grope at her, it was to keep her warm. She wasn't sure whether to be glad or unhappy about the kind of treatment she was getting from Mark. No man, not even Hank, had ever talked to her the way Mark did, as if he assumed she could follow his reasoning and understand what he meant when he used scientific terms. The funny thing was that she did understand what he meant—most of it, anyway.

It was lovely sitting beside Mark and listening to him talk. It felt good to be treated like a respectable and important human being again, after Hank's casual indifference. A little of Willi's tough, defensive outer shell began to melt that night while she sat with Mark's arm around her, looking at the stars and trying to remember all their names as he recited them. When he finally took her home, she was afraid he would break the spell by asking to spend the night, but he only brushed his lips across hers as he had done the day before and said he would see her on the morrow.

Inside her apartment once more, Willi turned on the tree lights and gently touched the star Mark had placed on the topmost branch. She left the other lights off while she undressed. The little white bulbs were illumination enough. They shone like miniature stars, and even after she pulled the plug and crawled into bed in the darkness, the street lamp outside her window sent a ray of light to shine upon the silver star at the top of the tree.

"Mark's star," she murmured. It was the last thing she saw before she closed her eyes.

Chapter Twenty-Five

It was the oddest Christmas Day India could ever remember. The sensation of jarring discrepancy she had felt upon first returning to the twentieth century had gradually faded over the last two days. She knew exactly where and when she was living, but the empty place in her heart where Theu's vital image had once dwelt was still an aching wound.

Mired in the grey pain of mourning, her only source of pleasure on that holiday lay in watching the easy way in which Mark and Willi talked and laughed together as they prepared the Christmas feast. India was pleased by the changes she noticed in her friend. Willi was wearing her usual black leather miniskirt, on this day topped by a bright green turtleneck sweater, but there was a new softness to her makeup, and her flamboyant red nail polish was gone. Instead, Willi's nails were a quiet shade of pink. The biggest change of all was that Willi's former sadness, the remnant of a difficult and impoverished girlhood, was missing from her eyes. And not once during that entire day did Willi call India *kid* in her old, tough way.

As for Mark, when he was not devoting all his attention to Willi, he spent his time probing India's memories about what had happened to her. He did it with delicacy and skill, by repeatedly steering the conversation onto the subject of the previous Sunday and then asking tactful questions. Whenever India tried to divert him, he went along for a while, talking about other things, but he always returned to his primary topic of interest. Dinner was over and the three of them were sitting in the living room, where logs blazed in the fireplace and the tree Willi and Mark had brought glittered in the bay window, when India decided that the best way to handle Mark's curiosity was by direct confrontation.

"I wish you would leave the subject alone," she said. "It is very difficult for me to think about that day, much less talk about it."

"I'm not prying," Mark told her. "There is a more serious reason behind my questions. I was hoping you would have some information that would help to stop Hank before he causes more trouble and puts someone else into danger. I know what Hank was trying to do—Willi told me as much as she could about his private project. From what she said, and from what I saw in Hank's office, I have been able to make a couple of intelligent guesses. There have been a few other projects based on theories like Hank's, begun by people like him, working alone and not fully understanding the damage they could cause. You cannot go back and tinker with the past. If you try, the changes you make, no matter how small, will mushroom exponentially until they alter the world we know. That's why I have called in a friend of mine, who is going to try to locate Hank and talk some sense into him."

"Will he go to jail?" asked Willi.

"Not unless the university decides to press charges against him for copying all those keys and for diverting material from the storeroom to his own use. It seems that the project was entirely his own, and had nothing to do with the university, or his actual job there. There are no laws against what Hank was trying to do. That's why my friend's investigation will have to be unofficial." Mark paused, watching his hostess's reaction to what he had said. "What is it, India? You have the strangest expression on your face."

"I was wondering if the world has already been changed by what happened last Sunday. If it has, we'll never know it, will we? The changes will just be part of our past and will seem perfectly natural to us. I can tell you this much, Mark—I cannot regret what happened, and if I had to live that time over again, I would

probably say and do exactly the same things."
They were both staring at her as if she had said
something completely outrageous. India
pressed her lips together, imposing silence on
herself, vowing not to say another word on the
subject, or about Hank."

On the Saturday morning after Christmas,
Hank came to see her. He was standing on the
front porch when India opened the door to take
her mail out of the box.

"I'm leaving town," he said. "I can't get near
Willi because that Brant guy is always hanging
around her, so I decided to ask you to tell her
good-bye for me."

"There are people looking for you," she said.

"I know. Some friend of Brant's wants to talk
to me. I plan on disappearing before he catches
up with me. I've been fired—did Willi tell you?
And they fined me for the keys I had made. They
said it was to cover the cost of changing all the
locks."

"I'm sorry you were fired, Hank, but you
should have expected it." She stood back, letting
him into the front hall. "Do you need anything?
Can I help you in some way?"

"I could use a cup of coffee." He followed her
toward the kitchen, looking about with interest
as he walked down the hall. "Nice house you
have here. It's pretty big for one person, isn't it?
You must get lost in all these rooms."

"What will you do now?" India asked when

they sat at the kitchen table sharing cinnamon buns and coffee.

"I'll find another job, somewhere far from Cheswick. How are you doing, India? No residual aftereffects? When I asked about you in the history department, they told me you've been sick."

"I'm all right now. I just needed a few days to sort out my thoughts."

"What about the big retirement party for Professor Moore on Monday night? Are you going to it?"

"I haven't decided yet," she said.

"You ought to go," he told her. "It would do you good to get out of this mausoleum. Look, India, would you consider giving me those floppy disks to play around with?"

"No," she said. "I would not. I told you that on Sunday night."

"Then I'd better leave before Willi or her new boyfriend arrive." Hank gulped the rest of his coffee and picked up an extra bun before rising from the table.

"Have you got any leads on new jobs?" India asked.

"Maybe." His sharp, distrustful eyes met hers, then veered away. "I'll find something. And I'll try again. I'll keep experimenting until some day I'll succeed in a way that will make all of you sit up and take notice."

"You still don't understand, do you?" India cried. "What you are trying to do is dangerous—

potentially very destructive to people's lives. Hank, you have to stop!"

"Oh, come on, now." He was completely unrepentant. "You know I gave you the greatest adventure of your life. Well, so long, India. Do me a favor, will you? Forget to say good-bye to Willi for me. Don't tell anyone I was here."

She stood in the doorway, watching him go down the walk. When he was too far away to hear her, she whispered after him, "It *was* a great adventure. Good-bye, Hank."

Shortly after noon of that same day, Willi appeared carrying a garment bag.

"Mark asked me to go to Professor Moore's retirement party with him," Willi announced. "I want your opinion on the dress I just bought. Isn't this weird? Just a little over a week ago, *I* was giving *you* advice on how to dress."

A week ago for you. For me, it was six months ago. India did not say what she was thinking. She followed Willi upstairs to the second floor, into her own bedroom. There she sat upon the padded windowseat while Willi modeled the dress for her. Charlemagne prowled across the room, pausing to rub against Willi's legs before he jumped up beside India and promptly fell asleep.

"What do you think?" asked Willi, twirling around twice for India's inspection. The dress was pale turquoise with a draped bodice, long sleeves, and a short, flaring skirt. "It's not my usual style, but I thought something elegant might be nice for a change. I may let my hair grow out, too.

"India, you haven't heard a word I've said. What's wrong?" Pushing Charlemagne out of the way, Willi sat down next to India.

"I can't seem to adjust," India said. "I can't eat, I don't sleep well, and when I do sleep, I have nightmares."

"This has gone on much too long," Willi declared. "I think you ought to see a doctor."

"Are you suggesting a psychiatrist? If I did talk to one, if I told everything, I would probably be locked up." India sighed. "Some things never change."

"All right, fine, if you won't go to a doctor, then just talk to me about what happened when you disappeared. I won't repeat what you say, not even to Mark," Willi promised. "This is the first time in our lives that you have refused to tell me about something that's bothering you."

"I can't."

"India, I told you this a couple of weeks ago, before all this mystery started, and now I'm telling you again. You have to get on with your life. For starters, why don't you dump this outfit?" Rising from the windowseat, Willi picked up the green tunic and trousers India had folded and placed on her bureau on her first night at home. "Who would ever believe this thing is less than a month old? It looks like a reject from a detergent commercial. What's this in the pocket?"

India had been scratching Charlemagne's

ears and thinking how badly the lazy cat's name suited him. She looked up just as Willi pulled out a handful of dried flowers.

"Violets," India said. "White violets. He gave them to me one spring afternoon."

"He? Who, the man I saw you with? The one with the sword?" Willi watched her friend with dawning understanding. "You left him there. That's why you're grieving again. Oh, India, I'm sorry." She gave the flowers to India, but as they passed from her fingers to India's, they began to disintegrate, crumbling until India held only a small pile of grey powder in the palm of her hand.

"Dust," India said, looking at the powder. "Like everything else from that time. Like love itself."

"No, that's not true." Willi crouched before India, looking up into her face. "Those flowers are only *things*. Love doesn't die like that, it lives on in your heart. And you did love him, didn't you? But you have to go on, India, and you have to keep hoping. There will be some kind of answer for you, just like there was for me when I first met Mark. I'm certain of it."

Pushed by Willi's insistence and compelled by her own affection for Professor Moore, India decided she would go to the retirement party being held the night before New Year's Eve.

"I'm glad to see you have recovered from the flu," Professor Moore said to her when she greeted him in the receiving line. Turning to Willi, he said, "I am delighted to see you again under these more pleasant circumstances, Miss Jones, and I am most pleased to note that you came in with Mr. Brant. I trust you have learned your lesson and will have nothing more to do with that questionable character, Mr. Henry Marsh."

"I haven't seen Hank for more than a week," Willi replied.

"Good evening, Mr. Brant," said Professor Moore. "When will your brother arrive in Cheswick?"

"He's flying in from Europe tomorrow," Mark said. When Professor Moore turned to speak to newly arrived well-wishers, Mark said to India, "Willi and I are driving to the airport to meet Theo's plane. Would you like to join us? It would be an informal way to introduce yourself to your future boss."

"No, thank you." India could not keep out of her voice the sudden tension she felt at Mark's suggestion. "I prefer to wait until the university officially reopens next week."

"Are you sure?" She could tell by the look in his eyes that he knew there was something strange behind her refusal.

"Please don't press me," she whispered. "Just let me ease back into normal life in my own way."

"Whatever you want." His smile was encouraging, his hand on her arm a sign of warm friendship. It was almost like having Marcion back again. "Call me if you need me, India. I mean that. Day or night, call me."

Not wanting to intrude upon the new intimacy between Willi and Mark, India had insisted on driving herself to the party. Later, on her way home, she thought about Mark and Marcion, Willi and Bertille. Inevitably, her thoughts drifted to those other friends from the past, Hugo and Danise. In the twentieth century, she knew no one like either of them. She thought she knew why. It was because neither of them had ever had children. Marcion and Bertille, having married, had surely produced children, and Theu had left his young son behind when he died. But Hugo had died too soon, and Danise had seemed headed for the convent life at Chelles, so their genetic material had not survived into later generations. How sad that such dear people should be lost to the world.

Still deep in thought, India pulled into her garage and entered the house through the connecting door. She walked from the back entry through the kitchen and into the front hall to hang up her coat before it struck her that something was wrong. She was not sure how she could tell—a whiff of shaving lotion in the air, one or two objects moved just a little out of their usual positions, or some more subtle clue—but she knew that during her absence, someone had been in the house.

She quickly discounted the possibility of a burglar. Her grandmother's silver tea service sat in plain sight on the dining room buffet, the television was still in its cabinet, and when she hurried upstairs, none of the bedrooms had been disturbed and none of her jewelry was missing. Nothing had been taken from the house except—*except*—

"Hank!" India almost flew down the stairs to the study. There, with trembling hands she opened the locked drawer where she had stored the two floppy disks and the notebook. They were gone. Frantically, she searched the room, knowing all the while that she would not find them. Giving up at last, she dialed the number Mark had given her. She was afraid he might still be with Willi, but he answered at once.

"You said to call anytime." She told him what had happened, told him, too, about Hank's Saturday visit, which she had previously not mentioned to him. "Now I wish I had told you. It was just an excuse for Hank to get inside the house and look around, wasn't it? Mark, he asked me not to tell anyone he had been to see me, and then he urged me to go to Professor Moore's party."

"So he could be sure you would be out of the house for a few hours, giving him enough time to search the place," Mark finished the thought for her. "Hank is so damned clever, he probably had no trouble at all picking the lock on your door or on the drawer in your study, and then relocking them both."

"We have to get those floppy disks back," India cried. "And Robert's notebook. Mark, he's sure to try to recreate what happened to me. Someone has to stop him."

"Let me check on this. I'll get back to you as soon as I can." Mark hung up, leaving India to wait in restless concern until the telephone rang some forty-five minutes later.

"It's being taken care of," Mark told her. "We've got a good man on the job, and he's on Hank's trail right now. I talked to him; he's planning to watch Hank for a few days in case Hank contacts someone else engaged in a similar project. That way, we might catch two birds at once. This means you won't get your property back for a while, but you don't have to worry about Hank anymore."

"Thank you, Mark. I knew I could count on you."

"Anytime. Sure you won't change your mind and go to the airport with Willi and me tomorrow?"

"I don't think so."

"My brother is not as bad as you might suppose after meeting me," Mark teased. "Give him a fair chance, and you two could become good friends."

But when Willi stopped by to see India on New Year's Day, her report on Theodore Brant was not encouraging.

"You can tell Mark and his brother really love each other," Willi informed India, "but Theodore Brant is not at all like Mark. He has been teaching in Europe, and I guess they are more formal there, because he seems to be a bit uptight. If I were you, India, I would walk carefully around him until you know him well."

"Is his wife uptight, too?" India was surprised to find herself holding her breath until Willi answered.

"Mark says she died a few years ago," Willi said. "At least you will have that much in common with him. You'll meet him on Monday. You *are* going back to work on Monday, aren't you?"

"I need the job, and I have no logical reason for leaving it," India replied. "On Monday I will have to walk into the history department office and meet my new boss. But not yet. Thank heaven, I still have a few days left."

During those few days, India faced the fact that where returning to work was concerned, her courage was rapidly failing. Emotionally bruised by what had happened to her, still devastated by Theu's death, she was terrified of meeting Theodore Brant, fearing that he would prove to be as much like Theu as Mark was like Marcion. She did not know how she could deal with a man who looked and sounded and acted like Theu, but who did not know her and who would treat her like the stranger she would be to him. It would be like losing Theu a second time.

Much as India wished she could do so, she could not stop the passing of the days. Monday arrived, the university was scheduled to reopen after the holiday vacation, and she could no longer put off going to work. Armoring herself in the tightest self-control she could muster, deliberately wearing the cheerful cranberry skirt and sweater Willi had chosen for her on a night that seemed years in the past, she returned to the history department office.

Classes had not started. Registration for the new semester was still in progress, so there was no one else in the office that morning. In the outer office there was no sign as yet of anything belonging to Theodore Brant, and the substitute secretary, who had taken over for India during the days before Christmas, had left her desk clean and neat. When the mail came, India sorted through it before taking the important-looking pieces into the chairman's office, entering the room for the first time in more than two weeks.

Professor Moore had been endearingly absent-minded, leaving books and papers scattered about in great disarray and keeping the file cabinet so full that its contents constantly spilled out onto the floor. Now that he was gone, the room looked bare, with books precisely lined up on the bookshelves, the file cabinet drawers closed, the venetian blinds tilted at just the right angle to let in plenty of light without glare.

India laid the mail in the center of the desk, lining up the edges of the papers until the pile was neat. Without warning, her hands began to shake.

"I have to get out of here," she muttered, starting toward the door. She had almost reached it when she stopped, her eye caught by the picture on the wall. No, it was not a picture. What the foot-square frame contained, what the glass covered, was not a picture at all, but a jagged, triangular section of chain mail. She stepped closer to see it better.

She could not breathe for the sudden pounding of her heart. At the long edge of the metal links, where the armor had been torn, the head had broken on a single rivet, and the rivet itself had been partially torn out of its link.

India could not stop herself. She placed one finger on the glass, covering the spot where the broken rivet was.

"Be careful, you'll smear the glass."

"Oh!" She spun around to face the man who had come into the office so quietly that she had not heard him.

"Theodore Brant." He nodded briskly. "I presume you are the elusive department secretary? Mrs. Baldwin, isn't it? I understand you've been sick. I hope you are feeling better, because we have a lot of work to do."

"Yes," she faltered, uncomfortable under his steady, deep blue gaze. She recalled Willi's warning to be careful until she knew this man. "I'm sorry about the glass. I'll clean it right away."

Having prepared herself to encounter a remnant of the long-distant past, she was bitterly disappointed to discover that Theodore Brant did not look like Theuderic of Metz. The man before India was several inches taller than she, in his mid- to late thirties, and obviously in perfect physical condition. His hair was dark and curly, like his brother's. He wore a nicely tailored grey suit, a white shirt, and an expensive-looking striped tie. Very conservative, very cool, more like a banker than a college professor—and there was not a trace of fire or warmth in him. He was not a bit like Theu.

India thought her heart would break. It was indeed like losing Theu all over again, but not in the way she had expected. She had been foolish to allow herself any hope at all. Theu was dead—long dead and buried—and it was time for her to accept that fact.

Theodore Brant walked across the room to stand beside her while he looked at the chain mail on the wall. Amazingly, his cold expression relaxed, as if he were seeing an old friend, and his blue eyes warmed. India's heart skipped a beat when he glanced toward her.

"I didn't mean to frighten you," he said. "It's just that I don't want this to be damaged in any way. Perhaps I shouldn't have brought it here to the office, but I like to look at it, and I'm not at home very much. Are you interested in antique armor?"

"Only in chain mail." When he looked surprised, she sought for an acceptable reason for a statement she had made in haste and emotional pain. "My late husband was a medievalist."

"Oh, yes, I did hear something about that."

He touched the frame, straightening it. "This piece is from the eighth or ninth century."

"Eighth," India said.

"It's a rare piece because iron that old has usually oxidized until it is a ruined mess of rust. For some reason, this has been well cared for over the centuries."

"Where did you get it?" India asked.

"It has been in my family for generations. Tradition has it that it was once worn by an illustrious ancestor. Unfortunately, I have never seen any proof of that claim. Still, I have felt an attachment to those links ever since I was a boy. My grandfather had them mounted in that frame, and I used to sit in his library making up stories about the man for whom the armor was made and the battles he fought wearing it. I guess that's why Grandfather willed it to me." His voice trailed off, as if he was a little embarrassed at having spoken so openly and so emotionally to someone he did not know.

"Theuderic of Metz," India said, feeling oddly compelled to speak and with her voice remarkably steady considering the way her heart had just gone on a wild roller coaster ride. "He died at Roncevaux."

"Do you know something I don't?" he asked.

"I believe I do," she said, smiling for the first time in weeks. Her heart settled down and began to beat steadily once more. From somewhere deep inside her a reviving happiness began to grow, along with the certainty that

Theu was not gone, not lost and dead in some far-distant past. He was with her and he always would be.

Theodore Brant watched her with a question in his eyes, and India found herself regretting the days when she had avoided meeting him. But that was all she regretted. Nothing else.

"It's a long and complicated story about an incredible adventure," she said to him. "When I know you better, I may tell you about it."

"Why do I have the feeling that ours is going to be an interesting association?" His blue eyes were laughing now, all his initial coldness vanished. One corner of his mouth quirked upward in a half smile, and suddenly she recognized in him the humor and spirit of the man she would love until time ended.

"You have no idea," she told him, "just how interesting you are going to find me."

Epilogue

September, 1992.

It was a lovely wedding, albeit a quiet one. The bride had insisted on having it that way. The small, gothic-style church was decorated with white roses and many tall candles, and the bride wore an ankle-length cream lace dress. The fifty invited family members and guests noted that the usually self-possessed groom was extremely nervous.

The reception was held at a nearby restaurant that had been remodeled from an old mill, and all through the golden late September afternoon, the guests danced on a deck extending out over the rushing stream and the waterfall that had once powered the mill.

"Nice place," said the best man to the maid-of-honor. "This is like dancing in a giant tree house. When it gets dark, we'll have a great view of the stars."

"It is beautiful," Willi replied, smiling into his eyes.

Mark pulled her closer, resting his cheek against hers while they moved slowly to the music. Willi's hair had grown out of its tough, spiky cut until it hung to her shoulders in soft curls. Her grey eyeshadow made her eyes look large and dark. The pale green chiffon of her gown drifted about her ankles.

"You're my girl," Mark murmured into her ear. "Always have been, always will be. I knew it the first moment I saw you."

"I knew it, too." Willi snuggled a little closer to him. "Right away, I felt as if I had known you forever. Amazing, isn't it?"

On the other side of the deck, India shook hands with a departing couple, then glanced toward Willi and Mark.

"They look so happy together," she said.

"They can't possibly be as happy as I am," her new husband told her, slipping an arm about her waist. He spared one quick look for his brother. "I have a feeling there will be another wedding soon. I think Mark plans to make your best friend into your sister."

"It's about time," India said, laughing at her own private joke.

"Speaking of time, shouldn't we be making our getaway about now?" Theo's tender expression as he regarded his wife held the promise of all the wonders of love still unexplored and awaiting them.

"Yes, my dear love," India said, taking his hand. "It is time. Our time. At long, long last."

Author's Notes

Late in the summer of 778, the Saxons did revolt against their Frankish overlords, taking advantage of Charles's absence in Spain, as many of his nobles had feared they would. It required swift action and much hard fighting to subdue them that autumn. But the Saxons were a determined people. Eventually they rebelled yet again, and stubbornly continued to fight for their freedom for another quarter of a century before they were finally conquered.

The story Theuderic recounts to India, of men who come in flying machines from a land called Magonia, is a tale that was current in Europe during the late eighth and ninth centuries. It seems that even in those days, more than twelve hundred years ago, there were rumors of mysterious unidentified flying objects.

Of the twin sons born to Charles's wife Hildegarde at Agen during the summer of 778, the smaller died in early autumn. The second boy, Ludwig, later rebaptised as Louis, was made King of Aquitaine by his father. Unlike his older brothers, he outlived his father, and on the death of Charles in 814, he became the second emperor of the Carolingian empire. He is known to the French as Louis I, Louis the Pious.

New Mexico October, 1992.

"Has anyone ever told you that you are crazy?"

"All the time. But I never pay any attention, because I know I'm right." Henry Adelbert Marsh regarded his visitor with cool arrogance. The man facing him was of average height, with dark hair and nondescript features except for the startling blue eyes that lifted his appearance far out of the ordinary. Hank Marsh wasn't one to be unduly impressed by a person's looks—he wasn't all that handsome himself—but he was annoyed with the man, and he was curious. He met the blue gaze with open defiance. "What I want to know is how you found me. I covered my tracks pretty damned well."

"You did. I'll give you that much. I lost you for a long time. It took me months of searching and a lot of trouble to discover just where you were hiding." Ignoring the woman who was the third person in the room, Bradford Michael Bailey moved a little farther into the back bedroom of the house, his eyes on the computer that filled the better part of the space. There could be absolutely no doubt; he had found his quarry at last, and Hank was up to his old tricks again.

"As it happens, I am something of a detective. An historical detective, since I'm an archeologist. I enjoy the challenge of a difficult search. And I was given a few clues to help me find you. Do you remember Mark Brant? Or India Baldwin?"

"India sent you after me?" Hank's arrogant mask slipped a bit. "I never thought she'd talk. She was so adamant about forgetting what happened last Christmastime."

"You mean, about you accidentally sending her far back in time? How could anyone ever forget living through such an experience? No, India didn't talk. My friend Mark figured out what had happened. He's the one who sent me after you."

"I knew that guy was trouble the first time I saw him," Hank muttered. "O.K., now you've found me. What do you want with me, Bailey?"

"The name's Mike. I've learned enough about you during the last ten months to put us on a first name basis. I assume this is your latest machine." Mike took a couple of steps toward the computer, noting the additional components and the power enhancers. He was no stranger to computers. Archeologists found them remarkably useful. "You have made some interesting changes to this thing, haven't you? Are you hoping to prove some wild new theory? Or are you still working on the old one?"

At this point, the young woman who owned the house, and who had let Mike in when he claimed to be Hank's friend, inserted herself between Mike and the computer. From his investigations into Hank's whereabouts, Mike knew her name was Alice. She was small and thin, with dark hair scraped back into a tight ponytail. She wore no makeup and her expression was grimly intense. It occurred to Mike that she would be a lot prettier if she would lighten up a little. But perhaps her interest in Hank was more scientific than romantic. It certainly seemed that way.

"Leave Hank alone," Alice ordered. "And you stay away from my computer, too. Our theories and what we are doing are none of your business. You don't have any right to intrude on our privacy."

"Did you know your friend here is a thief?" Mike said to her. When Alice glanced toward Hank, Mike took another step in the direction of the computer. "Hank has stolen the property of this India Baldwin we've just mentioned, who is the friend of a friend of mine. I have been sent to collect and return that property."

"Hank is no thief," Alice protested. "He's a great and misunderstood scientist."

"He broke into India Baldwin's house and

took two floppy disks and a notebook that belonged to her. Then Hank left town with those disks and the notebook. If that's not stealing, I don't know what is. But if he'll return her property, India has promised she won't press charges against him."

"You can't interfere with important scientific work," Alice cried, apparently oblivious to the legal implications of what Hank had done. Mike decided he wasn't going to get anywhere with her. Alice was on Hank's side, and she probably wouldn't budge from her position without a good scare.

"Hand over the disks, Hank. And the notebook." Mike put out his hand, waiting. "If you give them to me, I won't call the police. Refuse, and you are going to be in trouble with the local constabulary for possession of stolen property and for trying to recreate a dangerous accident. That is what you are trying to do here, isn't it? You want to repeat the accident that happened to India. You intend to try to send someone else back to the eighth century. Are you going to use your friend Alice as the guinea pig? Or are you planning to go yourself this time?"

"He knows, Hank." Suddenly, Alice looked frightened. "I don't want to go to jail."

"Shut up, Alice," Hank ordered. "He doesn't know anything. He's bluffing."

"Wrong," Mike informed him. "I know everything about your theories and your experiments. Now, ask yourself where I got the money to trail you across the country for all these months. Does it begin to dawn on you that I'm not acting solely on my own initiative? There are some very important people who are annoyed by what you are trying to do, Hank. After I leave here, you may have some other visitors. I don't think they'll be as pleasant as I am, or as patient with you. Now, come on, hand over the evidence and you'll be in the clear when other people come searching."

"Are you saying the federal government is after him?" Alice squeaked, backing away from Hank. "I didn't ask for this kind of trouble."

"Last chance, Hank. Hand over the disks." Mike paused for a moment, watching Hank, who stood unmoving and glaring at him. "All right, time's up. If you aren't going to give me the disks, then I'll just have to take them. Here's one. I guess the other's in the machine, isn't it? Now, where have you hidden the notebook?" As he spoke, Mike picked up one floppy disk from the shelf beside the computer and pocketed it. He reached toward the computer to remove the second disk.

"Don't touch that thing!" Hank yelled. "It's all set up and ready to go."

"Then turn it off and give me the disk," Mike demanded. "The notebook, too."

"No way!" Hank shoved at Mike, trying to get him away from the computer, but Mike caught his arm in a tight grip.

"Knock it off, Hank. I don't want to hurt you.

Just hand over the disk and I'll leave." Knowing he was the stronger man, Mike released the furious scientist. Doing so was a mistake.

"You aren't going to stop me," Hank declared. "Not you or anyone else, including the government. I can just imagine what the Feds would do with my material. Damn it, I'm sick and tired of uninformed idiots trying to interfere with my work!" With that, he clenched his fist and took a wild swing at Mike, who ducked. Hank was not a fighting man. The punch missed Mike's chin with plenty of room to spare, and Hank's fist slammed into the computer.

"Ow!" Hank cried, nursing his aching hand. "Get out of here. Just leave me alone."

"I can't do that." When Mike did not move, Hank and Alice came at him at the same time, but from different directions. Mike was concentrating on what Hank might do, so he wasn't expecting Alice's attack, and he didn't want to hit a woman. He tried to sidestep Alice while at the same time fending off Hank. As a result of his misplaced chivalry, he was pushed backward until he was up against the computer. He put out a hand to steady himself.

His hand went through the computer screen, vanishing into the solid surface. The computer screen appeared to be undamaged, but Mike could no longer see his own hand and arm.

"Hey! Come back here. You're not the one who's supposed to go," Hank shouted.

But Bradford Michael Bailey was beyond stopping what was happening. He could not believe what was happening, so at first he did nothing to help himself. Within half a second it was impossible for him to do anything anyway, because his own body would not follow his commands. Incredibly, he was being pulled into the computer. He saw an orange blur first, then an odd blackness with bright-colored numbers whizzing through it. His head ached and his ears popped as if he were falling fast, which he was.

He came out of the blackness into empty air. Then he was tumbling downward through tree branches. He grabbed at them to try to stop his precipitous fall, but some of the branches broke and his hands slipped off others as he plummeted toward the ground.

He knew he was going to die. Oddly, his life did not pass before his eyes. All he saw were tree leaves and branches, a few rocks below awaiting him, and the too solid earth on which those rocks were resting.

He hit the ground hard, knocking all the air out of his lungs. His head cracked against one of the waiting rocks. Unable to move or breathe, Mike fell into blackness again, a different kind of blackness that time, a sucking, greedy darkness that engulfed him in an instant, snuffing out his consciousness.

Francia
Spring, A.D. 779.

At first Danise thought the man was dead. He lay perfectly still, prone on a pile of leaves and branches, and when she turned him over she saw that his face was swollen beyond recognition.

Not that she would have recognized him if he had been in the best of health. She had never seen anyone wearing such strange clothing. His breeches were made of a coarse dark blue fabric, worn and washed until it was in threadbare state and had faded to near whiteness in places. The knees were torn and bloodstained. She would have thought him a peasant save for the stitching. Danise, no mean needlewoman herself, had never encountered stitches so tiny or so close together—two rows of them at each seam—and there were little pouches set into the garment near the waist, perhaps to hold his personal belongings. His upper body was covered by a short tunic of matching fabric, open down the front. Beneath it he wore a round-necked blue shirt of some soft material. His hair was black and straight. All this she saw in a moment, before her servant Clothilde spoke.

"Is he breathing?" Clothilde knelt in the leaves beside her mistress and pressed a hand against the man's chest. "His heart is beating. He is warm."

"Poor man." Danise let her fingers touch his face softly, so as not to hurt him further. His nose had been bleeding, but it had stopped. In addition to his scraped knees he had scratches on his face and hands and a nasty lump on the left side of his head. Danise could find no open wounds to require immediate staunching of blood. If he had any more serious injuries, they must be internal.

"How could a stranger come so close to the royal camp and not be stopped by Charles's guards?" asked Clothilde.

"I don't know," Danise said, "but he fell from a tree. Those are fresh spring leaves he's lying on, on top of the old leaves from last autumn. Look up, Clothilde. You can see from the broken branches up there the path by which he came to this spot."

"He was in the treetop, spying on us?" Clothilde gasped. "We must alert the guards at once."

"No." Danise spoke sharply. "We don't know that he was spying. He may have thought *we* would do *him* harm. We can't call the guards. They would think as you do, and be rough with him. He looks too badly hurt to endure such treatment. Clothilde, I think by the fine seams on his clothing that he must be a foreign noble. Look at them; no peasant woman could make stitches so small or so straight. I believe he has been traveling for a long time, if such sturdy fabric is so badly worn. Therefore, until he can tell us who he is, we would be wise to treat him as a visiting noble.

"I will stay here, to watch over him," Danise went on. "You must find my father or Guntram, who will know where my father is. We will need a litter to take him back to the camp."

"Savarec would not want me to leave you alone," Clothilde protested.

"One of us must go, for we cannot leave him by himself," Danise pointed out. "And, Clothilde, be discreet. Don't talk to anyone but my father or Guntram. Be careful to avoid Sister Gertrude. You know how she loves to make a fuss."

"How am I to do that?" Clothilde demanded, standing and planting her hands on her wide hips. "That nun has eyes like an eagle."

"You and I together have avoided her eagle eye often enough," Danise responded. "I know you can do it, Clothilde. Just be quick. I fear he must be badly injured, or he would have wakened by now."

Left alone with the stranger, Danise took off her light spring cloak and used it to cover him. Then she sat beside him, gently stroking his hair.

"Why did you climb so high in the trees?" she murmured to him. "Was it to look over the landscape and thus find your way? Were you intending to come to Duren to meet with Charles?"

Since the man remained unresponsive, Danise settled herself more comfortably to await the arrival of help. Despite Clothilde's qualms, she was not the least bit frightened to be alone in the forest. There could be no danger to her there, so close to the Frankish encampment.

Charles, king of the Franks, had called the Mayfield, the great spring assembly of Frankish nobles, to meet at Duren on the River Rur, about two days' journey east of Aachen. The choice of place was deliberate, to demonstrate just how powerful the Franks were to the ever-restless Saxon tribes who lived on the eastern borders of Francia. Still, Duren and the forests surrounding it were safe. If they were not, Charles would never have allowed his beloved queen to accompany him there, for Hildegarde was seven months gone with her sixth pregnancy in eight years of marriage, and she was not at all well.

Nor, if Duren were unsafe, would Savarec have summoned his daughter Danise to meet him at the royal court. Danise had made the journey from the convent school at Chelles, near Paris, to Duren in the company of her usual chaperone, Sister Gertrude, her personal maidservant Clothilde, and two men-at-arms whom her father had sent to protect her along the way. She had seen her father only briefly on her arrival the previous night, before retiring to the tent Savarec had provided for his women-folk next to his own tent.

Duren was but a small settlement, so the Franks had established a town of tents on a broad space cleared between river and forest. There they would live during the weeks of May-field, feasting out-of-doors in the fine spring weather, and enjoying the contests of skill in wrestling, weaponry, and riding put on by the younger warriors. Meanwhile, in the huge royal tent or on the open field, the nobles would meet with Charles to decide whether another campaign was necessary against the Saxons. While the men conferred, the women, too, would meet, renewing old friendships and making new ones.

The annual assembly was also the time when Frankish nobles traditionally arranged marriages for their children, and Danise very much feared Savarec had called her to Duren for that reason. At nearly eighteen, she was almost too old to be wed.

The man beside her moaned, diverting her thoughts from herself to him. He raised one hand to his face, then moaned again.

"It will be all right," she told him, catching

his hand. "Help is coming soon. We will take good care of you."

He grew still at the sound of her voice, and she thought he was trying to frown. It was hard to tell for sure, since his face was so swollen, but his expression seemed to change and he winced.

"Just lie still," she advised.

He muttered a few words in a language she could not understand, then said a word she did know.

"Angel?"

"*Ange?*" she repeated. "Oh, I comprehend. You think you are dead and I am an angel? I'm afraid not. I am far from being an angel."

He grew still again—listening to her, she was sure—and then he opened his eyes.

They were blue, the deepest, purest, most penetrating blue she had ever seen. In his sorely damaged face, swollen and bruised and streaked with dirt and scratches and blood from his injured nose, those eyes were like torches in a dark forest. Not even the famous piercing blue gaze of Charles, king of the Franks, had ever affected Danise the way this unknown man's eyes did.

"Who are you?" she whispered, caught and held by light and color and unmistakable intelligence. When she saw the puzzled expression invading the blue depths, she repeated her question, speaking slowly and carefully, hoping he would understand her.

He said something and started to shake his head. The movement elicited a groan of pain. The blue eyes closed and he slipped away from her, back into unconsciousness. Only then did Danise realize she was still holding his hand, clutching it in both of hers, pressing it against her bosom. She let it go, laying it upon his chest and stroking the limp and dirty fingers with her own white ones.

"Don't die," she whispered. "Please don't die. I want to know you."

About the Author

Flora Speer is the author of six historical romances and three futuristic romances. *A Time to Love Again* is her first time-travel romance.

Born in southern New Jersey, she now lives in Connecticut. In addition to doing the research for her books, her favorite activities include gardening (especially flowers and herbs used in medieval gardens), needlepoint, amateur astronomy and following the U.S. Space Program. She also loves cats, long walks, and the pleasures of good conversation with dear friends.

She enjoys receiving letters from readers and faithfully promises to answer each one. Readers may write to:

Flora Speer
P.O. Box 270347
West Hartford
CT 06127-270347

Please include a stamped, self-addressed envelope.

THE MAGIC OF ROMANCE
PAST, PRESENT, AND FUTURE....

Dorchester Publishing Co., Inc., the leader in romantic fiction, is pleased to unveil its newest line—Love Spell. Every month, beginning in August 1993, Love Spell will publish one book in each of four categories:

1) *Timeswept Romance*—Modern-day heroines travel to the past to find the men who fulfill their hearts' desires.

2) *Futuristic Romance*—Love on distant worlds where passion is the lifeblood of every man and woman.

3) *Historical Romance*—Full of desire, adventure and intrigue, these stories will thrill readers everywhere.

4) *Contemporary Romance*—With novels by Lori Copeland, Heather Graham, and Jayne Ann Krentz, Love Spell's line of contemporary romance is first-rate.

Exploding with soaring passion and fiery sensuality, Love Spell romances are destined to take you to dazzling new heights of ecstasy.

COMING IN AUGUST 1993
HISTORICAL ROMANCE
WILD SUMMER ROSE
Amy Elizabeth Saunders

Torn from her carefree rustic life to become a proper city lady, Victoria Larkin bristles at the hypocrisy of the arrogant French aristocrat who wants to seduce her. But Phillipe St. Sebastian is determined to have her at any cost—even the loss of his beloved ancestral home. And as the flames of revolution threaten their very lives, Victoria and Phillipe find strength in the healing power of love.

_0-505-51902-X $4.99 US/$5.99 CAN

CONTEMPORARY ROMANCE
TWO OF A KIND
Lori Copeland
Bestselling Author of *Promise Me Today*

When her lively widowed mother starts chasing around town with seventy-year-old motorcycle enthusiast Clyde Merrill, Courtney Spenser is confronted by Clyde's angry son. Sensual and overbearing, Graham Merrill quickly gets under Courtney's skin—and she's not at all displeased.

_0-505-51903-8 $3.99 US/$4.99 CAN

COMING IN SEPTEMBER 1993
HISTORICAL ROMANCE
TEMPTATION
Jane Harrison

He broke her heart once before, but Shadoe Sinclair is a temptation that Lilly McFall cannot deny. And when he saunters back into the frontier town he left years earlier, Lilly will do whatever it takes to make the handsome rogue her own.

_0-505-51906-2 $4.99 US/$5.99 CAN

CONTEMPORARY ROMANCE
WHIRLWIND COURTSHIP
Jayne Ann Krentz writing as Jayne Taylor
Bestselling Author of *Family Man*

When Phoebe Hampton arrives by accident on Harlan Garand's doorstep, he's convinced she's another marriage-minded female sent by his matchmaking aunt. But a sudden snowstorm traps them together for a few days and shows Harlan there's a lot more to Phoebe than meets the eye.

_0-505-51907-0 $3.99 US/$4.99 CAN

A TIMESWEPT ROMANCE

Timeswept passion...timeless love.

REFLECTIONS IN TIME

ELIZABETH CRANE

When practical-minded Renata O'Neal submits to hypnosis to cure her insomnia, she never expects to wake up in 1880's Louisiana — or in love with fiery Nathan Blue. But vicious secrets and Victorian sensibilities threaten to keep Renata and Nathan apart...until Renata vows that nothing will separate her from the most deliciously alluring man of any century.

_3254-6 $4.50 US/$5.50 CAN

A TIMESWEPT ROMANCE

Timeswept passion…timeless love.

PASSION'S TIMELESS HOUR

VIVIAN KNIGHT-JENKINS

Propelled by a freak accident from the killing fields of Vietnam to a Civil War battlefield, army nurse Rebecca Ann Warren discovers long-buried desires in the arms of Confederate leader Alexander Random. But when Alex begins to suspect she may be a Yankee spy, the only way Rebecca can prove her innocence is to convince him of the impossible…that she is from another time, another place.

_3296-1 $4.50 US/$5.50 CAN

Bestselling Author of *Time-spun Rapture*

A hard-eyed realist and a fanciful optimist, Adam Berwick and Bethany Rose Stewart are the unlikeliest of lovers. But from the moment he stumbles into Wildcat Hollow to retrieve a stolen horse, Berwick is determined to take the beautiful girl away with him. And although Bethany has waited all her life for a handsome prince to rescue her from her father's endless abuses, she could never have guessed that reality would outshine her secret dreams.

_3284-8 $4.50 US/$5.50 CAN

SPEND YOUR LEISURE MOMENTS WITH US.

Hundreds of exciting titles to choose from—something for everyone's taste in fine books: breathtaking historical romance, chilling horror, spine-tingling suspense, taut medical thrillers, involving mysteries, action-packed men's adventure and wild Westerns.
